THE SECRET INGREDIENT

ALSO BY JANE HELLER

Female Intelligence

Name Dropping

Sis Boom Bah

Crystal Clear

Princess Charming

Infernal Affairs

The Club

Cha Cha Cha

THE SECRET INGREDIENT

JANE HELLER

ST. MARTIN'S PRESS
NEW YORK

 For information, address St. Martin's Press, 175 Fifth Avenue, New York, N.Y. 10010.

www.stmartins.com

ISBN 0-312-26172-1

First Edition: February 2002

10 9 8 7 6 5 4 3 2 1

For my friend Ruth Harris

Acknowledgments

Writing this book was truly a joy, thanks, in large measure, to the efforts of the following people:

Julia Grossman, who was my gracious and supportive tour guide while I tried to decode Los Angeles. You are the best, and I'm thrilled that we reconnected!

Howard Papush, who provided vital details about his city, along with his unflagging friendship.

Lieutenant Edward T. Kreins of the Beverly Hills Police Department, who is as engaging as he is informative.

Michael Barrett, who's not only the hippest cop in Westport, Connecticut, but who came up with the idea for this book's prologue.

David Reznick, who knows everything there is to know about snakes and has since he was six years old.

Ken Halama, who filled me in about hiking in southern California, especially the Mt. Baldy area.

Dale Carlson, whose expertise in the hospitality industry was crucial in making the heroine's career authentic as well as amusing.

Allison Seifer Poole, who can find the answer to just about any question. Thanks, too, to those whom Allison consulted on my behalf: Jim Elmer, David Ogden, and Mary Theroux.

Arlene Sanford and Devra Lieb, who entertained me while I was in L.A. doing research and whose stories are the stuff of funnier books than mine.

Jennifer Enderlin, who has been and continues to be my trusted editor and friend. Thanks, too, to her colleagues at St. Martin's Press who have worked so hard to broaden my readership.

Ellen Levine, who can only be described as the most caring and competent literary agent on the planet.

Louise Quayle, whose voice on the telephone always signals good news and cheers me up enormously.

Amy Schiffman, who tirelessly represents my books to the show biz community and will someday make us both rich.

Renée Young, who is an endless source of both creativity and generosity and who is never stingy about sharing either of them.

Kristen Powers, who designed my website so that even computer-challenged folks like me can navigate it.

Michael Forester, who did triple duty as husband, sounding board, and research subject. *The Secret Ingredient* pokes fun at marriage, and he allowed ours to be the butt of my jokes.

And thanks to everyone who let me badger them about a title for this book. Special gratitude to Mort and Sheila Lowenstein and Paul and Judy Hartnett.

THE SECRET INGREDIENT

PROLOGUE

If only he would change . . . If only I could change him . . .

Is there a wife on the planet who doesn't harbor such thoughts occasionally?

Go on, admit it. There's at least one characteristic about your husband that you're dying to change, isn't there? More than one, I'll bet—everything from the way he forgets to cap the tube of toothpaste to the way he forgets your anniversary. And why is this the state of affairs? Because at some point—even if your relationship got off to a promising start, even if your union seemed destined for greatness, even if your man has genuinely admirable qualities—there comes that inevitable period of dissatisfaction in every marriage or romantic partnership when minor irritants become mega-irritants; the inevitable realization that he is no longer writing you intimate little notes, surprising you with bouquets of flowers, rendezvousing with you in the middle of the day for a roll in the hay; the inevitable moment when you look at him as he's splayed out on the sofa, fiddling with the TV remote, feeding his face with something disgustingly artery-clogging, oblivious to your very existence, and you wonder, Who the heck is this bozo? Where's the prize I won? And how do I get that guy back? What is also inevitable is that you will decide that the trick to getting him back is by *you* fixing *him*. It's an automatic reflex on our part, an irresistible impulse, a foolhardy descent into what psychotherapists call "magical thinking."

There. I've said it. *Magical*. The M word. The word that figures prominently in the story I'm about to share with you, the story involving my own marriage.

It was a marriage that began well, as most marriages do, with an auspicious first encounter to kick it off. People always say that love comes calling when you least expect it, and that was certainly the case with us.

How did Roger and I meet? He rescued me on the 405—the "dreaded 405," as southern Californians refer to the freeway whose traffic is the stuff of nightmares, particularly at rush hour. My car had overheated, and I'd managed to navigate it across six lanes to the shoulder, after which I'd climbed out, planted myself on the pavement in the blistering August sun, and prayed for some good Samaritan to help me. (I appreciate that many women know exactly what to do when their cars break down—women who can reel off the name and purpose of each hose and belt and wire under the hood—but I am not one of them. I don't even know how to fill my own gas tank; among my favorite words in the English language are *full serve*.)

So there I was, sweltering, stewing, speculating about how I would ever make it back to my townhouse in Santa Monica before dark, when a car pulled up behind mine and a man got out.

Be careful what you wish for, I thought as he walked toward me, setting off an orgy of "what ifs" in my head. Like, What if he's a serial murderer whose M.O. is that he pretends to be a rescuer of women but then abducts them, drags them back to his lair, and kills them by some hideously inventive method?

"I see you've got a problem with your car," said the man, who wore a friendly, if not downright cheerful, expression.

I squinted, gave him the once-over. He was about my age—thirties—and handsome, although hardly GQ cover-model material. He was in the six-foot range, lean but broad-shouldered, and he had curly brown hair, a prominent jaw and nose, and, to the right of his mouth, a very deep dimple, an indentation I found quite adorable. He was nicely dressed too—well-tailored sport jacket and slacks, open-necked shirt, sporty loafers. And, when he removed his sunglasses, he revealed a pair of soulful, thoroughly captivating green eyes. Still, I couldn't let my guard down. Ted Bundy wasn't bad-looking either.

"Yes," I said. "I think the engine overheated. A little red light went on, and the next thing I knew the car smelled like some oily fish that was left on the grill too long."

He laughed.

"What's so funny?" I asked.

"You," he said. "You have a funny way of describing things."

"How can you tell?" I said. "I only described one thing. Maybe the way I describe other things isn't funny at all."

"Maybe, but let's try you out," he said. "How would you describe me, for instance?"

"How would I—" This was weird. Weird, but interesting. "Well, for starters, you have a sinkhole in your cheek."

He laughed again, running his fingers over his dimple. And then he gave *me* the once-over, his green eyes skipping over my body, which was as thrilling as it was discomforting. "Back to business," he said, as if reminding himself to be a Boy Scout. "I'm sure you'd prefer dealing with your car problem to discussing the peculiarities of my face."

Not necessarily. I liked his face. "Right you are," I said. "Do you know how to fix my engine?"

"Fix it? Sorry. I'm a real estate attorney, not a mechanic. But I'd be glad to lend you my cell phone so you could call for a tow."

"That would be great. I would use my own cell phone, but, like the car, it isn't working. It's just not my day, I guess."

"The day's not over yet. Stay positive. Let's walk back to my car and you can call from there."

I followed Mr. Positive to his car, a silver Mitsubishi something-or-other, but I refused to get in.

"What's wrong?" he said.

"How do I know you're not going to kidnap me?" I said.

He laughed again. "I don't usually have to kidnap women to get them to go out with me."

Go out with him? That wasn't what I'd meant, obviously. But since he mentioned it and since I was unattached, the idea was rather appealing, provided he wasn't one of America's Most Wanted.

I peered inside his car. No weapons that I could spot. No drops of blood. No newspaper clippings of his heinous crimes. I did see a shopping bag full of children's toys resting on the backseat and was curious about it.

"Are you married?" I asked.

"Why?" he said. "Are you proposing?"

"No. I was wondering if the toys were for your kids."

"For one kid. I'm in the Big Brother program and my Little Brother is a six-year-old. I get together with him once a week."

So he was a lawyer with a conscience. A lawyer with a conscience who was also attractive and single. Maybe he was right; the day would turn out better than I'd thought.

I got in his car and called AAA. "They said they'll be here in forty-five minutes," I reported after I'd finished with the dispatcher, "which means it'll be more like two hours." I reached for the door handle. "Thanks for the phone. I really appreciate it. Take care."

"Hey, where are you going?" he asked as I was about to return to my poor excuse for an automobile. "I don't even know your name."

"Oh." I grabbed his hand and shook it. "It's Elizabeth."

"Nice to meet you, Elizabeth. I'm Roger. And I don't intend to let you wait on the dreaded 405 for two hours by yourself. We're in this together. So which will it be? Your car or mine?"

He wanted to wait with me? What was *that* about?

"What's wrong now?" he said. "You're staring at me."

"Sorry. I was just wondering why you don't have to be anyplace." Like back at the federal prison before bed check.

"Who said I don't have to be anyplace?" He picked up his cell phone, punched in a number, and told someone named Samantha that he wouldn't be able to make the movie after all.

"Am I hearing things or did you just cancel a date?"

"Actually, I think I just cancelled a relationship."

"Cancelled a—" I felt guilty. Okay, no, I didn't. I was beginning to really like this guy.

"Listen, I know this is going to sound crazy, Elizabeth, but have you ever had a hunch that you were in exactly the right place at exactly the right time with exactly the right person?"

"That's a pretty heavy thing to say," I remarked, counting all the *exactlys*. Roger was either a kook or a catch, and I was definitely sticking around to find out which one.

"I don't want to scare you," he said lightly. "Why don't I put on some music while you digest my question. Do you like Eric Clapton?"

"Who doesn't?" I said, settling into the passenger seat of his car as he popped in a CD.

"How about something to drink? I've got bottled water in the cooler."

"Water would be wonderful, thanks."

He reached into the backseat, retrieved two plastic bottles, and handed me one. Then he clinked his bottle against mine. Well, not clinked; plastic doesn't really clink. "Here's to being in the right place at the right time with the right person."

"May I ask *you* a question, Roger?"

"Fire away."

"What makes you think I'm the right person?"

He took a swallow of water before answering. "Because my heart is leaping around in my chest in a way it's never done before. Of course, I could be going into cardiac arrest, but since I'm only thirty-four years old and I keep fit and eat healthy and try not to indulge in type-A behavior, my guess is I'm falling in love."

I couldn't believe this. I absolutely could not believe this. Let me add, though, that I wanted very much to believe it.

"So you do think this is crazy," he went on. "You're too cynical to buy the whole love-at-first-sight thing, is that it?"

"Well, sure I'm cynical. You don't even know me. And while I'm very grateful for your help today, I don't know you either."

"Do you have any desire to know me?"

"Yes."

He smiled. "Then why don't I get started?"

While we sat in his car for two-and-a-half hours, he told me about himself, let me know him, injecting the story with charming, self-deprecating jokes. What I learned that day about Roger Baskin was that he was a good, kind man to whom the words "What can I do to help?" came naturally; that he considered it a no-brainer that he would volunteer in the Big Brother program instead of spending his free time on a golf course; that, because his parents had died of cancer within a year of each other, he had a maturity about him, an understanding of how to be alone without being lonely. I learned that he loved the beach and swam in the

Pacific when it was too cold for most mortals; that he loved camping and slept under the sky even in crummy weather; that he loved dancing and had earned the nickname "disco king" back in college. I learned that he was smart—not an intellectual, but bright, quick, well educated; that he was a partner in his law firm and worked hard but not compulsively; that he was successful but not one of those awful strivers who is consumed by his place in some pecking order. Mostly what I learned about Roger, by the end of those two-and-a-half hours, was that I wanted to marry him. And so I did marry him, a mere eight months later. We anticipated that we would enjoy a long and happy life together.

Six years into the marriage, however, our relationship took the unfortunate turn I hinted at earlier.

What happened was this: I, Elizabeth Baskin, an otherwise risk-adverse, play-it-safe sort, had the brazenness, the impudence, the gall to mess with Mother Nature, and the result was a total disaster.

No, I did not have a botched face-lift. My miscalculation was far more serious—a truly bad, bad thing.

I'm not suggesting that I was a paragon of virtue before I committed this act. I had my faults, just like the next person. I spent too much money on my clothes. I had a habit of employing sarcasm whenever I was trying to mask my true feelings. I was often suspicious of people, as I demonstrated during my first interaction with Roger. And—this was, perhaps, my most glaring shortcoming—I was obsessively neat. (I viewed my Dustbusters with the kind of reverence others reserve for their televisions.)

But on the whole, I was a decent woman, not somebody you would point to and say, "Watch out for that one." What's more, I'm not so sure that, if you'd been in my situation, you wouldn't have done the same bad, bad thing that I did. *If only he would change . . . If only I could change him . . .* You've uttered those words, remember? You have. It's possible that you, too, would have used a little magic, reached for the quick fix, resorted to the identical strategy I did—the bonehead move that riled Mother Nature and sullied my marriage to Roger, the nice, sweet man who'd saved me on the 405.

Oh, come on. Just hang on a second, would you? I swear this won't be yet another sob story about a woman whose husband took a powder. Not in the conventional sense.

No, this tale has legs. But I suppose the only way to prove it is to dispense with the throat-clearing, spill my guts, and let you make the call about me. Am I worthy of redemption? Did I get what I deserved? Would you have done the same bad, bad thing if you'd been in my Manolo Blahniks?

PART ONE

CHAPTER ONE

Bye, Roger. I'm off to the airport," I said to my husband one Tuesday morning in March. (I've decided to begin the story here because it's the morning I became aware that I wanted to kill Roger. Well, not *kill* him, exactly. Just slap him around a little.) "Roger?"

There was no response from him. Not even the slightest flicker. It was as if he were alone in our three-bedroom house on the corner of fifteenth and Idaho in Santa Monica, as if he didn't have a wife of six years who was about to leave on a business trip, as if he had morphed from a husband who takes his marital responsibilities seriously into a husband who takes his marital responsibilities for granted. Such a shame, wasn't it? Especially after our dreamy start on that freeway?

"Roger," I tried again. "I *said* goodbye."

He was sitting at the kitchen counter, reading the *L.A. Times*, drinking coffee, and eating an English muffin. There were crumbs everywhere, including those pesky little seeds that regularly slough off the underside of English muffins. I was itching to grab the nearest Dustbuster, but there wasn't time. I was running late. The Town Car from Ascot Limo was picking me up any minute to take me to LAX.

"Oh, are you going now, hon?" he said sweetly, innocently, turning his head in my direction at last, answering with a mouthful of food. His question sounded more like *Ohyougonaha*? I often thought of hiring a translator for those precious moments when Roger spoke while he ate.

"Yes. I'm taking a nine o'clock flight, remember?" I had only told him that ten thousand times.

"When will you be back?"

"Thursday night," I replied impatiently. I had told him that too. I'd told him where I was going and what time I was going and when I would be home, but he hadn't been paying attention. Not for a long time. When we were first married, he hung on my every word, not to mention hung up his clothes, and now he did neither. He was always too busy, too tired, too something, and, as a result, I was always carping. "I really wish you'd listen to me when I talk to you, Roger."

He took a sip of coffee. Slurped it, actually. A renegade drop dribbled down the side of his mug onto the counter. I hated how tempted I was to wipe it up.

"And *I* really wish you wouldn't go off on a trip on such a harsh note," he countered. "Besides, I do listen to you when you talk to me. I'm allowed to forget the details, aren't I?"

He honestly didn't get it, didn't get the disconnect that had occurred between us. Or if he did, he didn't want to face it—or, God forbid, have a conversation about it.

"You never used to forget the details," I said wistfully.

"Sorry, hon. You know how tied up with work I've been."

Tied up with work. Ha! Roger had become a card-carrying workaholic. When we were first married, he couldn't wait to get away from the office so he could be with me. Now, the reverse was true, or at least it seemed that way.

"Is it really work, Roger?" I said. "Is that what's distracting you? Or is it that the thrill is gone? That our marriage is in trouble?"

"Elizabeth. Don't start that again."

"Why not? You've changed. I can't help that I notice it."

"I haven't changed. It's just . . . just . . . I don't know . . . reality, I guess. People get bogged down by the routine of marriage, the everyday-ness of marriage, the blah-blah-blah of going to the office and dealing with the house and figuring out whether it's our turn to have the neighbors over. It can't be the way it was when we were first married. It never is."

"That's not true. There are plenty of couples who've been married a long time but act like they're still on their honeymoon."

"Name one."

I thought for a minute, taking a quick inventory of all our friends, many of whom were no longer our friends because they'd gotten divorced, remarried, and moved on to other friends. "I can't. Not right this second. But that doesn't mean there aren't any."

"Elizabeth." He said this with a patronizing tone. "I appreciate that you have high standards and demand the best of everything and everybody, but marriage *isn't* a honeymoon. It isn't supposed to be."

"I don't believe that. I refuse to believe that. Maybe what's really going on between us is that you're having an affair."

First, he did the jaw drop. Next, he did the eyebrow arch. Then, he did that thing people do with their neck where they sort of extend it forward and hold it there, to register their shock and disbelief—and buy time.

"Nice stall," I said.

"I'm not stalling," he said. "I'm just stunned by your question. I'm processing it."

"What's to process? A yes or no will do."

"Elizabeth. What's gotten into you?" He shook his head, so as to indicate that he thought I was emotionally unstable. "Of course I'm not."

"Not what?"

"Having an affair, for God's sake!"

"Would you tell me if you were?"

"Okay, stop this." He put his hand up, like a school crossing guard. His palm was smudged with newsprint. His fingertips were glistening with margarine. The cuff of his shirt revealed a small coffee stain. I had an impulse to haul him over to the sink and hose him down. "I'm sorry I didn't remember what time your flight is leaving this morning. I'm sorry I didn't remember when you're scheduled to come home. I'm sorry if you feel I haven't been as attentive as I should be. But I am not having an affair. I am in love with my wife. And I would appreciate it if she would let me finish my breakfast."

"Sure. Okay. Fine."

The truth is, I didn't really suspect him of having an affair, despite my accusation. When men have affairs, they generally dress spiffier, log in more time at the gym, wear too much cologne. Roger, on the other hand, had slacked off in the area of his personal grooming. Remember the lean and rangy guy who'd rescued me on the 405? Well, sorry to report that he had sprouted baby jowls, not to mention an actual gut. Plus, the hair on his head was beginning to thin while the hair in his nose was beginning to grow, and don't even get me started on his hopelessly dated wardrobe. No, I didn't think he was cheating on me. I was just trying to be provocative in an effort to shake him up, get him juiced, snap him out of his coma, rekindle his old spark. I would have been devastated if he'd admitted he'd been sleeping around. He'd been acting like a clod lately, but he was *my* clod.

"I love you too, you know," I said out loud, inching my way over to him. "That's why it hurts me so much that we've drifted apart."

"We haven't drifted apart. I'm right here, hon." He smiled, showing off the dimpled grin that had made me weak-kneed at our first meeting.

"If we haven't drifted apart, then why does it feel as if we're just going through the motions?" I said. "Can you deny that we don't even communicate?" Sure, I knew relationships went through stages, passages, whatever you want to call them; that the adrenaline rush didn't last forever. But I wasn't ready to forfeit excitement for contentment. Not yet, anyway.

"We're not drifting apart and we're not going through the motions and we communicate as well as can be expected," said Roger.

"As well as can be expected? What's *that* supposed to mean?" I said, my stomach twisting as it always did when we fought.

He swatted the newspaper at some invisible bug. "Don't put me on the defensive, Elizabeth. I hate when you do that."

"Then tell me what you meant by that last remark."

"Nothing. Let's just forget I said it."

I was about to argue that I couldn't forget it and why should I forget it and once people say something it's too late to take it back, but I heard the doorbell.

"There's the car," I said. "I've got to go. I'll call you when I get to Seattle."

"Right."

"Right? Is that the best you can do? What if my plane crashes and 'right' turns out to be your final word to me? Is that your idea of communication, Roger? Is it? Because I remember a time when you said beautiful words to me—words full of poetry and depth and intimacy. What happened to them, huh? Tell me that, if you can." I had become unhinged and it was unattractive of me, but the guy was making me nuts.

"Elizabeth." Roger extended his hand to me.

"What?"

"Come here."

"Why?"

"Because I don't think you should leave like this."

"How should I leave then?"

"By walking over here and letting me kiss you goodbye."

Letting him—oh, well, why not, I figured, surprised and delighted that he was the one initiating the physical intimacy for a change. He *had* said "kiss," so my assumption was that our lips would make contact and that our tongues might even get involved. For a couple who hadn't had sex in months, that was pretty hot stuff.

"Roger," I murmured, my voice softening, my body relaxing. I sidled up to him, rubbed his thigh, and puckered up.

"Travel safely, hon," he said, then deposited a dry little peck on my cheek.

Yeah, on my cheek. How about that for heat, huh? Now, do you see what I'm talking about?

Where was the passion? The lust? The saliva? Where was the man who was so demonstrative when we were in the throes of our courtship? The man who claimed I turned him on, rang his chimes, lit his fire? The man who was so gallant, so chivalrous, so endearing the day he picked me up on that damn freeway? Was he still in there, still inside that body? Or had he been replaced by somebody's old-fart uncle? He was only forty at that point—just two years my senior and hardly ready to be carted off to an assisted living facility. So where was the guy I married? How was I going to save him? How was I going to save us?

CHAPTER TWO

Welcome to the Worthington Hotel Seattle, Ms. Stickler," said the navy-blue uniformed woman at the registration desk. "How are you this afternoon?"

"I'm fine, thanks." I made a mental note of her cheerful greeting and, especially, her meticulous appearance. No visible tattoos. No obscenely long nails. No moussed tendrils obscuring her vision.

"We have you staying with us until Thursday," she said, pulling up my reservation on the computer, "in a deluxe non-smoking room with a king-size bed and a view of the city's historic Pioneer Square. Oh, and it's a quiet room on a high floor, well down the hall from the elevator, as you requested."

"What about the non-allergenic foam pillows?" I asked. "I indicated when I made the reservation that I'm sensitive to feather."

"All taken care of. It's noted right here." She pointed to the computer screen.

"And the case of Evian? Has that been delivered to the room? I couldn't possibly rinse my hair with anything else."

"Yes, it has been delivered. Are there other requests?"

"Not at the moment."

"Then here is your registration packet containing your room key and the key to the mini-bar. The bellman will bring up your luggage and tell you about our health spa, our conference area, our beauty salon, and all our other amenities. If there's anything we can do to make your stay with us more enjoyable, please don't hesitate to alert the front desk, Ms. Stickler."

"I'll be sure to do that." I turned away, glanced at my watch, and nodded approvingly. The check-in was well under five minutes. Check-ins must never exceed five minutes, including waiting in line. Oh, and she used my name twice during her presentation. Very, very efficient.

Okay. I'll stop here because you're thinking I'm some high-maintenance monster who more than deserves the big chill her husband's been giving her. You're also wondering why the woman at the front desk called me Ms. Stickler instead of Ms. Baskin. Let me explain.

For starters, Elizabeth Stickler was my name when I was on a job. It was my code name. My alias. The name on my *other* American Express card. Anonymity was crucial, you see.

No, I wasn't a spy. At least, not for the government. I was one of seventy-five inspectors for America's Most Luxurious Properties, aka AMLP, the trusted source for millions of discerning and demanding travelers. A sort of upscale AAA or Mobil Guide, AMLP rates the country's poshest hotels and resorts—we're not talking about Motel 6's here—and publishes the results in an annual newsletter to subscribers. As an inspector, my mission was to visit each establishment within my territory, armed with AMLP's exacting Standards Manual, register under my false name, spend two nights at the property, and pronounce judgment on everything from the quality of its bed linens to the ability of its staff to attend to my every need, no matter how unreasonable or burdensome. If the property passed our rigorous test, I recommended to my supervisor that it be awarded AMLP's coveted Five Key distinction. If it failed to meet the company's set of criteria, it was downgraded to Four Key status—or lower.

What I'm saying is that I wasn't a random pain-in-the-ass who regularly times registration check-ins just for the heck of it. I was a professional pain-in-the-ass, a fusspot for a living, a person who was paid to be a stickler (hence, the code name). I earned my money jetting from swanky hotel to swanky hotel in pursuit of perfection, which sounds like an utterly fabulous job, right? And it was—until I realized that my pursuit of perfection was an asset in my career but a liability in my personal life. Husbands are not hotels. If only I'd figured that out sooner.

After the bellman escorted me to my room, hung my garment bag in the closet, informed me about the hotel's facilities, and filled my ice bucket, he left me alone to do my work. I fished my trusty Standards Manual out of my carry-on bag and started making notes.

I assumed I wouldn't find much to fault about the Worthington Seattle. An up-market chain on the order of Ritz-Carlton and Four Seasons, the Worthington properties were uniformly top-notch, and the Seattle hotel had undergone a recent renovation. I was almost certain it would maintain its Five Key rating, but that remained to be seen.

My initial impression was an extremely positive one. I surveyed my room and found the décor casual yet elegant. It was furnished with a mix of antiques and clubby, traditional pieces, and on the coffee table rested a vase of orchids. A thoughtful touch.

I drew the draperies and took in the view, which looked out onto

Seattle's bustling historic area, with its waterfront and ferry terminal beyond. No surprise how lovely it was, as the Worthington hotels were known for their spectacular settings.

I pulled my light meter out of my bag (all AMLP inspectors carry one, as well as a little pocket thermometer, to measure the temperature of the hot food from room service) and gave high marks to the excellent lighting in the room. I checked the lampshades too and was pleased to see they were made of a translucent off-white fabric and were shaped to prevent heat build-up. Do you know what happens when there's heat build-up? Yellowing from bulb wattage, that's what. A definite demerit.

I moved on to the bed. It was king-size, as advertised, and the pillows were, indeed, foam-filled, not feather. I pulled the bedspread down farther, to make sure there were no stains on its underside (hotels are always trying to pawn off stained spreads on unsuspecting guests), then felt the blanket, which was one-hundred-percent wool, not one of those disgusting velour numbers, thank God. And then I checked the sheets, which were billed as three-hundred-count Egyptian cotton linens from Italian maker Frette. Hmmm, I purred as I ran my hand over them. I'm going to sleep well in this bed.

I ducked under the mattress—no dust bunnies. I opened the door of the closet—no shortage of hangers and all made of a natural wood finish, not wire. I plugged in the iron—no cheesy model but a full-size steam iron complete with an automatic shut-off button.

I scribbled in my manual. So far, so good.

The mini-bar, too, was in excellent order, as was the writing desk, which contained hotel information, a welcome letter, and room service menus, as well as a range of stationery options and a ballpoint pen, all imprinted with the hotel's name and logo.

Then it was time to inspect the bathroom, often a hotel's Achilles' heel. If there were going to be weaknesses, it was in the bathroom where you'd most likely find them.

This bathroom was enormous. Hanging on two hooks near the large whirlpool tub were the requisite fluffy white terry robes. On the vanity top, which was made of granite, was a display tray offering an array of Aveda Spa products, a boxed shower cap, a hair dryer, a sewing kit, a lint remover, a custom tissue-box cover, a shaving mirror, and two drinking glasses.

As for the toilet, which was housed in its own little alcove, it looked sparkling clean. But—and I actually gasped when I spotted this—the roll of toilet paper affixed to the tiled wall had not been repointed after the last guest had vacated the room! Whatever was the housekeeping department thinking! What's more, there were actually a couple of stray hairs on the floor, and they were definitely not mine!

I noted these lapses in my manual and continued with my room inspection. I checked to make sure that the phones were free of finger marks or other substances; that there was no debris under the sofa cushions; that the television was easily viewed from the bed and in good working order. And so forth.

I unpacked, drank some Evian (I wasn't really planning to rinse my hair with it), and called downstairs. Now that I had completed my inspection of the room, it was time to play Torture the Concierge.

I know that sounds like an unnecessarily mean-spirited little game, but it really was part of my job—to test the I-can-make-it-happen skills of the concierge staff.

Why? Because, given millionaires out there looking for luxe, it's essential that high-end hotels make people feel pampered, cosseted, well tended to—or risk losing them to the competition.

Of course, things have gotten out of hand in this area, what with so much money floating around and the sense of entitlement that accompanies it. For many concierges at the finest properties, it's becoming harder and harder to draw the line between serving a guest and indulging a lunatic.

In the old days, for instance, concierges simply procured restaurant reservations or theater tickets or a limo. Now, they've got to track down the laptop you left in the trunk of a taxi, or search the earth for the specific brand of dark German beer you absolutely *must* use as shampoo, or send up a chest full of dry ice so you can ship breast milk home to your baby while you're on a business trip. Oh, the stories that circulate within the hospitality industry! There's the one about the concierge who was asked to acquire parts for a guest's AK-47; the one about the concierge who was asked to give a guest an enema (he declined but located someone outside the hotel to perform the service); the one about the concierge who was asked to fill a guest's bathtub with melted Godiva chocolate. And, speaking of randy guests, there are loads of stories involving the notorious "towel drop," where the concierge is called to the room and discovers that the guest is nude except for a towel, which he or she then drops accidentally on purpose.

I felt sorry for these concierges, but as I've explained, I had a job to do, so I dialed.

"Concierge desk. This is Scott speaking. How may I help you, Ms. Stickler?"

Warm, cordial greeting. Friendly but not overly familiar. "Hi, Scott. I have a favor to ask."

"Go ahead, Ms. Stickler. That's what I'm here for."

"I would like a pashmina throw for the bed in my room. However, I suppose ordinary cashmere will do if you can't get the pashmina."

"I see." Scott would be wondering how to accomplish this, since the department stores were closed by this time.

"Is that going to be a problem?" I asked, wishing I could give him a hint that his answer could determine whether his hotel would keep its fifth Key. But staying undercover was essential in order that I be treated like any other guest.

"No. No problem at all," he said, recovering beautifully. "I will see to it personally."

"That's very kind of you, Scott. When can I expect the throw to be delivered to the room? I'll be going downstairs for dinner in a few minutes. It would be wonderful if the throw could be here when I get back."

"Of course," said Scott, as if I'd just asked him to send up a can of Pepsi. Perhaps I had made the game too easy.

"Thank you. Oh, there's one other thing."

"Yes?"

"Well, actually it's a little embarrassing."

"I'm here to help, Ms. Stickler."

"All right. I just remembered that it's my husband's birthday on Thursday—can you imagine a wife forgetting her own husband's birthday?"

"Certainly I can." He was very sweet.

"So the situation is that I must send him something and have it arrive in Santa Monica the day after tomorrow."

"No cause for concern, Ms. Stickler. What would you like to send him?"

"Um, let me think." I let him sweat for a second. "My husband is an avid reader, mysteries in particular. Tony Hillerman is a favorite author of his."

"Then why don't I send him one of Hillerman's books for his birthday?"

"That sounds like a fine idea, Scott. Thank you."

"My pleasure. I'll just jot down your home address and your husband's name, and first thing tomorrow morning I'll have someone here at the hotel purchase Hillerman's latest book and ship it out by overnight mail. We have a wealth of fine bookstores here in Seattle. This won't be a problem at all."

That's what you think. "You said 'latest book.' I'm afraid there's a tiny detail I neglected to mention, Scott."

"Yes?"

"My husband is not only an avid reader but an avid collector. What I'm saying is that you're going to have to find a first edition of one of Hillerman's books, signed by the author, and make sure that *it* arrives in Santa Monica by Thursday."

It wasn't Roger's birthday on Thursday and he wasn't a collector of signed first editions, but I used this ruse frequently when playing Torture the Concierge. You should see the hard-to-find goodies he's been sent over the years. There was the time I claimed he was an aviation enthusiast (he got a replica of a P-51 Mustang). There was the time I claimed he loved tennis (he got tickets to a WTA tournament in Manhattan Beach). There was the time I claimed he was Macedonian and was yearning for a gift that would remind him of "the old country" (he got baklava from a Balkan bakery around the corner from the hotel). Why Roger had become so lackadaisical about our marriage was beyond me. It had to be sort of fun being my husband, didn't it?

"Well, the need for a signed first edition does complicate the task a bit," said Scott. He exhaled. The strain was beginning to show. I was rooting for him though. Especially after the housekeeping snafu in my bathroom.

"So you won't be able to help me after all?" I said, sounding crushed.

"No. No. It's not that." He paused. He was trying not to crack. "Why don't you let me research this matter while you're enjoying your dinner? Would that be acceptable?"

Excellent, Scottie. Never say die. "Yes, that would be acceptable."

I hung up. Only minutes later, as I was freshening up to go down to the restaurant, Scott called back.

"Oh, good. I caught you," he said excitedly, slightly out of breath.

"Yes. I was just leaving the room."

"Here's wonderful news: I've had success with our birthday crisis." *Our* birthday crisis. AMLP gives high marks to a concierge who makes the guest's problem his problem. "As I told you, Seattle has some incredible bookstores, including an antiquarian bookstore. I got in touch with its owner—I was able to reach him at home, actually—and he has in stock a first edition of a novel called *The Fly on the Wall*, published in 1971 and signed by Hillerman. The price is three hundred dollars, plus shipping and handling." He was practically panting.

"My, I'm so relieved—and appreciative, of course." There would be a nice big tip for Scott. Thank God I didn't have to pay for these trips myself.

"Thank you, Ms. Stickler. Thank you. Now, if you'll just give me the necessary information I'll take care of the rest."

I gave him Roger's name (Roger Stickler, not Roger Baskin), our address, and my Stickler Amex number.

"Then we're all set," he said.

"All set."

"Enjoy your dinner, Ms. Stickler. Oh, and may I add my own wishes for your husband's happy, happy birthday."

"I'll pass them along, Scott."

"He's a fortunate man to have a wife who takes such pains to find just the right gift. He must feel very lucky."

If he does, he's not letting on, I thought glumly.

CHAPTER THREE

The Worthington Seattle boasted three restaurants. For my first meal at the hotel, I chose to dine at its top-of-the-line spot, Elliott's, named for Seattle's Elliott Bay. I didn't have a reservation, but that was the restaurant's problem.

"Hello," I greeted the maître d', who was not in a tuxedo, as was once standard for high-end hotel restaurants. He was wearing a white shirt with hidden buttons that went all the way up to his Adam's apple (sort of a modern twist on the old Nehru jacket) and black slacks. The Worthington was going for edgy as opposed to stuffy, apparently. "I'm a guest in the hotel and I'm absolutely famished. Anything available? Preferably near the music?" There was a combo playing "cool jazz" of the type you hear in elevators and dentists' offices.

"Let me check," he said. "Would you give me a moment?"

I'll give you *three* moments, dude. According to the AMLP manual, the host or maître d' must seat diners within three minutes of arrival.

While I waited for him to produce a table, I glanced around the room to determine whether the facility was well ventilated and well lit, whether the tabletops were adorned with attractive centerpieces, whether there were telltale food remnants on the floor, et cetera. During my visual sweep of the place, I inadvertently made eye contact with a man who was dining alone—a stupifyingly handsome man, in his forties, I guessed. He had dark wavy hair and awesome cheekbones and he was dressed in a very snappy blue suit, and he not only nodded at me with a sort of sly, I'm-here-alone-and-so-are-you half-smile, he actually raised his wineglass to me. I was so startled that I swallowed wrong and started choking on my own spit.

Real swift, Elizabeth, I thought, ducking my head in embarrassment. It wasn't as if I wasn't a pro when it came to traveling by myself and fending off the occasional joker. That goes with the territory. But this joker looked awfully suave and sophisticated compared to the previous ones, and I was thrown by his attention, suspicious of it—well, and flattered by it, sure.

He's coming on to me because I'm a blonde, I rationalized, and blondes always turn heads, no matter what they look like. (I was, of course, a brunette with an excellent colorist.) Or maybe all those hours at the gym are finally paying off, I mused, wincing in pain at the mere thought of the crunches and the heel diggers and the other masochistic contortions I put myself through in an effort to be at my best. I worked hard on my appearance the way I worked hard at my job, which was also the way I worked hard on my marriage. It was all about control. I had the sad little notion that if you kept your body fit and your house clean and your closet filled with designer clothes, the moving van wouldn't show up at your door and take everything you cared about away.

"I can seat you now," said the maître d', interrupting my descent into neurosis. I snuck a peek at my watch. Three minutes on the nose, luckily for him.

I followed him to a table in the section I'd requested. After he pulled out the chair for me, I sat down and waited to see if he'd unfold my napkin and place it on my lap. He did.

"Your waiter will be with you shortly," he said before departing.

I nodded, then gave the table the once-over. The cloth was without stains, tears, or frays. The flowers in the centerpiece were fresh, fragrant. The glassware was free of cracks, chips, or, my personal favorite, lipstick grease.

The waiter came, took my drink order, returned with my drink, told me the specials, took my dinner order, and left. I checked my watch. According to the AMLP manual, waiters must serve the first course within fifteen minutes of ordering and the main course within twenty minutes after that.

While I was waiting for my food, I sipped my wine and tried to appear completely nonchalant as I turned my head this way and that, in search of the cutie who had smiled at me. I couldn't find him. Perhaps he'd finished his dinner and left. I felt a pang of disappointment.

Dinner was delivered in a semi-professional fashion by my server. I say "semi-professional" because his thumb was dangerously close to the salad greens as he was depositing the plate in front of me. Manual or no manual, the last thing I want to think about as I'm about to eat *anything* is where some guy's thumb has been. The other faux pas he made was to rush over with my main course, his fingers protected by a white cloth, and warn, "Now this plate is very, very hot, so be careful." What is it with waiters these days? Are they your mother? The plate—and the food sitting on it—is *supposed* to be hot, so why the news bulletin? What's more, when they tell you how hot the plate is, your automatic impulse is to touch it, to see whether it's hot or not. My opinion is that they should just shut up about this particular aspect of the meal and get on with their business.

Griping aside, the food was wonderful, and I enjoyed my dinner immensely. I was about to order a decaf coffee and go back to the room when guess who appeared at my table.

"I couldn't help noticing that you're here alone," said the handsome man who hadn't vanished after all.

I was stunned, absolutely nonplussed that he had materialized at my table, but I didn't choke on my spit this time. "Your powers of observation are astonishing," I said, resorting to sarcasm, as was my habit when I was caught off balance. Actually, it was his face that was astonishing. He was even better looking up close—deep brown eyes, full lips, a lightly tanned complexion. And I found his voice very seductive; it was one of those Clint Eastwood whispers that's soft yet assertive.

"And to think that I worked on that line for the last hour," he said with a chuckle.

I smiled, hoping none of my dinner was wedged between my teeth. "I'm delighted that you spent so much time on it. Would you like to sit down?" I was amazed by my boldness, amazed and energized by it.

"I was hoping you'd ask. I'm here alone too, and I'm in the mood for an after-dinner drink. How about joining me?"

As I indicated, it wasn't unprecedented for a man to hit on me when I was on the road, but the last one who did was singularly unappetizing. He waltzed up to me at a hotel in Denver and asked, "What's your sign?" Needless to say, my answer was, "Do not disturb." No, what was unusual was that this guy was enormously attractive and had a smooth approach. More to the point, I was lonely and had a little buzz going and was feeling neglected by my husband, so what was the harm?

"Please. Sit down," I said, figuring I'd have a drink, make chitchat, and head back to my room.

"Thanks. My name's Chris. Chris Eckersly." He leaned over the table to shake hands, then sat.

"Elizabeth Bas—" I stopped. "Elizabeth Stickler. Nice to meet you, Chris. Are you here on business?"

"Yes," he said. "I'm from Kansas City, but I have clients in Seattle. I'm an investment banker."

At this juncture, the waiter stopped by and asked if he could bring us anything. Chris ordered a cognac for each of us. I'm not a huge fan of liqueurs—they give me a headache—but I didn't protest. I was "going with the flow," as they say.

"What about you, Elizabeth?" he asked me. "Are you here on business?"

"Yes," I said. "I'm a rep for a skin care company." I made up a dumb name. It was something like Dermaco. "We have terrific products."

"Then you must use them on yourself. You have lovely skin—and a lovely face to go with it."

Whoa. A compliment of a personal nature. Did I have a lovely face? It was probably lovelier than average, especially when I smiled. Roger used to say I was beautiful when I smiled.

The waiter brought the cognacs. I took a whiff of mine, remembered about the headache, and decided to just swirl the liqueur around in the glass instead of actually drink it.

"So you work for a skin care company and you travel a lot, but you haven't told me where you live," Chris remarked.

"L.A.," I said.

"Ah," he said. "La-la land. Do you party with the movie stars?"

"No, I do my dry cleaning with the movie stars. I run into them at Brown's Cleaners near my house in Santa Monica; they're dropping off their gowns and I'm dropping off my bedspreads."

"Poor Cinderella. And what does your husband do?"

So he'd checked out my left hand and noticed my wedding band. "He's a real estate attorney."

"Then he must be a busy guy. The real estate market is booming in southern California, I hear."

"Yes, he's been very busy lately." Too busy. And not just because the market was booming but because Roger was such a pushover, letting the other lawyers dump their workload on him. In the early years of our marriage, I'd thought his eagerness to take on everybody else's burdens was rather sweet and unselfish. Now, I resented how much time he was putting in at the office—time he could be spending with me. "How about you, Chris. Are you married?" I knew the answer. I'd checked out his left hand too.

"I am indeed, for ten years. To my high school sweetheart, the love of my life."

Then what are you doing here with me, big boy? "You have a bunch of kids, I'll bet."

"Four. Meredith's a great mom."

But Meredith isn't as exciting to you as the women you meet in hotel dining rooms, is that it, Chris? She's the love of your life, but she resents you for not being around to help with the children? "You must miss your family when you travel."

"I do." He sipped his cognac. "That's why I'm so grateful that you walked into the restaurant tonight. You're really taking my mind off my loneliness, Elizabeth."

"I'm glad I could help." Okay, so he was full of it. It was fun to be flirted with for a change. Roger never flirted with me anymore. His idea of making advances was paying the mortgage early.

He cocked his head to the right, gave me that sly smile again. "Would it be fair to say that I'm helping you too? That I'm taking your mind off *your* loneliness?"

"It would be fair to say that." I wasn't encouraging him exactly. I was just going with the flow again.

Chris raised his brandy glass. "Here's to pleasurable distractions. Drink up."

Oh, why not, I decided. So what if I got a headache. Wasn't that why Extra-Strength Tylenol was invented? I took a couple of sips of cognac and felt the warm liquid slide down my throat. Nice.

"Tell me more about you, Elizabeth," Chris prompted, moving his chair around the table so he could sit next to me instead of across from me.

"What would you like to know?" I replied, involuntarily batting my eyelashes at him. *This* was what was missing in my marriage—the frisson of sexual tension, the sense of unpredictability, the fact that a man was dying to get into my pants.

"Your opinion on health care, gun violence, tax cuts, the color of my tie. Anything you want to talk about would be just fine with me."

I leaned in closer to examine his tie. "What color is that anyway?"

"I believe the salesman called it burnt sienna. Remember that crayon from the Crayola box?"

"Of course." We both laughed. Given enough alcohol, almost anything is funny.

We continued to drink (Chris ordered another cognac for himself), listen to the music, flirt. It was clear to me—and probably to everyone in the restaurant—that he was deeply interested in getting laid. And brother, was I tempted. Well, not tempted, exactly. I wasn't such an easy mark. I was a married woman and I loved my husband and I had every intention of hanging on to him, no matter how dreary our situation had become. When I say "tempted" I mean simply that I allowed myself to imagine myself in Chris's arms, to picture us together in his hotel room, to envision us cavorting in the same playful, intimate way in which Roger and I used to cavort.

But in the end, sitting there with a stranger only made me want Roger, only made our inability to connect in the past year more depressing.

"I've got to go," I said abruptly, getting up from my chair. "It's late and I really should—"

Chris put his hand on my arm. "I wish you'd stay, Elizabeth."

His eyes were pleading. Oh, to be desired like that—even if the guy *was* half in the bag—was a major turn-on. Still, I wouldn't cave.

"I'm sorry, Chris. This was a lot of fun, but it's time for me to go to bed."

"By yourself?"

I nodded.

"Why?" he said. "We could keep the fun going. Think about it."

I had. That's what unnerved me. "It was nice meeting you," I said. "Thanks for the cognac and the company. Enjoy the rest of your stay in Seattle."

Before he could protest further, I was gone.

As I rode up in the elevator, which, I was careful to note, was outfitted with the plush carpeting, the crystal lighting fixture, the wood panelling, and the fire and safety features that were obligatory for AMLP's Five Key hotels, I realized how much I needed to speak to Roger, to hear his voice, to remind myself that our marriage was worth fighting for. We were just going through a stale period, that was all. Nothing to worry about.

The minute I entered the room, I rushed for the phone and dialed our number. It was eleven-thirty. Roger would either be sprawled in front of the television set watching Leno or standing in front of the refrigerator grabbing a late-night snack. I smiled proprietarily when I thought of him. My sweetie. Everything would be all right between us. I would make it all right.

The phone rang several times before the answering machine picked up.

"Hey, honey. It's me," I said, hoping he was nearby and was only screening calls. "Pick up, okay? Pick up, Roger. I'm calling to say good-night."

Nothing.

"Okay, so if you're in the bathroom or something, here's the number at the hotel." I had given it to him before I left, but I repeated it. "Call me back so we can check in. I love you, Roger."

I waited a few more seconds to see if he'd pick up, but since he didn't I hung up.

Where could he be? I wondered. He hadn't mentioned any plans for the evening. And he didn't usually work this late.

I tried the number again. After two rings, Roger picked up.

"Hi," I said, relieved that he was home. "Where were you before?"

"Before what?" He sounded groggy, out of it.

"A few seconds ago. I called and left a message."

"I was asleep. You woke me up."

"Oh. Sorry. Why did you go to sleep so early?"

"It's not early. It's the middle of the night."

"No, it's eleven-thirty." There. Another example of the change in Roger, another example of how marriages lose their punch over time. When we were first married, he had the stamina of a Labrador retriever. He'd be up for dancing at eleven-thirty. He'd be up for taking a walk at eleven-thirty. He'd be up for having sex at eleven-thirty. In those days, eleven-thirty was not considered *the middle of the night*. Now, he could barely keep his eyes open past Leno's opening monologue. Where, oh where, was my frisky puppy?

"Is everything okay up there?" he asked.

"Everything's fine," I said, proud that I hadn't succumbed to Chris's charms. "I just wanted to tell you I loved you."

"I love you too, hon. How's the hotel?"

"It's too soon to tell whether they'll keep their Five Keys. There've been a couple of missteps. Tomorrow will be the real test, when I inspect the entire property."

Roger yawned loudly, into my ear.

"You sound riveted," I said. "How was your day?"

"Hectic. I took Frankie Rollerblading after school." Twelve-year-old Frankie Wheeler was his Little Brother in the Big Brother Program. "And in between, I had back-to-back closings. The last one was on a house up the street from us, just north of Montana. The buyers paid one and a half million for it."

"And it's a teardown, I'll bet."

"Naturally. The house is dated and needs a little TLC, but it's got good bones. The buyers could easily renovate it or redecorate it and it would be more than livable. Instead they're going to bulldoze it so they can build a palace on a lot the size of a postage stamp. It's nuts."

"I know."

"So when are you coming home?"

Here we go again, I thought. This would make the zillionth time I'd told him. "Thursday," I said. "My flight lands around four, so how about a nice romantic dinner together after you get home from the office? Doesn't that sound enticing?"

No response.

"Roger? Are you there?"

"Yeah. I just—"

"Fell asleep, right?"

"Sorry. Don't take it personally."

"How else am I supposed to take it? No one but you falls asleep when I'm talking." Chris certainly hadn't.

"Look, I'm really beat, Elizabeth. I'd like to talk but I can barely see straight."

"You never used to be so tired. Maybe there's something wrong with you, health-wise."

"No, I'm fine. I had my annual physical last month. The doctor said I had the body of a teenager."

A teenager on downers. "Well, since you'd rather go to sleep than catch up with me, I guess I'll get off," I said, feeling rejected and resentful in equal measure.

Not a peep out of him.

"Roger?"

Still nothing.

"Wake up, would you please!"

"What's going on?"

"You fell asleep again. It would be nice if you'd stay up long enough for us to say goodnight to each other, the way we always did whenever I'd be away on a trip."

"Goodnight, Elizabeth."

"So I'll see you tomorrow, okay, honey? And we'll have that dinner? Just the two of us?"

Nothing. Well, not exactly nothing. I heard the light wheezing that had become the warm-up act for Roger's snoring.

" 'Night," I said dejectedly and hung up.

No, it did not occur to me to pick up the phone and ask the hotel operator to ring Chris's room. I believed in the sanctity of marriage. I believed in remaining true blue. I believed in being exactly what my mother wasn't—a woman who could hold on to her man.

It's not that Mom was a horror or anything; it was just that she had a rather short attention span. By the time my sister, Brenda, and I were in high school, she'd been married and divorced three times, which had meant new houses, new schools, and new friends, not to mention new fathers. What happens to a little girl who grows up amid such chaos? She either becomes the sort of adult who creates chaos, because it feels familiar, or she becomes the sort of adult who desperately tries to control her environment, because she's scared to death of chaos. Guess which path I chose? While my sister flitted from city to city, job to job, and man to man (unlike our mother, she was not a fan of marriage and had yet to take the plunge), I graduated from UCLA, stayed in the Los Angeles area, was hired by AMLP as a public relations assistant, and, after revealing myself to be a perfectionist as well as a loyal employee, was entrusted with the position of inspector.

In other words, I'd spent my grown-up years with one company and one husband. And I intended to keep it that way. I would fix Roger, not junk him for some other guy. Yes, I would improve him. In the parlance of real estate professionals, he was not a teardown but a renovation project, and, as his wife, I was the likely architect for the job.

CHAPTER FOUR

Despite the comfy mattress and fancy bed linens, I slept fitfully, dreaming at one point that Roger had not only forgotten my travel schedule, he had forgotten my name.

Feeling a little wrung out, I ordered breakfast from room service—a mixed experience. Yes, my call was answered within the required three rings, and yes, I was greeted in a courteous fashion and given a time estimate for delivery, and yes, the meal was delivered within five minutes of the time promised. However, there was no morning newspaper with my breakfast, the server did not offer to pour my coffee, and, according to my pocket thermometer, my egg-white omelette was not the proper temperature. Worst of all, the flowers on the table were wilted. Very disappointing.

I spent the day inspecting all other areas and aspects of the hotel, and noted additional infractions. In the health club, for example, there were nicely appointed lockers and changing rooms but no fresh towels. The sundries shop was stocked with guide books on Seattle but was out of toothpaste and deodorant. And the hair salon—God, I wish you could have seen me. When I arrived for my appointment, I explained to the stylist that I wanted a shampoo and blow dry. "Just blow it out straight," I told her. "Nothing poofy." She ignored me. By the time she was done, I was sporting a Dolly Parton 'do.

The following morning, as I was standing in the lobby waiting to check out, I ran into Chris Eckersly, whom I had successfully avoided up to that point.

"Well, well," he said with a slight curl of his top lip. "If it isn't Elizabeth Stickler, the lady who seduces you and then does a vanishing act."

Uh-oh. So he was the type who cops an attitude when women don't leap into bed with him. "How are you, Chris?" I said in my most professional, detached voice. I wanted to block out the memory of ever meeting him. "I'd love to stay and chat but I've got a plane to catch."

"That's a shame," he said. "I was hoping we could have dinner together tonight, pick up where we left off, put a different ending on the scene this time."

Sheesh. What a letch. "As I said, I've got a flight to catch."

"Back to Santa Monica? That's where you live, isn't it? With your real estate lawyer hubby?"

Me and my big mouth. Well, I certainly learned my lesson. No matter how dispirited I was about my relationship with Roger, I would not invite another man to buy me a liqueur.

"Next!"

It was the clerk at the check-out desk, advising me that it was my turn to settle up.

"Goodbye, Chris," I said hurriedly.

"Goodbye, Elizabeth," he said. "I'll be seeing you."

In your dreams, I thought, wondering why strangers who seem perfectly pleasant when you strike up a conversation with them in dimly lit bars and restaurants always end up being so creepy in the light of day.

After I checked out, I took a taxi to the airport and wrote up my evaluation during the flight back to LAX. Sad to say, I was recommending that we downgrade the Worthington Seattle to a Four Key property, given the breaches I've enumerated. AMLP's Five Key properties were hotels and resorts that demonstrated perfection in every way. This establishment did not. Did I feel guilty about depriving them of their fifth Key and, possibly, putting a dent in their business? Sure. There were times when I wished I were back in AMLP's public relations department where it wasn't my job to take the temperature of egg-white omelettes. But now I was being paid to protect the consumer, and I was damn good at it. A little too good at it, you're probably thinking.

My plane landed early, so I took the limo home, dropped my bags off at the house, hopped in the car, and drove to Fred Segal. A former ice skating rink that had been transformed into a shopping emporium with dozens of individually leased boutiques under one roof, it sells everything—from clothes and jewelry to soaps and stationery—and is incredibly popular with the trendoids. Not a department store, not a mall, Fred Segal is, as the locals say, "a concept." Anyhow, I was thinking ahead to my romantic dinner with Roger that night and wanted to pick up something sexy to wear. I settled on a long, black, silky, sleeveless number with slits up the side, the back, and the front. What I'm saying is that I paid a lot of money for not a lot of dress. I had vowed to renovate Roger and the first step was to rewire his libido.

By the time he got home from the office, I had slipped into the dress, set the table, lit a few candles, dimmed the lights, opened some wine, and readied the platter of the Cantonese duck I'd taken out from Chinois on Main, a nearby restaurant also popular with the trendoids.

"Wow. Look at you," said Roger as he stood in the foyer eyeing me. His suit was rumpled, his face needed a shave, and there was a red stain on his tie. Ketchup, I guessed.

"You like the dress?" I said, modeling it for him.

"What there is of it." He smiled, dumping his bulging briefcase on the floor. "Come here and let me see it up close."

I sauntered over to him, lifting my hair off my neck, vamping. "Want to feel it?" I said suggestively. "It's silky."

He ran his hands over my hips, then pulled me to him. "Welcome home, hon."

"It's good to be home," I said, thrilled that this was going so well. I was even more thrilled when Roger lowered his head and kissed me on the mouth. It was a hot kiss, a moist kiss, the kind of kiss I'd been pining for.

"And thanks for doing all this." He nodded at the dining room. He had caught a glimpse of the candles and the table and the wine.

"My pleasure. Are you hungry?" I was being deliberately ambiguous here. If he wanted to postpone dinner and go straight to the bedroom, I was all for it. If he wanted to eat dinner and have sex afterwards, I was all for that too. I wasn't going to push. Not much, anyway.

"Now that you mention it, I'm starving. I had a burger for lunch but that was hours ago."

I was right—ketchup. "Then why don't you sit down," I said, taking his arm and walking him into the dining room. "I went to Chinois on Main and bought their Cantonese duck, your favorite."

"That was sweet of you, Elizabeth, especially with all you had to do today." He kissed me again, rubbed up against me. I could feel his gratitude through his trousers. Yes, this was going extremely well.

I poured him a glass of wine, then scurried into the kitchen where I had dinner warming. I brought it out and served it to him, spooning it onto his plate in a manner I hoped he would find sensual, not servile.

Then I asked him if there was anything else he needed. The right answer would have been "You," but I settled for "No, this is great, hon."

We chatted while we ate—it was an actual conversation as opposed to me trying to pull information out of him—and I was positively giddy with the sense that Roger's apathy, or more accurately, his disappearance into old farthood, had been only temporary.

For example, he filled me in on what was going on in his office, shared juicy tidbits with me about his partners just like he used to.

"David's got a new girlfriend," he reported.

"Did he remember to tell the current girlfriend this time?" I kidded.

David Durston, the "frat boy," as we had dubbed him, was aggressively single and had dated practically every woman in southern California. Roger was forever putting up with his middle-of-the-day trysts, covering for him when he failed to show up at closings. David had a good heart, Roger believed, in spite of all his running around. They'd been friends since law school and they couldn't have been more different. While Roger was the dependable one, who never minded working hard or late, David was the salesman who never failed to bring in a new client. He had the personality, and Roger had the stability, and together they built a firm.

"Guess what this one does for a living?" said Roger.

"She's a nuclear physicist."

"Nope. She's a baby whisperer."

I laughed. "What the heck's that?"

"She's like a horse whisperer, only with infants. She communicates with them and then tells their mothers what's really on their minds."

"So she translates *goo-goo gaa-gaa* into 'Mommy, I feel abandoned every time you leave me with the nanny?' " I sighed. "Only in L.A."

"Brad's going to Tuscany for two weeks," Roger went on, speaking of another of his partners. "Gerta rented them a villa."

"Didn't they just come back from a vacation in Europe?"

He nodded. "But you know Gerta. She says she feels 'stifled' here in America."

Brad Weiner was a pleasant man and a good lawyer but he had a major problem—his wife. No one knew exactly where she was from—her accent was vaguely German, vaguely Swiss, vaguely Scandinavian—and she offered a different version of her heritage every time she was asked about it. She was one of those people who professes to hate the United States, yet has no compunction about taking advantage of its goods and services. Her latest adventure in capitalism was shooting lessons, because, she said, America was such a violent and dangerous place, and owning and operating a gun was one way to make it less violent and dangerous.

"How's Carrie?" I asked, referring to the fourth and most recent of the partners.

"Feisty, as always," said Roger.

Carrie Toobin was a single mother who had started out as a paralegal at the firm, gone to law school at night, passed the bar, and become a first-rate lawyer. She was fiercely loyal to "the boys," as she had nicknamed Roger and David and Brad, and they rewarded her eventually by making her a partner. She was a little rough around the edges—there was entirely too much gum-chewing going on, in my opinion, as well as a tendency to wear skirts that barely covered her ass—but people who wrote her off as a floozy were the dim ones.

Roger and I ate together and drank together and laughed together, and being with him in such a convivial atmosphere gave me hope that the guy I met on the 405 was still in there.

"How about I do the dishes?" he volunteered when we were finished with dinner. There. Another flash of the early days, when he was thoughtful and considerate and not only did the dishes but took out the garbage.

"How about we leave the dishes for later?" I suggested. "I've got something else in mind for us."

"Dessert?"

"Not exactly." I sat on his lap, ran my fingers through his hair. "What about a little trip to the bedroom?" I know I said I wasn't going to push, but the timing seemed right and Roger seemed ripe.

"Now you're talking." He smiled enthusiastically, lasciviously. I was immensely optimistic.

He kissed me, helped me up from the chair, took my hand and led me down the hall toward the bedroom.

"I'll be there in a minute," I whispered, nodding at our fluffy queen-size bed. "I just want to freshen up."

"I'll meet you between the sheets," he said, winking at me. "Don't be long."

"I won't, hon." I kissed him, tingling with anticipation—and relief. He was back. Dear God, he was back.

While he undressed and slipped under the covers, I stood in front of the bathroom mirror and prepared to make myself utterly irresistible. I wanted to drive him crazy with desire so that he would deem this night the standard by which all nights would be measured; so that, should he be tempted to slide back into the body of the distracted, sexless creature I'd been living with, he would remember how fabulous it was between us; so that, should he be conflicted about whether to make mad, passionate love to me or labor over a real estate closing contract, there would be no contest.

I lifted the black dress over my head and gave my naked body a quick once-over. Underarms shaved? Check. Legs shaved? Check. Cellulite gone? Not in this lifetime.

"You coming, hon?" Roger called out to me.

"In a sec," I said, loving the eagerness in his voice. I especially loved that he had left the lights on in the bedroom. He wanted to *see* me as well as feel me.

I gargled with a capful of Scope after flossing out the Cantonese duck. I dabbed perfume behind my ears, on my throat, between my breasts, along the inside of my thighs. I brushed my hair forward, over my face, then let it fall back into what I hoped was a sort of mussed up, disheveled, bedroom-y look. I applied a fresh coat of lipstick, mascara, and blusher. There was nothing else to do. I was ready.

Yes, I mused, nodding approvingly at my reflection. Roger will be powerless to resist me.

I undulated into the bedroom, my stride somewhere between a strut and a slink. "Here I am, baby," I said, several octaves lower than I normally spoke. "All set to make your fantasies come true."

At first I thought Roger said something.

"What was that, sweetheart?" I whispered as I climbed into bed next to him. He had taken off his clothes and was stretched out on his back, his head resting on two pillows, his arms folded across his chest, *his eyes closed*. "Roger? You're not asleep already, are you? Tell me you're not." My heart sagged with disappointment.

"Not asleep," he mumbled.

I wasn't so sure. I cozied up to him, nibbled his lips, ran my tongue along the folds of his ear, massaged his chest, moved my hand down to his—

Swell. *It* was asleep, no question about that. I couldn't believe my luck. Yes, Roger had just eaten a meal but not a heavy meal, and yes, I had just been primping in the bathroom but only for a couple of minutes, so what was the goddamn problem?

Well, I was not taking this lying down. I sat up, straddled my husband, grabbed—no, I was more tender than that—his penis, and began to stroke it, commanding it to wake the hell up.

"Come on, Freddy boy," I urged as I stroked. That was what we called Roger's pecker: Freddy. Also, mushroom cap, pinkie, and Sylvester. Don't ask me why couples pick names for the man's organ. It seems cute when things are going well in the sex department but absurd when they're not. "Come on, Freddy. Let's get you feeling good. That's it. That's it. Okay, we've done it. My, what a big, big boinger you are."

And so he was. It took long enough, but eventually Freddy (and Roger) had risen, and shortly thereafter, sexual intercourse was achieved. If that sounds clinical, I intend it to. Oh, sure, there was cuddling afterwards—for about a nanosecond. Roger nuzzled me, told me he loved me, then fell deeply into the land of wheezing and snoring.

What are you supposed to do with a man who was once a perfect mate but is now a perfect drag? You could hire a hit man, but that would be a different book. You could also walk out on him, but that would be a different book too. I went in another direction, as I've indicated. Stay with me.

CHAPTER FIVE

On Saturday afternoon, while Roger was burying himself under a pile of papers at the office rather than burying himself under the sheets with me, I had lunch with my sister, Brenda, one of the "trendoids" I referred to earlier.

At thirty-two, Brenda was old enough to have outgrown her slavish devotion to fads but, instead, made her living from it. After bouncing from job to job, she had finally landed in the editorial department of *In the Know*, a Los Angeles–based magazine that's a cross between *In Style* and a Liz Smith column—a publication brimming with such life-and-death matters as how Hollywood's biggest stars conceal their acne.

I love Brenda dearly and was thrilled when she settled down in L.A. after tearing around the country, but I was mystified by her obsession with celebrity culture even as I was amused by it. I mean, she honestly believed that the fact that Jennifer Aniston moisturized with rose oil qualified as news.

We met at a small, noisy restaurant called Kay 'n' Dave's, which isn't chic but *is* trendy. (Brenda says there's a big difference.) Situated on the border of Santa Monica and Brentwood, where, by the way, Brenda rents a condo, it offers what Kay 'n' Dave call "fresh, healthy Mexican," which means that they don't cook with lard. All I can say in that regard is that Michelle Pfeiffer was there the day we were, and there was no lard on her that I could detect.

"Michelle always orders the arroz con veggies, even though it's not on the menu anymore," Brenda whispered, as if this information were right up there with nuclear arms secrets. "It's Mexican rice mixed with roasted vegetables, topped with melted cheese and guacamole and served with flour tortillas."

"I know what it is, Brenda," I said. "I've had it here many times. We non-celebrities are allowed to eat too."

"Well, *excuse* me. Touchy today, aren't we?"

"Sorry." I was touchy and grouchy and horny, none of it Brenda's fault.

We both ordered the arroz con veggies and chatted about this and that.

"So how's everything with you?" she asked finally, after a long riff involving Hollywood stars and their beauty and health regimens. Nick Nolte, she confided, was injecting himself with specially formulated vitamin tonics. Salma Hayek was fastening her hair back with colorful twist-ties, the kind that seal garbage bags. And Shania Twain was keeping her skin supple with nightly applications of Bag Balm, a product that numbs cows' udders so they don't feel pain while being milked. Was I ever out of the loop.

"I'm not so great," I admitted. "Roger hasn't been himself lately. He's insensitive and inattentive and doesn't seem to care about me."

"Don't be ridiculous, Elizabeth. Roger adores you."

"*Used* to adore me. For the past year—"

"You and Roger have been having problems for an entire year and I'm only hearing about it now? I'm your sister, for God's sake!"

"Please don't get huffy, Brenda. I didn't want to talk about it before. I wasn't ready to admit how upset I've been."

"But you're ready now?"

"I'm so ready I'm about to burst."

"Then go ahead. Tell me."

"Well, it's just that Roger has been treating me as if I'm not very interesting to him. He doesn't listen. He doesn't initiate conversation. He doesn't initiate sex." I told her about Thursday night's fiasco. "And he doesn't pay the slightest attention to his appearance the way he used to. He's gained weight and he hasn't bought new clothes in ages and he leaves crumbs all over the kitchen, not to mention on himself. He's not the person I married, Brenda."

"Is that all?" She snorted. "No guy is the person anybody married, Elizabeth. They all change after they walk down that aisle. Why do you think I'm still single?"

"Because of Mom," I said. "You're afraid of repeating her mistakes."

"Bullshit. I'm still single because I'm waiting for George Clooney to propose." She smiled, and when she did, I felt as if I were looking in a mirror. She had the same wavy blond hair as I did (we went to the same colorist now that she was living nearby), the same blue-gray eyes, the same crooked two front teeth. She was a younger, thinner version of me—the resemblance really was startling—but our approaches to life couldn't have been more different. "The truth is, I've seen what goes on between couples, and it's not for me."

"What, exactly, goes on between couples, in your opinion?" I said, eager to hear this one.

"I call it 'the settling-in phenomenon.' Men get fired up in the beginning of a relationship—because they're in the hunt—but once the challenge is over, they revert to form."

"Which is?"

"The way you're describing Roger. They stop listening, stop talking, stop turning on the charm. They *settle in*. From then on, all they care about is getting paid and getting laid."

"Roger doesn't care about getting laid. I already told you—*I'm* the one who had to jump *his* bones the other night."

"Maybe he's depressed," said Brenda, who became an expert on the subject after Marie Osmond announced she was a sufferer.

"Maybe, but I thought depressed people lose their appetite. If Roger were here with us at lunch, he would have eaten your order of arroz con veggies *and* mine. And he would have gotten most of it on his shirt. No, I think he's just become a bored, boring, boorish husband, and I didn't see it coming."

"Elizabeth, aren't you being a little hard on poor Roger? He was never the life-of-the-party type, not even when you two started going out. He was sweet and dependable and had his own interests and let you have yours. If you wanted the personality kid, you should have married someone else."

"I'm not saying I want the personality kid. I hate those exhausting loud-mouths who have to be the center of attention. They suck all the air out of a room. No, what I want is Roger, the way he used to be—quiet, but a wonderful companion and friend and lover."

"And he's not any of those things anymore?"

"No. For example, he used to like the same music I do—rock 'n' roll, disco, reggae. Guess what he listens to now? *Classical*."

"Snooze music."

"Right. And he used to love going out on weeknights—to restaurants, to the movies, to the pier, to clubs. Now he just works late, and when he doesn't work late, he plants himself in front of the television with a bag of Cheetos. The family-size bag."

"Not good."

"And he's so moody. You'd think *he* was the one with PMS."

"Also not good."

"He doesn't even like to talk about starting a family anymore, even though he knows how much I want to have kids."

"Gee, I'm so sorry to hear this, Elizabeth. Have you considered marriage counseling?"

"I've considered it, but Roger won't go. Whenever I confront him with the fact that we've drifted apart, he denies it. He really thinks everything is fine the way it is."

"Well then, what *are* you going to do? You're not planning to leave him, are you? Because if you are, you'd better snap out of it." She jabbed her fork in my face when she said this.

"Snap out of what?"

"Snap out of whatever fantasy world you're living in." She put the fork down on the plate and leaned back in her chair. "Elizabeth, I'll try to make my point one more time. Roger is probably in the settling-in phase of your marriage. If you walked out on him and married someone else, you'd run into the same problem with the new guy sooner or later. Besides, there's no such thing as a perfect husband. Even if you made up a list of everything you'd ever want in a mate—he should look like a Greek god; he should earn a million dollars per year, not including bonuses and/or stock options; he should speak three foreign languages fluently; he should paint landscapes or write novels or sculpt nudes; he should come up with imaginative gifts for your birthday; he should love you in the precise way you would like to be loved—you'd wind up cutting a deal. You'd compromise. You'd choose a man who meets *most* of your needs. So I'd stick with Roger, if I were you. He's not perfect, but he's not a prick."

"Brenda." I sat back and grinned at her. "Where did all this world-weariness come from at your age?"

She shrugged. "I just view what happens with celebrity relationships as a microcosm of real life. Do you actually think that when Soon-Yi Previn was growing up, her dream was to marry a man who looked like Woody Allen? No. She cut a deal. She came away with a package she could live with."

"Well, *I* didn't 'cut a deal,' as you put it. I fell in love with Roger. And you're right—he's not a prick, which is why I have no desire to leave him. He doesn't beat me. He doesn't drink too much. He doesn't even go crazy when I run the vacuum cleaner while he's watching a football game. It's just that he's not the man he used to be, and, well, I can't explain it except to say that the magic is gone."

"Then do something to get the magic back."

"I did—on Thursday night—and I bombed."

"What about using a little magic to get the magic back?"

"Brenda. You're not making sense."

"I am so. You know the saying 'fight fire with fire?' Well, there's another saying—'use magic to get magic.' "

"I must have missed that one."

"Listen, Elizabeth," she said, growing excited. "I'm onto something here, something that could save your marriage, something I would never have heard about if I didn't work at the magazine."

"What you hear about by working at that magazine is that capri pants are out this year and wide-leg pants are in. I don't see how that information, vitally important though it may be, can save my marriage."

"If you stop being so sarcastic, I'll tell you how."

"I'll do my best."

"What I heard about is that there are people right here in L.A. who are using magic to make their lives better."

I rolled my eyes. I told you Brenda was the one who liked chaos. "Okay, so which celebrity is a member of Wicca, or whatever that organization of witches is called?"

"No, not that kind of magic. I'm not encouraging you to put a spell on Roger." She paused. "Not exactly."

"What do you mean, 'Not exactly?' "

She motioned me closer. When our heads were practically touching as we sat across the table from one another, she whispered very dramatically, "There's this doctor in Beverly Hills."

I laughed. "I get it. The doctor is a plastic surgeon and you're suggesting he work his 'magic' on me. A little nip, a little tuck, a couple of implants, and Roger will be panting for me, is that it?"

"No. It's Roger who needs the makeover. And I'm not talking about plastic surgery."

"Then what the heck *are* you talking about, Brenda?"

"I'm talking about Dr. Gordon Farkus. He's a specialist in life enhancement."

I shook my head, swallowed my giggles. "Where do you come up with this stuff?"

"Just listen to me. Whether you call him a life enhancement specialist or a plain-old Dr. Feelgood, he has an extremely successful practice. Tons of celebrities go to him."

"For what?"

"For magic potions. Well, they're not magic potions, of course. They're custom formulations."

I stared at her blankly.

"Let me lay it out another way," she said. "You know how top makeup artists mix customized blends of products for people like Halle Berry and Courteney Cox and Drew Barrymore? To deal with their specific complexion issues?"

"No, I do not. What's more, don't say things like 'complexion issues.' It's silly."

"Fine. What if I told you that Dr. Farkus could create a mixture that would turn Roger into the husband you've been craving—a potion that would help him achieve peak performance in every aspect of his life? Would *that* be silly?"

"How on earth would he do that?"

"By determining what nutritional supplements Roger is lacking, identifying the herbs that counteract the deficiencies, and then combining them into a specialized life energy formula. The man is a genius, Elizabeth. Everybody goes to him."

And the quack probably rips them off, I thought. "So he works with herbs, you say?"

"Yeah, but not just regular herbs. He only uses very exotic herbs that originate in some rain forest."

"Then he doesn't prescribe actual drugs or medicines?"

"No. Apparently, he was Harvard-educated and went the traditional doctor route before changing the direction of his practice. Now he's the herb guru. The stars can't live without the brews he conjures up for them."

"Okay. Let me get this straight. You're suggesting that Roger go to see Dr. Farkus, who will then send him home with a cocktail of mystery herbs that, when taken as prescribed, will turn him into the man of my dreams?"

"Elizabeth, if Roger won't go to a marriage counselor, he's certainly not about to go to an herb doctor."

"Right. So why did you tell me about the guy in the first place?"

"Because *you're* the one who should go to see Dr. Farkus."

"Me?"

"Yeah. You schedule an appointment—don't be put off by the long waiting list, there are always cancellations—and tell the doctor about Roger's problems. Farkus will make up one of his customized blends and you'll sneak it into Roger's orange juice the next morning. Then, presto—your hubby will be 'fixed.' Like magic."

I couldn't believe what I was hearing. "You're saying that I should drug my own husband—behind his back? Very nice, Brenda. Very, very nice." See what I mean about my sister?

"Oh, chill out. You wouldn't be drugging Roger. You'd be herbing him. The worst that can happen is that the herbs don't work and Roger doesn't get any better and you're out a few hundred bucks."

A few hundred bucks. I could pick up a Prada handbag for that kind of money. Well, on sale. "So the fact that I'd be giving him these herbs without his consent doesn't trouble you?"

"No. And it shouldn't trouble you. From what you've told me, you tried to convince him that the relationship has deteriorated, and he dismissed the idea. You tried to talk to him about going for marital counseling, and he wasn't receptive. You tried to seduce him after a romantic dinner, and he fell asleep. He's backed you into a corner. He's forced you into making a choice. You either put up with him the way he is or slip Dr. Farkus's magic formula into his orange juice."

I was speechless, a million thoughts scrambling around in my head, cancelling each other out.

The idea of my actually being able to change Roger, improve him, rekindle his old spark, merely by adding some all-natural herbs to his diet, was breathtaking in its simplicity. What if Dr. Farkus's potions really *were* effective? What if Roger could be restored to his peak? What if he suddenly became attentive again, playful again, the adoring husband again? How fabulous would that be?

On the other hand, how could I put something in his food without telling him? That wasn't the sort of stunt I would normally pull. I had my faults, as I indicated earlier, but I also had scruples, integrity, common sense! It wasn't like me to go around dropping substances into people's drinks, as if I were a deviant boy hoping to score at a nightclub. How could I ever look Roger in the eye if I gave him the herbs? How could I expect him to trust me if he found out?

Still, what would be the harm, when you got right down to it? So I'd be serving him some healthy herbal supplements—*for his own good.* What would be the difference between me and the mother who sneaks some puréed cauliflower into her kid's mashed potatoes? I'd be helping my husband to lead a better life. It would be an act of altruism, of love.

"Hello, Elizabeth?" Brenda was waving her hand in front of my face. I was so deep in thought I'd forgotten she was sitting there. "You don't have to make a decision about this today," she said. "I just wanted to give you the scoop about Dr. Farkus so you'd have the option of going to see him."

"I appreciate that."

"The thing to keep in mind," she said as she signaled for the check, "is how society is trending."

"Please, Brenda. Not an anecdote about how celebrities are getting botox injections to immobolize their sweat glands."

"Oh, come on, Elizabeth. I'm not that single-minded." Right. "The point I was making is that our society is trending—and has been trending for a while now—toward instant gratification, toward quick fixes. That's why therapy is out and medicine is in. If we aren't satisfied with our mood or our appearance or our sex drive, we pop a pill. In your case, what you'd be doing with Roger is giving him herbs to quick-fix his mood, his appearance, his sex drive, and anything else that needs enhancement. No biggie. To sum up, instead of worrying about your marriage twenty-four/seven, you'd be taking control of it. What could be wrong with that?"

"Maybe nothing. But maybe things between Roger and me will improve on their own and I won't need any help."

"Possible but doubtful. Look, why don't I get you the doctor's phone number anyway? As I said, he has a long waiting list for appointments, so you might want to make one, just to have it. You can always cancel."

"I don't know, Brenda."

"What's not to know? You want Roger to perk up, don't you? Well, there's a doctor with an office only twenty minutes away and he's more than capable of doing the job. Picture how happy you'll be when Roger emerges from his funk and starts wooing you again, making you feel like you did when the two of you were courting, acting like the man you fell in love with."

I found myself choking up at the very notion. I did love Roger. He had so many qualities I respected and admired. He just needed a little perking up, as Brenda said. "That would be wonderful," I replied.

"So I *should* get you Dr. Farkus's phone number?"

"I suppose it couldn't hurt," I said, honestly believing it couldn't.

CHAPTER SIX

The following Tuesday I flew to Arizona to inspect the Phoenician Paradise, an AMLP Four Key property that had been angling to be upgraded to a Five Key rating. Its general manager had sent our corporate office numerous and rather desperate letters requesting a re-evaluation—such was our clout within the hospitality industry—and I was finally being dispatched to give the place a look.

Unfortunately, the news wasn't good for the Phoenician Paradise. The turkey in the club sandwich that arrived with my room service lunch was clearly turkey *roll*, complete with that jellied stuff of undetermined origin. What's more, there was something green—I shudder to think what—stuck to one of the prongs of my fork. But the hotel's fatal flaw revealed itself during Torture the Concierge. I had given Carlos, one of the hotel's three concierges, the rap about it being Roger's birthday in a couple of days, and he had seemed up to the challenge of finding a gift on such short notice—until I announced that Roger's passion was taxidermy.

"I'd like to send him a stuffed animal," I said, "and I'm not talking about a plush toy."

Carlos was undone. "I wouldn't even know where to look," he said.

"Why don't you ask around?" I suggested. Well? All sorts of people had stuffed birds and fish and antelope heads over their fireplaces, didn't they? It wasn't my thing, but to each his own.

In the end, Carlos couldn't make it happen. We ended up sending Roger a tie with coyotes on it, and the Phoenician Paradise did not get its Five Keys.

As usual, I felt guilty about being the spoiler. I rooted for these hotels to make the grade, really I did, but AMLP didn't pay me to look the other way when I discovered a problem.

"You're the best inspector we have," enthused Preston DeWitt, my supervisor at AMLP, after I'd submitted my evaluation and the Phoenician Paradise had been notified of our decision. "If a property has an imperfection, you'll be the one to spot it. You're top drawer, Elizabeth."

Top drawer. Preston wasn't British, just affected, snooty, like most of AMLP's upper management. The company was all about projecting the same impeccable manners and service and appearance that their Five Key properties were supposed to project, and Preston fit the mold perfectly. I don't think I'd ever seen him with a wrinkle in his suit or a hair out of place or a shoe that hadn't been shined, and I had never heard him raise his voice. He was a cool, steely customer behind all the pleasantries, and he wouldn't be the first person I'd call if I were ever in a jam, but we understood each other. My being a stickler made him look good and he returned the favor by sending me out on jobs.

"Thanks for the compliment, Preston," I said.

"No thanks necessary," he said. "The only little negative here—and I'm only mentioning it so we can prevent similar problems from cropping up in the future—is that the Paradise figured out who you really are right after you checked out."

"How?" I said. This didn't happen often. I was so careful to protect my true identity.

"We'll never know for certain," said Preston, "but my guess is that the valet parking attendant searched the glove compartment of your rental car and got 'Elizabeth Baskin' off your driver's license."

"Well, at least it happened *after* I checked out," I said with relief. "No harm done, because I was able to evaluate the property as Elizabeth Stickler, average hotel guest, and get the information we needed. It doesn't matter now if they know I'm Elizabeth Baskin and that I work for AMLP. You can just assign someone else to inspect the property the next time they're up for evaluation."

"Yes, of course, but my concern is that the Paradise's general manager, an irritating gentleman named Art Yarnell, is absolutely incensed about not getting a fifth Key and he holds you responsible. He knows your real name now, as well as your home address, and he just might write you a nasty letter or some such thing."

"Not to worry, Preston. I can handle a nasty letter. But thanks for the heads-up."

Nasty letters were the least of my problems. I was consumed with whether or not I should contact Dr. Farkus in Beverly Hills. Brenda had given me his phone number. I'd written it down and stuck the piece of paper in a drawer and then made myself crazy wondering if I should call him or not. On the "minus" side, I was not a trendoid, and flocking to some Dr. Feelgood's office along with the rest of the L.A. trendoids felt dopey, and what good could a bunch of herbs do for Roger anyway. On the "plus" side, I was not a happy wife, and seeking help from a doctor with a successful practice might not be dopey, and maybe the right concoction of herbs *would* enhance Roger's life and, therefore, mine.

I decided to give myself the weekend to decide—a weekend that got off to a rocky start, as it turned out.

I had hoped that Roger and I might go out together on Friday night, see a movie, have dinner, something. But when he came home early that afternoon and immediately began gathering up his tent and sleeping bag and hiking boots, I knew there was no movie in my immediate future.

"What are you doing?" I asked as I stood over him, hands on hips.

"Packing," he said.

"I can see that, Roger. For what?"

"I'm taking Frankie camping at Mt. Baldy. I'm picking him up in a half-hour, so I've got to move it."

I wanted to strangle him. Yes, it was heartwarming that he never shirked his responsibilities to Frankie, his Little Brother, and yes, Mt. Baldy was a mere fifty miles from downtown L.A. so it wasn't as if he was leaving for Thailand, but *he hadn't told me he was going.*

"You're taking Frankie camping and you don't even have the courtesy to let me know beforehand?" I said through clenched teeth.

He glanced up from his packing. "Oh. Didn't I mention the trip?"

"*No!*"

"Gosh, I'm sorry, hon. I could have sworn I told you. We're only going for tonight, though. We'll camp out at the Manker Flats, do some hiking tomorrow, and be back by late tomorrow afternoon. You're welcome to come if you want to. We'd both love to have you with us."

Roger knew damn well that I despised camping as much as he enjoyed it. When we were first married, I went with him—once—and promised myself I'd never go again. I ask you, What's fun about dealing with insect bites and altitude sickness and nocturnal visits from bears, never mind about trying to sleep on the wet, cold, hard ground? I was an inspector for AMLP, for God's sake! A stray hair on the bathroom floor was enough to make me postal!

"Thanks, but I'll pass," I said, hurt as well as angry. Why couldn't Roger have told me he was going camping with Frankie? Why didn't he treat me like I mattered? Why did he have to be so disengaged? Yes, I was proud of the way he had become a real father figure to a boy whose own father was never there for him. Roger had been a stablizing force in Frankie's life and I respected him for that, loved him for that. As I said, Roger had admirable qualities, which made his behavior toward me all the more frustrating.

"Are you sure, Elizabeth? It would be great to have you along," he said.

"I'm touched," I said, heavy on the sarcasm. If he wanted to have me along, why hadn't he mentioned that he was going? "But I'll stay here. You *are* planning to be back in time for David's party tomorrow night, I hope." I was referring to David Durston, one of Roger's partners, the serial dater who had recently started dating the baby whisperer. Saturday was the baby whisperer's birthday, apparently, and he was throwing her a little soirée at the house he'd recently purchased. David changed houses almost as often as he changed girlfriends.

"I'll be home tomorrow about four," he said. He took my hand, a sheepish look on his face. "I'm sorry about tonight, Elizabeth. I really thought I told you."

I mumbled something, then shut up and watched him pack. And as I did, I began to feel the fear—not the anger and the hurt, but the *fear*—that Roger's forgetting to tell me about his trip might be more than an inadvertent slip-up; that it might really be about his not loving me, about his not wanting to be married to me anymore.

It can't be that, I thought, the panic kicking in, along with the denial. He does love me. He says so all the time. He just needs to be perked up, jazzed up, enhanced, and once he is, our problems will be history.

Yup, I was growing closer to making that fateful phone call.

David Durston's house defied gravity. It was perched way up in the Hollywood Hills on a tiny, nearly vertical street that could only handle cars single file. A 1930s bungalow, it had once been partially destroyed by fire and was, therefore, available for sale at a reasonable (for southern California) price. David had turned it into a sexy house, but it was hanging off a cliff and wouldn't be my idea of shelter, should there be an earthquake or a mudslide. Of course, I wasn't the risk taker David was. At least, not yet.

The party was quite lively, as David's parties always were. A congenial host, he was handsome in a boyish way. He wore his hair longer than most lawyers in town and his skin was smooth and pink, as if he was still too young to shave, and he was a relentless grinner. I often wondered, when I looked at David, if he really found life so entertaining or if the grin was sort of a tic.

As for his girlfriend, the baby whisperer, she was an attractive redhead named Lucy Corliss, and unlike his previous conquests, she was bright and articulate and had no interest whatsoever in becoming an actress, although she did have aspirations of writing a book about her experiences as a baby whisperer. The only thing wrong with her, as far as I could tell, involved her skewed sense of spacial relations. She was one of those people who stands too close to you, puts her face right in yours during a conversation, which is awkward at best.

Brad and Gerta Weiner were at the party, of course, and were both dressed in pink.

"I am extremely tired of za black everybody vears in zis country," she explained in the accent I kept trying to place but couldn't. "Vhy must vee be made to feel as if vee go to a funeral everyday? Only in America, eh?"

"Actually, Gerta, it's not only in America," I said, feeling defensive on behalf of my country whenever I was around her. "Black is popular all around the world."

"Not vhere I am from," she insisted.

"And where, exactly, *is* that?" I asked, poised to play the game we always played, Guess Gerta's Native Land.

"You have never heard of it, I promise you. It's a tiny country high in za mountains."

"Which mountains?" She was not getting off so easily this time.

"The Shoenhoffer mountains."

"I see," I said, nodding. Shoenhoffer mountains, my ass. The second I got home I was going straight to my almanac. "They sound German. Are you German, Gerta?"

She chuckled. "People in America assume I am German, but I am not." She chuckled again. "You know, if Americans vould only study languages za vay vee do in Europe, zey vould have a broader knowledge of ozer countries."

"You know, if Europeans vould only brush zeir teeth twice a day za vay vee do in America, zey would have fewer cavities."

No, I didn't say that out loud, just in my head. I was about to pursue Gerta's heritage further when Carrie Toobin came along, Carrie being the remaining partner in Roger's firm.

"Hey, Elizabeth. Great to see you." She extended her arms to me and we shared a hug. She was spilling out of her low-cut blouse, as usual, and I hoped the hug hadn't dislodged a breast or two.

"It's great to see you too, Carrie," I said. "How are the kids?"

"A handful." She sighed. "They're spending the night at my mother's. In case I get lucky tonight."

Lucky with whom? I wondered, glancing around the room. Every man there was either married or in a long-term relationship, except for David, and he was involved with Lucy for the time being. Besides, he was one of her colleagues. She regarded him and Brad and Roger as her mentors, her saviors, the people responsible for allowing her to pull her life together and support her family. Maybe she was meeting someone after the party and was hoping to get lucky with him, I mused. In any case, she and I talked for a while. Then Roger and I mingled among the other guests. Then there was dinner and the presentation of Lucy's birthday cake and the blowing out of the candles, followed by dancing on David's patio.

"Okay. Up, up, up," I said to Roger as I clapped my hands to the beat of the music. "Let's get out there and show them how it's done."

He smiled but nixed the idea. "Not tonight, hon."

"Oh, come on, Roger," I said jauntily, tugging on the sleeve of his shirt. "Just one dance. You're the disco king, remember? How about shaking that booty?"

"How about sitting with me and watching the others? I'm still digesting all that birthday cake."

See? He *was* acting like an old fart! And who asked him to have two helpings of the cake? It wasn't even good. "Dancing is the perfect way to work off the calories. Let's go." I tugged at him again.

"Sorry. I just don't feel like dancing. But you go, hon. I'm sure you can find a partner."

That did it. "*You're* my partner," I said. "Or at least you used to be." And off I went in a snit. Not that I pranced onto the patio to dance by myself. I stormed off to David's powder room and sat there on the toilet sulking, wondering why Roger was avoiding any sort of intimacy with me. Maybe Brenda was right when she said that all men turn into slugs as soon as the hunt is over; that once they've snared their quarry, they crawl back into the cave and hibernate. Or maybe Roger was looking to snare some new quarry. Either way, I wasn't about to stand by and let my marriage fail.

I emerged eventually—other people were entitled to use the facilities—and sat in a corner watching everybody else enjoying themselves. It was all pretty ho-hum stuff until a seriously inebriated Gerta ripped off her clothes and dove into David's swimming pool.

"Everybody join me!" she shouted as she splashed.

Nobody joined Gerta, who backstroked around like Esther Williams until Brad finally fished her out.

"Well, what did you think of that little scene?" I said to Roger during the car ride home, trying to make conversation even though I was still mad at him.

"You mean Gerta?"

"Of course I mean Gerta."

He shrugged. "She's always doing something unpredictable. She enjoys keeping people off balance."

"She's the one who's off balance, getting smashed and then swimming around naked. She really should watch her drinking."

Silence.

"Brad must have been mortified," I went on, undetered by his unresponsiveness. "I can't imagine how he stands it."

"He didn't seem mortified," said Roger.

"How could he not have been?" I said.

"Because he loves Gerta and accepts her the way she is."

A not-so-thinly veiled reference to my not accepting Roger the way he was, obviously. "What did you think of David's girlfriend?" I asked, eager to change the subject.

"She was interesting," he said. "She told me she has a master's degree in child psychology."

"Did you think she was attractive?"

"I didn't think about it one way or the other."

"Oh, please, Roger. You're not blind. You had to form an opinion of some kind."

"Why? It was a superficial encounter at a party. I didn't do a study of her."

"I know, but people usually form initial impressions. I was asking you if your initial impression of Lucy was that she was an attractive woman."

"And I said I didn't form that sort of opinion. I wasn't checking her out. I'm a married man, remember?"

"Please. Married men aren't dead men. You're allowed to think a woman is attractive."

"I can't believe you're angry because I didn't come on to David's girlfriend."

"Who's talking about coming on to her? You don't even come on to *me*." I'm sorry to say I was yelling at this point.

"Ah, so it's back to you, isn't it, Elizabeth. Back to how disappointed you are in me, in our marriage." He was keeping his voice down, but I could see the veins in his neck standing out even in the dark of the car.

"Look, I only wanted to talk to you about tonight, share tidbits, exchange gossip. It's part of being a couple. You go to a party and then compare notes while you're driving home. When we were first married, you and I used to—"

"Stop. I'm not in the mood for yet another lecture on how things used to be. Not tonight."

"Fine. Then what *are* you in the mood for? I'd really like to know."

"This." He turned on the radio—to a classical music station, of course—with the volume way up. He was tuning me out, literally.

Well, that was the last straw. While he was navigating the car along San Vicente Boulevard, I was rehearsing my appointment with Dr. Farkus. I had to go to see him. You can understand that, can't you? I didn't want to argue with Roger anymore. I hated that I had become a nagging wife, one of those hostile, quick-to-criticize, resentful shrews. I wanted the old Roger back, but I also wanted the old *me* back—the kindler, gentler, happier me, the me that was secure in his love. I had to make a change, to fix the situation. Why not use a little magic to restore the magic? Wasn't that what Brenda had suggested? Worst-case scenario: The herbs wouldn't work and I'd have wasted my money. It wouldn't be the first time *that* happened; I had old outfits in my closet with the tags still on them. So there was really nothing to lose by calling Farkus. Not a thing.

CHAPTER SEVEN

At nine o'clock on Monday morning, ten seconds after Roger left for work and five seconds after I Dustbusted up the poppy seeds that had skipped off his bagel onto the kitchen floor, I called the office of Gordon Farkus, M.D.

"Dr. Farkus's office," said a woman whose voice was a lilting, rich singsong.

"Hello," I began warily. I still wasn't thrilled about going behind Roger's back—or about putting our lives in the hands of some herb guru—and so it occurred to me to be nervous. "I'd like to make an appointment with the doctor."

"Lovely," said the woman, who identified herself as Andrea, Dr. Farkus's receptionist. (She pronounced it And-REY-a.) "May I ask who referred you to us? As you know, our phone number isn't listed."

I wasn't sure how to handle that one. Brenda had explained that Farkus's practice was all very hush-hush, very insiders-only, and since I was clearly not an insider, I was at a loss, momentarily. "I was referred by Goldie Hawn," I said, picking a name at random. Well, not *that* random. She lived in L.A. and was often featured in Brenda's magazine. She wasn't a bad guess, I figured.

"How nice," Andrea said warmly. "Miss Hawn has been very generous with her referrals, and we appreciate that."

Boy, this receptionist was really friendly, not at all what you'd expect from a chichi place. Usually, the more exclusive the establishment, the more abusive the gatekeeper.

"Let me check our appointment book and see when we can fit you in," she said. "What is your name, please?"

"Elizabeth Baskin," I said. "I understand that you have a waiting list, but I'm hoping it isn't too long. I really need the doctor's help. As soon as possible, in fact."

"Yes, I'm afraid we do have a waiting list for appointments, but since you've been referred by Miss Hawn, I'll be sure to find an opening for you. How's this Thursday morning at eleven-fifteen?"

Being Goldie's pal definitely had its advantages. "It's perfect," I said. "I'll be there."

"And we'll look forward to seeing you, Miss Baskin. Or is it Mrs. Baskin?"

"Mrs.," I said. "And my insurance is with—"

"I'm afraid the insurance companies don't cover our services," she said. "Dr. Farkus practices a type of alternative medicine that our health care system has yet to recognize, unfortunately."

"Of course," I said. "I should have realized that."

"But if money is an issue, I suppose we could—"

"It's not an issue," I cut her off. "Whatever Dr. Farkus charges, I'll pay it."

"All right then. I've got you down for eleven fifteen on Thursday morning, Mrs. Baskin. You have our address?"

Oops. Brenda hadn't given it to me. "My, I seem to have lost the piece of paper Goldie wrote it on. Isn't that careless of me."

"Not a problem. We're at 435 North Roxbury, Suite 106. It's a four-story brick building right off Wilshire in Beverly Hills. There's a parking lot next door."

"I've got it. Thank you, Andrea."

"You're very welcome, Mrs. Baskin. Give our best regards to Miss Hawn when you speak to her."

"Will do."

I was early for the appointment. I was always early when I was anxious, and I was definitely anxious about seeing Dr. Farkus. While sixty percent of me was certain that I was taking a positive, proactive step toward saving my marriage, the remaining forty percent had its doubts. As a result, for a halfhour prior to my appointment, I sat in my car in the parking lot on Roxbury, blowing on my palms to dry the sweat. At eleven-ten, I got out, walked to the four-story brick building next door, and went inside.

It was a snazzy building, as medical offices go, with varnished wood panelling and lush green carpeting and polished brass nameplates on all the doctors' doors. I wasn't the real estate expert Roger was, but I knew a high-rent address when I saw one. Farkus's fees were probably off the charts.

I breathed deeply as I wandered down the hall. To my right were the even-numbered offices: SUITE 100, MARTIN PODEROFF, M.D., UROLOGY; SUITE 102, ORRIN RADISON, M.D., CARDIOLOGY; SUITE 104, LINDA DELANO, M.D., HEMATOLOGY. All reputable-sounding doctors with reputable-sounding practices. And then, in Suite 106: GORDON P. FARKUS, M.D., LIFE ENHANCEMENT. *Life Enhancement*. What kind of specialty was that, for God's sake? I felt like a complete idiot even contemplating walking in the door, but I was there and Andrea had been nice enough to give me an appointment right away and I could always change my mind about herbing Roger if Farkus was too weird.

I opened the door, stepped inside his office, and stood on the threshold for a moment, taking it all in. The waiting room was exquisitely decorated—opulent yet tasteful, stylish yet comfortable, everything I looked for in my Five Key hotel lobbies. There were plump sofas upholstered in fabulously expensive fabrics; actual antique tables, not reproductions; handpainted lamps; a creamy ecru rug with a needlepoint border. There was even a scent I couldn't place—sweet but not sickeningly so; perfumey but subtle; suggestive of a restorative balm but not the least bit medicinal; the essence of one of Dr. Farkus's mysterious herbs, perhaps. And then there was the music that emanated from the recessed speakers on the wall. No run-of-the-mill doctor's office tunes. No golden oldies. No "cool jazz." Just an ever-so-soft tinkling of a harp. Or was it a triangle?

I must add that the waiting room was packed with high-profile people and that even I, who lived in Los Angeles, where sightings of celebrities are commonplace, was impressed. Off to the right, in the corner, was Wendy Winters, the NBC News correspondent. To her left, a few feet away, was Angela Clay, the singer everyone had dubbed the new Whitney Houston. And in the back of the room, *way* back, was—I kid you not—Lanie Duquette, the gorgeous Australian actress who was in Spielberg's new movie.

Boy, I thought. Dr. Farkus must be a master at what he does if he's got all these superstars venturing out of their gated estates to see him. I chuckled to myself as I wondered if they had come for magic potions for their husbands or themselves. Maybe I wasn't the only one interested in putting some zip into my partner. On the other hand, there weren't just famous females seated in the waiting room. I also spotted an extremely well-known action hero, plus the host of TV's longest-running game show. For a second, I felt as if I'd walked into one of the big Hollywood talent agencies by mistake.

Yeah, this Farkus *must* be good, I decided, when I had finished gawking and was starting to relax a little. I approached the reception desk, where Andrea, who was older than she'd sounded—in her early sixties, perhaps—greeted me after I introduced myself.

"Mrs. Baskin. So glad to have you," she said. "Would you care for a beverage? We have all sorts of coffees, teas, waters."

"I'm fine, thanks." She had a tender, mothering quality about her, which was probably a job requirement, given that Farkus's clients were the type who were used to being fawned over. "I assume there are forms for me to fill out? Since I'm a new patient?"

"Not necessary," she trilled. "You'll discuss your needs with Dr. Farkus and he'll formulate a preparation based on your conversation. And then you will be billed accordingly. All very simple, isn't it?"

"Very." I'd never been to a doctor who didn't require you to write your medical memoirs.

"He's running a bit late, so why don't you sit down and make yourself at home. I'll come for you when it's time."

I thanked her again and eyeballed the waiting room, in search of an empty seat. I would not be sitting with the glamorous Lanie. She had barricaded herself in, hogging the spaces on either side of her by loading them up with scripts, and I wasn't about to ask her to move them. The only seat that was free was over by the door, on the loveseat that was already occupied by a woman about my age—a non-celebrity like me.

"Hi," I said to her. "Is this seat taken?"

"It is now." She smiled, patting the cushion next to her as encouragement for me to sit there.

I sat, got comfortable. I was about to scan the coffee table for a magazine when the woman struck up a conversation with me.

"I'm Clover Hinsdale," she said, grabbing my hand and pumping it. "This is my first appointment with Dr. Farkus and it feels like I've been granted an audience with the Pope. Have you been here before?"

Clover Hinsdale. Wasn't that the sort of name you gave a thoroughbred race horse? Like, Clover of Hinsdale Farm. Or was I thinking of Clydesdales? "No, this is my first time too. I'm Elizabeth Baskin."

"Real nice to meet you, Elizabeth. Real pleasure." She was southern, with the fried-green-tomatoes accent to prove it. She was a brunette, her hair straight except for the bouncy curls at the ends, and she was very thin, pale, a fragile flower. And, though her mouth was too wide for her face and her chin a little recessive, she had an openness about her appearance that was appealing. I imagined her growing up on one of those plantations, being tended to by her mammy. "How did you find out about the doctor, if you don't mind my asking?"

"I don't mind at all." Actually, I was glad to have someone to talk to about Farkus, someone who hadn't been nominated for an Oscar. "My sister works for *In the Know* magazine. She told me about Dr. Farkus's practice and gave me his number. How did you find out about him, Clover?"

"From the lady who lived down the street. She said she came here because she wanted to feel more empowered."

"And Dr. Farkus helped her to feel more empowered?"

"Oh my, yes. About two months after she drank his special potion, she upped and left her husband for the man who installed her Direct TV. She was sweet but slutty, bless her heart."

I love that about southern women. They can say the most insulting things about a person and never get called on it, just because they tack that "bless her heart" business at the end of the sentence. "So you're here hoping the doctor will help *you* to feel more empowered?"

"Lord, no." She laughed. "I'm originally from Kentucky. We don't talk about being 'empowered' back there. We talk about getting what we want, whatever it takes." She leaned in closer, lowered her voice. "I probably shouldn't tell you this, Elizabeth, but I'm here on account of my husband. He's the one who needs Dr. Farkus's help and I'm gonna get it for him."

Well, what do you know? Another nice, normal wife out to save her marriage. Suddenly, I didn't feel so conflicted about what I was doing in that office. Suddenly, I had a buddy. "To tell you the truth, Clover, I'm here to get one of Dr. Farkus's concoctions for my husband too," I confided.

She gave my arm a conspiratorial squeeze. "Then we're in this together, aren't we?" She giggled. "I was really on the fence about coming here—I'm not crazy about the idea of going behind Bud's back—but things between us have gotten so bad that I couldn't hold off."

"Bud's your husband?"

"Sure is. His real name is Buchanan, but everybody's always called him Bud. He's got a car dealership—well, three car dealerships—in Los Angeles County. If you're ever in the market for a Cadillac, you let me know, you hear?"

"Thanks, Clover. How long have you and Bud been married?"

"Seven years, most of them happy years. But a good while ago I began to get annoyed with him. He was taking me for granted, not talking to me, not listening to me, not making love to me the way he used to. I woke up one morning, took a long, hard look at him, and thought, What happened to that nice fellow I married and how do I get him back? That's why I'm here today, Elizabeth. I'm hoping that Dr. Farkus will get me my husband back."

I couldn't believe this. It was absolutely uncanny. Here was a woman whose words echoed my own, whose disappointment in her husband echoed my own, whose plan of action echoed my own. I wanted to unburden myself to her, to share with her what I'd been going through. And so I did.

"My sister says Roger is just in the settling-in phase of our marriage," I reported at the end of my account. "But I think it's more than that. I think there's a vicious cycle that goes on in marriages. The man starts to withdraw and the woman starts to complain. Then *her* complaining makes *him* withdraw even more, and *his* withdrawing makes *her* complain even more. And so on. The way out of this cycle, in my opinion, is to bring the man back to his original state before the withdrawal, to turn him back into the person who was attentive and loving and fun to be around at the beginning of the relationship. I don't know what Dr. Farkus means by 'life enhancement' or what he puts into the cocktails he dispenses, but my hope is that he'll be able to transform Roger into the man I married. If he can do that, then he truly is a magician and worth every dime I'll have to pay him."

"Dime!" She laughed again. "I think we'll be shelling out more than dimes for his services." Her expression grew somber. "Of course, there's always the chance that you and I are just a couple of women who weren't meant to be with our husbands in the first place and that time has only made our incompatibilities more obvious. Do you ever consider that possibility, Elizabeth? That you and Roger weren't cut out for each other?"

"No, because we were compatible in the beginning. With the exception of camping, which has always been his idea of escape and my idea of punishment, we enjoyed the same things. There's no question that our personalities are different, but on the whole we meshed very well. Now, we don't mesh at all."

Clover patted my hand in sympathy. "I can't remember the last time Bud chose me over the World Wrestling Federation."

I sighed. "Mine never misses an episode of *Everybody Loves Raymond.*"

"How am I ever going to get pregnant if Bud's stuck to the chair in front of the TV?"

"I hear you. Roger and I plan to have a family, but with every year that passes, the likelihood of making babies with him becomes more remote. Which is another reason why it's imperative that I *enhance* him—sooner rather than later."

Clover and I continued to chat, commiserate, get to know each other. We were both grateful that Dr. Farkus was running late because it gave us a chance to air our grievances against our husbands, validate our points of view. Finally, it was Clover's turn with the doctor.

"Good luck," I said after Andrea had come to get her. "I'll be pulling for you."

"Thanks. Listen, why don't we plan to meet for lunch after you're finished here?" she suggested.

"Great idea. What about Barney Greengrass, since it's around the corner on Wilshire? You could reserve us a table and I'll get there as soon as I can."

"You're on."

After she went off with Andrea, I tried to concentrate on an article in *Los Angeles* magazine about ostrich-egg chandeliers. Twenty more minutes went by. When I thought I couldn't *be* more fidgety, Andrea came for me. "Dr. Farkus will see you now, Mrs. Baskin."

"Oh," I said, nearly leaping off the loveseat. "But I didn't spot Mrs. Hinsdale coming out."

"She's with one of our staff members, in the preparation staging area."

The preparation staging area. What was I getting myself into?

"Ready to meet with the doctor?" she asked.

"As ready as I'll ever be," I said.

CHAPTER EIGHT

Here we are," said Andrea after she led me down a long hallway and into a small but lavishly appointed room in which two wing chairs faced each other. "This is one of Dr. Farkus's communication rooms. He'll be with you shortly."

Okay, so most doctors have examining rooms, and this doctor had communication rooms. That didn't scare me. I wasn't a fan of those dreadful spaces furnished with nothing but a waxed-paper-covered slab. Besides, Farkus wasn't going to be examining me in the literal sense; he was going to be listening to my husband's symptoms and then prescribing a curative recipe of some sort.

While I waited for the herb guru to put in an appearance, I perused the walls of the room and checked out all the diplomas. There was the undergraduate degree from Yale, then medical school at Harvard, an internship and residency at Mt. Sinai, then a fellowship back at Harvard with a specialty in gastroenterology.

Very reassuring, I mused after taking a second look at the gastroenterology diploma. No matter what he throws into those potions of his, at least they won't upset Roger's stomach.

I was pondering what had led Farkus to abandon conventional medicine for alternative medicine when he made his entrance.

"Mrs. Baskin," said an extremely tan man. Tan skin, tan hair, tan suit. I don't think I'd ever seen anyone so monochromatic. He was in his forties, I guessed, and quite the hipster—ponytail, diamond stud in one earlobe, necklace with some sort of pagan symbol dangling from it, bare feet. Yeah, that last one surprised me too, talk about unorthodox. I wondered about the hygiene involved in practicing medicine with bare feet. Doctors were supposed to wash their hands, but what about their lower extremities?

"Hello," I said, still processing the feet but trying not to stare at them, although I did notice a toe ring.

"Why don't we have a seat." He gestured toward the two wing chairs. His manner was rather formal for someone who went without his shoes. "You've come on the recommendation of Miss Hawn?"

"That's right," I lied. "I'm very grateful that you made time to see me on such short notice."

"That's what I'm here for," he said. "Now. Why don't you tell me how I can help."

"All right." While he took notes, I told Dr. Farkus about my problems with Roger, about the changes in his behavior, about my hope of injecting new life into him, to restore his old zest. "Of course, I would have preferred that Roger came here himself," I added at the end of my litany of complaints. "I don't feel entirely comfortable with the fact that I'll be giving him your preparation or potion or whatever you call it without his knowledge."

"It doesn't sound as if he's left you much choice," said Dr. Farkus, who, apparently, had no compunction about whipping up herbal remedies for people he'd never met. "Once he has undergone my treatment, he'll thank you for taking the initiative, believe me."

"So you think you can help Roger? I mean, you've helped other men with similar symptoms?"

Dr. Farkus smiled. His teeth were crooked but not tan, like the rest of him, fortunately. "I have helped many, many men with similar symptoms. In fact, my clients have given this particular preparation a nickname: stud stimulant."

Oh, brother. "What, specifically, do you put into this, um, stud stimulant?" I asked. "My goal is to perk Roger up, not turn him into one of those high-testosterone crazies."

Dr. Farkus gave me a puzzled look, as if my concerns were totally frivolous. "Leave this to me, Mrs. Baskin. We're going to transform your husband from zero to hero within a matter of weeks—without an ounce of testosterone. You won't recognize him."

"I won't recognize him?" Maybe this wasn't such a hot idea. Roger wasn't a zero. He just needed enhancement.

"There's no need to panic, Mrs. Baskin. I only meant that you'll be delighted with the results. But to answer your question about the actual ingredients that will be used in your husband's customized preparation, they will be all-natural, additive-free products to which I have access, due to my extensive travels in Central America and my close relationship with the natives there. In particular, I have tapped into a rain forest in Honduras, about two hundred miles from the capital city of Tegucigalpa."

Tegucigalpa. He reminded me of Gerta and her Shoenhoffer mountains. Hopefully he wasn't full of it, the way she was.

"This rain forest," he continued, "contains the highest concentration of life energy on the planet and, as a result, the most potent nutritional supplements, which is why my preparations work so well and so quickly."

"But with regard to the specific needs of my husband—"

"As I was about to explain, what I will be creating for your husband will be a blend of herbs that stimulates the endrocrine system—the adrenals, the thyroid, the hypothalamus, and the gonads—in an effort to relieve his stress, bolster his immune response, regulate his hormones, increase his physical energy, sharpen his mental clarity, strengthen his muscle tone, and rekindle his libido."

"Is that all?" I joked.

"Actually, it isn't all." He flipped through the pages of his notepad. "I see from my transcript of our conversation that you mentioned a small bald spot on the back of your husband's head."

"Yes. It's hereditary. I suggested that he try Propecia, but maybe you have a better idea."

"Indeed I do. There's an herbal equivalent that will be much more effective and I'll be glad to add it to the mix. You also commented that he had gained some weight."

"Oh, that. Well, he's not obese or anything. It's just that he used to be so nice and thin and now he's gotten a little jowly. He's not watching his diet and he's given up exercising for the most part."

"Then we'll add a very potent herb that will control his weight and balance his metabolism."

I shook my head in amazement. "Gosh, you're sure this preparation you'll be creating won't have any harmful side effects? It sounds too good to be true. I guess what I'm asking is, We won't be putting some sort of *spell* on him, will we?"

Dr. Farkus's eyes narrowed. I had insulted him. "Mrs. Baskin," he said with a patronizing tone, "I've been trained at the best schools and hospitals in this country. I've been a medical doctor for most of my adult life. But it wasn't until I traveled to the Honduran rain forest and witnessed the miraculous powers of the herbs that are indigenous to the area that I learned what real healing is about."

"Of course. I was only—"

"Did you happen to see all those people in the waiting room?"

"Yes. I couldn't believe that Lanie Duquette was actually—"

"Some of them are very prominent, Mrs. Baskin. They don't interrupt their busy schedules to visit a doctor unless the doctor has the credentials that I have—plus the results that I achieve."

"I'm not questioning your ability, Dr. Farkus. It's just that I can't believe my dreams are about to be realized. It's all so thrilling."

He softened. "Yes, it is thrilling. The fact that I've been able to create preparations such as the stud stimulant—as well as its antidote—has been a professional triumph for me."

"Its antidote?"

"Yes, the precise herbal recipe that counteracts the preparation, all the preparations. I'm a great believer in the yin and yang of life, Mrs. Baskin, that every reaction has an equal and opposite reaction. One must have the power to negate as well as the power to create, don't you think?"

I didn't know what I thought, except that I'd never met anyone quite like Dr. Gordon Farkus.

"Now, let's finish up," he said. "Andrea will escort you back to our preparation staging area, while I will be in my lab mixing your husband's powder."

"It's a powder? I'm just asking because I was picturing a liquid."

"*Spells* come in all varieties," he said with a wink, throwing my word back at me. "Your husband's comes in the form of a soft, yellowish powder."

"How interesting."

"I'm prescribing one packet of powder in his coffee or orange juice or whatever he drinks with his breakfast in the morning. You should see changes in him within two weeks, as his body begins to absorb the preparation."

"Two weeks! That's wonderful! Does the powder have a taste or odor? We can't have Roger suspecting anything."

"No taste and no odor. He won't have any idea what you're giving him. He'll only notice the changes in his behavior and overall sense of well-being."

"Great. One more question, Doctor. How long will the effects of the powder last?"

"It varies with each person, but in a man of your husband's age, I would estimate it will last ten to twelve months—long enough to make an enormous improvement in your marriage and enable you both to rediscover the joys of being together."

"Ten to twelve months?" I hadn't barged my way in to see Farkus for just a year of a new-and-improved Roger. I wanted more time to rediscover the joys of being together. I needed more time. "Could you by any chance sell me additional packets of the powder, Dr. Farkus? You said that the effects of your potions vary, depending on the person. I'd hate to have to keep troubling you for additional quantities in the future."

He chuckled. "If you don't mind paying for them, I'm happy to sell them to you. I'll make up three packets and you can use them as a backup."

I thanked him profusely, let Andrea take me to the staging area, and waited for my set of three stud stimulants, which were packed together into a—what else?—tan shopping bag.

After that, I was presented with the tab.

"This is for today," said the woman in charge of billing.

I smiled and glanced at the number in the last column—and nearly fainted. I won't be vulgar and tell you the exact amount Farkus charged me for the visit and the stud stimulants, but suffice it to say I wouldn't be doing any serious shopping in the near future.

"Are you all right, Mrs. Baskin?" she asked.

"I will be," I said, pulling out my checkbook. As soon as I get my Roger back.

✧

By the time I arrived at Barney Greengrass, the über-deli on the top floor of Barney's department store, the lunch crowd had packed the place, particularly the men-in-black crowd. Hollywood agents, all of them. You could tell by the way they talked to their cell phones instead of to the person across the table. I wondered if any of them had been a client of Dr. Farkus and, if so, if they'd tried his stud stimulant. Please, God, I prayed, don't let Roger start wearing Armani T-shirts and using words like "platforming," "branding," or "synergy."

"Elizabeth!" Clover waved at me. She'd secured a table in the back.

I hurried over. "Well, I've got *my* stash. How about you?" I said excitedly, holding up my shopping bag.

She held up hers. "Sit down, friend. We're celebrating."

She had ordered a bottle of Dom Perignon. And, yes, delicatessens in L.A. serve champagne. I hoped she was treating, given my newly meager bank account. "Excellent idea. Pour me some, Clover, and tell me what you thought of the great and powerful Gordon P. Farkus."

She filled my glass. "First, a toast. To his so-called stud stimulant. May it save our marriages."

"Here, here," I said. We clinked glasses. "It just occurred to me—if Farkus gets the ingredients for the stud stimulant from a rain forest in Honduras, maybe we should move there. I mean, can you imagine all the stimulated studs running around that country?"

We both broke out laughing and didn't stop until a waitress came to take our order.

"I'll have your special powder," Clover told her. "I mean, your special *platter.*"

That brought forth another round of giggles. Eventually, we settled down, ordered lunch, and swapped Farkus stories.

"Other than the bare feet, he seemed sort of normal," I said.

She shook her head. "Where I come from, it's not normal for men to wear a ponytail. He's probably gay, bless his heart."

"Not necessarily, Clover. Plenty of straight men wear their hair that way."

"Not in Kentucky—unless they're fixing to whack you with an ax."

"Seriously, I was impressed by Farkus's credentials. With those degrees from Harvard, he can't be a total snake oil salesman, can he?"

"We'll find out soon enough. How many packets did you buy?"

"Three. He wanted to sell me one but I figured why not go for it."

"You and I are two peas in a pod, Elizabeth. I bought three packets too."

"Come to think of it, he was the one who suggested the three packets. I expressed my concern that one might not last long enough and he said, 'Why don't I sell you three? As a backup?' "

"That's exactly what he said to me," she confirmed.

"Well, at least he's consistent. Now let's see if he knows what he's doing. I was planning to give Roger the first packet in his orange juice tomorrow morning."

"Same here with Bud."

"If Farkus is the magician everybody claims he is, then in a couple of weeks you and I are going to be two very happy—and, I might add, sexually fulfilled—wives."

"Amen to that."

We clinked glasses a second time and drank to our impending good fortune.

CHAPTER NINE

I was in the kitchen bright and early the next morning, preparing Roger's breakfast—especially his glass of orange juice—before he was even out of bed. I didn't want to take any chances that he might catch me stirring the powder into the juice.

"You're serving me breakfast. What a nice surprise, hon," he said when he finally staggered into the kitchen, his eyes encrusted with sleep crud, his hair matted to the right side of his head, his boxer shorts slipping below his ever-expanding love handles. He was a sight to behold, let me tell you. I was counting the days until the stud stimulant kicked in.

"Well," I said cheerfully, "I'm your wife, don't forget. It's only natural that I'd want to help you in any way I can." Even if it's in the form of a yellow powder. "How about throwing on some clothes, though."

"Why? I was planning to shower and dress after breakfast. Or do you have a problem with me walking around like this in the privacy of my own home?"

"Oh, humor me, Roger. By the time you're presentable, I'll have everything ready."

He grumbled a bit but went back to the bedroom—and returned wearing a Lakers jersey that must had been shoved into a drawer and was now wrinkled to the point of being pleated. The man had lost all fashion sense.

"Here's your paper," I said, handing him the *L.A. Times* as he saddled up to the stool at the counter. "And here's your orange juice, nice and cold and freshly squeezed, just the way you like it."

"Great, but I think I'll start with coffee. I need a wake-up badly."

I'll say. "Why not drink the juice while I'm getting the coffee, Roger. It'll wake you up. It's very tart." Okay, so I was a little over-anxious. But why couldn't he just swallow the powder, for God's sake! The sooner he drank it, the sooner it would work.

He shrugged, picked up the glass, and brought it to his lips.

Here goes, I thought expectantly, as I watched the liquid slide down his throat. Glub, glub, glub.

"Hey, you're right. That *was* tart," he remarked when he'd finished the juice, down to the very last drop. "Bitter, almost."

And the herb guru said there wouldn't be any taste. Well, maybe it was just Roger being fussy. "Here's your coffee. And your toasted English muffin."

"Thanks." He started munching away, seeds skittering onto the counter, a coffee spill on the Lakers jersey—the usual. "What's on your schedule today, Elizabeth?"

"I've got a meeting with Preston about the hotel he's sending me to next."

"Which hotel's that?"

"Roger." I tried to reign in my impatience. After all, it wouldn't be long before he would actually *remember* the things I told him. "I'm inspecting the Mansion on the Square, the new hotel in San Francisco that I mentioned to you the other day."

"When are you going?"

"The week after next," I reminded him. "Monday."

No reaction. Just a lot of chewing and slurping.

"Do you ever mind that I travel so much for my job, Roger?" I asked, since we hadn't discussed the subject in ages. "Does it ever bother you that I'm always flying off somewhere?"

"Do I begrudge you your career? Of course not. I've got mine. There's no reason why you shouldn't have yours."

"That's very evolved of you, but I guess what I'm really asking is do you ever *miss* me when I'm not here?"

He turned the page of the newspaper, didn't even look up at me. "If you're feeling guilty about traveling, forget it, Elizabeth. By the time I get home at night, I'm so brain dead I don't even know you're gone."

"That's flattering."

"I didn't mean it the way it sounded."

"How did you mean it, Roger? Why don't you just come out and admit that you don't miss me at all. Not the way you used to."

He slammed the paper down and glared at me. "Please. I have a lot on my calendar today. I've got closings one right after the other, then a dinner sponsored by the Board of Realtors."

"You're not coming home for dinner?"

"No. Didn't I—"

"*No!*"

Well, there's no point in reporting the rest of the argument. You know how it went.

My meeting with Preston was brief and uneventful, with the exception of the subject of Art Yarnell, the general manager of the Phoenician Paradise, the hotel I'd recently denied a Fifth Key.

"The man is absolutely beside himself," said Preston, holding up the letters Yarnell had already dashed off to various people at AMLP's headquarters, complaining about me. "He claims you judged his hotel unfairly, that you put some of his employees in danger of losing their jobs, and—he's most perturbed about this—that you put him in danger of losing his job."

"What's AMLP's position on this?" I asked, hoping the company wasn't taking Yarnell's side and that *I* wouldn't be in danger of losing *my* job.

"We believe in you, Elizabeth, in your impeccable eye for perfection. We support you one hundred percent. However, we don't care for Yarnell's tone. The man sounds a bit unbalanced."

"At least he's not writing to me directly," I said.

"No, but that could be next. Be sure to let us know, will you?"

I said I would, but frankly I wasn't worried. There had been plenty of unhappy hotel managers as a result of my inspections over the years, and none of them had ever lost it, professionally. Besides, I was totally focused on my marital situation and didn't have time for some crabby guy in Phoenix. I had a crabby guy in Santa Monica to deal with.

A week went by, with no change in Roger. Before flying up to San Francisco, I checked in with Clover. She hadn't noticed anything different about Bud, either.

"No difference at all," she confirmed. "The other night we got into bed and instead of making love to me, he snuggled up with the latest issue of *Car and Driver*."

"That's horrible, but we can't get discouraged. We've got to give this project time, give the potion time. Once I'm back from San Francisco on Wednesday, it'll be just over two weeks since we slipped Roger and Bud the powder. Let's regroup then and see where we are, okay?"

She agreed and off I went to inspect the Mansion on the Square. Billing itself as a European-style boutique hotel, it was once a grand turn-of-the-century estate that had been completely refurbished. I was impressed with its contemporary art deco design and proximity to San Francisco's Union Square and Nob Hill. However—and there always seemed to be a "however" lately—I was not impressed with the hotel's concierge service. I explained to Wendall, the concierge in question, about my husband's birthday and the urgency of a gift and the fact that Roger was a Freudian analyst to whom I wanted to send a new couch for his patients—something with a whimsical, imported, slightly West Indian flair. And do you know what that snot Wendall said? "I'm sorry, Mrs. Stickler, but the Mansion on the Square is not Pier One." The nerve of him speaking to a guest like that. Five Keys for his hotel? Over my dead body.

I arrived home from my trip, bursting with curiosity over whether Roger's enhancement had taken effect while I was gone. I called him at the office the minute I walked in the door.

"Hi, hon. I'm back," I said after his secretary put me through. "How are you?"

"Fine, but I can't talk, Elizabeth. I'm about to go into a meeting."

Swell. No "It's great to hear your voice" or "How was your flight?" or "I'm so glad you're home." Nope. No change that I could detect.

"Would you like to do dinner and a movie tonight?" I asked. "Or just dinner? We could have a bite, then take a moonlight walk on the beach." Something romantic, in other words. Something other than you falling asleep in front of the tube.

"Sorry, hon, but I'm staying late at the office," said Roger. "Brad's in Tuscany with Gerta, David's got a date with Lucy, and Carrie's been home with her kids ever since they came down with the chicken pox. Someone's got to keep this place afloat."

So it was business as usual with Roger. My heart sank. Farkus was a rip-off artist and I was a moron for letting him rip me off. I couldn't wait to let Brenda have it for even suggesting I go to see him.

But first I called Clover, who was even more dejected than I was.

"Nothing," she said. "Not even a hint of anything different, especially in the bedroom. I could have handcuffed myself to the headboard last night and Bud wouldn't have noticed."

"The blockhead."

"What should we do?" she said. "Storm over to Farkus's office and demand our money back?"

I thought for a minute. "There's another possibility."

"Which is?"

"We bought those two other packets of the stud stimulant as a backup, remember?"

"Right, so the effects of the potion would last longer. But what good are the extra packets if what's inside them doesn't even work?"

"We don't know for sure that it doesn't work. We only know for sure that the dose Farkus gave us didn't work. Maybe our husbands are more resistant to the herbs than other men. Maybe they need a stronger concentration of the powder. I say we should dump the other two packets into their orange juice tomorrow morning and find out once and for all whether we've been conned."

"You mean, just give Bud and Roger the rest of the stuff? All at once?"

"You bet. Farkus said the powder was all-natural, non-toxic, so it's not as if we'd be putting their health at risk. We'd just be moving the process along. I can't take another day with that insensitive, unresponsive spouse of mine."

"I suppose it wouldn't hurt to give them the other two packets," she conceded. "If what's in them is some phony-baloney placebo, there's no harm done. And if what's in them is as potent as Farkus claims, our husbands will be enhanced to the max."

"So you'll do it?"

She sighed. "There's nothing to lose, I guess."

The next morning, before Roger emerged from the bedroom, I had already mixed the two packets full of Farkus's preparation into a tall glass of orange juice.

He parked himself at the kitchen counter. "Here's your juice," I said with an ostentatious display of nonchalance.

"Thanks." He drank it all down in one long ingestion. "Jeez, that's bitter."

I ignored the comment and busied myself around the kitchen. Roger read the *L.A. Times* and I read *Travel and Leisure*, he ate an onion bagel with cream cheese and I ate Special K with fat-free milk, and he made no attempt at conversation and I made no attempt at conversation. A normal morning in the Baskin household, in other words.

"I'm taking a shower," I announced when I had rinsed the dishes and stacked them in the dishwasher. "See you later."

Roger grunted a reply of some sort and picked his teeth.

I went off to the bathroom, hung my nightgown and robe on the hooks on the back of the door, and stepped into the shower. I was sitting on my little bench—we had one of those enormous, hedonistic, top-of-the-line stall showers with his and hers seats and jets spraying at all angles—and pondering my next move if Farkus's "magic" proved to be nothing but hocus bogus, when I heard something, heard someone, heard someone *humming*.

"Hello?" I called out.

It wasn't the housekeeper's day to clean, I knew. And she was the only one with a key, not to mention the only one around the house who hummed. Roger used to hum, but that was back when—well, never mind.

The humming progressed into an actual melody, with lyrics and a beat. To my utter shock and amazement, it was Roger's voice I heard, and the song he was singing (while he was snapping his fingers) was "Boogie Oogie Oogie," the '70s dance hit by Taste of Honey. I *told* you Roger was the disco king! Who else would even remember that song?

"Yeah, baby," he crooned. "Get down. Boogie oogie oogie. Get down. You gotta gotta gotta . . ."

I was stunned, absolutely blown away. He was actually doing some serious bumping and grinding while he was singing!

I stood up slowly, warily, as if unsure whether or not I might be hallucinating, and pressed my nose against the glass. It was pretty fogged up, but I had no trouble identifying Roger's body—his *naked* body—and it was headed my way!

"Hey there, Lizzie," he said flirtatiously.

Lizzie? He hadn't called me that since we were first married.

"Better watch out, little Lizzie, 'cause here I come."

The next thing I knew, Roger was opening the shower door and hopping inside, invading my steamy space, which was soon to become even more steamy.

Before I could react, before I could even attempt to make sense of what was happening, he was grabbing my bar of soap and lathering me up—my neck, my shoulders, my breasts, my thighs, my buttocks, my pubic hair. I couldn't believe how sensual he was and how completely in charge of the action. I heard myself moan, felt myself melt with every stroke of his hand, felt my old desire for him not only spring back to life but overtake me. He was the man I married all right (not counting the love handles), and I watched hungrily, breathlessly, blissfully as he lathered himself up—all of him—and began to press his soapy, slippery body against mine.

"Get down. Boogie oogie Lizzie."

"You want me to lie down?" I said between gasps.

He laughed. God, it was wonderful to hear the carefree ring in his voice again. "No, silly. I want you exactly where you are, so I can do this."

He lifted me onto him then, wrapped my legs around him, positioned me so that I was straddling him.

"There," he murmured. "That's it." He backed us against the wall, keeping us from falling on our wet asses.

For an instant, I worried that Roger wouldn't be able to hold me up for long and that we'd go crashing onto the tile floor. No, I didn't weigh all that much, but he wasn't in the greatest shape, remember.

"How about this?" he said, lowering me down to the little shower seat I'd been sitting on, as if he had read my mind. "Better?"

I nodded. *Better* didn't begin to describe how I was feeling. It was all so unexpected, this lustfulness of Roger's, this re-emergence of his playful, attentive, giving side. I really didn't know what hit me.

"You're so beautiful," he said. "Every inch of you."

He was telling me I was beautiful too? I couldn't remember the last time he'd paid me that kind of a compliment.

"And so lucious to touch," he added.

With my legs still hugging his back, he stood over me, thrust himself inside of me, made me forget there had ever been a harsh moment between us.

"I love you, Lizzie," he groaned as the water and the soap and the sex comingled. "Oh, yeah. I do."

"I can't get over the change in you, Roger. It's so—"

He began to move faster then, the squishing of our moist bodies providing most of the sound effects. We clung to each other, our hearts racing, racing, racing until—

Well, I still can't believe that we did it in the shower that morning, even as I'm flashing back on it, even as I'm telling you this story. I mean, we'd never done it in the shower, not even when we were dating.

I had no idea whether the sudden and dramatic and desperately hoped-for enhancement of my husband was triggered by those two extra packets in his orange juice, or whether the first packet had simply, finally, coincidentally kicked in. All I knew with any certainty was that Roger had returned, and that I was beyond ecstatic.

CHAPTER TEN

After Roger left the house for work, I drifted onto my bed in a state of euphoria—and exhaustion, to tell you the truth. I was out of practice in terms of sex that was even remotely acrobatic, and I felt spent, my legs still wobbly, my lips raw (all of them). Whatever Dr. Farkus had put into that cocktail of his sure was potent. He really *was* a magician, I decided, and it was no wonder that his waiting room was packed with people willing to shell out big bucks for his potions.

I sighed with the memory of Roger's kisses. To see the tenderness in his eyes again, to feel his need for me, to hear him call me "beautiful"—well, let's just say that all was right with the world for the first time in a long time.

Of course, I was itching to find out if Bud had responded to the powder the way Roger had, so I reached for the phone and dialed Clover's number.

"Any change?" I asked, not wanting to blurt out my good news in case she didn't have any of her own to report.

"Just a sec," she said, then lowered her voice to a whisper. "Bud's still home. He's in the kitchen making up a shopping list."

"For what?"

"For groceries." She giggled. "He insisted on cooking me dinner tonight."

"Oh, Clover," I said excitedly. "I have a sneaking suspicion that Bud's enhancement took effect this morning. Am I right?"

"Are you ever. One minute I had my butt sticking out of the refrigerator while I was checking to see how much milk we had left. The next minute Bud came up behind me and told me I had a 'precious little rear end.' Those were his exact words. I was so caught off guard that I dropped the milk and spilled it all over the floor. Then—listen to this one—Bud said, 'How about letting *me* take care of that, cutie pie.' Cutie pie! He hasn't called me that since we were first married! What's more, he got down on his hands and knees with a sponge and wiped up my mess! You don't know Bud, Elizabeth, but I'm telling you—he hasn't helped me around the house since he bought himself that La-Z-Boy four years ago."

"That's incredible," I said, sharing her sense of exhilaration at her husband's transformation.

"And then he volunteered to cook us a romantic dinner."

"Does he know how to cook?"

"Not really, but he's been in there studying my mama's recipe for fried chicken. He said he's making a shopping list, going to the store, and coming back with a whole bunch of surprises for me."

"Doesn't he have to work today?"

"He probably should, but he said he doesn't want me out of his sight. Oh, can you stand it, Elizabeth? This is everything I prayed it would be. Bud is just like he was when he was courting me."

I was thrilled for Clover, naturally. Thrilled for both of us. It was while

I was lying there being so thrilled that it occurred to me that I had forgotten to thank the person responsible for this merriment.

"Hi, Brenda," I said when she picked up the phone in her office.

"Well, if it isn't my long-lost sister," she said. "I haven't heard from you in over two weeks. I thought you'd dropped off the face of the earth."

"I'm sorry," I said. Brenda was one of those sisters who keeps score of who calls whom and how often. "I've been traveling. And things have been a little crazy at home."

"Crazy how?" she asked. "The last thing you told me was that you were conflicted about calling Dr. Farkus and making an appointment."

I know, I know. I really should have filled her in immediately after I went to see Farkus, but I wanted to work out my thoughts without interference. And once I did work them out, I had my new friend Clover to confide in. "That's why I'm calling, Brenda. To tell you what happened."

"I'm listening," she said, still hanging on to her attitude.

"I did go to see Dr. Farkus," I began, prepared to give her a play-by-play of the events of recent weeks.

"Oh!" she squealed before I got any further into the story. "Who was there? In the waiting room, I mean? Anyone famous?"

"Yes, Brenda, but this is off the record. I'd hate to be the snitch who lands them in your magazine."

"Just tell me, Elizabeth. I'm curious, that's all."

"Well, there was Wendy Winters and Angela Clay." I dropped a few more names, then the big one.

"Lanie was there?" She shouted this in my ear.

"Yes."

"Was she alone?"

"Yes."

"What was she wearing?"

"I didn't notice."

"What was she doing while she was waiting?"

"Reading."

"Reading *what,* Elizabeth?"

"How should I know? Look, don't you want to hear about me? About *my* experience with Dr. Farkus?" Brenda wasn't just starstruck. She was star stuck.

After I finally managed to tell her about Roger's reaction to the stud stimulant, she squealed again. "I'm so happy for you. And for Roger too. This is incredible news."

"And it wouldn't have been possible if you hadn't tipped me off about Dr. Farkus. I don't know how to thank you."

"I know how. You can have me over for dinner some night and I can get a look at my enhanced brother-in-law with my own eyes."

"It's a date."

Later that afternoon I was stretched out on the massage table at Burke Williams Day Spa on the corner of Broadway and Fourth. I'd been going to the Santa Monica pleasure parlor for my weekly rubdown for the past year, but would now be forced to cut such indulgences out of my budget, due to Dr. Farkus's exorbitant fee. Not a bad trade-off, all things considered. I'd rather have a loving, sexy, attentive husband than a weekly massage, however divine, wouldn't you?

I was in that wonderful space between hypnotic stupor and old-fashioned relaxation when one of the staff at the spa said I had a phone call.

"You sure it's for me?" I said.

"He asked for Elizabeth Baskin," she said.

He? What man would be calling me here? I wondered as I climbed off the table and padded to the nearest phone.

"Hello?" I said.

"Hey, Lizzie."

"Roger?" He never called me at the spa. He never remembered the name of the spa. He never remembered where I went on which day of the week.

"You sound surprised," he said, his tone lighthearted, mischievous, like the Roger I used to know.

"I am. Everything all right?"

"Everything's groovy." Groovy? "For some reason it popped into my head that you have your weekly massage there this afternoon. So I thought I'd call to tell you I love you."

"Aw, that's so sweet." And such a one-eighty from the guy who hated to be disturbed at the office.

"I've been thinking about you, about our little tryst in the shower this morning, and I was wondering if you're up for another go-around."

I smiled, felt my face grow hot. This was amazing, unbelievable, a miracle. "You never know what tomorrow morning might bring," I said coyly.

"Who's talking about tomorrow morning?" he said. "I meant now."

"Oh. Well, I already washed and blow-dried my hair, Roger, so I'm not really up for another shower."

"Then we'll find someplace else to 'express ourselves,' " he suggested with a chuckle. "I could meet you at home in, say, fifteen minutes."

"Won't the others mind that you're leaving work so early?" I asked.

"After the hours I've spent covering their asses? I doubt it." He laughed. "I don't know what's gotten into me, but to hell with my responsibilities at the office. All I want to do is be with you."

I know what's gotten into you, I thought, feeling both proud that I had brought about the changes in Roger's behavior and guilty that I'd left him out of the process. I found it interesting that while the stud stimulant had certainly increased his libido, as Dr. Farkus had assured me it would, it was also responsible for getting him to remember my schedule of appointments and to call me on the phone just to say "I love you" and to choose to spend time with me instead of slaving away at his job. Perhaps there would be many, many other benefits of the potion. I could hardly wait to discover them.

Roger met me at the house. He walked in the door carrying a bouquet of roses—yellow ones and pink ones and white ones, along with a few sprigs of baby's breath.

"I remembered that you think red roses are a cliché," he said, presenting them to me.

"I can't get over how nice you're being to me." I was touched that he went to the trouble of stopping at the florist—and flabbergasted that he remembered what I'd once said about red roses. Even *I* didn't remember I'd said that.

"Why wouldn't I be nice to you?" he said, as if genuinely puzzled by my statement. I had to remind myself that he didn't know he'd been herbed. "You're a wonderful woman, Elizabeth. You deserve flowers and so much more."

"Thank you, Roger. That's a lovely sentiment."

I was about to bring the roses into the kitchen and put them in a vase of water when he took them from me. "Let me," he said. "I don't want those elegant hands of yours getting scratched by the thorns."

I didn't respond. I just followed him into the kitchen, shaking my head in astonishment.

He was clipping the ends of each rose and placing them strategically into the vase when I noticed that he was wearing a suit I hadn't seen before—a crisply pressed, impeccably tailored, very fashionable gray suit without even a single remnant of food caked onto the fabric.

"Roger?"

"Hmm?"

"Is that a new suit?"

"Oh. Yeah. Do you like it, hon?"

"It's gorgeous. Where'd you get it?"

"Saks." He spun around and smoothed his lapels, preening for me. "I don't know why, but I found myself looking in the mirror this morning and thinking, You need new threads, Rog. So I canceled the client I was supposed to take to lunch and drove to Beverly Hills. I bought this baby the second I laid eyes on it. I managed to convince them to do the alterations while I was trying on shoes."

I glanced down at his feet, which were sporting a pair of buttery leather Cole Haan loafers in place of his beat-up, ten-year-old Ballys.

"Very spiffy," I said admiringly. I was delighted that he was finally embarrassed enough by his old wardrobe to buy some decent clothes. "But didn't the client get upset when you canceled lunch?"

He shot me a wide grin. "If there's a choice between looking good for my Lizzie or sucking up to some client, there *is* no choice."

I didn't know what to say. I was too blissed out for words. Imagine if *your* husband was suddenly speaking and acting and looking exactly the way you'd been wishing he'd speak and act and look. It would be a complete shock to your system, right?

"There," he said when he'd finally arranged and rearranged the roses to his satisfaction. Martha Stewart couldn't have done it any better. "Perfect, aren't they?"

"They are," I agreed, marveling at the fact that Roger had never been a big fan of flower arranging.

He turned to me, pulled me close. "*You're* perfect, Lizzie." He nibbled on my earlobe. "Let me show you how perfect."

He was ready to go again, judging by the bulge in his snazzy new pants. "Okay, show me," I challenged, inhaling his musky cologne. That's new too, I thought, as he kissed my neck. He must have bought it at Saks along with the suit and the shoes.

"My pleasure," he whispered, then released me abruptly. He moved the vase of roses off the countertop, collected the cuttings and the florist paper and deposited them into the garbage, and sprayed the entire surface with Fantastik. "There. All set. Not a speck of dirt anywhere."

Now I was *really* taken aback. Roger was cleaning the kitchen counter? The same Roger who had become pathologically incapable of cleaning anything, including himself?

He lowered his head and kissed me on the mouth, first gently, then with greater urgency. "You're so beautiful," he said again, as he had that morning in the shower. "I have this unquenchable thirst for you. Isn't that something?" Oh, it was something all right. With the deftness he had exhibited earlier, he peeled off my clothes, then his own, and draped them over the back of a chair—neatly. And then he said, "Ready?"

I smiled and clasped his hand, figuring he was about to lead me into the bedroom.

Wrong. He jerked me back, put his hands on my waist, and hoisted me up onto the kitchen counter.

"What are you doing?" I asked, confused as well as cold, given that the countertop on which my naked tush was now resting was made of eighteenth-century limestone.

"What am I doing? Preparing to make love to my wife," said Roger, climbing up onto the counter and assuming the position.

"Up here?" I said, both excited and alarmed. Excited, because Roger was obviously in touch with his adventurous, playful side again. Alarmed, because the limestone, which was durable and attractive and had just the right patina for the country French look I was trying to achieve in the kitchen, was also distressed and bumpy and likely to carve permanent dents in my skin.

"Oh, yeah, Lizzie girl," panted Roger, his breathing as hard as his Freddy. He lowered himself onto me, careful not to crush me, and made love to me so slowly and skillfully that I forgot about the limestone. Sort of.

"How about a walk on the beach?" he suggested when we were done, bouncing off the counter and landing on his feet with the agility of a gymnast. "Are you up for it, hon?"

I smiled. Weakly. "What about after dinner?" I suggested, hoping for a quick nap—on an actual bed.

"Sure. Why don't I take you to The Lobster down on the pier. We could walk on the beach afterwards, get a good workout."

I'd already had a workout. Two of them. "Sounds wonderful," I said, not about to refuse his offer, especially since it was precisely the kind of evening's entertainment I'd been nagging him about.

The Lobster, a contemporary, multilevel seafood restaurant on the site where a funky old lobster shanty used to be, was right across the Pacific Coast Highway from the Santa Monica Pier. It was both an expensive destination for tourists and a popular local hangout, with plenty of atmosphere and excellent food.

"You look radiant," said Roger, who was gazing at me across the table.

"It's easy to look radiant when you're happy."

"I'm happy too," he said. "I feel like a new man for some reason."

You don't want to know the reason, I thought. "How are your crab cakes, Roger? You've hardly touched them."

"They're a little mayonaise-y, plus there's all that breading on them. Not exactly low-cal."

That didn't bother you before, I mused, picturing the Big Macs he'd been scarfing down. "Are you watching your weight now?"

"It's about time that I paid more attention to my body, isn't it? As a matter of fact"—he nodded at my entrée, Louisiana prawns with dirty rice—"I don't think that was the most slimming item you could have ordered, Elizabeth. You might want to skip dessert."

I blinked. Roger was advising me on *my* weight? *I* wasn't the one with the jowls! Still, I had been complaining that he never noticed anything I did, never showed much interest in the little details of my life, and now here he was commenting on my choice of a dinner entrée. I couldn't very well get huffy about it.

After the meal, we strolled hand in hand along the sandy beach, just like we used to when we were first married. It was the beach that had drawn us to Santa Monica, and our house was only blocks from the ocean.

"This is so invigorating," said Roger, breathing in the cool night air.

"It is," I agreed, floating on a cloud, still basking in the luscious afterglow from our matinee on the kitchen counter. I had wanted heat. I'd gotten heat. I had wanted passion. I'd gotten passion. I had wanted saliva. I'd gotten saliva. I felt like the luckiest woman on the planet, my husband having been restored to me in the most miraculous, magical way. How many wives ever get to experience such a turnaround?

"It's so invigorating," he continued, "that it's given me a second wind. What do you say we check out that club on Hollywood Boulevard?"

"What club, Roger?" I tried unsuccessfully to stifle a yawn. It was eleven-thirty, our usual bedtime.

"It's called Perversion. David told me about it, and for some reason the name didn't go in one ear and out the other as it normally would."

"Don't you have to be up early tomorrow morning for work?"

"Sure, but tomorrow's tomorrow." He kissed me. "Why not live in the moment?"

What could I say? This was the Roger I'd been yearning for, and now I had him.

We lived in the moment. We drove over to Hollywood to a club that is, indeed, called Perversion. It's got three dance floors, each featuring a different kind of music. In the first room there's goth; in the second there's industrial; and in the third there's both techno and trance. If you're completely in the dark about all this, don't feel bad; I was too. I spent most of my time in hotel rooms, not nightclubs, and was, therefore, not acquainted with the various subsets of music.

When we got to Perversion, it was clear (at least to me) that Roger and I were hopelessly out of place. For one thing, we were overdressed. For another, we did not have purple hair. For a third, we did not know how to dance to goth, industrial, techno, or trance. Not that Roger was deterred.

"Hey, come on, hon. Let's get out there and mix it up," he said, dragging me onto the dance floor—the dance floor that featured industrial.

"They're not playing 'Boogie Oogie Oogie,' " I reminded him as he began to do his disco thing. "This is a completely different style of music."

"Loosen up, hon," he said, rotating his hips. "Just move to the groove."

I moved to the groove. People were snickering at us. I saw them. But Roger was oblivious, enjoying himself like a kid. He would have kept dancing until dawn if I hadn't pleaded with him to call it a night.

"It's one o'clock in the morning," I pointed out.

"So? I heard a guy say they're open until three," he replied.

"Roger. I love that your batteries have been recharged and that your spontaneity has returned—it's been so long since you've wanted to do things on weeknights—but you've got a busy day at work tomorrow and I've got a million errands to run."

"You're right, hon. We should go. Besides, I think I need to be alone with you right now."

"Alone with me?" Was he seriously considering another—

He wrapped his arms around me, kissed my chin, brushed my hair back with his fingers. "Alone with you, Lizzie. As in, you and I are about to take intimacy to a new level."

No sooner were we inside the house when he started nuzzling me, licking me, kneading my breasts, right there in the foyer.

"You are so sexy," he said. "You drive me crazy with desire."

You are so sexy. You drive me crazy with desire. Weren't those the words I'd been dying to hear? Well, now I was hearing them, only I was so worn out that they were coming in only faintly.

"Let's get you into bed," said Roger, swooping me up in his arms, carrying me into the bedroom, and setting me down on top of our queen-size Serta.

"Thanks for the lift," I said torpidly, about to pass out with my clothes on.

"I get the distinct feeling you're not into making love right now," said Roger, who was standing over me, observing my eyelids growing heavier and heavier by the second.

When there was no response from me, he jiggled my arm a little, then watched it flop lifelessly beside me. "I *said* I get the feeling you're too tired to make love with me, Elizabeth."

When there was still no response from me, he leaned down and whispered into my ear, "Earth to Lizzie. Is she in there? Does she want to come out to play?"

I would have answered him, of course. I would have come out to play too. But I was unable to speak, let alone stroke his Freddy. I had crashed, and was on my way to a sound and decisive sleep. It had been quite a day.

CHAPTER ELEVEN

The next few weeks were heaven. Roger courted me, came on to me, campaigned for me. Gone was the apathy. Gone was the forgetfulness. Gone was the tension between us. (Also gone, albeit more gradually, were his bald spot, his jowls, and his gut.) Rather than avoid me or ignore me or dismiss me, Roger wanted to be around me day and night. We cuddled up by the fireplace and sipped wine. We took long walks on the beach and held hands. We went to the movies, worked out at the gym together, wrote each other howlingly bad love poems. Picture a really sappy music video and you've got the idea.

And I wasn't the only one singing a happy tune. Clover was beside herself with joy because the stud stimulant had worked its magic on Bud too.

We were both so eager to show off our husbands that we arranged to have dinner together, the four of us.

"Great. Let's meet them at Spago," Roger suggested when I had proposed the date. (When he'd asked how I'd met Clover, I told him that she and I had struck up a conversation at Wild Oats, the health food store on Montana and Fifteenth, and became fast friends over the bean curd.)

"Spago?" I arched an eyebrow. "You always hated that place. You said only phonies went there—people who wanted to see and be seen."

"I did say that, didn't I." He scratched his head as if bewildered by what had popped out of his mouth lately. "I guess I've changed my mind for some reason." He laughed, flicked a speck of lint off his brand-new Armani T-shirt—his black Armani T-shirt. Well, not *everything* about his transformation was positive.

Clover and Bud were up for driving to Wolfgang Puck's Beverly Hills outpost too. Apparently, Bud relished the thought of seeing and being seen, now that he had dropped a few pounds and perked up his wardrobe and been to a colorist for highlights.

Everybody hit it off really well at dinner. Clover and I sat there beaming while our husbands pulled out our chairs for us and ordered our drinks for us and discussed the various menu options with us. What a difference a potion makes, I thought. The last time Roger and I had been to Spago he'd made fun of the menu. "Caviar pizza?" he'd said. "Who the hell would order that?" This time, *he* ordered it.

"What's it like owning car dealerships?" I asked Bud, hoping to get to know my friend's husband better.

"Aw, let's not talk about business tonight," he said in his Kentucky drawl. "I'd rather talk about my cutie pie here." He planted a wet smooch on Clover's lips. "She's the most important thing in my life."

Clover blushed. "Bud's the important one in our household. He's doing all the cooking," she announced. "He never used to give a hoot about what I put on the table. Now he comes home from work early every day, reads my cookbooks, picks a recipe, runs to the store to buy the ingredients, then puts them all together and serves them on our best china. He's an artist in the kitchen, Lord love him."

"What's your specialty?" Roger asked Bud with genuine interest.

"Probably my soy-mirin-glazed Chilean sea bass with wasabi mashed potatoes and lemongrass-cilantro sauce," said Bud. "I started out cooking southern, but I've moved on to Pacific Rim."

Clover winked at me. I winked back.

"Roger's not a big one for cooking," I said, "but he's developed an incredible eye for home decorating. For ages I tried to convince him that we needed to spruce up the house, and he had zero interest. Now he practically devours the shelter magazines. He wants us to redo the master bedroom first, don't you, honey?"

Roger leaned over and licked my ear. The words "master bedroom" must have gotten his mojo working again, not that it took much these days. He was as charged up, turned on, and demonstrative with his affection as a horny teenager.

The four of us were laughing and talking and having a wonderful evening when I happened to glance across the restaurant and make eye contact with a familiar face. A familiar *male* face. Let's see, I thought. What movie was this guy in? Or was he the star of a TV series? I couldn't believe I even cared. Brenda was the one who would have cared.

And then it hit me. I remembered where I'd last seen the familiar male face, and it wasn't in a movie or on television. It was in the lobby of the Worthington Hotel in Seattle.

Yup, there he was, Chris Eckersly, the man with whom I'd had cognac but not sex. What in the world was he doing in L.A.? He was from Kansas City, or so he claimed.

Well, I had two choices. I could slouch down in my chair and pray he wouldn't see me, pray he wouldn't strut over to the table and fill Roger in about our brief encounter in Seattle. Or I could get up and go speak to him, diffuse the situation. Not that I had anything to feel guilty about when it came to Chris Eckersly. I had behaved honorably that night, thanking him for the liqueur and then high-tailing it up to my room before there was even a hint of impropriety. Still, the last thing I needed was some jerk bragging to my husband that I'd been flirting with another man, with *him*. Not with my marriage going so well.

"Hon? Are you all right?" said Roger, who must have noticed that I had tensed. He noticed everything now.

"Fine. I'm fine," I said. "But I think I'll run off to powder my nose. Be right back." I had chosen option number two.

As I rose from my chair, Clover did the same. "I'll come with you," she said.

Damn. What is it with women, anyway? Why must they trot off to the bathroom in pairs? I didn't want her tagging along. I was on a mission. "They only have one stall here," I lied, "so you might as well wait until I come back. Otherwise, you'll have to stand outside the ladies room door and you'll end up feeling self-conscious while every single person in the restaurant is staring at you."

"Oh." She sat back down. "All righty then."

I walked toward the restroom, en route to Chris's table, hoping he would explain what he was doing in my neck of the woods.

He was dining alone I saw as I approached him. Probably scoping out the place for some lonely woman to slither up to.

"Well, if it isn't Elizabeth Stickler. What a surprise," he said, as if it weren't a surprise at all.

Making sure Roger wasn't looking, I drew closer to Chris and exchanged a few pleasantries with him. "Are you here on business?" I asked. "To see a client?"

"In a manner of speaking." He smiled, ran his eyes over me. "Small world, isn't it?" Too small. "I suppose that's hubby over there? The one in Armani?"

"The one with the curly brown hair is my husband," I said frostily. "He and I are out with friends tonight."

"Sounds chummy. How about inviting me over for a drink? A cognac, maybe?" He said this leeringly, tauntingly. "You could introduce me as the man you picked up in Seattle. I'm sure that would go over big."

"I didn't pick you up in Seattle," I hissed. "You picked me up."

"No, actually you invited me to join you. Let's at least get our facts straight."

"Look, Chris. I don't know why you have such an attitude about that night, but if I did or said anything wrong, I apologize. Now, let's forget we ever met and move on. Okay?"

He shook his head and mock-pouted. "And I thought you liked me."

"I'm sure your wife likes you. Her name is Meredith, isn't it?"

"I'm not married, Elizabeth. I only told you I was married so you'd think we had something in common, so you'd loosen up around me. Not a bad strategy, huh?"

This stopped me cold. So he was a liar as well as a sore loser. "What about the wedding ring you were wearing?" I checked his left hand. "The wedding ring you're still wearing?"

"I told you. Pretending to be married is a surefire way to get married women to relax. And once they relax, it's a guaranteed score. Or at least I thought I would score with you. There we were, enjoying ourselves, and the next thing I knew you were cutting out on me."

"Chris, let me say once again that I'm a happily married woman, and if I gave you any other impression when we were in Seattle, I'm sorry. Very sorry. Now, I'd better run. Bye-bye."

I hurried off to the ladies' room, cursing myself all the way. If only I had mentioned my marital problems to Brenda sooner, I would have gone to see Dr. Farkus sooner and Roger would have been enhanced sooner and my life would have improved sooner and I wouldn't have felt the need for the attention of a creep like Chris! Oh, well. That would be the last of him, I was certain.

When I got back to our table, Roger asked, before I even had a chance to sit down, "Who was that guy you were talking to, Elizabeth?"

As I said, Roger noticed everything now. "He's one of the training managers at AMLP," I told him. "I hardly know him." Well, the second part was true.

Speaking of AMLP, Roger was so attached to me, after having been enhanced, that he insisted on coming with me on inspections.

"The thought of spending nights alone, without your body next to mine, is pure torture," he said one morning as I was telling him about an upcoming trip.

What a hottie, I smiled to myself. Before I'd slipped him the powder, he hadn't given a flip whether I was home or not. "I'm not sure Preston would approve of your coming with me," I said.

"Then don't tell him," he said. "I'll register as Mr. Stickler and keep a low profile. During the day I'll let you conduct your inspections of the properties, and during the night I'll help you achieve the orgasms of your life."

Not a bad deal, I thought, savoring the idea of having more quality time with Roger. We agreed that he would accompany me to two of the hotels I'd been assigned to evaluate. It hadn't bothered me, such was my state of bliss, that his being away with me also meant his being away from the office. He was entitled, I thought, wasn't he?

The first jaunt was fun—I felt naughty that I was sneaking him along on my business trip. Instead of returning to a lonely hotel room at the end of the day, I returned to a husband who catered to my every whim. A wife's dream.

After the second trip, however, I was less enthusiastic, to put it mildly, and decided that I would go it alone from then on.

What happened was this—Roger was beginning to wear me out, sexually. In fact, it was at the new Peachtree Resort and Spa in Atlanta where we had our very first fight since his enhancement.

It flared up after I had just put in seven arduous hours inspecting the property. I'd come back to the room, taken off my clothes, and slipped into bed, in anticipation of a nice, quiet nap before dinner, when Roger pounced on top of me, aroused yet again.

"Lizzie, honey. I've been waiting for you," he said and started nibbling on my right shoulder.

"Roger!" I snapped. "What do I look like to you? The *other* white meat?"

"Hey, what's the problem?" he said cluelessly and started to go for the left shoulder.

I bolted up, covered myself with the sheet. "You. You're the problem. You're into having sex a gazillion times a day."

"I am, aren't I?" He assumed that bewildered look again, and while I felt for him, I also resented him. I'd hoped for a lover and I'd ended up with an animal. "I can't seem to help myself," he said.

"Well, try, because I just can't keep up with you. There are moments when all I want to do is be left alone."

My God. I couldn't believe I'd said that. *All I want to do is be left alone*? How could I have uttered such a thing? How could I have meant such a thing? But I did mean it. For so long I had yearned for Roger to lavish his attention on me, to be more romantic with me, to initiate lovemaking—expertly and often. But now that he was lavishing his attention on me and being more romantic with me and initiating lovemaking, it was too much. I couldn't handle it. Not several times a day and not on the Travertine marble floor of the hotel bathroom (yes, we'd done it there that very morning, right smack in the middle of my inspection).

Roger backed off and left me to my nap, but he sulked throughout the remainder of the trip. As we were standing at the registration desk, waiting to check out of the hotel, he muttered to me, "I certainly hope you'll get over what's bothering you, Elizabeth, because I'm a man, and we men have our needs."

"Excuse me?" I said, hoping the clerk wasn't listening to this.

"My point is that I'm back in touch with my sexuality, and it won't be denied. If you're not willing or able to be my partner in every sense of the word, I—"

"You what?"

"Nothing."

"Come on, Roger. Say it. If I can't match your energy and stamina in the bedroom, you're going to find someone who can. Isn't that what you're insinuating?"

"Mrs. Stickler? Do you want to see a copy of your bill or not?" asked the registration clerk, looking embarrassed for me, sorry for me. This was not supposed to be happening. Roger was not supposed to become so enhanced that I would lose him to another, equally enhanced woman. No, that was not the scenario I'd paid good money for.

Another problem surfaced soon after we got home. Roger continued to spend time away from the office, and his absences were pissing off his partners. In his altered state, he'd become positively obsessive about his appearance and was now a regular at the gym, keeping himself in tip-top shape; a regular on Rodeo Drive, buying himself the finest in apparel and accessories; a regular at the Burke Williams Day Spa, where *I* could no longer afford to go but where *he* was having weekly thermal seaweed wraps.

"What's with him these days?" asked David, who was one to talk. For years he skipped out on the others to frolic with his conquest du jour. Now he was calling me to express his dismay over Roger's adventures. How ironic.

"He's just taking better care of himself," I replied, trying not to sound defensive. I was responsible for David's complaints, I knew. If I hadn't tampered with Roger's body chemistry, he'd be the same old workaholic, and David and I wouldn't be having this conversation.

"Yeah, well, he looks great, no doubt about that. He's got all the secretaries swooning over him, not to mention Carrie. She's the only one who's not mad at him for being out of the office so much."

Isn't that special, I thought. I mean, sure I was happy that Roger was trim and well groomed and wearing suitable clothes again, but did I really want to think about all those women at work drooling over him? Did I really want to think about Carrie Toobin—Carrie *Boob*in, I called her when I was feeling catty—drooling over him?

"Brad tells me zat Roger has a new hobby," said Gerta, who called one day to invite us to dinner.

"A new hobby?" I said. "What is it?"

"Himself." She laughed. Cackled, really. "Brad cannot believe za change in Roger. He says Roger alvays looks at himself in za mirror, making sure everyzing is perfect."

I didn't know how to respond. I had noticed the same tendency in Roger. And not just with regard to himself. He'd become a perfectionist when it came to the house too. I'm telling you, the man could no longer walk by a picture on the wall without stopping to straighten it. In the kitchen, for example, he'd not only alphabetized all the spices in the spice rack and organized the pantry by food group, but purchased an entire and very expensive set of copper pots from the Williams-Sonoma catalog and hung them on gleaming brass hooks above the stovetop. I came home from a trip and couldn't find anything because he'd rearranged the entire room.

"What are you putting in your husband's orange juice in the morning?" Carrie kidded when she called one afternoon, looking for Roger, who was having a manicure.

"I'm not putting anything in his orange juice," I said indignantly, having done just that, of course. "Why do you ask?"

"Because he's acting like a raging hormone," she said.

I panicked, picturing Roger groping every woman at the office, including Carrie.

"Seriously, he's got almost too much energy lately," she said. "Is he downing those dietary supplements that are so popular with athletes?"

"Not that I'm aware of," I said. "But then I don't monitor Roger's intake of food and beverages."

"Are you angry about something, Elizabeth?" she said.

"No. Why would I be?" I said. I wasn't angry exactly. I was just a tiny bit fed up with people wanting to know what was wrong with Roger, particularly after I'd spent my hard-earned money to make everything *right* with Roger.

The most distressing conversation, though, was the one I had with Frankie Wheeler, Roger's twelve-year-old Little Brother, the day he stopped by the house.

"Hi, Elizabeth," he said as he stood at the front door, having ridden his bicycle all the way up from Venice Beach. "Is Roger real sick?"

"Sick? No, he's fine, sweetie," I said, giving Frankie a big hug. He was small and extremely young-looking for his age, as well as lonely and desperate for affection. His mother worked around the clock, cleaning office buildings as well as waitressing, and even on those rare occasions when she was home, she was preoccupied and indifferent to Frankie's needs. As for his father, as I've said, he was a no-show most of the time. And when he *was* around, he was a snarling, foul-mouthed type who took his failures out on everyone else. Since Frankie was six, Roger had been his support system, but now the boy was at my house, wondering whether his Big Brother, like the others he cared about, had abandoned him too.

"If he isn't sick, how come he hasn't driven me places and done stuff with me?" asked Frankie, his face contorted with hurt. He had brown eyes and a button nose, and his blond hair was shorn in a buzz cut. He was adorable enough to be the kid in the cereal commercial and so good-natured for a boy with such problems at home. It broke my heart to think that Roger was shirking his responsibilities to Frankie now because of his enhancement. Instead of zealously keeping their weekly dates, as he had for so many years, Roger had been passing them up in favor of his workouts, his spa treatments, his shopping excursions, and other manifestations of his quest for perfection. In fact, the day that Frankie had stopped by he was having a consultation with an orthodontist, of all things.

"I'm thinking of getting braces," he had announced to me the week before as he lingered in front of the bathroom mirror, studying his smile.

"What in the world are you talking about?" I'd responded, growing more and more perplexed by his behavior.

"My teeth," he'd said. "They're not perfectly aligned. I should probably get them fixed."

"At your age?" I'd said. "You've lived with those teeth for forty years. Why fool with them now?"

"Because it's never too late to make improvements, Elizabeth."

Right. Fortunately, when the orthodontist he'd gone to see had explained the procedure for straightening his teeth, including the fact that he'd be walking around looking like a goofy kid while the braces were on, Roger had bagged the idea.

Meanwhile, here was Frankie Wheeler, munching on the sandwich I'd made for him, sitting at the kitchen counter, asking me again why Roger hadn't been spending time with him.

"So he's been real busy with work?" he said.

"Work and other things," I said. "I'm sure he'll call you and tell you what he's been up to. And when he does, you guys can plan another camping trip or something. You know how much Roger loves camping."

He nodded but wasn't convinced. "Maybe he's taking another kid camping. Maybe the new kid is more fun than me."

"Oh, Frankie." I couldn't stand this. I threw my arms around him, gripped him tightly. "Roger loves you even more than he loves camping. There's no other kid in his life, believe me, sweetheart. He's just going through a hectic period." Well? How was I supposed to explain the situation to a twelve-year-old child when I didn't fully understand it myself? All I knew was that Dr. Farkus had promised to transform Roger into the perfect husband and that, while the initial results were wildly successful, the more recent effects were downright upsetting. At first, Roger *had* become the perfect husband. But now, "perfect husband" seemed to be about making *himself* perfect, about gratifying his own pleasure. Hadn't I made it clear to Farkus that I wanted to perk Roger up, not turn him into a man who shared few, if any, of the same values as the man I married? Had I somehow miscommunicated my goal at the time of my appointment? Or was Roger simply having a bad reaction to the stud stimulant?

I got my answer the next time I called Clover, who confided that Bud was spending hours trading online through Charles Schwab.

"All of a sudden, he's obsessed with proving how much money he can accumulate," she said. "He claims that he can't be a perfect husband unless he's making a killing. What the heck's he talking about, Elizabeth? He's a car dealer, not a stockbroker."

Yes, a pattern had emerged—Clover was seeing a similar reaction in Bud.

"Oh, and here's another thing," she added before we hung up. "He's way too into sex. I told him I'm just not up for it every hour on the hour, and do you know what he said?"

"I'm afraid to hear."

"He said, 'Well, then I just might have to find me someone who *is* up for it.' " She groaned. "This will probably sound crazy, but I'm actually having second thoughts about the fact that I gave Bud the powder."

"It doesn't sound crazy at all," I said, having had second thoughts myself.

"You don't suppose Bud will go out and find someone else, do you?" she said plaintively. "The point of this whole operation was to save my marriage, not destroy it."

"I don't know what Bud will do, Clover. I've got my own problems to deal with," I said, thinking of Carrie Toobin and the secretaries at the law firm and the entire female population of L.A., all of whom were potential threats to my marriage now. "Let's just see how things go for a while."

"Okay." She paused, not ready to end the conversation. "I was wondering, though."

"Wondering what?"

"If maybe we overdosed them. Maybe they're acting like self-involved idiots because of those two extra packets we put in their juice."

"Maybe those two extra packets did make the initial dose more potent. But I think there's good news and bad news here. The bad news is that this 'perfect husband' attitude of theirs isn't likely to disappear right away. The good news is that it isn't likely to get any worse."

CHAPTER TWELVE

But it did get worse. Much worse. Not only was Roger on a quest for his own perfection, he was now on a quest for mine, finding fault with me in precisely the same way and for the same reasons that I had once found fault with him.

Here were my demerits, according to him.

I was a dud in bed, both because I often fell asleep the minute my head hit the pillow at night and because I wasn't daring enough for his taste. Please. I was more than capable of satisfying a *normal* man—a man whose idea of "daring" was not having sex while bungee jumping.

I did not keep up with fashion trends. Since *he* was the big shopper now and came home every day looking like a walking window display, suddenly *my* clothes were under scrutiny. "Boat neck sweaters are so over," he sniffed when I emerged from the bedroom wearing one. "What were you thinking, Elizabeth?" *That you're turning into a huge asshole* was what I was thinking.

I did not keep the house clean. Well, that one was so absurd it was laughable. I mean, he was talking to the Queen of the Dustbusters, the picky AMLP inspector, the professional stickler. I could spot a spill or a smudge or a stain a mile away. Besides, our cleaning lady did a fine job. Between the two of us, the house was a goddamn museum.

I did not keep myself clean. Yup, he was actually on that kick now. He said I didn't shave my legs often enough, didn't wash my hair often enough, didn't floss after each and every meal the way I should. Oh, and he wasn't crazy about my breath. Ha! I was the one who was never without Tic Tacs! Once, after we'd been to dinner at Drago, another trendoid favorite in Santa Monica, he said I smelled of garlic. "You're supposed to smell of garlic after you eat in an Italian restaurant," I said. "Not if you order properly," he said. *Order properly*. Really. The guy had taken the "perfect husband" thing and gone Stepford with it.

Rather than continue to run down his list of complaints about me, let me offer up an actual incident for you.

I had been trying to have Brenda over for dinner so she could get a look at the enhanced Roger, and she finally found time in her busy schedule to come on a Tuesday night. I served penne primavera, a green salad, and a round of hearty peasant bread, and the three of us were sitting there eating it when Roger said to me, "You've got sauce on your chin, Elizabeth."

"Thanks." I wiped my chin with my napkin.

A few more minutes went by. Brenda was in the midst of one of her unburdenings about the stars—Peter Fonda wears bulletproof trifocals, she was telling us—when Roger broke in. "The penne's not al dente, the way I like it," he said to me. "How long did you cook it?"

"Ten minutes," I said.

"Eight minutes would have been preferable," he said.

"The package said ten minutes," I maintained. "Ten to twelve minutes."

"Well, it tastes soggy to me," he said.

"It tastes fine to me," said Brenda, who went back to her story about Peter Fonda.

More time passed. Again, Roger interrupted. "There are crumbs on your placemat," he said to me, then pointed to the area around my plate. "When you tore off a piece of the bread, you produced crumbs."

I had *produced crumbs*. "Not to worry," I said, determined to remain chipper, since we had a guest. "I'll un-produce them after dinner."

"You're going to leave them there while we're having coffee and dessert?" he said with an amazed and disgusted expression on his face, as if I had suggested that he stick his head in doggie do. Don't think I wasn't tempted.

"They're crumbs, Roger. They won't bite," I said.

Yes, indeed. We had switched roles, he and I. Before his enhancement, I would have barked at him about the crumbs, or possibly Dustbusted them up while he was still eating.

After dinner, Roger excused himself, explaining that he had some ironing to do.

"Ironing?" Brenda said when we were alone.

"You heard him," I said.

She cracked up laughing. She couldn't breathe she was laughing so hard.

"This isn't funny, Brenda," I said. "You wanted to see what Dr. Farkus's powder did to Roger? Well, now you've seen. My husband has turned into such a perfect husband that nothing's good enough for him. *I'm* not good enough for him."

She sobered up, patted my hand. "He's acting totally bizarre, no question about it. I can't believe he got so upset about the crumbs."

"Ah, yes. The crumbs." I sighed. "But do you know why he left the table to do some ironing? Because he's got a new client—a bodacious Victoria's Secret model who's selling her house in Westwood and wants him to handle the closing. I can tell whenever he has a meeting with her. The night before, he irons."

"God. You don't think he's cheating on you, do you, Elizabeth?"

"I don't know what to think anymore. I'm petrified every time he leaves the house now. He's told me in no uncertain terms what a disappointment I am. What's to prevent him from finding someone who isn't?"

"Love," said Brenda. "He loves you, Elizabeth, and he always has, right from the moment he rescued you on the freeway."

"Then why is he treating me this way?"

"Because of the powder you gave him."

"The powder you talked me into giving him."

"You're blaming me for this?" She looked indignant. "You weren't blaming me when things were all kissy-face between you two. Then you were thanking me. So don't you dare make me the scapegoat."

"Oh, Brenda. Forgive me. I'm so rattled by Roger's behavior that I don't know what I'm saying."

She nodded sympathetically. "You're forgiven. Have you told Mom about this?"

"Are you kidding? Our mother isn't exactly the one to turn to when it comes to marital advice."

"True, but she's experienced with men. She's had plenty of them."

"Let's not go there, Brenda. I've got enough trouble with mine to think about hers. In any case, I haven't breathed a word of this mess to her or to anyone else, except Clover, the woman I mentioned to you. Who would believe me?"

"I believe you, now that I've actually seen the new Roger." She tsked-tsked. "Such a pity. Dr. Farkus is a true genius. The problem here isn't that his stud stimulant didn't work, it's that it worked too well."

"Too well?"

"Yeah. You wanted Roger to be more energetic sexually, and now he is—only you didn't mean *that* energetic. You wanted him to be more attentive to you, and now he is—only you didn't mean *that* attentive. You wanted him to be more aware of his personal grooming, and now he is—only you didn't mean *that* aware. And you wanted him to—"

"I get the picture, Brenda. It's pretty gloomy, isn't it?"

She was about to respond when Roger bellowed at me from somewhere in the house.

"E-liz-a-beth! Would you please come here right away?" he said.

"Where are you, Roger?" I called out.

"In our bathroom."

I shrugged at Brenda, told her I'd be back in a second. When I returned, she asked me what the emergency was all about.

"He found one of his hairs on the floor, under the sink," I said. "He wondered what it was doing there."

"God. Talk about a tight sphincter."

"This is all my fault," I said. "Before I gave him the potion, he'd been shedding his hairs all over the bathroom floor and didn't even notice. It was like having a dog in the house. And now he summons me upstairs because he finds one hair? It's madness, pure madness."

"The kind of madness you get paid for."

"What?"

"You get paid to find hairs on the bathroom floor when you're inspecting hotels. That's your job, Elizabeth. In a weird way, it's as if Roger has turned into you."

"Oh, stop it, Brenda. That's not fair. I get paid to check for hairs on the bathroom floor because I'm a consumer advocate, not because I'm a maniac. I get paid to be the eyes and ears for millions of high-end travelers—people who spend a lot of money on their accommodations and expect the very best. And I don't just check for hairs. I make sure every aspect of a property meets AMLP's high standards."

"Right. And now Roger has taken on your high standards."

"AMLP's high standards."

"*Your* high standards, Elizabeth. You wouldn't be so good at your job if you weren't so anal yourself."

"I am not anal! I'm neat. I'm organized. I'm—"

"You're just like Roger, the way he's being now. Think about it. I know you'll kill me for saying this, but maybe Dr. Farkus is more of a magician that we ever suspected. Maybe he created a specific potion that would change Roger in such a way that it would force you to confront your own flaws. Maybe the potion was intended to show you how Roger wasn't the only one responsible for the problems in your marriage."

My mouth dropped open. I was stung by her remarks. "Meaning?" I challenged.

"You get my meaning." She patted my hand again. "Just think about it, let yourself think about it. You're my sister and I love you, but you can be a tremendous tight-ass, Elizabeth. It's possible—just possible—that you're getting what you deserve."

"Getting what I—"

Well, I asked her to leave, naturally. She had hurt my feelings. First, Roger was picking on me. Now my own sister was. Thank goodness I had my job to count on. When Preston telephoned to say he was sending me on a trip to Dallas it wasn't a moment too soon, as far as I was concerned.

The Rancho Miramar in the heart of Dallas was a new property that had been receiving a lot of hype in the travel media. Preston was counting on me to give it the AMLP once-over and cut through all the public relations spin. But I couldn't concentrate on my work, not from the minute I arrived at the hotel. Not only did I forget to time the check-in, which was unpardonable enough, but I left my Standards Manual at home, a truly dumb move. I felt like a moron when I had to call Preston and ask him to overnight me another copy. He wasn't pleased.

"This isn't like you," he said after I confessed my blunder. "You're usually so efficient, so competent, so—"

"So perfect?" I said, cringing when I uttered the word.

"Yes. But I suppose everyone is entitled to a lapse here and there," he conceded. "Write up your evaluation, we'll take a look at it, and if we feel your report was compromised, we'll send someone else to re-do the inspection."

I thanked Preston for being so understanding and went about my business. But, as I said, I had trouble focusing on the job. How could I make myself care whether there were dust bunnies under the bed when Roger was probably at home right that very minute, checking whether there were dust bunnies under *our* bed! I couldn't make myself care. I only cared about my marriage, about whether Brenda's assessment of me was accurate, about whether it had been my own behavior over the past few years that had caused Roger to withdraw, about whether Dr. Farkus had somehow concocted a potion that projected my worst characteristics onto those of my husband. Most of all, I was consumed with the fear that, thanks to the powder, Roger had become so dissatisfied with me that he would leave me for another woman. I so fearful, in fact, that I forgot to play Torture the Concierge during my two-night stay at the Rancho Miramar in Dallas. As a result, my inspection of the property was not only compromised but incomplete.

"Are there problems at home?" Preston asked after I'd turned in my work. He seemed to be searching for a reason for my sudden ineptitude.

"It's nothing I can't handle," I said, hoping this was true.

"Or is it the awful business with Art Yarnell?" he said.

"You mean the general manager of the Phoenician Paradise?" I said.

"Yes. I thought I told you about his latest efforts to discredit you."

"No. You didn't tell me."

"Well, let's just say that the level of his rage has escalated. He's demanding that we fire you, Elizabeth. What's more, he's threatening to pass along your code name and physical description to other hotel managers, which would effectively limit your ability to inspect future properties."

I panicked. "So I'll change my code name, wear a disguise, do whatever I have to do," I said, thinking I should write Mr. Yarnell some nasty letters and see how *he* liked being harassed.

"Look, Elizabeth, the main point I wanted to make is that we can't afford another of your missteps. We're depending on you and your sharp eye for detail. You won't let us down, will you, dear?"

"No, Preston. Of course I won't."

But I did let him down, let the whole company down, and I wouldn't have if I hadn't become unglued over the latest fiasco with Roger.

On the eve of a trip to Savannah to re-inspect a Five Key property there, he didn't come home until two o'clock in the morning.

"Where have you been?" I demanded when he walked in the door looking ridiculously full of pep.

"I was with Nikki," he said.

"Who the hell is Nikki?" I said.

"My new client. The one who's selling her house in Westwood."

"The Victoria's Secret model?"

"Yes."

I had trouble swallowing. "What were you doing with her all night?"

"Dancing," he said, as if there were nothing inappropriate about this answer. "Nikki knows the owner of a new club in West Hollywood. I told her I'd like to try it out, so we did. And, wow, was it ever fabulous, Elizabeth. Great lighting, great D.J., great action."

Great action. I'll show you action, you dope. I had the urge to wind up and sock him.

"Is there a problem?" he had the nerve to ask.

Breathe, I coached myself. And remember that he doesn't know what he's doing. It's the powder that's making him act this way, the powder *you* gave him. "The problem is that you've been with another woman, dancing, while I've been sitting here worrying."

"Why were you worrying? I left you a message on the machine, telling you exactly where I was." He heaved a big, impatient sigh, as if I were the villain. "You used to yell at me when I didn't call to tell you my plans. Now I call and you yell at me anyway." Another sigh. "I even invited you to come and join us, although I figured you wouldn't show up, because you go to bed so much earlier than I do. I don't know what's wrong with you lately, Elizabeth. Your energy level just isn't what it should be."

Right, compared to the bionic man.

To be fair, I hadn't checked the answering machine that night, which was another example of how I was slipping mentally. In the past, I was compulsive about checking for messages—God forbid I should miss a call from Preston about a trip (or from Neiman Marcus about a sale).

"Roger." I calmed down, moved closer to him. "You're not having an affair with this Nikki person, are you? Please tell me you're not."

"I'm not," he said rather unconvincingly. "She and I are having fun together, that's all."

"Fun?"

"F-u-n. Fun. Surely you can dig down in your memory and recall the meaning of the word, Elizabeth. It's when people do things together, go out during the week, have a good time."

My God. Brenda was right, I thought. I *was* getting what I deserved. I had nagged Roger about doing things with me during the week instead of coming home and zoning out. And now look. He was doing things during the week, all right, but not with me. For all I knew, Nikki wasn't his only playmate, either.

"I love you, hon," I said, in a tone that had a pathetic, pleading quality to it.

"I love you too," he said. "But—"

"But what?" I braced myself. Maybe he *was* having an affair.

"You have something on your cheek."

"Something—" I brought my hand up to the spot he'd pointed to.

"It's brownish. Brownish orange."

"Oh." I felt it, identified it. "I didn't feel like cooking tonight, since I was by myself for dinner, so I had peanut butter on a bagel. I must have gotten some on my face." Not the crime of the century, was it?

"I see," said Roger, recoiling slightly. "Well, I'd better get ready for bed. I'm going to sleep in the guest room if that's okay."

"Because I got peanut butter on my cheek?" I said.

"No. Because your snoring is keeping me up," he said. "The wheezing too."

Yes, I was getting what I deserved.

I was up the entire night wrestling with my thoughts. Why couldn't I have left Roger the way he was? Why did I have to tamper with Mother Nature? Would I have to wait out the effects of the potion, or was there something I could do to reverse them in time to save my marriage, never mind my job?

I say "my job" because I screwed up again when it came to my trip to Savannah the next morning. I had stayed awake so late rehashing my conversation with Roger that by the time I finally fell asleep, I was out cold and didn't hear the alarm clock go off and missed my flight. When I arrived at the hotel, I learned that they had given away my room, which I had forgotten to guarantee, just as I had forgotten so many things in recent weeks. I'm telling you, I was messing up royally. Preston actually scolded me, which he had never done in all my years with AMLP.

"Let's get our act together, shall we?" he said in that noblesse oblige way of his.

"I'll do my best," I promised, thinking that holding on to both my husband and my career was going to be a tall order.

CHAPTER THIRTEEN

Needing moral support as well as another perspective on the situation with Roger, I drove over to Clover's the next morning. She and Bud lived in Bel Air in a Mediterranean-style house on Stone Canyon Road, near the Bel Air Hotel. It was a large, lavishly appointed house in an extremely pricey neighborhood. Either car dealerships were more lucrative than I thought or Clover had brought family money to the table. Kentucky horse money, I decided.

"Elizabeth. Thank goodness you're here," she said when she opened the front door. She had that look—the same look I saw when I caught a glimpse of my own reflection in the mirror. A look that combined exhaustion and anxiety, not to mention a few missed appointments at the hair salon.

We hugged each other tightly, two women bonding over the predicament we were in, the predicament we'd put ourselves in.

"We'll fix this," I said into her boney shoulder.

"How?" she wailed.

"I don't know yet."

We disentangled and went inside the house, landing eventually in her airy sunroom, where we sat and drank coffee and commiserated.

"Last night was the worst," said Clover at one point. "Bud didn't come home until midnight. He claimed he was at a wine tasting. I'm asking you, Elizabeth, Who has wine tastings at midnight? Not only that, Bud doesn't even like wine. He's been a beer drinker since I've known him. His big joke was, 'It takes a Bud to drink a Bud.' " He was never known for his sense of humor, bless his heart."

"Did he explain why he was at a wine tasting until midnight?"

"He just said he has so much energy that he feels like a kid again."

"Sounds like Roger," I said, and told her about the dancing-with-Nikki incident. "If I didn't know better, I'd write this off to a good old-fashioned midlife crisis—just a couple of men who are afraid to face their own mortality, so they're overcompensating."

"Some midlife crisis," said Clover. "Oh, by the way, Bud has taken an interest in opera. Bud! He used to think opera was just a bunch of fat people standing around howling in foreign languages. Now he says it's 'the highest form of artistic expression.' This was the same guy who refused to see movies with subtitles. I'd be thrilled about this except that he leaves me out of it. 'You wouldn't understand' was what he told me the last time he went to the opera. Of course, he came home that night wanting kinky sex, and when I said no, he got furious. Maybe there's a connection."

"Do you think you can hang on until the effects of the powder wear off?" I said. "That's the question I keep asking myself."

"No, Elizabeth. I don't think I can hang on, because the new Bud is much harder to take than the old Bud. The truth is, I'm about to go out of my mind."

"I hear you, Clover. I can't hang on either," I said. "I'm so upset about the way Roger's been acting that I haven't been able to concentrate at work. And I'm not the only one who's upset. His law partners are resenting the time he's been spending away from the office, and the twelve-year-old boy who depends on him is crushed by the kiss-off he's been getting. But what's most disconcerting, to be honest, is that there are women out there who are lusting after *my* Roger, and why shouldn't they? He's got his fancy wardrobe now and his sculpted body and his exfoliated complexion, plus he gives off an I'm-a-sex-machine vibe. When we walk down the street, all these babes are craning their necks to get a good look at him. The other day I turned around and yelled at one of them, 'You're gonna need a chiropractor if you keep that up!' If this is what it's like being married to a man who's 'enhanced,' I don't want any part of it."

"Neither do I. So what should we do?"

"Go back to Dr. Farkus."

"Go back to the great and powerful wizard?"

"That's right. We should call the office and speak to Andrea and make an appointment with Farkus. Then we'll see him and explain that our husbands are having an adverse reaction to his stud stimulant. And—this is the important point—we'll tell him we want him to sell us the antidote."

"How do you know there is an antidote?"

"He mentioned it. He said that, in addition to whipping up customized potions, he also whips up their antidotes—the specific herbal formulas that cancel everything out. I remember distinctly."

"I guess it makes sense. There are prescription drugs that counteract the effects of other prescription drugs, so why not herbs that counteract the effects of other herbs?"

"Precisely. And once we get the antidote, we'll give it to Roger and Bud, and everything will be the way it was."

She smiled. "I feel hopeful for the first time in weeks."

"Me too. Of course, this antidote won't be cheap. We'll have to come up with more money for it."

"It'll be money well spent," she said jauntily, as if finances were not a concern. "Oh, to have Bud back—the Bud who doesn't chew me out for falling asleep before eleven—will be a beautiful thing."

"Okay. So we've made the decision?"

"Absolutely."

"Great. You call."

"Me?"

"Sure. You've got that sweet Southern accent that people warm up to. I bet *you* can charm Andrea into giving us an appointment soon so we won't be stuck at the bottom of their waiting list."

She shook her head. "You're the one who told her you were referred by Goldie Hawn and then got in to see the doctor a mere three days later. *You* call."

I'd forgotten I'd admitted that little tidbit to Clover. It was during one of our celebratory conversations, when we were rejoicing over the positive changes in our husbands. Little did we know what was in store.

"Fine. I'll call. Where's the phone?"

Clover walked me into her kitchen, which was more square footage than my entire house, and handed me the phone. I pulled Dr. Farkus's number out of my wallet and dialed.

"That's funny," I remarked after getting a computer-generated voice instead of Andrea's. "It was a recording saying that the number is no longer in service."

"You must have hit a wrong button. I do that sometimes. Bud tells me I need glasses, but then Bud tells me I need a chemical peel too. Which is why I want the old Bud back, the one who doesn't notice every little flaw."

I dialed the number a second time—and got the same recording.

"Here," said Clover, grabbing the phone. "Let me try."

She dialed, waited, listened. "I don't understand this," she said after being told by the computer lady that the number had been disconnected. "Do you think Farkus moved his office?"

"That must be it," I said, "although the one on Roxbury was pretty nice."

"Maybe he needed more spacious quarters. Maybe he brought in an associate or two, since he has so many patients."

"Right. But then why wouldn't he keep the same phone number, or at least arrange to have the recording tell us the new one?"

Clover giggled. "Why don't you call your friend Goldie and get the new phone number from her?"

"Ha-ha. I guess the only way to get the new number is to call my sister. She was the one who told me about Farkus in the first place."

I took the phone back from Clover and called Brenda at *In the Know*.

"You got a recording?" she said when I explained the situation.

"Yes," I said. "We're wondering if Dr. Farkus moved his office."

"Let me ask around and I'll call you back. What's the number there?"

I gave her Clover's phone number. "Listen, Brenda. We're counting on you. We really need to get the antidote to the stud stimulant so our husbands will stop acting like creatures from another universe."

"Creatures from another universe," she mused. "I feel like I'm on an episode of *The X-Files*."

She called back twenty minutes later.

"Well?" I said.

"Nothing," she said. "We're about to close our special issue on 'Food Favorites of the Famous and Fabulous,' and no one has the time to focus on Dr. Farkus."

"Great."

"But you know what I think?"

"I'm all ears."

"Sometimes the phone company screws up. They did it to me once. My friends kept calling me and getting a recording saying my number had been disconnected. They assumed it was because I hadn't paid my bill that month. I was mortified. But it turned out there was just some kind of glitch in the computer. If I were you and your friend and I were in as big a hurry to get my husband un-enhanced, I'd hop in the car, drive over to Dr. Farkus's office, and nail down the appointment in person."

I thanked Brenda for her advice and relayed it to Clover, who agreed.

"His office is only five minutes from here," she said. "Let's just go. We'll take my car, schedule the appointment, and have lunch afterwards."

"As long as it's someplace cheap," I said, thinking of what the antidote would likely cost.

We parked in the lot next door to 435 North Roxbury and made our way toward the medical building. Feeling optimistic for a change, we laughed, linked arms, fantasized about having our husbands restored to us. When we reached the heavy wooden door to the building, skinny little Clover pulled it open it and then continued to hold it open for me. "After you," she said, bowing.

"Why, thank you, ma'am," I said, mimicking her accent. "Bless your heart."

We marched down the hall until we came to Suite 106.

"Well," I said, nodding at the polished brass name plate that announced GORDON P. FARKUS, M.D., LIFE ENHANCEMENT. "It certainly doesn't look like he moved his office."

"No, it sure doesn't." She turned the doorknob, but it wouldn't budge.

"That's weird," I said. "Why would they lock the door?"

Clover checked her watch. "Maybe they're closed for lunch."

"They weren't closed for lunch the last time we were here. You and I both had appointments about now."

She shrugged and tried the door again. No go.

"Maybe it's stuck," I said and knocked discreetly. No answer.

"Maybe we should knock a little harder," said Clover, who proceeded to pound on the door with her fist, which proved that she was much stronger than she looked. A regular steel magnolia.

"Hey! What's all the racket about?" said the woman who emerged from Suite 104, the office of Linda Delano, M.D., Hematology. The woman wasn't wearing a white lab coat, so I assumed she wasn't Dr. Delano herself. On the other hand, Dr. Farkus didn't wear a white lab coat—or shoes.

"Who are you?" I asked, hoping she could solve the mystery of the locked door, whoever she was.

"Laurie Vaughn," she said. "I work for Dr. Delano next door. What's with all the pounding?"

"Sorry about that," I said. "We're patients of Dr. Farkus's and we were just trying to get in to see him."

Laurie Vaughn snorted. "Good luck then. He's gone."

"Gone for the afternoon?" asked Clover.

"No. Just gone," she said.

Clover and I looked at each other, stricken.

"Are you saying that he moved his office to another location?" I asked, feeling my throat start to close up.

"I'm saying he left town," the woman replied. "Well, I don't know that he left for good, but the gossip is that he shut down his practice and skipped out on everybody, including the landlord of this building."

"But that can't be," said Clover, her lower lip quivering. "His name is still on the door. He wouldn't have just—"

"I'm only telling you what I heard," Laurie Vaughn maintained. "Dr.

Delano is the one who spoke to the landlord, who said that Farkus didn't even clean out the office. He and his staff may have vanished, but they left rooms full of furniture and filing cabinets. The landlord isn't allowed to touch the stuff either; the law says he has to let it sit there for a certain number of days in case Farkus comes back to claim it. I guess it's harder to evict a tenant than it is to find one."

"I can't believe this," said Clover. "It doesn't make any sense."

"No, it doesn't," I said. "Why would he take off without informing his patients?"

Laurie snorted again. "Oh, he told his patients, I'm sure of that. Maybe he didn't tell you two ladies, because you're not his bread and butter, no offense. But I guarantee you, he shared his whereabouts with his celebrity patients. He knows they can't live without their 'preparations,' or whatever he calls them."

I tried not to feel slighted by her remark. "I still don't understand why he would just up and leave," I persisted. "He had a thriving practice."

"And an illegal one," said Laurie.

"Illegal?" Clover squeaked.

"That's the rumor. Well, I've gotta get back to work. Sorry to be the one to break the news, ladies."

I couldn't speak. I absolutely couldn't utter a word. I watched silently as Laurie scurried back inside Dr. Delano's office, my mind exploding with visions of Roger remaining a jackass forever.

Clover wasn't doing much better in the communication department. She was staring up at the ceiling and muttering something unintelligible.

"Illegal?" she said finally. "What did she mean, Elizabeth?"

" 'Illegal' usually means 'against the law,' " I snapped, then apologized immediately, forcing myself not to lose it. Besides, it wasn't Clover's fault that the two of us were stranded outside Farkus's door, stuck with husbands we no longer recognized. "It could mean anything," I said in a more upbeat tone. "Maybe Farkus was way overdue with his rent. Maybe he wasn't reporting his income on his tax returns. Maybe he had underage employees toiling in his *preparation staging area.* I don't care what he was up to. All I care about is getting the antidote for Roger and Bud."

"How in the world are we going to get it if Farkus is gone?" said Clover, before dissolving into tears. Some steel magnolia.

I gave her a hug, patted her back. "Don't cry," I said. "There's got to be a way."

"Then what is it?" she said between sobs.

"Well, according to Laurie, Farkus left his office intact, left the *contents* of his office intact. She mentioned filing cabinets, didn't she?"

"So?"

"So the antidote must be in them. Farkus had to keep files on his preparations, right? What doctor doesn't keep files? I'm betting there's a wealth of information inside that office—on Farkus's patients, on his stud stimulant, on the formula for counteracting the effects of the stud stimulant, even on the supplier of his super-duper herbs."

Clover wiped her tears, looked at me. "But how are we supposed to get at these files?"

I cocked my head at her. "How do you *think*?"

Her eyes widened. "By breaking in?"

"Duh."

"But that's against the law!"

"Right, as in 'illegal.' " Okay, so I shouldn't have been sarcastic. It was a reflex of mine, as I've explained. "Look, Clover. I've never committed a crime in my life, never even gotten a speeding ticket. I was a solid citizen before I met Dr. Gordon P. Farkus. But now I'm in this mess up to my neck, and so are you. We have no choice but to get that antidote and give it to our husbands. If we don't, our marriages are over. You realize that, don't you?"

She nodded. "I just wish I'd left well enough alone, left Bud alone."

"I know, but we can't turn back the clock. We have to move forward, fix the problem, fix our husbands. And the only way to do that is to break into that office and grab what we need. You heard Laurie. She said Farkus ran off without his furniture and his files. She also said the landlord has to let it all stay there, but only for a certain period of time. I say we break in there tonight."

"Tonight?"

"Yes. Why, do you and Bud have plans?"

She scoffed. "Bud has plans. He's taking ballroom dancing lessons."

"And you're not taking them with him?"

"Nope. He says I have two left feet. Funny how he never used to complain about that. Of course, he complains about everything now. I'm a total washout, if you ask him."

"Which is why we have to get that antidote, Clover. Before Bud destroys your self-esteem. Now, are you with the program or not?"

She shrugged. "I'm with it, I guess. But how does a person break into an office? This isn't the kind of activity I'm familiar with, Elizabeth."

"As I said, I'm not exactly a hardened criminal myself, Clover." I smiled, tried to cheer her up. "Why don't we discuss it over lunch," I suggested. "Breaking and entering is probably harder to plot on an empty stomach."

The plan was hatched in the Polo Lounge at the Beverly Hills Hotel. We decided that if we were going to get nabbed for our misdeeds, we might as well make our last meal a swell affair.

By the time we downed our appetizers, entrées, and desserts, we'd named me as the designated mastermind and Clover as the person in charge of the props, and we'd plotted the caper about as well as two amateurs can plot a caper.

At ten-thirty that night, while Roger was out disco dancing and Bud was learning the tango, I drove over to Clover's house, picked her up, and took us to the parking lot on Roxbury. Dressed in black, which, of course, is a good color for people who want to be stylish as well as for people who want to escape capture, we walked briskly down the street to Farkus's building.

"Oh, great," I muttered when we discovered that they locked the front door after hours.

"Now what'll we do?" Clover asked me, since I was the designated mastermind.

"There's a call box." I pointed to the small box to the right of the building's front door. It listed the names of the doctors who leased office space inside, with corresponding buzzers. "Maybe someone's working late and we can get them to let us in." I walked backward, into the street, gazed at the building, and saw that there was a light on in one of the offices. "Yup. There's someone up there. I'll just keep pressing the buttons until the person answers."

"And then what? What makes you think they'll let you in?"

"Desperation."

I pressed several of the doctors' buzzers, until someone finally answered.

"Yeah?" a man called out through the intercom.

"Oh, hi. This is Laurie Vaughn from Dr. Delano's office in Suite 104. Can you buzz me in? I forgot my key and I've got to get into the doctor's office. It's kind of an emergency and she asked me to take care of it."

"No problem, Laurie. Stop up and say hello if you've got time."

"Thanks for the invite," I said, as if this man and I were pals.

He buzzed the door open, and Clover and I were in.

"Wow. I never would have remembered Laurie's name." Clover smiled, her eyes glowing with new respect for me.

"I'm good with names. Now let's see if I'm good with locks."

We tiptoed down the hall and stopped when we reached the infamous Suite 106.

"Okay," I said after a deep breath. "Let's try the bobby pin."

Since she was in charge of the props, Clover fished into her bag and handed me prop number one. I didn't have a lot of faith in bobby pins as instruments for picking locks, but they worked on TV.

I crouched down beside the doorknob, bent the bobby pin, and tried to stick one end of it inside the lock, wriggling it around until I heard the lock catch.

"I think you did it!" Clover whispered excitedly.

I shook my head. "I didn't do anything except break the bobby pin. It snapped in two."

"Oh."

"Let's try the steak knife."

She handed me a gleaming sterling silver knife, its handle decorated in a tasteful scrolls-and-beads pattern. "This looks like an heirloom," I remarked.

"It is," she said wistfully. "Mama left me all her silver when she passed."

I nodded. I felt guilty using Mama's silver for breaking and entering, but I had a job to do.

I wedged the blade of the knife between the door and the jam, hoping to trip the lock. After several minutes, the only thing I tripped was Clover, who fell on her ass after stumbling over my foot.

"Why in the world did you wear those shoes tonight?" she hissed, glaring at my Ferragamos.

"The same reason you wore your Stuart Weitzmans," I countered. "Those heels are so narrow we can probably pick the lock with *them*."

"All right. I'm sorry," said Clover, as we both simmered down. "I take it the knife isn't working. Want to try the screwdriver?"

I tried the screwdriver. Then I tried the tweezer. Then I tried the paper clip. All without success.

"How about the credit card?" said Clover, since we were nearly out of props.

"Might as well."

She handed me her American Express card. Her platinum American Express card. I stuck it between the door and the jam and swiped it up and down, up and down until—

"Hey!" I said, trying to keep my voice low. "I got it! We're in!"

Clover squeezed my arm. "You're a genius, Elizabeth."

"Not yet. There may be a security system. Let's hope it's not armed."

I turned the door knob very slowly, very quietly, and poked my head into Farkus's waiting room. When I didn't hear any alarms blaring, I motioned Clover to follow me inside. "Farkus must have left in such a hurry that he forgot to set the security system."

She gave me two thumbs up.

Once we were both inside the office, I closed the door gently behind us. "I need the flashlight now," I said.

She rummaged in her bag and handed it to me. I turned it on and directed the beam of light around the room. It was just as Laurie Vaughn had said: All the furnishings were in their place, exactly as we had remembered them. Nothing was missing, not even the expensive artwork on the walls.

"They must have left in quite a hurry," said Clover. "I'm still wondering why, aren't you?"

"Not at the moment. What I'm wondering is where they kept the antidote and all the rest of Farkus's recipes. Let's take a little tour of the premises."

Huddled together, two black-clad, high-heeled wives on a mission, we headed for the back rooms of the spacious office where, we were hoping, we would find the filing cabinets.

"There!" said Clover when she spotted them. "They're right there!"

"I see, I see," I said, moving toward them, wishing we'd brought two flashlights so I could comb through one set of files while Clover riffled through another.

"Where do we start?" she asked, looking lost.

"With the letter *B* for Baskin. I assume he had a file on me. Or maybe on Roger."

I flashed the light onto the first filing cabinet. When I opened the top drawer, I gasped.

"What?" said Clover. "Elizabeth! What is it?"

"Look."

She lowered her head and saw what I saw. "Oh my Lord!"

"Yup. They may not have taken the antiques in the waiting room, but they sure took the files," I said. Just to make sure, I opened every drawer, one after the other. All traces of Farkus's potions, not to mention his patients, had disappeared.

"Maybe he kept the formulas somewhere else," said Clover.

"Let's keep looking."

We checked everywhere—in the drawers in Farkus's personal office, in the drawers in his communication rooms, in the drawers of Andrea's desk—and found nothing. Not an index card, not a computer disk, not a scrap of paper, nothing that would give us the information we needed.

"Obviously, he grabbed the important stuff and ran," I said, as dejected as I'd ever felt in my life. "What isn't obvious is why he ran and where."

Clover started in with the tears. "What are we going to do now?" she said, dabbing at her eyes with the sleeve of her black turtleneck.

I was about to reply when two uniformed cops, their guns drawn, burst into the room.

"Police! Drop everything!" barked one of the officers, whose badge confirmed that he was one of Beverly Hills's finest.

Clover screamed, nearly destroying my hearing. My outcry wasn't quite as high-pitched.

"You heard me!" he boomed. "Give it up! Everything on the floor! Now!"

Since we had no weapons to speak of (not counting Mama's steak knife), Clover let her Kate Spade handbag slide to the floor while I dropped the flashlight.

"Now you can explain what the hell you're doing here," shouted the other officer.

Clover tried to answer the cop, but her southern drawl deserted her. So I told him that we were there to save our marriages. Not being the warm and fuzzy type, he cuffed us and read us our rights.

PART TWO

CHAPTER FOURTEEN

You know how people say, "Never get sick on a weekend, because the doctors are all playing golf?" Well, I've got a new one for you: "Never get arrested on a weekend, because the *lawyers* are all playing golf." What's more, the court is closed on weekends, so you can't get arraigned, which means that, unless you put up bail money, you're stuck for three days in what's called a type-one facility, aka jail. The Beverly Hills jail, in my case. No, it's not Sing Sing, but it's not a Five Key hotel, trust me.

After the cops burst in on Clover and me in Dr. Farkus's office (the security system had been armed, it turned out, as well as outfitted with a silent alarm), they read us our rights, paid no attention to our apologies, our excuses, or any other attempts at gaining their sympathy, and drove us to the police station, which was smack in the swanky part of town, surrounded by leafy streets and gated estates. Talk about an odd juxtaposition. There, we were searched, fingerprinted, and booked on suspicion of burglary.

"But we didn't take anything," I protested when it was explained to us that burglary was a felony, carrying a much stiffer penalty than, say, walking the dog without a leash.

"No, but you gained illegal entry to the building with the intent to commit larceny," said one of the officers.

"Burglary. Larceny. Goodness gracious, what harsh language," said Clover, doing her southern belle bit. "We didn't mean any harm. At least *I* didn't."

I should add here that Clover had decided, at some point during the evening, that our arrest was my fault, since I'd been the designated mastermind. "Mrs. Hinsdale may not have meant any harm, but all the props we used to gain access to Dr. Farkus's office belonged to *her*," I said in retaliation.

She started crying, so I said I was sorry. We tried to hug each other, to demonstrate that all was forgiven, but the handcuffs made the gesture impossible.

"Get 'em into the jumpsuits," the arresting officer instructed the jailer, a woman who was the size of a refrigerator. Her name was Lou, and I couldn't tell if she wanted to kill us or kiss us.

"Put these on," she said, handing us our new outfits.

"Orange isn't a good color for me," I said of the jumpsuit. "I'd really prefer the blue one I've seen on several of the other inmates."

"No can do," said Lou.

"Why not?" I said. "This *is* Beverly Hills, after all. If the jail doesn't have the blue in my size, you can always call another jail and have it sent. That's how it works at Saks."

Lou leered at me with uncertain intent. "The blue ones are for people who commit misdemeanors. Orange is for felons. Like you, babycakes."

Babycakes. Well, I'd been whining about intimacy. Now, it appeared, I'd be getting some.

"I'm not wild about the orange, but it's the fabric I really don't care for," Clover complained. "It's scratchy. My skin's very sensitive and has been since I was a child."

Lou smirked. "If your skin's so sensitive, you're gonna love the soap in the shower here. It's like washing with sandpaper."

"*The* shower?" I said. "There's only one?"

"Yeah," said Lou. "It's the community shower and there's no curtain. You can play hide the soap with the other gals and have yourselves a ball. Now, put the jumpsuits on. Both of you."

We donned our orange numbers, endured a few more procedural indignities, and were herded upstairs to our cells. When I walked into mine, I took stock of it, and I must say I was not impressed. It was a dreary little gray cubicle that was badly in need of a decorator. To the left was the bed—and I use the term loosely. It was a wafer-thin mattress on a concrete slab. No headboard, no blanket, not even a decent reading lamp. To the right was their idea of a "sitting area"—another concrete slab complete with an ancient issue of *Soldier of Fortune*, and a stool on which to sit while reading, its base bolted to the floor. Moving over to the area near the door, there was a stainless steel sink and matching toilet, sort of an all-in-one combo. No, it wasn't an actual bathroom, but, after doing a quick inspection of it, I didn't spot a single stray hair, which spoke well of the jail's housekeeping department. Of course, the toilet paper hadn't been repointed after the last occupant had vacated the room, but I was just glad there *was* toilet paper.

"Can you possibly open the window a little more?" I asked Lou, who was hovering in an unseemly fashion. The cell boasted a single window over by the bed. It was louvered, its slats barely cracked to let the air, never mind the city lights, in.

"Nope," she said. "You're lucky you get any light at all in here. You can thank the government for that."

I inquired as to what the government had to do with interior design.

"They passed the Blue Sky Law," she said. "It means we're supposed to give you some 'natural light.' We used to have regular windows that opened all the way, but the inmates kept mooning the residents, so we had to put the louvered ones in."

Mooning the residents of Beverly Hills. How delightful. The notion prompted me to ask, "What sort of criminals spend—sorry, *do*—time here, Lou?"

"All kinds. This weekend your cellmates will run the gamut from prostitutes and petty thieves to drug dealers and murderers. We're booked solid."

Just like a hotel, I thought, then remembered with a jolt that I was supposed to inspect a hotel that very weekend, a chichi resort up in Santa Barbara. My God, what had happened to me, to my sense of responsibility? Preston was counting on me to do my usual thorough job, and I had forgotten I even had a job! How would I explain? How would I make it up to him? How would I get out of jail without him hearing I was ever in jail? How would I get out of jail—period?

"Clover," I said, as I stood outside the door of her cell, which was right next to mine, thank God. "We've got to get out of here. We really do."

"I know, but how?" she said. "Our lawyers aren't around, remember? Yours is in Pebble Beach for the weekend. Mine is in Cabo San Lucas."

"Then we'll call other people to bail us out."

"Who?"

"Well, the obvious choices are Roger and Bud."

She nodded. "You call Roger first."

"Right." I thought for a minute. "There's one little problem with calling Roger: I'll have to tell him the truth about Farkus. He'll ask how I managed to land in jail and I'll have to come up with an explanation and he'll divorce me because of it. I can't let that happen, Clover. Not when this whole mission was about preserving my marriage."

"And mine. Bud will go bonkers if he finds out about Farkus," she said. "On the other hand, *I'll* go bonkers if I have to spend the weekend in this pit."

I shuddered, trying to imagine the conversation with Roger. *Hello, honey. I'm in jail because I tried to un-herb you. Could you please pick me up? Oh, and bring a pile of cash?* No, it wasn't an option. As unappetizing as jail was, having Roger leave me was worse. "I can't call Roger," I said.

"And I can't call Bud," she said.

"Okay. What about your fancy friends in Bel Air? Wouldn't one of them be willing to put up the bail money?"

"If I tell them I'm in jail, I'll be the talk of the neighborhood and never get invited to another cocktail party in my life. Besides, they're world-class gossips. They'd be whispering in Bud's ear about this in a Kentucky minute." She paused. "What about your sister? How about calling her?"

"It's worth a try," I said, hating to drag her into this mess but having no other choice. Feeling scared and hopeless and thoroughly exhausted, I asked Lou if I could make another phone call. She said I could.

"Brenda? It's Elizabeth," I said when she picked up. I was surprised and relieved that she was home on a Friday night.

"Hi," she said. "Can I call you back? I'm watching Angelina Jolie on *20/20*. She's telling Barbara Walters how she went off the deep end once."

"*I'm* going off the deep end *now*! I need your help, Brenda."

"Sure, sure. I'll put the TV on mute. Is this about Roger?"

"Isn't everything? Look, here's the situation. I'm in the Beverly Hills jail with my friend Clover. We broke into Dr. Farkus's office tonight and the police showed up."

"You're kidding."

"I wish I were."

"But when we talked earlier, you didn't know where Farkus was. You said his number had been disconnected."

"Well, it turns out that Farkus and his employees left town in a big hurry but didn't bother to take their furniture and their filing cabinets with them. So Clover and I broke into the office, hoping we could find the antidote to the powder we gave Roger and Bud. Instead of getting lucky, we got arrested."

"Oh, Elizabeth. What do you want me to do?"

"Come and bail us out of here. Will you, Bren?"

"What's the bail?"

This would be the hard part, I knew. Brenda was a working girl. "Actually, it's fifty thousand dollars. For each of us."

She whistled. "Did you kill somebody during this break-in?"

"Of course not. That's just the going rate for burglary."

"I don't have that kind of money sitting around, Elizabeth. I wish I could help you but I can't."

I sighed. "Maybe you can help in another way. Tell me how to convince them to let us go. I'm too tired and hungry to think straight."

"My suggestion would be to make a deal with them. On shows like *N.Y.P.D. Blue*, the perps are always making deals."

"Clover and I are not 'perps,' Brenda."

"Do they have you in the jumpsuits yet?"

"Yes."

"Then you're perps. Now, listen. Tell the police that you and Clover want a meeting with the D.A."

"The D.A.? It's Friday night. He's probably having a caviar pizza at Spago."

"He'll drop whatever he's doing if he thinks he's got a hot case on his hands. I've seen this over and over on cop shows."

"But Clover and I aren't a 'hot case.' We broke into a doctor's office, that's all."

"You're not following me, Elizabeth. It's up to you to give them the *impression* that it's a hot case. Ask to talk to the detectives. Then tell them you have incriminating evidence against Dr. Farkus—information you'd like to share with the D.A. because you think it will help them bring a dangerous criminal to justice."

"A dangerous criminal? Farkus may have turned Roger into the jerk of all time but he's not on a Wanted poster."

"How do you know? He didn't leave town for no reason. He left because he was in trouble."

"Now that you mention it, a woman who works for the doctor in the office next door to Farkus's said his practice was illegal."

"See? Maybe he overdosed somebody with those herbs of his and now he's on the lam."

"I doubt it, but even if it were true, how would it get Clover and me out of here?"

"You tell the detectives that you have information that's crucial to their investigation of Farkus. And when they ask you what the information is, you invent it."

"Brenda." She was trying to be supportive, I knew, but she had to get a life outside the entertainment business before it was too late.

"As I said," she went on, "it's done all the time on TV. You give them something, they'll drop the charges against you."

"Right, but if we're not up to inventing information, what do we give them? We don't know anything about Farkus."

"Oh, yes, you do."

"What?"

"The names of the celebrities you saw in his waiting room."

"Why would the cops care about celebrities?"

"Because everyone cares about celebrities, Elizabeth." She said this as if she genuinely believed it, poor thing. "Just try it. See what happens. Get the detectives in and tell them you're willing to spill everything you know about Farkus—and that you want to make a deal with the D.A. so you can get the hell out of there."

Before I could pump Brenda for more suggestions, Lou told me to get back to my cell. Apparently, dinner was being served.

Dinner was room service—cell service, to be more accurate. The meal Lou delivered that Friday night was a nuked TV dinner featuring Salisbury steak as the entrée.

"Mine's not hot enough," said Clover from inside her cell.

"Neither's mine," I called out. "What *is* Salisbury steak anyway?"

"I don't want to think about it," said Clover. "I only want to get out of here."

"That's not going to happen. Not tonight, anyway. Brenda doesn't have the bail money."

There was no response.

"Clover? Are you okay?"

"Now I am. There was a bone in my Salisbury steak. I was spitting it out."

"A bone in your—" I was incensed on Clover's behalf and moved swiftly into AMLP inspector mode, banging on the door of my cell to attract some attention.

"What's the problem?" said Lou, who arrived a few minutes into my tirade.

"Mrs. Hinsdale and I would like to send back our dinners," I said. "They're ice-cold, and the beef has bones and gristle and God knows what else in it."

"Really? I'll rush right into the kitchen and tell the chef." She laughed and took the dinners away—for good.

"I'm starving," said Clover about an hour later.

"Me too," I said. "But we've got bigger fish to fry."

"Please don't mention food."

"Sorry."

"I was just thinking that Bud will be worried sick about me when I don't come home tonight. And tomorrow night. And Sunday night."

"Roger will be worried too. Or, at least, puzzled by my absence. Maybe we should call them after all, Clover."

"But we decided we can't let them find out the truth."

"They won't find out. We'll just call them and say we're spending the weekend at each other's house. I'll tell Roger I'm at your place. You'll tell Bud you're at mine."

"What if they want to see us or talk to us over the weekend? I know you travel all the time, Elizabeth, but Bud's not used to having me take off like that."

"Bud's not the same Bud," I reminded her. "He might not care that you're gone now that he's so busy with his cooking and his wine tasting and his ballroom dancing."

After more discussion, she called Bud and left a message on their answering machine, explaining that she would be spending the weekend at my house, and I called Roger and left the same message in reverse on our machine. And then, as I was about to fill Clover in on my conversation with Brenda, Lou stopped by to say it was time for beddy-bye.

"You can be with Mrs. Hinsdale tomorrow." She grinned. "And with all the other gals too. In the community shower."

Over the course of my career as an AMLP inspector, I had been to some pretty tacky resorts, some really ghastly places, but none with a "community shower." No, I had finally hit rock bottom in terms of accommodations. I had landed in the ultimate bad hotel.

CHAPTER FIFTEEN

I was ravenous by the time breakfast arrived the next morning—eggs, sausage, hash browns. I was so ravenous that after I scarfed it all down with the puny plastic spoon they give you, I asked Lou for seconds.

She laughed and said, "What do you think this is? The all-you-can-eat buffet at Denny's?"

After breakfast, I yelled next door to Clover, to see how she was bearing up. We commiserated about our lack of sleep (we both sat up all night, afraid of catching head lice from the mattress), about our fear of taking a shower with the other "gals" (we decided we could live with bad hair and smelly armpits), and about our inability to move our bowels (we agreed that having a jailer look in on us every half hour was more binding than drinking a bottle of Kaopectate).

Mostly, I told her about my phone conversation with Brenda and suggested we request a meeting with the detectives assigned to our case.

"Whatever will we tell them about Dr. Farkus?" asked Clover. "We only met the man once."

"Brenda's advice was to make stuff up," I said. "I'm willing. How about you?"

"Anything to get out of here."

Lou made note of our request and told us to "chill" while we waited for the detectives to show. She further explained that the place to chill was the jail's dayroom, where she took us and told us to "make nice."

When Clover and I arrived, there were four other female inmates making nice. No, not the way you're thinking. They were sitting around the table, deeply involved in a game of cards.

"They must be playing poker," Clover whispered.

"Actually, I just heard one of them say, 'Go fish.' "

"Well, I'm going to introduce us to them. Mama always said that a little smile goes a long way."

"Mama was never in jail, I'll bet. A little smile can get you in a lot of trouble in this joint."

Clover shook her head and sat among the card sharks, pulling me down onto the stool next to hers. "Mornin', everybody. I'm Clover Hinsdale, and my friend is Elizabeth Baskin. We're pleased to meet y'all."

Four pairs of eyes turned in our direction, none of them looking the least bit pleased to meet us. Well, except one.

"Hey, yourself," said a short, stocky woman who had numerous tattoos and was bald. "My name's Cherry Queen. What are you two in for?"

Hopefully, not a confrontation with you, I thought, wondering if Cherry had murdered anyone. That's the thing about being an inmate in jail, as opposed to being a law-abiding citizen. The people you interact with have much more colorful pasts than you do.

"We're here for breaking into a doctor's office," said Clover, making friendly conversation, the way she did with me in Dr. Farkus's waiting room.

"You sell or use?" asked Cherry, who was pretty friendly herself, although terrifying-looking.

"Sell or use what?" said Clover.

"Drugs."

"We don't have anything to do with drugs," I interjected, just to set the record straight. We had *herbed* our husbands, not drugged them.

"Then why break into a doctor's office?" said Cherry.

"It's a long story," I said. "What're you in here for?"

"Attempted murder," she said, confirming my worst fear.

"So you mean you tried to kill someone and failed?" I asked.

"Cherry Queen doesn't fail," she said, reminding me how funny it is when people talk about themselves in the third person. "If I'd wanted to kill the guy, I would have, believe me."

"Then what happened?" I said, oddly fascinated by Cherry, the way you can be oddly fascinated by a circus act.

"It went down like this," she said. "I was supposed to kill this guy, but my client changed the plan at the last minute. So I was, like, standing there in the guy's house with a gun in my hand, ready to plug him, when my beeper went off. The guy grabbed my gun and called the cops."

"When you say you were 'supposed to kill' this man, what, exactly, do you mean, Cherry?" I asked.

"I mean that I was hired to kill him. You know, like it was a job. I'm a hit woman."

A hit *woman*. The feminist in me was cheered to hear that we had broken through yet another barrier in the workplace. "So you get paid to murder perfect strangers?"

"Sometimes. Other times, I'm just paid to find them. You'd be surprised how many people try to disappear. I track them down and do whatever the client wants me to do with them."

"Well, bless your heart," said Clover, who couldn't think of an appropriate response, apparently.

"I have another question, Cherry," I said. "How much time will you do for this attempted murder, once you go to trial?" The thought of her being out on the streets didn't thrill me.

She laughed. "What're you kidding? No one can prove I did anything wrong. I was in a house with a guy and I happened to be packing a licensed gun. I'll be outta here on Monday. No big deal."

Speaking of deals, Lou picked that moment to summon us to one of the interview rooms so we could have our meeting with the detectives.

"Okay, whaddaya know about Gordon Farkus?" asked Detective Mike Wasluski once we had all taken our seats.

"We have information that could speed up your investigation of the doctor," I said. "And in exchange for that information, we want the charges against us dropped."

The other detective, Paul Dembo, said, "What makes you think we're conducting an investigation of Dr. Farkus?"

I smiled a smirky, know-it-all smile. "Oh, come on, Detective. He was breaking laws left and right. That's why he left town. Don't act as if you don't want to put him away for good. Not after what he did." Whatever that was.

When there was no response from either cop, Clover batted her eyelashes at them, then crossed and uncrossed her legs, like Sharon Stone in *Basic Instinct*. Not a bad tactic, except that it's tough to turn a guy on when you're wearing an orange jumpsuit.

"We can tell you all about his practice," I continued. "We've got the dirt on how much money changed hands, what claims the doctor made, what *went down*. I bet his other patients haven't been very forthcoming. Farkus was running sort of a private club over on Roxbury. My guess is that you won't get a word out of its members."

The detectives looked at each other and came to some sort of silent, cop-ish understanding.

"Why don't you tell us what you know and we'll decide if it's interesting enough to share with the D.A.," said Dembo.

"Oh, thank you, Paul," said Clover with a little sigh. "It's all right if I call you Paul, isn't it?"

"Call me whatever you want," he said. "Just give us the information."

"Then you *are* investigating Farkus," I said, sitting up straighter in my chair.

" 'Course we are," said Wasluski. "The guy's wanted in six states."

Clover gasped. "Wanted in— "

I kicked her under the table. "Only six?" I said nonchalantly. "I'm amazed he hasn't wrecked havoc in every state in the country." So they *did* need information on Farkus! Brenda was a genius! Not counting that she had recommended the crook in the first place.

"Only six states at the moment," said Dembo. "But the charges are piling up. For instance, he's wanted for larceny, since he's been taking money under false pretenses."

"False pretenses," I repeated with a nod, as if the words were old news to me.

"Yeah," said Dembo, "because he's been running around pretending to have a license to practice medicine when he doesn't even have a license to drive a car."

I tried not to make eye contact with Clover. I knew that she would be as unnerved by this little tidbit as I was, and it was crucial that we keep our game faces on.

"Yup. Farkus was a smooth operator all right," I said. "He had all those diplomas hanging on the walls of his office—the degrees from Harvard and Yale, among others. Boy, what a con artist." My God, so he wasn't even an M.D.? I had put my husband's life in the hands of a complete and total quack?

"And then there's the criminal impersonation charge," said Wasluski. "Those diplomas you're talking about aren't his, obviously."

"Obviously." I had to glance over at Clover then. She appeared to be in shock. Her color wasn't good and her left eye was twitching.

"His real name is Jerry Sheck," said Dembo, "and the closest he ever got to Harvard was working in their food service department."

I felt a horrible tightness in my chest. Oh, poor Roger. Poor, poor Roger. What had I done to him? And how would I ever make it up to him?

"And then there's the fraud charge," said Wasluski. "*All* the fraud charges. Mail fraud, check fraud—"

"That's okay," I said, cutting him off. I couldn't take it anymore. I got the picture. "Let us tell you what we know about him and maybe we can help."

"We're listening," said Dembo.

Clover and I told Detectives Wasluski and Dembo every detail about our visit to Dr. Farkus's den of iniquity—plus whatever embellishments we could dream up.

"What gets me is how this guy does it," said Wasluski, shaking his head at the end of our speech, which climaxed with a description of Farkus's celebrity-studded clientele. "He breezes into town and suddenly the movie stars are falling over each other to get an appointment with him."

"All it takes is a few medical diplomas, a little charisma, and a toe ring," I said with a cavalierness I didn't feel. "You know how it is. People will believe what they want to believe."

"*I* believed him," said Clover. "And, while he's a liar and a cheat, he did create a potion for my husband that worked. For a while."

"I can't wait until the lab has a shot at analyzing those so-called herbs of his," said Dembo. "Then we'll know exactly what he's been up to. But first things first—we really need to find the fucker."

No, *we* really need to find the fucker, I thought. Our marriages are toast if we don't.

⟡

While we waited for the detectives to speak to the district attorney on our behalf and render a decision, we huddled together in the dayroom and tried to make sense of our ever-worsening situation. It wasn't bad enough that we had gone behind our husbands's backs to have them enhanced. Now we had gone behind their backs to have them enhanced by a man who was not who he claimed to be, did not have any medical training whatsoever, and was wanted by the police in six states.

"I keep thinking things can't get any more horrendous, and then they do," I said, just as Cherry Queen and another of the inmates erupted into a nasty scuffle over which of them had actually won at Chutes & Ladders.

"You're a loser," said the black woman with platinum hair. "A stupid, asshole loser."

"You better shut that pussy mouth of yours," Cherry threatened, her fists balled up. "Or do you want a piece of me?"

"Ladies. Ladies. Please," said Clover, covering her ears. "Such language."

The black woman turned and glared at Clover. "Who asked you, bitch?"

"She didn't mean anything," I piped up, eager to defend my friend and ward off trouble.

"Is that right?" said the inmate, a menacing look in her eye as she approached us. "Maybe she should stay out of other people's business then. Maybe she should shut *her* pussy mouth."

"She'll shut it, she'll shut it," I said quickly. "She's really sorry for speaking up, and so am I."

"How sorry?" she said, sticking her face in my face. I could count her pores.

"Sorrier than I can describe."

"Prove it." She gave my shoulder a shove. I did not like the direction in which we were headed.

"Hey, lay off them," Cherry said suddenly, strutting toward the woman and spinning her around.

"Yeah? Make me, freak," the other inmate taunted.

The two of them went at each other in earnest then, punching, kicking, head-butting. Clover and I ran to get Lou.

When the fireworks were over, we thanked Cherry profusely for coming to our rescue.

"Don't worry about it," she said, nursing a large bruise on her hand. "The bitch had it coming to her."

"Yes, but you saved our lives," said Clover.

Cherry smiled. "I liked you two the first time I saw you. You got class, both of you."

"And you have—" I stopped, because I was trying to think of a reciprocal compliment and couldn't.

"Spunk," said Clover. "That's what you have, Cherry."

"Exactly," I said. "And because of your spunk, we avoided injury. We'll be eternally grateful."

"So you want to stay in touch?" she said. "Like, after we get out of here?"

Uh, *no*. "Sure, sure we'll stay in touch," I said, hoping to pacify her. She had a fearsome right hook.

Clover and I thanked her again and rushed back to the safety of our cells. Later, when Lou brought lunch, a beans-and-burritos sandwich of the type you see at Taco Bell, I asked if there was any chance I could substitute a glass of wine for the carton of apple juice. After that fight in the dayroom, I needed a real drink.

"No wine," Lou said with a roll of her eyes.

"Not even a little chablis?"

"Be thankful for what you have."

Well, if I'd been thankful for what I had, I wouldn't have ended up in the Beverly Hills jail.

◇

Saturday afternoon dragged into Saturday night, which dragged into Sunday morning, which dragged into Sunday afternoon. Clover and I tried to make the best of the weekend, but we hadn't slept, hadn't showered, hadn't had any alcohol, and we were getting pretty cranky.

"Where are those cops?" Clover demanded, sounding very close to cracking.

"How should I know?" I said. "I'm just as eager to get out of here as you are."

"Oh, really, Elizabeth? If you hadn't suggested the break-in, we wouldn't *be* in here."

"Not that again. As I keep reminding you, Clover, I didn't exactly have to twist your arm to commit burglary."

"Twist my arm? You want a piece of me?"

No, we did not come to blows. We were just cranky, as I said.

At six o'clock on Sunday night, Detectives Wasluski and Dembo finally showed up at the jail, and the news was good. We were free to go.

"That's it?" I said, emotionally and physically wrung out. "You're dropping the charges against us? We don't have to appear in court tomorrow?"

"Nope," said Dembo. "The D.A. agreed to cut the deal you asked for."

"Lord have mercy." Clover hugged both men enthusiastically, then told them that if they were ever in the market for a Cadillac, they should give her a call.

"We'll be giving you a call all right," he said. "As soon as we nail the would-be Dr. Farkus, there'll be a trial to convict him and you two will be witnesses for the prosecution."

I smiled and said sure we'd be witnesses and tell our story. But my gut churned. I had absolutely no intention of going public with the cold, hard facts about what I did to Roger. What I intended to do was get the antidote, give it to my unsuspecting husband, and pray he never learned the truth about the whole ugly business. Let someone else stand up there in that courtroom with their hand on a Bible. I had a marriage to save.

CHAPTER SIXTEEN

By seven o'clock on Sunday night, Clover and I were free women. We shed our orange jumpsuits, donned the black outfits we'd worn the night of the break-in, and bid farewell to everyone.

"My, that certainly was an experience," said Clover as we rode in a taxi to pick up my car in the parking lot on Roxbury. "An experience I have no interest in repeating."

"I couldn't agree more," I said, "although I'll really miss Cherry."

She laughed. "You can always call her if you get lonesome." Cherry had made us write down her phone number in case we ever needed her services. Her beeper number too.

After finding my car in one piece, thank God, I drove over to Clover's, dropped her off, and headed home to Santa Monica. While I was wildly happy to be out of jail, I was dreading my re-entry into civilian life. How would Roger react to my absence over the weekend? How would Preston react to my failure to inspect the property to which he'd assigned me?

How would I proceed in my quest for the antidote? Yes, Farkus was a big, fat phony, but whoever and whatever he was, he had whipped up a potion that had turned Roger into the husband from hell, and it was all my fault. I *had* to undo what I'd done, didn't I?

"Roger? I'm home," I said, standing in the kitchen, which, by the way, was spotless and reeked of one of those industrial-strength cleaning liquids, the kind that makes your eyes burn. Obviously, Roger had been a busy boy.

I heard footsteps, then a voice. "Elizabeth?"

"Hi, honey. I'm back from Clover's," I called out.

More footsteps. Eventually, Roger materialized in the kitchen—the "new and improved" Roger. Instead of appearing in his old Sunday night uniform, a wrinkled T-shirt, he was wearing an honest-to-goodness smoking jacket, a burgundy velvet number with black satin lapels. He looked handsome but ridiculous. I did not marry George Hamilton, after all.

"Elizabeth." His jaw dropped when he saw me. Oh, and he pinched his nostrils with his fingers, so he wouldn't have to smell me. "What on earth have you done to yourself? You look as if you've been sleeping on the street."

"What do you mean?" I said, reminding myself that he wasn't himself but some distorted version of the man I married.

He took an inventory of me, stepping around me in a wide circle, as if he feared he might catch something. "You're filthy," he said finally. "Doesn't Clover have a shower at that palace of hers?"

"Oh. Right." I was so focused on Roger's appearance that I'd forgotten about mine. "We decided to have a no-maintenance weekend. No shampoo. No makeup. Just us girls. It was a lot of fun."

"Then I guess you and I have an entirely different idea of what constitutes 'fun,' " he said.

Oh, Roger, I thought with a terrible, heavy sadness. Your idea of fun used to be camping, and one of the things you liked the best about it was roughing it, including not having to shower. Don't you remember how it was? Don't you remember how *you* were?

"What did you do this weekend while I was away?" I asked, not sure I wanted to know.

"I wondered where you'd gone, for one thing," he said.

"But I left you a message on the answering machine," I said.

"After you'd already made your plans with your friend. Without consulting me, I might add."

"I'm sorry about that, Roger. Listen, how about if I hop into the shower right now, while you order us a pizza. We could have a nice dinner together, catch up, snuggle in front of the TV."

"I don't eat pizza. Too many calories."

"All right. Then order whatever you like. I'll be back in a jiffy."

Encouraged by the fact that he wasn't rushing out to go dancing with Nikki or some new playmate and that we might actually spend a little quality time together, I hit the shower, washed my hair, let it dry naturally, in the wavy style Roger always prefered, and threw on a beige sweater and matching slacks.

"Hi," I said upon my return to the kitchen. "This better?" I spun around, so he could get a good look.

"Uh, yeah," he said sarcastically. "If you were a cocker spaniel."

"I don't— "

"The hair, Elizabeth. What's up with the curls? Is there a dog show in town?"

I felt my face burn with unadulterated rage. Okay, so he was under the influence of the stud stimulant and wasn't responsible for what he was saying, but I was sick and tired of this Roger, this critical, carping, compulsively neat person who was much more obnoxious in those departments than I could ever be.

"Forget dinner," I snapped. "I'll order myself a pizza."

"Go ahead," he said. "They're your thighs."

"Why you—" Oh, what was the use.

We stayed out of each other's way that night. I don't remember ever feeling so lonely. The man I loved was right there in the same house with me, and yet I couldn't reach him, couldn't bring him back.

And he wasn't my only problem. As I was going through Saturday's mail, I found a letter from Art Yarnell, the general manager of the Phoenician Paradise. I knew he'd been hounding AMLP about me, but I honestly didn't expect him to write to me directly, at my home address.

As for the letter itself, it was threatening, crazy, over-the-top—yet another rant about how I had singlehandedly damaged his reputation in the hospitality industry and how he was going to make me pay, whatever that meant. Another headache I didn't need.

Actually, the worst news came the next morning, when I called Preston to tell him that I hadn't been able to inspect the resort in Santa Barbara over the weekend.

"I had a family crisis," I said. "I couldn't leave town." I decided to omit the part about being locked up in a jail cell.

"You've been having a number of family crises lately, haven't you, Elizabeth," he said, without a trace of sympathy.

"It's been a rocky time," I admitted, "but I can run up to Santa Barbara later this week to do the inspection."

"I think we'll let someone else handle it," he said. "It sounds as if you need a little time to yourself."

"Let someone else handle—" I was too upset to finish the sentence. *I* had been the number-one inspector in Preston's territory. *I* was the one the company had entrusted with its most important evaluations. *I* wasn't about to be shoved aside while some Elizabeth Baskin wanna-be, someone who did not have my discerning eye, someone who didn't even know how to play Torture the Concierge, stole my assignments.

"You're due for a break, aren't you?" said Preston. "Why don't you take it now."

"I don't want a break." I was not on salary with AMLP. I was paid by the job. No inspections, no income.

"That wasn't a suggestion," he said. "It was a directive."

Obviously, a little begging was in order. "Please, Preston. Give me another chance. I'll prove to you that I've still got it. Send me out and see. You won't regret it, I swear you won't."

"Let's give it a rest for now, shall we? I'll contact you when we need you, Elizabeth."

He hung up. I tried to look on the bright side. No inspections for AMLP meant more time to find Farkus. The question was, How?

It was Brenda who came up with a plan.

"The bottom line is that Farkus has been the herb guru to the stars," she said over lunch at Ivy at the Shore, the sort of restaurant where ordering off-the-menu is a status symbol. So is asking the waiter where the olive oil was pressed and whether the wheat in the bread is organic and how long it would take to duplicate one of the recipes in The Zone. "They've been depending on him for their preparations as much as he's been depending on them to pay his bills. They've been his meal ticket, Elizabeth. Do you actually think he'd leave without telling them where they could reach him? He's probably making housecalls to their estates right this very minute."

"Not with the police breathing down his neck. On the other hand, I just remembered something. A woman who works in the office next door to Farkus's made the same point you're making, that his famous patients were his bread and butter and that he's probably still in touch with them."

"Of course he is. The celebrities you saw in his waiting room—Lanie Duquette and Angela Clay and Wendy Winters—have to be just as desperate for their potions as you are for that antidote."

"So I should call the celebrities and ask them where he is?"

"Elizabeth. You don't call celebrities. You call their *people*."

"Brenda, please. I've had a rough weekend. Don't start talking like a segment on *Access Hollywood*."

"I'm serious. At the magazine, we have to go through their P.R. reps. I couldn't get Lanie Duquette's phone number for you if I tried." She smiled. "But I know where she lives. I know where they all live."

"You do?"

"Yup. So if you and your friend Clover really want to find the elusive herb man, you should consider becoming a stalker."

I stopped chewing my grilled vegetable salad and gave her a look. "Have you forgotten that I've already been arrested once?"

"I'm simply saying you should hang around *outside* Lanie's house and Angela's house and Wendy's house—nothing creepy. You might get lucky and catch Farkus ministering to his flock."

"Sounds risky."

"I repeat: You wouldn't be stalking them in the usual sense; you'd be staking them out. It's worth a try, Elizabeth. How cool would it be if you were stationed outside Lanie's mansion and you saw Farkus drive up, a little black bag in his hand. You could corner the guy and tell him you'll call the cops unless he gives you the antidote."

"What if he never shows up at Lanie's house?"

"What if he does and you miss him?"

"It could be a huge waste of time."

"What else do you have to do? You said you got fired."

"I didn't get fired, Brenda. I'm taking a break, that's all."

"So you're taking a break. Take it on Lanie Duquette's lawn."

Well, I didn't have any other ideas. About an hour after I returned home from lunch, Brenda called with the addresses of Lanie, Angela, and Wendy. "You're all set," she said. "Let me know how it works out."

"I will," I said, "if I'm not incarcerated somewhere."

When I told Clover about the idea, she was surprisingly upbeat.

"I thought you'd reject it right off the bat," I said, "because of the way our last caper turned out."

"Elizabeth, honey, I'm not in a position to reject any idea that'll get Bud to act like his old self. Do you know what that rascal did after you dropped me off at the house last night? He left. He hadn't seen me since Friday and he left—right after telling me I needed a bath, not to mention electrolysis on my upper lip. The man had the mitigated gall to inform me that I had a very faint mustache!"

"Where he'd go after delivering that lovely remark? Ballroom dancing again?"

"Yes. He says that to be the perfect man, he should be perfect at ballroom dancing. And to think that all we wanted our husbands to be was more attentive."

"And now they're too attentive, scrutinizing us down to the tiniest hair follicle."

"Oh, how I wish we'd never messed with them, Elizabeth."

"Me too, Clover. But we did mess with them, and now we've got to clean up the mess."

"Right. Which celebrity are we staking out first and what time does the staking out take place?"

"Let's start with Wendy Winters, the NBC News correspondent. She lives around the corner from me. We can stake her out, come here for a quick sandwich, then stake her out again."

"Count me in."

CHAPTER SEVENTEEN

Boy, Wendy must be making big bucks at the network," I commented after Clover and I had walked from my nondescript ranch on Washington Avenue to Wendy's Spanish hacienda on La Mesa Drive. Her place was set on a lush piece of property off San Vicente Boulevard, where all the joggers jog, and near the Riviera Country Club, where all the golfers golf. As they say in Roger's business, location, location, location.

"Maybe she got the house in her divorce," said Clover. "She used to be married to that professional baseball player, didn't she?"

"Football player. She's single now, according to Brenda, who is an expert on celebrity romances. Single and not dating anyone."

"That will make our job easier."

"Why?"

"Because if a man shows up, it might be Farkus."

"Let's hope." I suggested that we position ourselves at the curb so we could spot cars coming into the driveway. "If it's Wendy who cruises in, we'll just say we were out here resting because you sprained your ankle during our morning walk."

"Or you could be the one who sprained your ankle."

"What's the difference whose ankle is sprained?"

"I just don't see why I'm the one who has to play the victim."

"The operative word here is *play*, Clover. You'd limp around a little, wince in pain, and that would be that. The point is, we don't want to get in trouble for loitering or trespassing or, God forbid, stalking. Don't you understand?"

"I understand, Elizabeth. There's no reason to be cross with me."

Gee, this is getting off to a great start, I thought. "Look, we're both on edge because of the way Roger and Bud are acting, but can't we try to remember that we're on the same team?"

"A team, right. Then stop being so bossy."

"I'm not—" I let it go. The last thing I needed was a spat with my accomplice.

We sat on that curb from nine A.M. until noon, without a sign of life from inside or outside the house.

"My butt's sore," said Clover. "And I could really use some food."

"Me too. Let's go back to my house. I'll make us lunch."

We trudged back to my place. We had a couple of tuna sandwiches and, against my better judgment, a bottle of chardonnay. By the time we returned to our stakeout post on Wendy's curb, we were both feeling a little logy, not to mention sunburned. We'd forgotten to apply the SPF-15, and after being out there in the broiling hot sun, we had noses the color of ripe tomatoes.

"I think I'm going to take a nap," said Clover, who could barely keep her eyes open.

I was about to argue that neither of us was taking a nap, that we had an important job to do, but I remembered her remark about my being bossy and held the thought. "Go ahead," I said. "I'll watch the house."

She nodded and pitched over, into the grass, out cold. Some accomplice.

I amused myself by speculating about why Wendy Winters had become a patient of Farkus's. Her life seemed perfect, as far as I could tell. She was a pretty, perky blonde in her forties. She was a rising star at the network, having made her name at the NBC affiliate in Chicago. She was a regular contributor to Brokaw's *Nightly News*, filed stories for *Dateline* occasionally, and appeared on the *Today Show* whenever there was breaking news from L.A. So what would prompt her to seek out an herbal elixir? Did she suffer from performance anxiety now that there was more pressure on her? Did she want to enhance her appearance because she was getting more on-camera time? Did she have sexual inhibitions following her divorce from the football player, who was rumored to have cheated on her with everything that breathed?

I was pondering the libido issue when I heard, then saw, a silver BMW convertible zip up the street and pull slowly into Wendy's driveway.

"Clover." I nudged her. "Wake up, for God's sake. I think that was Farkus."

She roused herself. "You actually saw him?"

"No, but whoever it was sort of looked like him."

"Was he tan?"

"Yeah, but that's not exactly a distinguishing feature in L.A."

"What should we do?"

"Wait until he leaves and catch him on the way out."

We continued to sit for what seemed like an eternity. The sun started to set and the bugs started to bite. I was not enjoying myself.

"I don't think it's Farkus," said Clover at one point. "He wouldn't be in there with her that long. He only spent ten minutes with me."

"We can't take any chances. We've got to stay here until he leaves."

"Says who?" she said in that hostile tone again.

"Come on, Clover. I'm not being bossy, just practical. I'd hate for our entire day to be a waste."

A waste is, of course, what it was. At seven forty-five, the man in the BMW emerged from Wendy Winters's house. We both got a good look at him and he was definitely not the herb guru. He was Steve Neroy, the weather guy on one of the local TV stations—the *married* weather guy.

"What do you suppose she was doing with him all afternoon?" said Clover.

"Not talking about the weather," I said. "Obviously, my sister was wrong about Wendy's social life."

"Oh, so Wendy is a tramp, bless her heart."

I nodded, thinking it was time to call it a night.

The next day we resumed our stakeout at Wendy's house, hoping yet again that Farkus might show. Not only did he *not* show, but one of Wendy's neighbors did—an elderly woman with a gnarly, arthritic forefinger that she kept stabbing in our faces as she was demanding to know why we'd been hanging around. We tried the sprained ankle bit on her, but she didn't buy it.

"I'm a liberal, always have been," she barked at us. "I support welfare and all the other government programs, but I draw the line at you homeless people parking yourselves wherever you feel like it."

Homeless people. Clover and I were far from homeless, but, if we didn't find Farkus soon, we just might be husband-less.

Since camping out on Wendy's lawn was no longer an option, we decided to cruise around her block the next day, just go around and around in Clover's car, maintaining a surveillance that would be effective but not attention-getting.

"This is a lot easier on the body than sitting on that curb," I said as Clover pulled her Cadillac up to the stop sign at Wendy's corner.

No sooner were the words out of my mouth when some hormonal teenager in a souped-up Camero slammed into the rear of the Caddy. He not only dented its fender but deployed its air bags.

"Omigod!" I screamed when the damn things inflated, nearly crushing me, not to mention breaking my nails.

"Lord have mercy!" said Clover from somewhere behind the big white blob that was pinning her to the front seat. I could hear her, but I couldn't see her. I felt around and was relieved to find her all in one piece.

We helped each other out of the car, no easy feat, then had it out with the kid, who was terrified that his parents would ground him.

We were the ones who were grounded, our surveillance of Wendy Winters shut down. Clover spent the next few days getting the car back to Bud's dealership and picking out a new Caddy, while I stayed home and contemplated the melodrama that was now my life. It was time, I decided, to pay a visit to another of Farkus's celebrity patients.

Angela Clay, the junior Whitney Houston, lived in the Holmby Hills section of L.A.—one of the most expensive and established areas, populated by old-guard studio executives and movie stars who didn't flinch at a ten-million dollar price tag. Angela's house, a mammoth European villa on Dalehurst Avenue, had a name—Glorywood—and was the sort of residence you'd expect for a twenty-four-year-old with a big voice and the recording contract to match.

Clover and I parked down the street and walked to Glorywood—tiptoed practically (the neighborhood has that sort of hushed, get-out-or-we'll-kill-you atmosphere). Surprisingly, there wasn't a gate in front of the estate, but there was "staff"—four very large black men in blue jeans and T-shirts, the T-shirts imprinted with Angela's face and the title of her latest CD.

"Wassup?" said one of them as we approached.

"Not much," I said. "My friend and I were just out for a walk this beautiful morning." It wasn't a beautiful morning. It was gray and drizzling—unusual for L.A.—and we'd considered postponing our reconnaissance mission but decided to forge ahead. We didn't have the luxury of time.

"So this is where Angela Clay lives," Clover mused.

"She might," said her security man or her cousin or her husband. He was part of her entourage, in any case.

"You wouldn't be wearing that T-shirt if she didn't live here," I pointed out.

He shrugged. "Okay, so everybody on Angela's team is wearing it. But her fans can wear it too. They're selling it at all the music stores."

"Is that so?" I pretended to act fascinated, but I wasn't. I was impatient, unwilling to spend hours skulking around Angela Clay's curb, as we had at Wendy's. I made a unilateral decision then and there that we should up the ante and try to get inside and talk to the lady of the house. "Listen, we'd love to meet Angela," I said. "Any chance we could ring the bell and say hello? Just for a second? You could frisk us, to make sure we're not packing."

Clover glared at me. Okay, so maybe I *was* bossy.

"Sorry," he said, not sounding sorry. "Angela's very busy."

With whom, I wondered? Her herb guru? "Then would you mind if we kind of hung out with you for awhile? In case she comes out of the house? It would be such a thrill for us, just to catch a glimpse of her."

"Nope," he said. "You gotta move along. I'll tell her you were asking for her, though."

"Speaking of asking," I said, refusing to budge, "could I ask you a question about Angela? About a friend of hers, actually?"

"What friend?"

"A doctor friend. She and I both go to him. His name's Gordon Farkus."

"What's the question? And make it fast."

"Has the doctor been here to visit Angela recently? Do you know if she's expecting him?"

"What she's expecting is about fifty people today," he said, showing genuine irritation now. "Her record company set up a promotional gig, where the fans who won some kind of contest are gonna get to have lunch with her. So why don't you keep walking. I can't let you block the entrance."

There wasn't much chance of that. The entrance was almost as wide as the dreaded 405.

"Fine," Clover said. "We'll leave. Right, Elizabeth?"

"Sure," I said, not wanting to cause a scene.

"Good chatting with you," she told the man as she linked her arm in mine. "Have a nice day."

We walked away, in the direction of my car.

"I guess we can cross Angela off the list," she said. "We'll never be able to stake her out with those watchdogs of hers."

"Come on, Clover. Don't be so quick to give up."

"Do you have a better idea?"

"Yeah, I do. The man said there was going to be a party, and I think we should add ourselves to the guest list."

"Elizabeth! What are you talking about?"

"I'm talking about Angela's lunch party. I say we hop in the car, go buy a couple of her T-shirts to wear, and reappear as her most ardent fans. Then we'll sneak into the house on the coattails of the real contest winners."

She didn't answer. She just looked at me as if I'd lost it.

"Are you coming or not?" I said.

"I can't let you go by yourself," she said after a few awkward seconds.

I hugged her. "It'll be an experience. You'll have something to tell your friends back in Kentucky."

"I already do," she said. "But they'll never believe me."

We drove to Tower Records on Westwood Boulevard, bought the T-shirts, put them on, and motored back to Dalehurst Avenue. Then we sat in the car, down the street from Angela's estate, and waited for a procession of stretch limousines to pass us, tipping us off that the guests were arriving.

"There they are!" said Clover, pointing at the limos.

"Okay. Stay calm. Our game plan is to merge with these people as they're getting out of the cars and then enter the house with them, mix ourselves in with the crowd, two T-shirted fans in a sea of other T-shirted fans."

"Oh, Elizabeth," Clover wailed. "I'm really not wild about this one."

"Relax. The worst that can happen is we get thrown out and end up back where we started."

We scurried up Dalehurst Avenue, just as Angela's guests were emerging from their chariots, and squeezed ourselves among them.

"Oh, Lord," Clover whispered, ducking her head and holding onto the back of my T-shirt for dear life.

"What is it?" I said, letting the others push me toward the door, like a wave moving onshore.

"What if someone asks me about Angela's music? I've never liked it."

"Then lie."

We crossed the threshold of Angela's grand manse, and the superstar herself was there to greet everyone. When it was my turn with her, she was all smiles.

"Welcome, Elizabeth," she said after I introduced myself. "I'm so glad you enjoy my records."

"Do I ever," I enthused. "You're the greatest, Angela."

"Thanks. Which of my songs is your favorite?"

"My favorite? Gosh, let me think." I didn't want to hold up the line, but, like Clover, I wasn't big on Angela's sound. There was entirely too much yelling and precious little singing. She once belted out the national anthem at a baseball game, and the song was practically unrecognizable. "To be honest, I can't pick one. They're all fabulous. Even your rendition of the national anthem was amazing." I could feel my nose growing.

"That's sweet," she said, then looked past me, indicating that my moment with her was up.

It was Clover's turn next, but she was still ducking her head and clinging to the back of my T-shirt, attempting to slip past Angela without being noticed.

"What's the matter with your friend?" Angela whispered to me.

"She's shy," I whispered back.

Angela patted Clover on the arm and motioned for us to proceed into the house. I was ready to celebrate that we'd been able to get inside when Clover, who wasn't watching where she was going, knocked over the Ming vase on the foyer table. It shattered in a zillion pieces and created quite a commotion and reminded me of when she tripped over my foot while we were breaking in to Farkus's office. What a klutz!

"Wassup?" said the same enforcer who'd been guarding the house earlier in the day. When he spotted Clover and me, he shook his head and reached for us. "Okay. Out. Both of you. Now."

He grabbed one of Clover's arms, then one of mine, and before we could apologize to Angela for crashing her party and smashing her vase, he lifted us out the door, onto the lawn, our feet never touching the ground until we were back on the street.

"Next time you try something like this, I call the cops and they throw you two in jail," he warned.

"There won't be a next time," I promised, cringing at the thought of that community shower.

⟡

As befitting an international movie star, Lanie Duquette owned houses all over the world, but, according to Brenda, she had recently sold every one of them—except the residence in which she was presently ensconced: her beach house in Malibu.

"She not only has great looks and her own money," said Clover, as she was driving us along Pacific Coast Highway toward Lanie's house, "but she's married to that dot-com billionaire. Why in the world would she need Dr. Farkus's potions?"

"I don't have a clue. But we saw her in that waiting room, so we know she was—and, hopefully, still is—a patient of his. Maybe we'll be able to charm our way inside the house and ask her."

"Inside the house? Not that again. You really shook me up when you switched gears at Angela's. I don't want to go through that same kind of mess."

"Then don't knock over a vase this time."

"Very funny. So you're thinking that we'll just waltz up to Lanie Duquette's house and she'll invite us in and we'll ask her point-blank if she knows where Farkus is—and she'll actually tell us?"

"Look, Clover. I want that antidote, and Lanie's our last hope of getting it. I'm willing to pull out all the stops, do whatever it takes. If you're not, I'll understand."

She shrugged. "I want the antidote too."

"Good. Now, Lanie's house is in Malibu Colony, which is a gated community, as you know. The trick here will be to slip past the guard in that gatehouse."

"How are we supposed to do that? Those guards are armed."

"I haven't figured it out yet. I'm praying something will come to me before we get there."

When we arrived at the Malibu Colony gatehouse at nine A.M., I announced us as Lanie Duquette's accountants, and we were promptly told by the guard that our names weren't on the list of approved visitors.

"The only ones allowed in there today are the pest control people," he said. "And they're not due until three-thirty."

"That's strange," I said. "Are you absolutely certain you don't have Elizabeth Baskin and Clover Hinsdale on your list? From the Los Angeles accounting firm of Baskin and Hinsdale? Miss Duquette's secretary scheduled a nine o'clock meeting with our client."

"Nope," he said. "You're not on the list. Only the pest control people."

Well, it didn't look as if I'd be able to talk our way in. "Miss Duquette doesn't have termites, does she?" I said as a throwaway line, since I felt frustrated and thwarted and at the end of my rope.

"I doubt it," said the guard. "It's just Western Exterminator, coming to do her monthly spraying."

I acted unimpressed by this news, but in fact I was extremely interested in it. A new idea was percolating, and the minute Clover and I were back in her car, I shared it with her.

"What would you think about posing as the pest control people?" I asked.

"Excuse me?"

"I said, What would you think about pretending to be the people from Western Exterminator? The guard told us they were on the list. They're supposed to be at Lanie's at three-thirty this afternoon for her monthly spraying. Why don't *we* show up instead? Say, around three?"

Clover didn't respond other than to stare at me.

"No, I'm not insane," I said. "This is do-able, Clover. We *have* to do it. We're down to our last celebrity patient. If we don't get in to talk to Lanie, what are our chances of ever finding Farkus and saving our marriages?"

"Right, but to pretend to be exterminators?" She buried her head in her lap.

"Look, this is a once-in-a-lifetime opportunity, Clover, and I don't intend to blow it."

I honestly didn't know where I was getting all the nervy attitude, except that the game of Torture the Concierge had forced me to be nervy over the years. Of course, the person I was torturing at the moment was poor Clover, who didn't seem too happy about this latest escapade.

Still, she went along. Since Bud was a car dealer and had connections in the car rental business, she was in charge of renting us a van. I had the task of popping into Lynton's Uniforms in Santa Monica and buying us some exterminator-type duds, then heading over to Home Depot in Hollywood and purchasing a couple of insecticide sprayer cans. Our duties completed, we reconvened at my house, donned our disguises, and drove back to Malibu. Never mind that the van Clover had rented was white instead of yellow, the color of Western Exterminator's vans, and never mind that the uniforms I had bought were light green, making us look like surgeons. We were ready. At three o'clock, we pulled into Malibu Colony and announced ourselves. There had been a shift change in the gatehouse and we were now dealing with the afternoon guard instead of the morning guard—a guard who hadn't seen us when we were accountants.

"Your appointment with Miss Duquette is for three-thirty," he said, checking his watch. "You're a half-hour early."

"Miss Duquette asked us to come early," I said in a gruff, no-nonsense voice. "She's got a dead animal that needs removal."

"Raccoon?" he said.

"Bobcat," I said.

Wordlessly, the guard waved us through.

Lanie's house was a contemporary masterpiece—one of those stark white jobbies that's got curves and angles and roof lines where you'd least expect them.

"I'll bet it's a real chore to do pest control here," said Clover, after maneuvering the van into Lanie's driveway.

"We're only pretending to do pest control," I reminded her. "Removing dead animals is somebody else's problem."

"Right."

We got out of the van, sprayers in hand, walked up to what we assumed was the front door—the house may have been architecturally important but the layout was a real jigsaw puzzle—and rang the bell.

"Don't be nervous," I whispered to Clover as we stood there waiting.

"If you're worried that I'm going to break something, forget it. I'll be fine," she said. "I'm excited about the prospect of meeting Lanie Duquette."

I was about to add that I, too, was looking forward to coming face to face with one of the great beauties of the silver screen when a woman who could only be described as dreary opened the door.

"Hello," she said without enthusiasm. "You're early, aren't you?" It was Lanie, all right, but she was hardly in glamour girl mode. Her skin was makeup-less and mottled, her eyes heavy with deep, dark circles under them, her hair dank, limp, lifeless. And her clothes—well, I would have expected something more stylish. Certainly not the baggy jeans and sweatshirt.

"Yes, Miss Duquette. We're a little early," I said, "but at Western Exterminator, we pride ourselves on our thoroughness, which means getting a head start whenever possible. Whatever you've got in the way of pests—roaches, fleas, ants, spiders, moths, silverfish, earwigs—we'll take care of it for you."

Lanie looked bewildered. "What, may I ask, is an earwig?"

She had me there. I was only reciting from Western Exterminator's ad in the Yellow Pages. "An earwig is the worst kind of pest," I said. "It's an insect that crawls into your ears and eats away at your hair, which necessitates the wearing of a wig. Hence, its name."

"How awful," she said. "Well, please. Don't let me stand in your way.

Oh, and after you've finished spraying, would you mind getting rid of the wasp nests under the eaves outside the kitchen? I think there are three of them."

Wasp nests? I was allergic to wasps! I wanted Roger back, but I didn't intend to go into anaphylactic shock to *get* him back! She'd have to leave that little matter to the professionals.

Clover and I entered the house and went from room to room, spraying the baseboards. When we were done, I said to Lanie, "All set now."

"So soon?" she said skeptically.

"We're fast as well as thorough," I said. "But before we go, would it be possible to have a word with you? About something other than pest control?"

"Something other than pest control, huh?" She narrowed her eyes at us, pulled a can of Mace out of a drawer and pointed it at us. Boy, I hadn't seen that coming.

Clover gasped. "Don't!" she cried. "We didn't mean any harm. Oh, please."

"Then start talking," said Lanie, tightening her grip on the Mace. "Why don't you begin by telling me who you really are and what you're doing in my house."

"Okay, but there's no need for you to defend yourself. Not from us, Miss Duquette. You're not in any danger. Really."

"Oh, no? I'm alone here today," she said. "The maid is off. So are the cook, the gardener, and the rest of them. I'm all by myself for a change, and it wasn't half bad until *this*."

Clover gasped again, this time because she'd accidentally bonked herself in the shin with her own spray can.

"Let me explain," I said and plunged in, confessing the whole story about Roger and Bud and Dr. Farkus, and how desperate we were to get our hands on the antidote. "We apologize for misrepresenting ourselves to you, Miss Duquette. We meant no harm, as my friend told you."

There were a few more exchanges—I had to convince her that Clover and I weren't criminals, just a couple of women with marital problems—but she finally lowered the Mace and returned it to the drawer.

"You're probably thinking I look like hell," she said, self-conscious suddenly. "People assume movie stars look like movie stars when no one's around. Well, here's a bulletin for you: We don't. Now, why don't we sit down and talk about Dr. Farkus, since that's why you're here. The truth is, he's been on my mind a lot lately."

Relieved that we hadn't been blinded by noxious gas, Clover and I followed Lanie into her living room, which had the warmth of a warehouse. It was enormous but barely furnished, with not a single memento or picture or knicknack. It was cold—as cold as Lanie's life turned out to be.

Without bothering to make chitchat, she unburdened herself to us. She explained that, despite her great success, she was an insecure woman who'd been to countless shrinks, astrologers, and motivational experts, all in a fruitless effort to boost her self-esteem. When she heard about Farkus from her publicist or her hairdresser (she couldn't remember which), she rushed to see him. He was wonderfully reassuring, she said, and concocted a special preparation for her, which she stirred into her morning coffee once a month.

"I felt completely enhanced," she said. "Happier than ever before."

"What did he put into your preparation?" I asked.

"Some herbs from a rain forest in Central America, or so he claimed. Personally, I think he put magic into those potions."

"Metaphorically, you mean," I said.

"No, literally. I think that's why he left town, because he was misunderstood, the way brilliant and talented men are often misunderstood. The police may accuse him of a myriad of crimes, including practicing without a medical license, but would any of us have gone to see him if he'd advertised himself as a magician instead of an M.D.?"

"No," I said, not knowing what to believe about Farkus anymore.

"Neither would I," said Clover.

"But now he's fled," said Lanie, "because the police have chased him away. I'm without my preparations and you're without your antidote."

"So he didn't give you any idea where he was going?" I said. "Clover and I thought that you of all people would have been on his forwarding address list."

"Not a word from him. Or from Andrea, his assistant."

"Well, we're determined to find him," I said. "And if we do, we'll be sure to tell you where he's hiding and how to reach him."

"I appreciate that. I'd hire a private investigator to find him, but I have to be so careful in my business. Those P.I.s are the worst gossips. If it got out that I had paid someone to search for Farkus—and why—I'd be in the tabloids in a heartbeat."

"We understand," said Clover. "It must be a burden to be so famous."

"The burden is that famous people are supposed to be happy," she said and turned toward the door.

As she was walking us out to the car, I thanked her for speaking so candidly with us and wished her well.

"Oh, before we go," I added, "I'm curious about something. How did you know we weren't real exterminators?"

She smiled for the first time all afternoon. "Because real exterminators don't usually spray houses with Avon's Skin So Soft."

Well, it was a good try, wasn't it? I mean, the stuff worked on mosquitoes.

CHAPTER EIGHTEEN

Clover was backing the van out of Lanie's driveway when I spotted a man coming out of the estate next door. He looked familiar. Too familiar.

"Clover!"

She slammed on the brakes, giving me a nasty case of whiplash. "What's the matter? Did I hit something?"

"No. See that man walking out of the house over there?" I pointed to the shingled, Cape Cod–style house just south of Lanie's.

Clover squinted. "I don't have my glasses on, but he doesn't look like Farkus, if that's what you're thinking."

"What I'm thinking is that he looks like Roger."

"Roger?" She peered at the man. "Now that you mention it, he does. Let me pull the van up to the house so you can say hello."

"*No!*"

She slammed on the brakes again. The discs in my neck were history.

"Stop doing that, would you?" I said.

"Sorry, but I figured you'd want to talk to your husband."

"Like this? How would I explain the van and the uniforms and the sprayers?"

"Oh. Right."

"But that's not the point. What's he doing coming out of that house, looking all spiffy and smiley at four-thirty in the afternoon? He should be at his office where he belongs."

"Instead of with a babe, you mean."

"What Babe?"

"The one coming out of the house behind him. Look."

I looked. Sure enough, Roger wasn't the only one emerging from the house. A tall woman with long black hair and even longer legs was right on his heels. "Okay, Clover. Drive a little closer, can you? I don't want them to see us. I just want a better view."

"I'll try, but this thing doesn't handle like a regular car."

She put the van in gear and eased her foot down on the accelerator. We were inching along Malibu Colony Road, toward the house in question, when suddenly the van started bucking and jerking like an out-of-control bronco. But the really bad news was that the direction of its bucking and jerking was straight onto the lawn of Lanie's neighbor.

"Hey. What're you doing?" yelled Roger, who ran toward the van, wagging his finger at us. The babe, an Asian beauty, was practically Velcro-ed to his side. I guessed he had moved on from Nikki, the Victoria's Secret model. There was no keeping up with the enhanced Roger.

"Great. Just great," I muttered, as my husband and his sexy companion approached.

"At least they're dressed," said Clover, trying to be supportive.

"Do you people realize you're on private property?" Roger demanded when he reached the van. He didn't recognize us at first. A second went by. Then another and another. Then we had liftoff. "Elizabeth? Is that *you* in there?" He was surprised to see me, needless to say.

"It's me, all right," I said cheerfully, the wheels turning in my head as I attempted to come up with a decent reason for the get-up and the van.

"And don't forget me," Clover chimed in. "How're you, Roger?"

"Fine. Fine. But what are you two doing here?"

"I could ask you the same question," I said, eyeing the Lucy Liu look-alike. "I thought it was real estate agents who showed houses, not real estate attorneys."

"This is Kim," he said, nodding at her. "She's a client of mine. She's purchased this house and is closing on it tomorrow. We were having a walk-through."

A walk-through, my ass. A *see-through* was more like it, judging by Kim's blouse, which was so gauzy and transparent you could see right through to her bra, *except that she wasn't wearing one*. "Since when do you do walk-throughs, Roger?" I asked. I'd never known him to bother with them.

"Kim asked me to," he said. "She's not fully invested in her realtor, in terms of the trust factor, so she wanted my input."

Brother. He never used to talk like that. It was one of the things I loved about him—that he didn't speak in legal mumbo-jumbo or even in L.A. mumbo-jumbo. And now here he was, sounding like a complete dope. "How nice for Kim," I said. "How nice for both of you."

"What about both of *you*?" Roger asked, nodding at Clover and me. "What in the world are you doing in that van, dressed in those uniforms?"

Clover glanced at me as if to say, "He's your husband. You think of a good one."

"We were at a birthday luncheon for our friend, who lives next door," I said. "It was a costume party, and we were supposed to dress up as people who've made a difference in her life. Clover and I decided to come as surgeons, because our friend had her fibroid tumors removed recently and the doctor was able to leave her uterus intact as well as her ovaries and her cervix." When you throw female organs into a story, men automatically lose interest, or so I hoped.

"What about the van?" said Roger.

"Oh, well, we couldn't very well arrive in an actual EMS vehicle," I said with a chuckle. "Renting a van was the next best thing."

"I'm confused," said Kim. "I thought Lanie Duquette lived in the house next door. That's what my realtor told me."

"Ah, but you're not fully invested in your realtor, in terms of the trust factor," I said. "According to our friend, Lanie Duquette lives in the house next door to *her*."

"Whatever," said Kim, whose smugness, along with her unnecessary brushing up against Roger, made me want to punch her.

"Will you be home for dinner tonight, Roger?" I asked him. "Or is this your night to take a spin on the space shuttle?"

Okay, so I was being sarcastic. I couldn't help it. I was dying inside. I was jealous of Kim and guilty about herbing Roger and frustrated at not being able to give him the antidote. I was also tired, extremely tired. Lying uses up a lot of energy, I discovered.

"No, I won't be home, Elizabeth," he said. "I'm having dinner with Kim tonight. We still have quite a bit of work to do before her closing tomorrow."

"I was under the impression that the lawyer did the work, not the lawyer *and* the client," I said.

"Elizabeth, please try to understand." Roger said this in a rather poignant way, almost as if he were the one trying to understand. His own behavior must have been bewildering to him, given that he didn't have a clue that he'd been enhanced. Yes, he'd been acting in an insufferable and thoroughly unacceptable manner, and yes, I was terribly hurt seeing him with other women, but I felt sorry for him, wished I could make it all better, was determined to make it all better.

I vowed yet again to get that damn antidote. Farkus had to be somewhere, didn't he? Maybe if we turned the search over to a professional . . .

I presented the idea to Clover as she was driving me back to Santa Monica in the van.

"You want to do *what*?" she said, slamming on the brakes, herniating the discs in both my neck and my back this time.

"Why not?" I said. "What choice do we have? You and I aren't equipped to conduct a manhunt for Farkus. I have to concentrate on reinstating myself as an inspector with AMLP, and you have to, well, do whatever it is you do." It occurred to me that Clover didn't really do anything. She didn't have a job, didn't play golf or tennis, didn't belong to a book group or an art group or a group that took nature walks. She didn't even sit on charity committees. Her entire life had been devoted to the care and feeding of Bud, and now that he was rarely home, she was a wife without a purpose.

"I agree that you and I aren't making any progress," she said, "but we just started."

"Clover, my husband is on the verge of cheating on me, if he hasn't already. And you don't really know where Bud goes at night, do you? I mean, do you honestly believe he's taking ballroom dancing lessons until all hours?"

She started to cry, which worried me. Her driving wasn't that hot even without the tears.

"So I think it's worth a shot," I said, referring to my idea. "I'm going to make the call as soon as I get home."

She nodded. She wasn't happy about what I had proposed, but she had to concede it might do the trick.

But there was more pressing business to attend to when I got home. As I was sorting through the day's mail, I came upon another letter from Art Yarnell, the crazed hotel manager. He had amped up his rhetoric this time, actually threatening to come to my house and confront me in person about the rating I'd given the Phoenician Paradise.

I considered calling the police about the letter, but, frankly, I'd had my fill of the police at that point. I also considered calling Preston, but, frankly, he'd had his fill of me at that point. I really thought that the best course of action was no action—to just ignore Yarnell and hope he'd start harassing someone else after a while—but instead I sat down and wrote him back. In my letter, I apologized for any distress I may have caused him or members of his staff. I also explained that I was only doing my job and stood by my assessment of the hotel, and suggested that if he really wanted to hold onto his position there, he should stop obsessing about me and start making the improvements that would bring about a Five Key rating the next time around.

There, I thought, as I addressed and stamped the envelope. Maybe that will shut him up.

I was about to place the phone call that Clover and I had agreed I'd make when my doorbell rang.

"Oh. David," I said, motioning for Roger's partner to come inside, then giving him a hug. "This is an unexpected treat."

"I probably should have called first," he said, more serious than I'd ever seen him. He was usually such a happy-go-lucky guy, a frat boy.

"Don't worry about it. You weren't interrupting anything. Can I get you a drink?"

"A drink would be great, Elizabeth. I think we should both have one, actually."

Uh-oh. It struck me then that David had never stopped by the house when Roger wasn't home and that his visit that afternoon had a sort of lugubrious quality about it. "Here," I said, handing him a scotch.

"You're not joining me?" he said.

"No. I have a feeling I'm going to need a clear head for whatever you came here to tell me. Have a seat." He sat on the living room sofa. I sat across from him in a chair. "Now. What's this about?"

"It's about Roger," he said after taking a swig of booze. "Roger and Lucy."

"Roger and Lucy? Lucy, as in your girlfriend, the baby whisperer?"

David nodded. "They've been seeing each other, Elizabeth."

I blinked, a sharp pain stabbing me in the left eye. "What do you mean, *seeing each other*?"

"They had lunch the other day. Lucy told me about it—the night she broke up with me. She admitted she's very attracted to Roger."

Who wasn't? I had turned a very nice-looking man into a hot piece of ass and now I was paying the piper. "So she broke up with you because she's attracted to Roger?"

"That's the message I got."

"I'm sorry, David. Really sorry. I know you were very fond of Lucy. But why are you telling me all this? Just because she had one lunch with Roger doesn't mean he's to blame for your break-up or even that they're having an affair. My guess is that she invited him to lunch, that he was too polite to refuse, and that nothing happened between them. Roger would never come on to a woman you were dating."

"Not the old Roger, I agree with you. But he's changed, Elizabeth. He's totally into himself lately, into what *he* wants. It's true that Lucy was the one who asked him to have lunch, but did he tell me about it? Did he ask me if I minded? Did he tell you about it? Did he ask you if you minded? The answer's no on all counts. I'm starting to wonder if Roger is the guy I always thought he was."

He isn't, I wanted to shout. But it's not his fault. It's mine and I'm about to take care of it.

I sank back in the chair. "Don't be angry with him, David," I said, feeling angry enough at him for both of us. If he did have lunch with Lucy and something did happen between them—no, there weren't enough hours in the day for him to be cheating on me with Lucy and Nikki and Kim and God knows who else.

"I am angry," said David. "Friends don't steal each other's women."

I tried to reason with him, tried to suggest that the lunch could have been an innocent, one-time meeting. He wasn't having any. He came to vent. When he finished his drink, he set it down on the coffee table and said, in a menacing tone I'd never heard from him, "Roger should watch it from now on, watch his back. You might want to tell him that when you see him, Elizabeth."

I had no idea when I'd see him, but David's words sent a chill through me. However jealous I was of all the women who were currently fawning over Roger, I wanted to protect him too, had a responsibility to protect him. Despite his easygoing manner, David could be a hothead, not the sort of person you'd want for an enemy.

No sooner was he out the door than I dug up the phone number I'd written on a piece of paper. I needed to find Farkus—and fast—before Roger's law practice crumbled along with his marriage.

I dialed the number and waited. When an answering machine picked up, I cleared my throat and began speaking.

"Hi, Cherry," I said, my voice surprisingly steady under the circumstances. After all, I never expected to actually *need* her phone number. But she'd taken punches for Clover and me in that dayroom. She'd been our protector. She'd bonded with us. It wasn't such a stretch to think she might come to our aid again, was it? "It's Elizabeth Baskin. You know, from the Beverly Hills jail? The blonde in the orange jumpsuit? Wow, that narrows it down, doesn't it? Ha-ha." A little nervous humor. "Maybe you remember my friend Clover, the brunette in the orange jumpsuit—the one with the southern accent. Anyhow, we have a job for you and it's pretty urgent. Please call as soon as you can."

I left her my number and hung up. Sure, it was possible that after being arraigned she was presently doing time for attempted murder and would never have the opportunity to listen to my message. But I doubted it. "I'll be outta here on Monday," she'd said when I'd asked her how long she expected to be locked up. "Cherry Queen doesn't fail."

I was counting on Cherry not to fail. She was a hit woman for a living, but she also found people for a living. That's what she'd told us. "I track them down and do whatever the client wants me to do with them," she'd said.

Yes, she's the perfect person for this assignment, I thought, never imagining that jail would turn out to be a swell place for networking.

CHAPTER NINETEEN

Cherry returned my call within ten minutes. She was on her car phone, she said, en route back to L.A. from Laguna Niguel.

"Laguna Niguel is lovely. Were you there on vacation?" I said, figuring that even hit women needed a break every now and then, especially after a stint in jail.

"No such luck," she said. "I was on a job."

"I see," I said, amazed that I was having a conversation with this person. The things people will do when they're desperate. "Well, as you've gathered from my message, my friend Clover and I would like to hire you."

"I hear you, honey. Are we talking about offing one of your husbands?"

"Absolutely not, Cherry." God.

"I was just asking because the job in Laguna was a husband. The wife hired me to blow his brains out."

Charming. What the hell was I doing? "No, Cherry. We'd like you to find somebody for us. In the dayroom at the jail, you said you do that sort of work, along with, well, the other."

"Sure I do. I find them, I plug them, whatever."

"We don't want this man harmed in any way. That's very important, Cherry. He's not to be roughed up or threatened or any of that. We just want to know where he is—as soon as possible."

"Got it. When do you wanna meet?"

"Meet?" I hadn't counted on actually having to lay eyes on her again.

"Yeah. You gotta give me the background on the guy, a photo if you have one, a description if you don't, any other particulars, plus the money. I get half up front, half when I deliver. In cash."

"Right." I couldn't bring myself to ask how much. Better to wait until Clover was present, since she was the one with the bucks.

Neither of us wanted to be seen with Cherry, so we agreed to meet at her place. I didn't have a lot of experience with hit women, but I had imagined that she would live in a rat hole with empty pizza boxes and beer cans and cigarette packs strewed everywhere. I couldn't have been more wrong.

"My heavens," said Clover when we entered Cherry's townhouse, a spacious duplex in one of Marina Del Rey's prime neighborhoods. Not only was her furniture fairly tasteful, but her view of the marina was one of the area's best. Obviously, Cherry was a success at her chosen profession. "Did you do the decorating yourself?"

"Who has the time? I used an interior designer," she said. She was still bald and sporting tattoos, but, out of the jumpsuit, she looked somewhat civilized. She was wearing a purple skirt and matching top and a pair of those short black boots. It wasn't my idea of a great outfit, but you see everything in L.A.

"Are these antiques?" I asked, referring to several of the pieces in her living room.

"No, they're knockoffs," she said. "They were expensive but I had a good year. Now, how about something to drink? I've got all kinds of booze. What'll it be?"

I looked at Clover, who mouthed the words, "I want to go home."

Over white wine and jumbo shrimp we discussed the job.

"The man we want you to find is a doctor," I said. "Well, he's not really a doctor."

"He just plays one on TV?" Cherry laughed at her little joke.

"He poses as one, yes," I said. "He pretends to have graduated from Harvard Medical School and all the rest, but he's never gotten a license to practice medicine."

"What's this nutcase's name?" she asked, taking notes as we talked. Her notebook was leather, her pen sterling silver. Nothing but the best for our Cherry.

"He goes by the name of Gordon P. Farkus," said Clover, "but his real name is Jerry Sheck."

"What do the cops in Beverly Hills have on him? Besides practicing medicine without a license?" said Cherry.

"Several types of fraud," I said, "plus criminal impersonation. I guess there really is a doctor named Gordon Farkus out there."

"Have you got a photo of this prize?" she said.

"No," I said. "He never advertised."

"But we can describe him to you," Clover added, and painted a pretty good verbal portrait of the man who'd sold us the powder.

Cherry asked us a lot more questions—she really seemed to know her business—and said she'd get right on the case.

"But how will you be able to find him when the police in six states haven't been able to?" I said. "He could be hiding in a shack somewhere."

"Not if his game is conning money out of rich people," she said.

"Look, stop worrying. It's like I told you before—Cherry Queen doesn't fail."

"I'm glad you're so confident," I said, "but, specifically, how do you go about finding someone who doesn't want to be found?"

She laughed again, wider this time, revealing a few shiny gold crowns. "You two don't *really* want me to tell you how this works, do you?"

"No!" Clover said, holding her ears. "Spare us the details!"

We spent a couple of hours with Cherry, who was rather entertaining, it turned out, then got down to the matter of money. We agreed that we'd bring her five thousand dollars in cash the next day as an advance, and another five thousand dollars when she found Farkus. It was a ridiculous amount of money for us to spend (Clover coughed up most of it), particularly after the sum we threw away on the potions, but we were convinced—Cherry had us convinced—that we would be more than satisfied with the results.

"I'm gonna make everything A-okay," she vowed, finishing off the bottle of wine. "You're gonna be happy you met me in that jail, you'll see."

We didn't see for several weeks, but then we didn't expect to. Cherry had warned us that finding a person takes time, and so we went about our business, fingers crossed.

While we waited, I tried to get back in Preston's good graces. I called him and asked if he would send me out on an inspection, promising that I had regained my focus and concentration and that my ability to evaluate a property was no longer compromised.

"Let's give it a little more time, shall we?" he said in his impossibly patronizing tone, as if I were mentally deficient or simply born without the correct pedigree. "We've assigned someone else to inspect a couple of properties over the next two weeks or so. I'd like to wait and see how he does before making a decision about you, Elizabeth."

"I'll tell you how he's going to do," I said, not backing down one iota. "He's going to make you wish you'd assigned *me* those properties, because he's not going to be the perfectionist I am—the stickler that AMLP subscribers depend on before deciding which hotels and resorts to book. Elizabeth Baskin doesn't fail, Preston." Well, the line worked for Cherry, didn't it?

"You may be right," he acknowledged, "but we recruited this man while you were going through your little fuzzy period, and now he's already on board with these two properties, as I mentioned. So let's have you take a bit more time off and we'll reassess."

Reassess *this*, I thought glumly.

Feeling lost, the entire day in front of me with nothing to do, I lit on the brilliant idea of trotting off to Roger's office to surprise him. Maybe he'll take me to lunch, I thought as I began to dress—unless, of course, he's already made lunch plans with Lucy, David's girlfriend, or Nikki, the nightclub hopper, or Kim, Lanie Duquette's about-to-be neighbor.

No, I won't be scared off by those women, I decided. Maybe my showing up out of the blue will shake Roger up, knock some sense into him, remind him that he loves me and I love him and everything will be all right between us. Sure, why not? I made a reservation at Michael's, a popular restaurant directly across the street from his office. It couldn't hurt to be prepared.

I arrived at Roger's building—233 Wilshire Boulevard in Santa Monica—at eleven-thirty, early enough to catch him before he dashed out to meet a client (or a lover, perish the thought).

"Oh. Hi, Brad," I said, running into Roger's partner in the lobby of the building. "How's Gerta?"

He scowled at the mention of his wife's name, which shocked me. They were as close as any couple I'd ever known. "Why don't you ask your husband how she is?" he said through tight lips.

"Ask Roger about Gerta? Why?"

"Hasn't he told you?"

"Obviously not." I braced myself.

"They're studying European art history together," he said. "Or, rather, Gerta is teaching him about it. Either way, they've gotten very chummy."

Chummy? With Gerta? *Roger*? While he'd never been as critical of her as I'd been, he'd shared my amusement at her mysterious heritage. I couldn't imagine that he'd choose her as his tutor.

"They're not really studying art, of course," Brad went on, his face flushing as he became more agitated.

"What makes you say that?"

"Well, for one thing, neither of them ever mentioned to me that they were planning to work together. I had to find out by accident. I came home one night and there he was, your perfectly attired and coiffed and cologned husband, huddled together with Gerta in the den. When I asked what was going on, they claimed she was lecturing him about Renoir."

"Maybe she was," I said, not wanting to believe what Brad was insinuating, no matter how much it hurt. Roger *was* on a self-improvement kick, thanks to the powder. Maybe he really did want to broaden his knowledge of art history.

"Then where was the textbook? Where was the evidence? Where was the proof that they were 'studying'? The only artwork I could see was Roger's masterful job of lying to his old friend and law partner."

I tried to calm Brad, to beg him to reconsider his accusation, but he stormed off in a huff, leaving me with conflicted emotions—the familiar push-and-pull of feeling angry at Roger and sorry for him too. And let's not forget the guilt trip I was putting myself through, the "if only."

This is horrible, I thought as I rode up in the elevator. First David is furious with Roger. Now Brad is too. The law firm can't possibly survive under that sort of strain, and if it doesn't, I won't be the only one in this marriage who's out of a job.

Thank goodness for Carrie, I decided. She always supported Roger, was grateful to him for promoting her to partner. She'll hold the firm together.

I got off the elevator, greeted the receptionist, and asked her if Roger was in his office.

"I think he's in with Ms. Toobin," she said. "Should I tell them you're here, Mrs. Baskin?"

"I'd rather surprise my husband if it's all right," I said. "I'm hoping he'll buy me lunch."

She smiled, clearly a supporter of wives who attempt to keep the marital flames burning. If she only knew how far I'd gone toward that end.

I thanked her and walked down the hall to Carrie Toobin's office. The door was closed, so I knocked.

"We're busy," Carrie called out. "Come back later. Much later." She laughed then—a girlish giggle is what it was—and before I could stop myself, I was pressing my ear against the door, trying to eavesdrop.

"Hey, that tickles!" I heard Roger say. "Let's see how *you* like it, Carriekins."

Carriekins?

She giggled again, even let out a little squeal.

No, I thought, peeling myself off the door. Not Carrie too. It was too much. It was all too much. I was losing Roger and he was losing his mind.

Without bothering to knock a second time, I barged into Carrie's office, my heart pounding. The two of them were sitting on the sofa, very close together, with their shoes off. Otherwise, they were fully clothed, thank God, if you counted Carrie's outfit as clothes. She was in one of her tits-and-ass suits, exposing everything but her brains.

"Sorry to interrupt your game of footsie," I said, "but I was wondering if you'd like to have lunch with me, Roger. That is, if you can tear yourself away from your *law partner*." I wanted to make it plain, because he was under the influence of the potion and didn't know better, that fooling around with a coworker—or a coworker's wife, for that matter—wasn't a good move.

Roger stood, came toward me, put his arms around me, and pulled me to him. I think he honestly meant to demonstrate that he was glad to see me and that his shenanigans with Carrie were platonic. We remained in the hug for several seconds, just holding on to each other, feeling each other breathe. It was as if he sensed that he wasn't himself, that he was, in fact, a man with dueling impulses. Out of the corner of my eye, I noticed that Carrie was smirking while Roger and I were embracing. I wanted to ask her what was so damn funny and why couldn't she dress like a lawyer instead of a hooker and didn't she have better things to do than tickle my husband's foot, but I kept quiet, speaking only to repeat my lunch invitation.

"I can't," said Roger. "I'm meeting a client for lunch. I *swear*."

Don't worry, honey, I thought, not dwelling on whether he was or he wasn't. I'll get you out of this mess. It's just a matter of time.

Three-and-a-half weeks went by and Clover and I still hadn't heard from Cherry.

"You'd think she'd at least give us periodic reports," I said.

"Maybe she doesn't want to get our hopes up," said Clover. "Maybe she waits until she's finished the job."

"Just the same, I'm calling her and leaving a message on her answering machine. We paid her a lot of money to find Farkus. An update on her progress isn't too much to ask."

Clover agreed. I left a message for Cherry saying we'd like to know whether she'd had any leads. Twenty minutes later, she returned the call.

"How amazing is that?" she said, sounding very upbeat. "You called me about five minutes before I was gonna call you."

"Oh, Cherry," I said. "Does this mean that you've found the man we're looking for?"

"Damn right," she said. "Meet me at my place in an hour and I'll give you his address. Oh, and don't forget the cash. This job was a tough one. I earned every dollar."

"Of course you did," I said, absolutely elated. "We don't know how to thank you."

"Just bring the money," she said. "That's all the thanks I need."

I hung up the phone and clasped Clover's hand, dancing her around the room. "It's finally happening," I said jubilantly. "We're going to confront Farkus, make him give us the herbs that'll counteract his stud stimulant, and get our husbands back. Oh, Clover. I'm so excited, so relieved."

"Same here," she said. "And to think I didn't go along with you about Cherry at first. I was wrong to doubt you, Elizabeth."

"That's okay. I wasn't exactly overjoyed about getting involved with a character like her. She just seemed like our only option."

"And she came through. That Cherry Queen sure doesn't fail, bless her heart."

"No, she sure doesn't."

We met Cherry at her townhouse in Marina Del Rey at six-thirty that evening. Everybody was in a celebrating mood. We drank wine, munched on hors d'oeuvres, yakked like a bunch of girls at a slumber party. Eventually, Cherry said that she had some people coming to talk to her about a job and that we'd have to leave.

"I hate to throw you ladies out, but you understand, right?"

"Of course we do," I said. "But you haven't told us where Farkus is. We can't let you go without that information, right?"

We all had a good laugh over that one.

"Your guy is hiding out here in L.A.," she said.

"In L.A.?" I said. "Then why did it take so long to find him?"

"Hey, I found him, didn't I?" she said.

"I only meant that he must have been keeping quite a low profile," I said, trying to placate her. She was a murderer, after all.

"He's keeping a low profile all right," she said. "He's staying at a private house in Hancock Park and never goes out. The address is 215 Arcade Avenue. It's just off Larchmont Boulevard."

"This is great, Cherry. Just great," I said, writing the address down, folding the piece of paper, and sticking it in my wallet for safekeeping.

"Glad to help," said Cherry. "Now, you got the money?"

Clover presented Cherry with a Bloomingdale's shopping bag filled with crisp one-hundred-dollar bills—fifty of them.

"Nice doing business with you ladies," said Cherry. "Good luck with your husbands."

Clover and I shook hands with Cherry Queen and hit the road, our spirits soaring.

"Let's go straight to Farkus's," I said. "Tonight. Right now."

"My thoughts exactly," said Clover. "No time like the present, before he decides to make a run for it."

I drove us to Hancock Park, a section of L.A. near Paramount Studios. As we cruised along Larchmont Boulevard with its attractive shops and restaurants, we kept a lookout for Arcade Avenue and couldn't find it. I asked Clover to check the map in my glove compartment.

"There's no Arcade Avenue in Hancock Park," she said after studying the map.

"There has to be," I said. "Let me turn the light on in here."

I flipped the car's interior light on and kept driving.

"I still can't find it," said Clover.

"It must be one of those tiny streets—a private road or something. That's why Farkus is hiding out there. Because it's so off the beaten path."

Around and around I drove, finally stopping to speak to a man walking his dog. "Would you please tell us how to get to Arcade Avenue?"

"No such street," he said. "Not in Hancock Park."

"But a friend of ours is staying in a house there. Number 215 Arcade Avenue."

"Your friend must have been yanking your chain. I've lived here for twenty years and I'm telling you, there's no Arcade Avenue."

I stared at Clover, my stomach turning over. "Could Cherry have been yanking our chain?"

"Lord have mercy, Elizabeth. Why in the world would she do that?"

"*For the money, Clover!*" I didn't mean to shout at her and I apologized right away. After all, I was the one who'd suggested we hire Cherry, but what if she had conned us, ripped us off, made us look like the two biggest dopes on the planet? "If she took our ten thousand dollars and we've got nothing to show for it, we're screwed."

"Now, now. Maybe you wrote down the wrong address. Or maybe Cherry gave you the wrong address by mistake."

"Yeah, and maybe Cherry wasn't in jail for attempted murder. Maybe she was there for swindling two other gullible women out of ten grand."

Clover's eyes widened. "You really believe she stole our money?"

"It looks that way. Damn! I can't stand it! She played us for total fools. Cherry Queen doesn't fail, remember?"

As was her habit, Clover began to cry. "We'll go back to her townhouse and confront her," she said. "We'll demand that she return our money or else."

"Oh, like she'll just hand it over to us? Fat chance."

"Well? We've got to do something, Elizabeth. We can't just walk away from ten thousand dollars."

She was right, of course. We had to at least try to recover the money. I turned the car around and headed down to Marina Del Rey. When we got to Cherry's place, I took Clover aside and said, "The important thing is to stand our ground with her. We can't wimp out, even if she gets huffy."

"Right."

"No chicken-shit stuff."

"Got it."

"Ready?"

"Yes, ma'am."

I rang the bell. A man answered. He was beefy, like Cherry, but without her generally pleasant disposition.

"Yeah?" was how he greeted us.

"We're here to speak to Cherry Queen," I announced.

"Who?" he said.

"Cherry Queen. She lives here. Tell her Elizabeth and Clover need to see her immediately."

"There ain't no Cherry Queen here," he said with a snarl. "*I* live here and I ain't in the mood for company."

"But we know Cherry lives here," Clover protested as he was about to slam the door in our faces. "We were with her earlier this evening, right in this very townhouse."

Just then the man was joined by three more men of similar size and demeanor. "If you two aren't out of my sight in about a half a second, me and my friends are gonna have to teach you how to act polite," he said. "When we're done doing that, we'll teach you how to show a man you're sorry. Ain't that so, boys?"

He and the boys nodded and drooled and did disgusting things with their tongues. I felt like I was in a scene from *Deliverance*.

I grabbed Clover's arm, told all four of them to go fuck themselves, then ran with her out to the parking lot.

"I don't understand," she said, really sobbing now. "Who were those men?"

"Who cares? The point is that Cherry doesn't work alone," I said. "She's got partners."

"Fine. So when we call the police, we'll have *all* of them arrested."

"We can't call the police, Clover. If we did, we'd have to admit that we hired a hit woman to find a man who's wanted in six states. That won't reflect well on us, trust me."

Her knees got wobbly then, as if she were about to faint, but I caught her in time and cradled her in my arms. "It'll be okay," I said, trying to soothe her.

"How?" she wailed, her tears soaking my shirt. "How will it be okay, Elizabeth?"

"I don't know, but we can't give up."

"*I* can. I can divorce Bud and move back to Kentucky."

"Oh, Clover. Please don't say that. I would miss you terribly if you left L.A. I couldn't have gotten through all these months without you. I need you to stay."

She picked her head up off my shoulder. "You do?"

"Of course. We're a team. We may not be the smartest team, but we're a team."

She nodded, wiping her eyes with the pretty white lace handkerchief she'd pulled out of her pocket. One of Mama's, I guessed. "Seriously, what will we do now?" she said. "How will we ever get the antidote? It's going to take a miracle to find Farkus."

"Then we're home free. I believe in miracles," I said, partly to cheer her up and partly because I did.

CHAPTER TWENTY

Needing money more than ever, I called Preston, prepared to pester him about sending me back out on inspections. But to my surprise and relief, I didn't have to pester him, because he was about to reinstate me anyway.

"The gentleman we used in your place wasn't up to the task," he explained. "He simply didn't have your discerning eye, and he certainly didn't have your creativity in testing the concierges."

"Thank you, Preston. I take that as a compliment."

"As well you should, dear." So he was back to calling me "dear." I was thrilled that he had come around. Now I'd be able to put at least *something* into my pathetic bank account. "Getting down to business, we have a property in Palm Beach we'd like you to inspect. It's the Seaborne Resort, a brand-new hotel with both individual villas on the beach and guest rooms in a twenty-story high-rise. It's got four restaurants, a golf course, tennis and croquet courts, the usual. You've probably heard about it through the grapevine. In any case, they've requested an inspection, and I'd like you to handle it, Elizabeth."

"I'm happy to, Preston." An understatement. "Leave it to me."

"I'd like to do that. Keep in mind, though, that you're on a probation of sorts. After those miscues of yours, you'll have to be on your toes from now on. No trouble, or I'm afraid we'll have to end our association with you."

"Everything will go smoothly," I pledged. "No trouble whatsoever."

All the buildings at the Seaborne Resort were pink—as pink as the pants worn by many of the men, who also wore green blazers and white shoes. The other thing I noticed right away was the attitude on the part of the staff, all of whom were snippy, snobby, just *too* pleased with themselves.

"Ms. Stickler, good afternoon," said the woman at the registration desk upon my check-in. She was so chilly my teeth chattered. "Lovely to have you stay with us at the Seaborne." Liar.

"It's lovely to be here, especially after the long flight," I said. "Is my room ready?"

"Let me see." She played with the computer, then glanced up at me. I could tell by her forced smile that the news wasn't good. "Apparently, the previous guest had asked for a late check-out," she said. "Housekeeping is doing the room as we speak."

"In other words, the room isn't ready," I said.

"No, but if you'd like to have tea and pastries in our Seaborne Club—complimentary, of course—I'll have the bellman store your luggage and let you know when the room has been cleaned."

"Why not just put me in another room?"

"I'm afraid there aren't any other partial oceanfront rooms available in the Tower. We're sold out in that category."

"Then upgrade me to an oceanfront room. Or switch me to a beach villa." No, I wasn't being a ballbreaker. Upgrades were commonplace at Five Key properties.

"I'm not permitted to do that, Ms. Stickler. Your room will be ready in just a few moments. Please enjoy some tea and pastries with our compliments. Again, our apologies."

Okay, missy, but I really wish you'd given me the upgrade. For your hotel's sake.

I trotted off to have the tea and pastries, which were well prepared and presented and accompanied by a serenade from a string quartet, but where was the local ambience? Where were the Key Lime tarts, the fruity drinks with little umbrellas, the steel drums? The Seaborne could have been in London, for God's sake.

After I'd been alerted that my room was ready—it had taken them a full hour to make this happen, which virtually eliminated the Seaborne from Five Key contention—I was gathering up my purse and getting up to follow the bellman when I spotted a woman who looked familiar. She was wearing a wide-brimmed straw hat and large, dark sunglasses and I could hardly make out her features, but there was something about her that rang a bell.

She's probably one of those Palm Beach socialites that are always turning up in magazines, I thought, trying to keep pace with the bellman, who needed to be told to slow down. Another demerit.

When he brought me up to my room, I discovered that the "partial" in partial ocean view was a wild understatement. My windows looked out over the garbage dumpsters, with only a hint—I mean a sliver—of the blue ocean beyond. What a disappointment.

I called downstairs to complain and was told, once again, that the hotel was "sold out in that category" and that an upgrade wasn't possible. I could have requested to speak to the manager, but why bother? This was the treatment the average guest would get—the treatment I was obligated to report.

I fished my Standards Manual out of my bag and wrote up my evaluation of the room, then phoned the concierge.

"Yes, Ms. Stickler. This is William. How may I help?"

"Well, I'm embarrassed to say that I forgot my husband's birthday. It's tomorrow and I haven't bought him a gift."

"My, that *is* unfortunate." He said this mockingly, as if he couldn't care less about me or my husband. "Is Mr. Stickler here at the hotel with you?"

No, he's in L.A., probably fending off the advances of an entire harem, I thought. "No, he's home in California," I said. "I really wish I could send him something that would arrive tomorrow."

"Well, we don't have to be a rocket scientist to figure this one out, do we?" He was unbearable. So condescending. "It's five o'clock, and Federal Express doesn't pick up until six. Plenty of time for you to go shopping. We can have you stop by our arcade here at the hotel, or we can pop you into our complimentary shuttle bus that takes our guests to Worth Avenue."

Nobody was *popping* me anywhere. He didn't get it. "I don't feel up to leaving the room just now. I was hoping *you* could buy the gift for my husband, William." Because that's what concierges offer to do. The nice ones.

"Oh. All right. What would you like me to buy? We have golf sweaters with our logo on them, down in the arcade."

"No, he's not a golfer, he's a bowler." I went this route frequently when I played Torture the Concierge. It was an excellent test for a hotel like the Seaborne, which allowed its employees to snub guests who weren't royalty. "Yes, I think I'd like you to buy him a new pair of bowling shoes. I know his size, so it shouldn't be a problem. All you have to do is contact the local bowling alley. They usually sell the shoes, the balls, everything."

"You want me to do business with a bowling alley? I'm not sure there *are* any in Palm Beach. It's just not that kind of town."

"And what kind of town might that be?"

"It's not Akron, I'll tell you that."

"I understand," I said, understanding that William was costing his manager another Key.

"But how about an ascot for your husband?" he suggested.

I declined as politely as I could, given that he was a pompous ass, and noted the incident in my manual.

Dinner was as un-Florida as the tea and pastries experience. Virtually every menu entrée was a fussy, dated, fifties-type dish with a capital letter in it—veal Oscar and beef Wellington and chicken Divan. What's more, the waiter asked me which "starch" I wanted, rice or potato. We weren't talking about a cutting-edge restaurant, let's put it that way.

Over coffee, I surveyed the other guests, and as I was doing so, my eyes landed on the same woman I'd been curious about earlier. She was sitting across the room, too far away for me to get a good look at her, and she was dining with a much younger man. (I figured her for sixty-something and him for thirty-something. He was young enough to be her son is what I'm insinuating.) Who is she? I wondered, certain that I'd seen her before. And why is it bugging me that I can't identify her?

She left the dining room minutes after I'd noticed her; otherwise I would have skirted past her table and given her a discreet glance or two. Maybe I'll see her again while I'm here, I thought, sipping the last of my coffee. Or maybe her name will just come to me, the way names often do.

✧

The next morning, I inspected the rest of the hotel—inside and out—and was about to go back up to my room to change into my bathing suit when I saw the woman again. She was walking toward the spa, sporting the same floppy hat and dark glasses as the day before. It was almost as if she were in disguise and didn't want anyone to guess her identity, which, of course, made me want to guess it all the more.

But I *have* met her, I confirmed, deciding that it was her mouth or her expression or her body language that I recalled from a previous encounter. The question was, *Where* had I met her? Through AMLP? At one of Brenda's *In the Know* shindigs? In Roger's office? At Clover's house?

Clover. Yes. The woman had something to do with Clover. I was getting warmer now. I could feel it. She was Clover's—what? Friend? Neighbor? Bible studies group leader? I couldn't remember, couldn't place the face, and it was driving me nuts for some reason.

I was sufficiently fixated on solving the puzzle—and not especially dying to test out the Seaborne's swimming pool—that I postponed my plans to go up to the room to change clothes and instead followed the woman into the spa pavillion.

Why not? I thought as I remained several steps behind her. I'm required to inspect *all* the hotel's facilities.

I pulled open the door to the spa and entered the building, just in time to watch the woman being escorted down a long hallway. So near and yet so far.

"Hello," said a receptionist in a pastel pink tunic that was clearly the Seaborne's signature shade. "Which of our services can we interest you in today?"

"I'll have what *she's* having," I said, nodding in the direction of the mystery woman. I'd never be able to catch up to her if I didn't hurry. She had a significant lead on me already.

"Beautiful," said the receptionist, who was much friendlier than the concierge. "May I have your name, please?"

"Elizabeth Stickler," I said quickly and told her my room number.

"Beautiful," she said again. "You're going to love the treatment you've chosen, Ms. Stickler."

"I'm sure I will," I said. "So let's get the show on the road, okay?"

"I'm delighted that you're so eager," she said. "You must have read about us in the women's magazines. There's a reason why they call the treatment the 'ultimate facial.' It's incredibly nourishing and rejuvenating for the skin—as good as a face-lift."

"Oh," I said warily. "I'm not ready for a face-lift. At least not yet." I was only in my thirties, not my sixties, like the woman I was tailing, the woman who was probably reclining on a table right that very minute.

She smiled. "I'm exaggerating. It's just a facial. But it's our Four-Level Facial, our top-of-the-line item. You'll feel like a new person when you leave here."

Little did I know how prescient that remark would turn out to be.

After I finally got her to can the selling job (she was sweet, but I was in a hurry, as I said), I was shown to the women's locker room and instructed to change into the spa's robe and slippers. Once in my pretty pink outfit, I was placed in the care of Giselle, my "aesthetician," who led me to one of the facility's five "gender-specific" spa rooms.

"Oh!" I said, when I saw a body lying on a table being ministered to by another facialist. "I hadn't expected to share a room."

"They should have told you up front," said Giselle. "All of our facial rooms are for two people. Is that all right with you, Ms. Stickler?"

"Sure," I said, checking out my roommate. I wondered if she could be the mystery woman, but there was no way to tell, since her head was wrapped in a towel turban and her face was covered in God knows what. "Is she having the Four-Layer Facial too?" I whispered. There was a New

Age-y CD playing. I got the sense we were supposed to meditate, not make chitchat.

"Yes, she is. Now, let's get you comfortable—and *quiet.*" Giselle adjusted my position on the table until I was flat on my back and absolutely still.

"First, I will apply the milk blend," she said, massaging a cool liquid into my skin. I felt my eyelids grow heavy and my muscles slacken.

"Next comes the seaweed mask . . ."

I was getting sleepy, very sleepy.

"And now the enzyme mask . . ."

Bliss, total bliss.

"And finally the mud mask, which will seal in and enrich the previous layers as it dries and hardens. Just relax and contemplate your serenity while your skin's cells are being reborn. . . ."

Whatever. Nighty night.

I was splayed out on that table, motionless, mindless, my face buried under a thousand pounds of goo, when I was roused out of my stupor by the voice of the woman next to me.

"I nearly fell asleep," she was telling her facialist. "Is it time to clean me up now?"

My God! I knew that voice! It was lilting, rich, singsong, and very, very familiar. There was no doubt that I'd heard it before.

I realized in short order that she *was* the mystery woman and that I'd been lying next to her for nearly an hour.

I lifted my head, which was tougher than it sounds, and studied her—with zero results. Her face was still covered in mud, among other treasures of nature. I would have to wait until she was wiped up.

I felt a tightening in my chest while I watched from my prone position as her facialist lifted off the now-dried mud mask, removed the remaining debris, and applied some moisturizer.

Just let me see her already, I wanted to shout, becoming extremely impatient. As I said, I didn't know why her identity mattered so much to me, but it did.

"All finished," said her facialist at long last.

"Thank you, Paloma. That was wonderful," said the woman.

I jerked my head up again to get a good look at her nourished and rejuvenated face, and when I did, I couldn't believe my eyes.

"Andrea!" I said.

At the sound of her name, she gave me a sidelong look. Then, as if the very last thing she wanted was to be recognized, she hopped off the table and fled the room.

"Andrea! Wait!" I cried out, hopping off my own table. "You can't just rush off like that! I've been searching everywhere for Dr. Farkus!"

"Ms. Stickler," said Giselle with dismay. "You mustn't leave before the treatment is finished. Your mud mask hasn't dried yet and you still have—"

I paid no attention and took off after Andrea. I couldn't go very fast—those terry slippers they give you at spas don't provide much traction—but I was in hot pursuit of Farkus's receptionist and nothing was going to stop me. After all the miserable months, all the dead ends, I'd finally gotten lucky. I wasn't about to give up now.

My face caked with mud, I chased Andrea out of the spa and across the pool deck and into the lobby of the hotel. We were quite a sight in our robes and slippers, as you can imagine. *I* must have been especially entertaining.

I'm not letting you get away from me, I vowed as I huffed and puffed to keep up with her. She was in better shape than I was, probably because she'd been *enhanced* by one of Farkus's potions. But I had a lot of incentive to catch her—she was going to save my marriage, whether she liked it or not.

She headed out of the lobby and straight into the Seaborne Club, where I'd been served the tea and pastries the previous afternoon. The string quartet abruptly stopped playing when they saw us racing through the room.

"You might as well throw in the towel!" I called out to Andrea, which was ironic, since I was the one still wearing the towel around my head. "You're not getting away from me! Not until we talk!"

"There's nothing to talk about!" she yelled back. "Leave me alone!"

"No way!"

I was gaining on her, I really was, when I inadvertently slammed into a waiter carrying a serving of vanilla ice cream. A guest must have requested his pastries à la mode, but *I* was the one who was à la moded. Upon impact, the bowl of ice cream glommed onto my face. I was now a human dessert—a mud pie, to be specific.

I apologized to the waiter—to everyone in the Seaborne Club, in fact—and continued on, picking up speed in order to narrow the gap between Andrea and me. I did not think about the scene I was creating or that Preston might hear about it or that I would flunk my probation. I thought about Roger, about undoing the wrong I'd done.

Andrea flew out of the building and onto the nearby golf course. The foursome that was standing on the green, about to putt, nearly croaked when they saw our twosome charging toward them. It was at that point that my mud mask finally hardened and cracked, a chunk of it falling off my face into the cup. In unison the golfers shouted, "A hole in one!" as I dashed past them.

I noticed that Andrea had lost a little steam then, which motivated me to run faster.

"Okay!" I called out. "The game's over!"

She didn't answer. She knew I was on the verge of overtaking her.

"It's over!" I said again, reaching out and grabbing the back of her pink robe. I tore the robe but held on to her. "You're not running anymore, Andrea."

"I told you to leave me alone, didn't I?" she said, her breathing coming in spurts. She was worn out and she knew it.

"I'm not leaving you alone. Not until you and I have a nice long chat."

"Why? What do you want? And how do you know who I am?"

"Questions, questions." I let go of her. "*I'm* the one who's asking the questions. And here's the first one: Where the hell is your boss?"

CHAPTER TWENTY-ONE

Nice digs," I said after poking around Andrea's beach villa, which was airy and spacious and sitting right on the sand. Of course, in keeping with the Seaborne's identity crisis, it was furnished with English-style wingbacked chairs instead of casual, island-y rattan, but I hadn't come to Andrea's villa to evaluate it; I'd come to interrogate *her*. "I take it from all this that business must be booming."

"What's that supposed to mean?" She was no longer the pampering, mothering, accommodating receptionist who had treated me so well at Farkus's office. She was a cranky, testy, suspicious woman who hadn't counted on running into one of his former patients in Florida.

"Well, these beach villas aren't cheap," I said, gesturing toward the spectacular view of the Atlantic. "I've got a hunch that you made off with a sizable bundle of cash when you beat it out of Beverly Hills."

"My finances are none of your concern."

"Ah, but you're wrong, Andrea. I'm concerned about everything that has to do with Gordon Farkus—or, should I say, with Jerry Sheck."

She gasped. "How do you know—"

"That he's been masquerading as someone else? As a doctor with degrees from Harvard and Yale? As an honest man instead of a crook? A little birdie told me."

"The police?"

"Good guess. I understand from the detectives in Beverly Hills that your pal Jerry is wanted in six states on a number of charges. Which makes you an accessory at the very least, Andrea." I scratched my face. My skin was itching like crazy after having left that mud mask on for so long.

"I had no idea what that man was up to, I swear I didn't. I only worked for him for a few months."

"Tell me another one."

"It's true."

"Then why didn't you go to the police when he skipped town? Why did you run off too? Now that I think about it, you and Jer are probably on the lam together. Maybe he's staying right here at the Seaborne, and you're in love *and* in cahoots."

"Please." She rolled her eyes. "He's young enough to be my son."

"That doesn't seem to be a problem for you. I saw you with a man in the dining room last night, and *he* was young enough to be your son."

She didn't respond, except to pout.

"Look, Andrea. I might as well be frank with you. I don't really care about the nature of your relationship with Sheck. I just care about finding him. If you tell me where he is, I'll forget we ever had this conversation."

"I don't know where he is."

"I don't believe you."

"That's your choice."

I sighed. Clearly, I had to take another tack with her. I decided to try the truth, possibly win her sympathy. I laid out the entire story of Roger and Bud—how Clover and I had given them three packets of the stud stimulant without their knowledge, and how we wanted—needed—the antidote in order to save our marriages.

"I'm begging you, Andrea." I was tempted to go down on bended knee, but I was exhausted after chasing her around the grounds of the Seaborne and chilled from sitting around all afternoon in that pink robe. "Can't you tell me where Sheck is? Can't you please?"

I examined her face to see if I'd moved her. I also checked to see if her skin looked nourished and rejuvenated. I couldn't tell on either count.

"It's a shame about you and your friend," she said finally. "But I can't help you."

I got angry. "You can't or you won't?"

"I don't know where Jerry is, all right?"

"But you know something. You wouldn't be hiding in Palm Beach if you didn't."

"What makes you think I'm hiding? Remember the young man you saw me with last night in the dining room? The one you said looked young enough to be my son? Well, he *is* my son. And he just happens to be the general manager of this hotel. I'm here because he invited me. How does *that* strike you?"

Her son was the manager of the Seaborne? That struck me as the best news I'd heard in a long time. I sensed a shift in the balance of power between Andrea and me. Suddenly, I was the one with the leverage.

"Thank you for sharing that little tidbit about yourself, Andrea," I said. "In return, I'm going to share a little tidbit about myself. My real name is Elizabeth Baskin, but the name I'm registered under is Elizabeth Stickler. And do you know why I'm using a different name as a guest of this hotel? Because I'm an inspector with AMLP, and we always travel anonymously."

"You're an inspector with AMLP?" She said this with genuine awe. As I've explained, the company has quite a reputation.

"Yes. I was assigned to evaluate the Seaborne, so here I am. Sad to report, my experience at the hotel thus far hasn't been positive, and my inclination is to give it a Four or even Three Key rating—certainly not the Five Key designation your son was banking on."

She gasped again. "But a Three or Four Key rating would kill the hotel's bookings. It might even cost my son his job."

I nodded. "I'm afraid you've hit the nail on the head, Andrea. High-end travelers won't even bother with a property that doesn't have Five Keys from AMLP. Not when they can afford—and demand—the ultimate in luxury and service."

She was silent for several seconds, mulling over my remarks. "I still can't help you," she said eventually.

"Why is that?"

"Because I don't know where Jerry is, as I've already told you."

"But you're not a complete innocent in this, are you, Andrea? You wouldn't have left town if you were, as *I've* already told *you*."

"I left town to visit my son," she maintained.

"Oh. So then it's okay with you that I place a call to the Beverly Hills police? They'd be very interested in getting a tip about where you are. They're putting together quite a case against Sheck, and they'd be thrilled to have one of his accomplices locked up."

When she didn't answer, I picked up the cordless phone in her villa, dialed information, and asked for the number of the Beverly Hills P.D.

"Don't!" She rushed up behind me, grabbed the phone out of my hand, and placed it back on the table. "Don't," she said again, more softly this time.

"Why not?" I said, watching her sink into a chair in defeat.

"Because I don't want to testify against Jerry," she said. "He's broken the law—we both have—but he's a decent man. He's trying to improve the quality of life of his patients."

"How touching."

"I'm serious. He's a magician in a way. He transforms people."

"Yeah, well, now he'd better un-transform people. Two of them, to be specific. Tell me where he is so I can get that antidote."

"I don't know where he is, but I—"

"Baloney," I cut her off.

"I was about to say that I don't know where he is, but I do have what you want."

"Excuse me?"

"Listen, Elizabeth. While I think Jerry is a wonderful healer, I can't become involved in some awful criminal trial. There's my son and his family to think of, as well as my own sanity. I have to protect myself in the event that the police do come after me. And the way to do that, I decided, is to hang on to Jerry's preparations. What I'm telling you is that I've got the antidote."

Now it was my turn to sink into a chair. "You've got the antidote?"

She nodded. "I figured that if the cops ever try to implicate me in this mess, I should have evidence against Jerry so I can cut a deal with them. You know, trade information for a lesser charge?"

"Yes, I know all about that." Too well. "But you couldn't possibly have stolen all those files out of the office and stored them someplace, could you? Not by yourself."

"I didn't steal the files. Not the hard copy anyway." She rose from her chair, went into the bedroom, and returned holding something in her hand. "But I did steal the recipes for the preparations as well as their antidotes and stored them on this."

She opened her hand to show me.

"They're on your Palm Pilot?" I said, my jaw dropping.

"Every single one. I had them on my big computer and then downloaded them onto my Pilot."

I was amazed by her revelation. "This is fantastic," I said. "But where are the actual herbs? The recipes are useless without them."

"Oh, no you don't." She wagged a finger at me. "You're not getting near the herbs until I get something from you."

"Which is?"

"A Five Key rating for my son's hotel."

Well, I'd figured this was coming. I'd hoped it was coming. It was the miracle I'd been praying for, the miracle I'd promised Clover. But if I gave the Seaborne its Five Keys when I believed that it deserved Three, I would be compromising my professional integrity, not to mention giving Preston a reason to fire me once and for all.

"Those are the terms," said Andrea. "You guarantee that the Seaborne gets a Five Key rating from AMLP, and I'll guarantee that you get your antidote."

"I need two antidotes. One for me, one for my friend."

"Two antidotes it is."

"And they're gratis. I'm not spending a cent on any more potions."

"Gratis? The herbs are expensive. They—okay, fine. Gratis."

Finally, I was saving money on this whole affair. "You must love your son very much to take such a risk," I said. "I could go straight to the police with the evidence you're giving me."

"You must love your husband very much to take such a risk," she countered. "You could lose your job if your boss finds out you've accepted a bribe."

So I'd lose my job, I thought. I'll have Roger back, my sweet, forgetful, rumpled Roger. He was far more important to me than AMLP; he was everything to me, in fact, and I'd never felt it as keenly as I did at that very moment.

"Here's the plan," I said. "I'm due to check out of here at nine o'clock tomorrow morning, by which time I will have written up my evaluation giving the Seaborne its Five Keys and sent the report off to my regional director. In exchange, by nine o'clock you will have delivered to me two antidotes, prepared and packed up and ready to administer. Do we understand each other?"

"We do."

"And you're absolutely, one-hundred-percent sure you know which herbs to mix together in which quantities?"

"I assure you, I have Jerry's recipe for the stud stimulant antidote, down to the last detail."

"Then I'll see you bright and early tomorrow morning."

"Right."

"Oh, there's one other thing I'd like to get off my chest, Andrea. I lied when I said that I was referred to Dr. Farkus by Goldie Hawn. I've never met her."

"From the sound of it, you've been doing a lot of lying, and you'd better be prepared to do some more. Once you give your husband the antidote and it cancels out the effects of the stud stimulant, he's going to express confusion about his recent behavior, and that confusion will prompt a barrage of questions. 'Why are there so many new suits in my closet?' he'll ask you. 'Why have I been spending so much time at the gym?' 'Why is there an attractive woman who thinks I'm leaving you for her?' Yes, Elizabeth, there *will* be such a woman. She's an inevitable consequence of the stud stimulant. What will you tell him about her? How will you explain?"

I didn't have an answer. I would cross that bitch when I came to her.

✧

At eight-fifteen the next morning she knocked on my door.

"Andrea," I said. She was carrying a pink Seaborne beach bag, and after I let her into my room she reached into it.

"Your antidotes," she said, holding up two packets of herbs. When I tried to swipe them, she pulled them back. "Uh-uh-uh. First things first. Let's see your evaluation."

I handed her the written report of my inspection. Her eyes followed the words down to the end of the last page, where, on the bottom line, it read "Recommendation: Five Keys."

"Satisfied?" I said.

"Very," she said.

"You should be. The Seaborne is far from perfect. Most of the people who work here have major attitudes, and the restaurant sucks."

"Not according to AMLP. They're giving it their top rating. Haven't you heard?"

"Yeah, yeah. Let's have the antidotes."

She turned them over to me. I sniffed the packets. "How do I know this is the good stuff?" I said, sounding like a drug dealer. "It could be dried oregano from the spice rack in the hotel kitchen."

"You'll just have to trust me."

"Not a chance." I'd learned my lesson from the Cherry Queen experience. "No. What I'll do is give the contents of one of the packets to my husband and see what happens. If there's no change in him, I'll not only call the police and tell them everything I know about you, I'll call my regional director at AMLP and tell him I made a mistake about the Seaborne."

"That won't be necessary," she said. "Those are the antidotes. Really. I'm not that stupid. I'm aware of what's at stake here."

"Good. How long will it take for them to work?"

"About a week to ten days. Your husbands should be un-enhanced by then."

"But will they *stay* un-enhanced? When Farkus—Sheck—sold us the stud stimulant, he said its effects would last for ten to twelve months. So how about the antidote? My friend and I need a permanent solution to our problem, Andrea."

"Once your husbands ingest the new preparation, it will expel the stud stimulant from their system. In other words, the antidote *is* permanent. Your worries are over."

"Well," I said, slipping the packets into my purse, "I guess this is goodbye, Andrea."

She smiled. "Thank God. I couldn't take another race through the lobby. You really tired me out."

I smiled too. "Why don't you head over to the spa for a massage? As long as you're here, you might as well take advantage of the facilities."

She nodded and left. Within the hour, I was at the airport in Palm Beach, anticipating my flight home to Roger.

We're almost there, my love, I thought, as I waited to board the plane. Within a week to ten days, our lives will return to normal.

CHAPTER TWENTY-TWO

"She just *gave* them to you?" said Clover after I hurried over to her house that afternoon and dangled the packets in front of her eyes.

"I had to do a little favor for her in return," I said, "but it's nothing for you to bother about." Why make her feel guilty about the fact that I'd virtually guaranteed my own dishonorable discharge from AMLP if Preston learned the truth about the Seaborne? It was my problem, not hers.

"And she didn't charge you for the antidotes?"

"Not a penny."

"Incredible." Clover giggled. "Deep down, Andrea is probably one of those women who commits crimes but has a heart of gold, bless her heart."

"Probably." As I said, there was no point in forcing her to face the harsh realities of life. "So, here's your antidote." I handed her one of the packets. "We're supposed to give them a week to ten days to work."

"Oh, Elizabeth." She hugged me. "Thanks for helping me get my Bud back. I owe you so much."

"Just keep on being my friend," I said, remembering Andrea's words of warning about the challenges that lay ahead, particularly the challenge involving the woman Roger may have led on while he was under the influence. "I have a feeling we're going to need each other now more than ever."

"Why? I thought our troubles were over."

I patted her. "Let's hope."

We each slipped the herbs into our husbands' juice the next morning. And then we waited. A week passed. Clover called to report no change in Bud's behavior.

"No change in Roger's either," I said. "Maybe it'll take another few days."

We waited and waited. And then we hit paydirt. I did, anyway.

I was in bed one night, reading. It was ten o'clock and I didn't expect Roger home for hours, given his boundless energy, so when I heard the garage door open, I was somewhat startled. A few minutes later, he walked into the bedroom and plunked himself down on the side of the bed next to me.

"Boy, am I tired," he said.

Tired? Roger, the super stud? "You do look a little ragged," I remarked. He had dark circles under his eyes and his hair was wildly disheveled. And, in a complete one-eighty from recent months, his clothes were wrinkled, his shoes scuffed, and his hands dirty. Upon closer inspection, I noticed that there was a large pink stain on his tie.

"I worked like a dog today," he said. "There was meeting after meeting in the office. If I never see another real estate contract, it'll be okay with me."

I cocked my head to get a better look at him, to try to judge whether I was witnessing the effects of the antidote or whether his comments were merely idle chatter. "So you didn't go to the gym today?"

"No. Who had time?"

"Or go shopping?"

He laughed. "I've got enough clothes to open a store of my own. I don't know why I've been on such a shopping kick. It's not like me, is it?"

I didn't answer, couldn't answer. I was transfixed by what I was seeing and hearing.

"I didn't even have time to leave the office for lunch," he went on. "I gulped down a sandwich at my desk."

"A sandwich?" He'd been eating salads ever since he'd started obsessing about his weight.

"Yeah, a pastrami on rye with Russian dressing."

Russian dressing. That explained the pink stain on his tie. But the pastrami was the real shocker. Before the antidote, the only meats he allowed himself were fish and chicken. I had my proof! My Roger had returned!

"How was your day, hon?" he asked, leaning over to finger-comb my hair off my forehead and then plant his lips there. The tenderness of the gesture nearly reduced me to tears. He hadn't kissed me like that, so warmly, so affectionately, since the stud stimulant had taken effect. It had certainly fired up his libido, rendering his kisses raw, hot, passionate, but it had taken away his gentleness, his humanity, and I'd missed that, missed all the qualities about Roger that had made me fall in love with him in the first place. How sad, I thought, as he caressed my face. What a fool I was.

"My day?" I could barely get the words out. I was trying so hard to keep my feelings in check. "It was fine."

"You know, I never asked you—how was that hotel in Florida you went to?" he queried. "Was it up to AMLP's standards?"

"Let's just say that it's getting a Five Key rating."

"Hey, it must be quite a place then. You're a pretty tough critic, Elizabeth."

I suddenly remembered that Brenda had described me in similar terms the night she'd come over for dinner and floated the theory that Farkus's potion had projected my overly judgmental personality onto Roger, that I was not only a tough critic but an unreasonably tough critic. Was that how he viewed me too? Was that who I'd become? Had my childhood—all those years of chaos and upheaval—shaped me into a person who was incapable of leaving well enough alone? Of leaving my husband's flaws alone? Of loving him unconditionally the way the men in my mother's life never seemed to love her? Yes, some of my complaints about Roger had been valid, I knew, but why had I chosen such a wrong-headed solution to our problems?

I lay there in that bed, attempting to sort out my feelings. Roger kept asking me what was wrong and I kept saying it was nothing.

"It can't be nothing," he said after a while. "I may not be the most observant husband in the world, but I can see that you're upset, Elizabeth."

"I'll be fine," I said, trying to pull myself together. "I guess I'm tired too."

"Then let's go to bed," he said, loosening his tie and taking off his clothes and letting them fall to the floor in a heap. No folding. No straightening. No checking for lint. Instead, he got under the covers and snuggled up next to me.

"This is a early night for you," I said, as he rubbed his toes against mine.

"It is, isn't it? I've been quite the night owl lately. God knows why."

I knew why, but I couldn't explain it to him. I would never tell Roger the truth. I couldn't. Now that I had him back, I could hardly risk losing him for good, could I?

"Elizabeth?"

"Yes, Roger?"

"It isn't just that I've been staying out late at night and leaving the office to go shopping and paying more attention to my appearance, is it? It's that I've been acting like an ass. Admit it."

When I started to protest, to stop him from what I prayed would not be an endless string of questions about his behavior, he silenced me with a kiss and continued on. "Maybe I've been in the throes of a midlife crisis, although I'm not sure I'm old enough for that."

"Sure you're old enough," I said offhandedly, desperate not to have this discussion. "People can have a midlife crisis at any age. Men, especially. You hear about it all the time—the sports cars, the workouts, the bimbos."

"The bimbos." He flinched, as if he were expecting a fight. "I wasn't unfaithful to you, Elizabeth. I swear on my life I wasn't."

"I didn't say you were."

"I know—look, I probably shouldn't be telling you this, because you're my wife and I don't want you to think you can't trust me—but it's just that for some reason, maybe the midlife crisis, I've been spending time with certain women, women I wouldn't have dreamed of bothering with. They seemed attracted to me and I was flattered by that and I might have let them believe—oh, I don't know what I'm talking about, I really don't. And I don't want to hurt you."

"You're not hurting me." Not now, not anymore. You're back, and that's what's important.

"I'm glad, because you're the person I need to confide in, the only person I can turn to—" He paused, as if he wasn't sure how to proceed. "Please shut me up if you think I sound completely off-the-wall, Elizabeth, but the situation is this." He paused again to take a few deep breaths. "Sometimes, over the course of the last few months, I've actually felt like I was someone else—the same me but stuck in some jerky guy's body."

"I don't—"

"No, let me finish. On these occasions, I'd do or say something totally self-serving and then kind of step outside of myself and go, 'What were you thinking, Roger?' It's been a weird time for me, really weird."

"How perplexing," I said, playing along, "but you've given me the impression that this 'stage,' or whatever you want to call it, is over. So why don't you just relax and forget it ever happened?"

"Forget it ever happened?"

"Yes. As long as you're feeling all right now."

"Wow. That's a switch. Usually you're the one who's in favor of analyzing everything."

"Maybe, but let's not analyze this. Okay, Roger?"

"Then you believe me when I say I didn't cheat on you with those women? I may have acted inappropriately, and if I did, I'm sorry, but I didn't have sex with them. Tell me you accept that."

"Of course I do." I had to. I was the one responsible.

"I can't get over how well you're taking this. I was all set to schedule a session or two with a shrink so that I could—"

"No shrink necessary." I put my arms around him and held him. "You just need a little TLC."

He smiled. "Is that what I need, Doctor?"

"Yes, indeed, Mr. Baskin," I said, sliding my hand under the covers in search of his Freddy. A little distraction, that's what he needed.

In an instant, the confusion, the befuddlement, the concern disappeared from his face and he moved closer. "I love you," he whispered. He kissed my neck, my chin, my cheeks, once again filling me up with his tenderness, and when his mouth found its way to mine, his fingers pried open the bottons of my nightgown. Suddenly, his hands were everywhere, moving slowly, sensuously, skillfully over my body, the tenderness building toward a more urgent desire.

"I love you too, Roger," I murmured. "More than you realize."

I wrapped myself around him, as aroused as I was grateful. Grateful that I had my husband back. Grateful that he had no idea what I'd done to him. Grateful that, with Farkus and Andrea out of the picture, there was no way for him to find out.

Life did return to normal—sort of. Yes, Roger came home after work every night instead of boogying on some dance floor until all hours, and when he did, he was his old sweet self—not the neatest English muffin eater, but that's what Dustbusters are for. The new wrinkle was that he was constantly bombarding me with anecdotes involving people who were reacting strangely toward him.

"David and Brad are barely speaking to me," he reported one evening. "The tension at the office is unbearable."

"Well, David's probably in a bad mood because he's between girlfriends," I said, hoping to skirt the subject.

"That's just it. He claims I actually caused his breakup with Lucy, the baby whisperer. You remember her, don't you, Elizabeth? She had the birthday party at David's house."

"Sure I do. During the car ride home from the party, I asked you if you found her attractive, and you didn't really have an opinion on the subject."

"Right. But I did have lunch with Lucy—one lunch. Do you mind that I'm telling you this?"

"You can tell me anything," I said. "But there's no reason to dwell on—"

"She called and invited me to lunch and I went. We had a fairly entertaining conversation and that was it. The next thing I knew, she was breaking up with David, and apparently he holds me responsible."

"His ego is bruised, that's all. He'll get over it."

"What about Brad? He seems to think that I've got the hots for Gerta. Isn't that ridiculous?"

"Totally."

"And yet he claims he caught us together in a compromising position. All I was doing at their house that afternoon was listening to her lecture me on the great artists of Europe. I don't know why I was there—as I told you, there have been moments over the past few months when I felt as if I were someone else—but Gerta must have given Brad the idea that I'm interested in her. Have you ever heard such nonsense?"

" 'Nonsense.' That's the perfect word for it. Now, why don't I pour you a drink and we can forget— "

"And that's not all," he went on, growing more agitated. "There's Carrie."

"What about her?"

"She's been acting like a cat in heat."

I chuckled. "Nothing new there, honey. She doesn't dress the way she does so she can spend her evenings alone."

"But she never used to come on to *me*, Elizabeth. I'm her law partner. It's unseemly for her to suggest that she and I have a relationship outside of the office."

I didn't have a quip for that one. I was out of easy answers for Roger. But he wasn't out of questions for me. Not by a long shot.

"There's this woman named Nikki," he said one night. "She was a client of mine. She sold her house in Westwood and I handled the closing."

"I remember, Roger. She's the Victoria's Secret model."

"Right. Do you also remember that she and I went club hopping a few times?"

"I do, but— "

"*Why* did I do that?" he demanded. "Why wasn't I club hopping with you? You must have hated me for that."

You bet I did. "No, honey. I was happy that you had someone to go with because I was a little under the weather a few months ago, remember? I had that thing."

"What thing?"

"That bug. I couldn't leave the house it got so bad."

"I don't—"

"It doesn't matter, because I'm fine now. But during that time that I couldn't leave the house, you and Nikki went dancing a few times and you really enjoyed yourselves. There's nothing wrong with that."

"Except that she keeps calling me, begging me to see her again. And I don't *want* to see her again, Elizabeth."

"It must be a chore to be so popular." I said this in a lighthearted manner, as a joke, to try to jolly him out of his dark mood.

"It isn't funny," he said. "There's another one."

"Another what?"

"Another woman who keeps calling me. Her name is Kim and she was a client too. She bought a house in Malibu and I helped her with—oh, wait. You met her. You and your friend Clover were dressed as surgeons for some costume party and you drove your van onto her front lawn as we were doing her walk-through."

"I remember her, Roger," I said, the guilt and the dread coming in equal waves. "She's very beautiful. Asian, right?"

"Yes. Well, I had a couple of lunches with her, spent time with her—innocent time—and now she's convinced I'm ready to divorce you and run off with her. What's *with* all these women? Are they nuts? It's not as if I'm some big stud."

Of course he was some big stud. Thanks to me and my brainstorms.

The next night, Roger was terribly upset about a conversation he'd had with Frankie's father, who had reappeared in the boy's life, as he often did, acting as if he'd never been gone.

"He was belligerent," Roger reported. "He accused me of not caring about Frankie because I missed so many dates with him. That's a lot of nerve, isn't it? He's the one who breezes in and out of the kid's life and *I'm* the villain?"

"The man's unstable and always has been," I said. "Don't pay any attention to him. You adore Frankie."

"Then why *did* I skip so many dates with him, Elizabeth? I know I did. I remember feeling crappy about it but doing it anyway. It's all part of this . . . this . . . weird period of my life. I just wasn't myself. That's the only way I can explain it."

Yes, yes, I felt horrible every time Roger brought up the subject of his "weird period," but I tried to tell myself that time would heal all wounds and that, eventually, his law partners, his women, Frankie's father would lose interest and find someone else on whom to focus their emotions.

In the meantime, I was dying to hear how Clover was faring with Bud now that he'd been un-enhanced, and so I met her for burgers at Kate Mantilini, a hot spot in Beverly Hills, not far from the scene of our crime.

"I'm getting all the questions too," she confirmed after I'd told her how Roger had been peppering me with them. "But the odd part is that Bud is still going to the opera and to the wine tastings and to the ballroom dancing lessons, and he's still cooking me dinner. I was sure he'd revert back to his old ways once I gave him the antidote."

"That *is* odd," I agreed. "I don't know what to make of it."

"All I can come up with is that Bud's a big, tall fellow. Maybe it'll take longer for the herbs to work their way through his body."

I was about to respond when I felt someone tap me on the shoulder. I turned around, and who was standing there smirking but Chris Eckersly, the jackass I'd declined to sleep with in Seattle.

"Hello, Elizabeth," he said, bowing slightly. "We meet again."

I was surprised to see him, to put it mildly. He was like a pebble you can't get out of your shoe no matter how hard you try. What the heck was he doing in L.A. again?

"Hello, Chris," I said, then introduced him to Clover as someone I'd met on one of my business trips. "What brings you back to our part of the country?"

"I couldn't stay away from you," he said, obviously getting a kick out of taunting me. I, on the other hand, was unnerved by the sight of him. Why would he keep showing up in L.A. when he lived in Kansas City? Or had he lied about that, the way he'd lied about being married? "How's hubby?"

"My husband is just fine, thanks," I said, wishing he'd move along.

"You tell him he's a lucky guy," said Chris. "Bye now, ladies."

He nodded at Clover and me and took off just as mysteriously as he'd appeared. The encounter was short but definitely not sweet. I didn't like the fact that he continued to turn up, seemingly out of the blue.

"Gee, he's too handsome for that brushoff you gave him," said Clover. "I wouldn't mind running into him in some hotel."

"Yes, you would," I said. "Believe me."

Apparently, it wasn't my day. When I got home from lunch and opened the mail, I found a letter from Art Yarnell. The first sentence, in which he called me a name that rhymes with "hunt," set the tone. It was clear that he had not been placated by my letter to him and was now feeling patronized as well as victimized. He vowed to make me pay—his familiar refrain. I crumpled the letter into a little ball and threw it in the trash. It was a nuisance, nothing more, I told myself. When I was a kid—a new kid in yet another new school—I used to get phony phone calls at night. The prankster would ask for me in a disguised voice, and when I came to the phone, he would curse at me. I was scared by the calls, afraid that the person would come to the house and harm me, but my mother said not to be. "The ones who call never do anything," she told me. "It's the ones who don't that you have to worry about." I assumed the same rule applied to letter writers.

✧

Roger and I had planned to have a quiet dinner together at home, and so I showered and primped and prepared for what I hoped would be a romantic evening. Ever since the antidote had reversed the effects of the potion, he and I had enjoyed a real closeness, a wonderful intimacy. We were friends as well as lovers, shared everything with each other (well, except for you-know-what), were partners in every sense of the word. It was almost as if we were newlyweds again—newlyweds who went to sleep before eleven.

"Hi, honey," I said, greeting him with a kiss as he entered the house. "Tough day?"

"Very, but I feel better already." He kissed me back. "Have I told you how great you've been over the last couple of weeks?"

"No, but I'm always up for a compliment."

"It's true, Elizabeth. I've been monopolizing every conversation lately, going on and on about the *phase* I went through and the fact that this person is mad at me now and that person is harassing me now, and yet you've been an absolute saint. You've listened. You've offered your opinion. You've made me laugh. You've helped me *relax*." His eyes twinkled when he said this, referring, I guessed, to our mutually satisfying sex life. "I just want you to know that I appreciate how supportive you've been and how patient. I love you. Very, very much."

"That was a beautiful speech," I said, resting my head against his chest, wishing I could capture the moment and freeze it in time. Yes, Roger and I were happier than ever, but I was living a lie. No matter how creatively I answered his questions, no matter how cleverly I changed the subject when I had to, no matter how carefully I navigated him through discussions of his "phase," I was living a lie and I was waiting to get caught. I just didn't expect to get caught that particular night.

We were sitting at the dining room table, eating the penne primavera I'd made (Roger not only didn't complain about the pasta being too soggy, he declared it the best he'd ever had and asked for seconds), when the doorbell rang.

"Who could that be?" he said.

I shrugged. "The kids who come around selling things are in bed by now. It could be the Jehovah's Witnesses though."

"Then ignore it. Maybe they'll go away."

If only I'd ignored it. When the doorbell rang again, I told Roger I thought I should see who it was. "Maybe it's Brenda," I said. "Maybe she spotted Barbra Streisand in the supermarket and drove over here to tell me."

"Barbra Streisand doesn't go to the supermarket," said Roger. "She has minions to buy her paper towels."

"She probably has minions to tell her minions to buy her paper towels."

We both had a good chuckle, then I walked toward the front door. I was still chuckling when I opened it.

" 'Evening, Mrs. Baskin."

I stopped chuckling. I nearly stopped breathing too. "Detective Wasluski. And Detective Dembo."

God, I couldn't believe they had just shown up like that. I had forgotten about them, to be honest. I had assumed they were pursuing their leads in the Farkus case and that was that. But now here they were, and I was seized with fear that my whole world was about to come crashing down on me.

"Who is it, honey?" Roger called out from the dining room.

"Nobody," I called back, then turned to the cops. "Couldn't you have called first?"

"You were charged with a felony, Mrs. Baskin," said Wasluski. "We don't have to be on our best behavior with you."

"Yes, but can't we do this another time? My husband and I are in the middle of dinner."

"Nope," said Dembo. "We've gotten some information about Jerry Sheck, and we need to check it out with you and Mrs. Hinsdale. We're paying her a visit next."

"She'll be thrilled," I said. "Look, I'm asking you nicely. Couldn't we do this tomorrow, when my husband will be out of the house?"

"Nope again," said Dembo. "You made a deal with us, Mrs. Baskin. If you don't like the terms, you can always go back to jail. I hear they've got a few vacancies."

"Hon? Everything all right?" Roger called out.

I couldn't answer him this time, didn't know how to. And when I didn't, he got up from the table and followed me to the door, his napkin still tucked inside his shirt collar. His pants, by the way, were dotted with tomato sauce.

"What's this?" he said when he saw the police officers. "Has there been a break-in somewhere?"

The cops looked at each other and laughed.

"Your wife's not the only one with a sense of humor," Dembo said to Roger. "But then you people probably think break-ins are one big joke."

"I don't understand," said my poor husband.

"Maybe Mrs. Baskin will explain it to you," said Wasluski.

CHAPTER TWENTY-THREE

The detectives' big news was merely that a private investigator, representing a disgruntled patient of Farkus's, had tipped them off to the pretend doctor's possible whereabouts, and they wanted Clover and me to stay in town should they need us as witnesses sooner than they thought. It could have been handled by a phone call. It should have been handled by a phone call. If it had been handled by a phone call, Roger wouldn't have sat there wondering what the hell was going on, and I wouldn't have been forced to tell him.

The challenge, I decided, once the cops had left and the moment of truth was upon me, would be to lay out the facts, all of them, no matter what Roger's reaction was. I owed him that much.

"I went to see this doctor," I began. We had moved back into the dining room, where our pasta looked timeworn, like Christmas trees after New Year's.

"Dr. Farkus, the one the detectives kept asking you about?"

"Yes. You see—"

"What kind of a doctor is he?"

"He calls his practice 'life enhancement.' "

Roger's left eyebrow arched. "You went to a doctor specializing in life enhancement? What in the world for? You don't need to be enhanced. You're fine the way you are."

Swell. So he was going to make this truly gruesome. I cleared my throat and ploughed on. "I went, Roger, because I thought *you* needed to be enhanced."

I let the words hang there, just for a second or two, figuring that if we got through that part—the part about my wanting to change him—the rest would be easier. It was wishful thinking, obviously.

"You'll have to explain that," said Roger. "I mean, really explain it."

"Yes, of course I will." I cleared my throat again. I was extremely nervous, and the throat clearing bought me some time to collect myself. "During the past year or two, I was feeling as if you had sort of shut down on a lot of levels. You didn't seem to care how you looked, how the house looked. You—"

"Give me a break, Elizabeth. This isn't about leaving crumbs on the floor, is it?"

"Only partially. The major issue was that you didn't seem to care that you were spending day and night at the office and then coming home in a coma, barely aware that I existed."

"Now, wait a minute."

"You said you wanted me to explain."

He shifted in his chair. "Go on."

"You didn't initiate conversation. You didn't listen when I'd try to talk to you. You weren't up for sex, at least not like you used to be. You'd sit in front of the TV and pass out most of the time."

"Okay, so this is all the stuff you were nagging me about. It's coming back to me now. You nagged me about it, and I resented it, resented you."

"You resented me and you withdrew from me, and I didn't know what to do about it. All I knew was that the man I fell in love with was slipping away, that our marriage was slipping away. I had to take some kind of action."

"This ought to be good."

"It isn't good, Roger. You have to prepare yourself for how good it isn't."

"I'm listening."

"Brenda told me about this doctor in Beverly Hills, a doctor with a very hush-hush practice. She said all the celebrities went to him. She said he created customized preparations for them, to help them with whatever problems they were having. She said that if I went to him and gave him a rundown of the things about you that needed enhancing, he would help me too."

"And you fell for that bullshit? I thought you were more sensible than that, Elizabeth."

"Usually I am, but I was very unhappy, very vulnerable. More importantly, I was very scared. I felt as if my husband—the engaging, attentive, sexy guy who'd rescued me on the 405—had deserted me, and I wanted him back."

He didn't say anything.

"I went to Dr. Farkus's office in Beverly Hills," I continued, "and that's where I met Clover. In the waiting room."

"You told me you met her at the health foods place."

"I lied." I'd been dreading this conversation for months, but now there was something liberating about finally having it, of cleansing myself of the lies that had been eating away at me. "She went to see Dr. Farkus because she thought Bud needed enhancing."

"*Enhancing*. You're both crazy. Why would anyone believe in that crap, let alone spend money on it?"

"As I was saying, we went to the doctor and told him about our problems with our husbands and he—"

"Let me guess. He gave you some exotic herbs and you mixed them into your orange juice and they were supposed to transform you into the perfect wives so we would pay more attention to you."

"Close."

"How close?"

More throat clearing. An actual coughing jag. "He gave us some exotic herbs and we mixed them into your orange juice and they were supposed to transform you into the perfect husbands so you would pay more attention to us."

He laughed. He thought I was kidding. "So the plan was that Bud and I would drink the herbs and immediately start cooking and cleaning and doing the laundry? Cut back on our jobs in order to conserve our energy for you and Clover? Be the ever-ready escorts? Service you sexually?" He laughed again.

"All of the above."

"Excuse me?"

"That was the general idea—that you and Bud would go back to being the men who courted us; the men who talked to us and listened to us and shared the household chores; the men who were up for going out at night instead of falling asleep in the Barcalounger; the men who made love to us, not once a month or, in our case, once every three months, but often and passionately."

The smile evaporated. "I didn't realize I was such a disappointment to you, Elizabeth. Apparently, I should have taken your complaints more seriously."

"Maybe you should have. Maybe if there'd been more communication between us this never would have happened."

"What wouldn't have happened?" He stared at me. "You didn't actually go ahead and buy any of this quack's herbs, did you? I just assumed that you were joking when you said you—"

"I gave you the herbs, Roger. I snuck them into your orange juice. I did."

He squinted at me. He seemed to be trying to determine if I was for real, if the words coming out of my mouth were for real. "You're telling me you put something in my juice behind my back, something you bought from this nut in Beverly Hills, something he ordered off the Internet, probably?"

"He ordered it from a rain forest in Central America."

"I don't believe this, Elizabeth. You thought I was such a dud that I needed enlightenment?"

"Enhancement."

"And then you were suckered into buying the product this guy was pushing and dumped it in my orange juice?"

"Yes, and it worked. It really did change you, Roger. Suddenly, you were calling me in the middle of the day to tell me you loved me. Suddenly, you were bringing me flowers. Suddenly, you wanted sex—any time, any place. Remember?"

He thought for a minute, some of our friskier couplings coming to mind, no doubt.

"But," I said, "just when I was congratulating myself on enhancing you, you became too enhanced. You had so much energy you began to wear me out. What's more, you started focusing on your own perfection, instead of concentrating on how you could be perfect for others. You bought tons of new clothes. You worked out nonstop at the gym. You got facials and manicures and—"

"And haircuts. Expensive haircuts."

"Yes." A flicker of understanding. It wouldn't be long before he processed it all. "Your personality and your values changed, along with your wardrobe. You were slacking off at work, rushing out to pamper yourself. You were picking on me at home, harping on every little thing I did. And you were ignoring Frankie, choosing to skip many of your dates with him so you could indulge your own pleasures."

"The women. You're referring to the women."

"Yes. After you became enhanced, you were like honey to the bees, Roger. They couldn't stay away from you. Not Nikki or Kim. Not Lucy or Carrie. Not even Gerta."

His expression was one of utter disbelief. "So it's because of *you* that they're all throwing themselves at me now?"

I nodded sheepishly.

"And it's because of *you* that David and Brad are furious at me?"

I nodded again.

"And it's because of *you* that Frankie's father accused me of being the scum of the earth?"

"Yes, but I—"

"So I went from being a fairly decent guy to a guy everybody's got a gripe against?"

"I wouldn't put it in quite those terms, but—"

"And the midlife crisis I've been moaning to you about, my self-described 'weird period,' was a result of your herbs?"

"Well, not *my* herbs. I was the one who gave them to you, but it was this doctor who—"

"Stop! Let me get this straight. You thought I was such a zero as a husband, as a *man*, that you sought medical help for me?"

"That's the thing. Farkus wasn't a medical doctor after all. He wasn't even named Farkus. That's why the police are after him, because his name is Sheck, and he's been pretending to be a doctor and practicing without a license and committing larceny as well as several types of fraud."

"That's great, Elizabeth. Just great. You sure know how to pick 'em."

I went back to nodding. And then I explained about wanting to nullify the effects of the herbs and breaking into Farkus's office with Clover and spending a weekend with her in the Beverly Hills jail.

"That was the weekend you claimed you and she were having a girls-only sleepover at her house," he said disgustedly.

"Yes." I held nothing back. I told him about trying to get the antidote, about Cherry, Andrea, all of it. "The only saving grace here is that you've responded to the antidote and reverted to your old self."

"The old self you were so intent on trashing. Some saving grace."

"Roger, please."

"Please what?" His eyes were brimming with tears now, and his voice was cracking. The net result of my truth telling was that I had shattered my husband's self-esteem, not to mention his heart. "Please don't be angry? Please don't be hurt? Please forgive you for betraying me? Is that what you were going to say, Elizabeth?"

He got up from the table, paced back and forth in front of my chair. He was breathing hard. He was wiping his brow. I had never seen him so upset. Never. I was dying to grab him and hold him and tell him I loved him, but he wouldn't have let me near him.

"You know what *really* gets me?" he said, half-yelling, half-gulping his words. "It's that I—oh, shit, this is the pits." He ran his hands through his hair, looked up at the ceiling. "It's that I understand why you were dissatisfied with me."

"You do?" This caught me by surprise.

"Yeah. I'm not a complete moron. I'm aware that I was burying myself in my job and avoiding intimacy with you. And I'm aware that I didn't give a damn about what I wore or how I wore it or whether or not I left a mess around the house. I forgot that marriage has to be worked at, Elizabeth. I took it for granted sometimes, took you for granted. I share the blame for letting the excitement fizzle out of our relationship."

Now I was the one who stared in disbelief. I never expected to hear him acknowledge his shortcomings.

"But so fucking what?" he said, finally making eye contact with me. "So I had faults. When you love someone, you accept that person, faults and all. That's what 'unconditional' means, Elizabeth. You've heard of that word, haven't you?"

"I—"

"See, the difference between us," he interrupted, "is that *I* loved you in spite of your imperfections and *you* didn't love me in spite of mine."

"But that's not how it was. I did love you, even though I—"

"Your imperfections, your character flaws, your high-maintenance personality," he muttered. "You think it's easy to live with a woman who would like to see 'Thou shalt not shed hairs' added to the Ten Commandments? You think it's easy to relax around someone who notices everything, scrutinizes everything, judges everything? You think it's easy to be married to a professional nitpicker? Well, it's not. It's not easy at all. But I loved you, in spite of your pickiness, your need to control, your need for order. I was willing to overlook your faults, to try to understand where they were coming from, instead of saying, 'Hey, Roger. How about making wholesale changes in Elizabeth so she'll turn into a perfect wife?' That would never have occurred to me. That just isn't what I'm about."

"Oh, Roger. I'm so sorry."

" 'Sorry' doesn't cut it."

"But I am. I've learned my lesson, I swear it. If I had it all to do over again, if I could rewind the tape, I would never have gone to Farkus, never have herbed you behind your back, never have jeopardized your trust in me. Please believe that."

"What I believe is that you're only sorry because you got caught."

"Oh, God. That isn't true."

"Isn't it?"

"No! I've changed, Roger. I'm not the woman I was when all this started. I don't want or need perfection anymore. I just want you. *I just want you.*"

I extended my arms to him, beseeching him to come into them, but he wouldn't, and the ache inside me, the emptiness, was unbearable.

"I can't talk anymore," he said after a long few minutes of silence. "I have to get out of here."

"What do you mean?" I panicked. He couldn't leave me. Not after what we'd been through. Not after we'd gotten everything out in the open.

"Just what I said. I need some time to myself."

"Out of the house? You're moving out?"

"Don't make this more dramatic than it already is, Elizabeth. I'm moving my things into the guestroom."

That was a relief. At least we'd be under the same roof and I'd have a crack at winning him back. "I'd like the opportunity to show you that I've changed," I said. "Promise me you'll give me that opportunity, Roger."

"I'm not making any promises," he said. "Not to you."

"But I *have* changed. I'm not the woman you were describing, the one who's so picky about everything, so perfectionistic. Not anymore."

He shook his head at me. "I don't see it, Elizabeth. I don't think you have it in you to change."

Following that parting shot, he stormed out of the dining room without even a backward glance.

Alone, shaken, miserable, I looked down at the table, at the hardened, uneaten pasta on the plates, and reminded myself to take it all into the kitchen and clean up.

Or maybe I wouldn't do any such thing.

Maybe I won't clean up until tomorrow, I thought. Maybe I'll let the food sit here, just let it get really funky.

"Yes, you're wrong about me," I said out loud, even though Roger was long gone. "I've changed and I'm going to prove it."

CHAPTER TWENTY-FOUR

While Roger and I continued to occupy the same physical space but rarely spoke to each other, Clover and Bud hadn't even had the big talk yet. He'd been at the theater the night Detectives Dembo and Wasluski stopped by to see her, and so she still hadn't told him the truth about Farkus.

"You really have to tell him," I said during a phone call. "There's always the chance that Roger will tell him. You don't want him to hear it that way, do you?"

"No. I'm just waiting for the right moment."

"There is no 'right moment.' He'll be upset no matter when you tell him, Clover."

Upset. The word wasn't strong enough. In the past, whenever Roger and I had a fight and then found ourselves in that awful aftermath, before the kiss-and-make-up took place, he would be all grumpy and pissy and sulky, and mutter at me under his breath. This time, there was a complete blankness about him, a deadness in his eyes. I'd pass him in the hall or cross paths with him in the kitchen, and he'd look through me instead of at me. I'd felt his anger before, but never this bitterness.

"Are we ever going to be okay?" I asked him as he was on his way out the door one morning.

"I'm not sure we ever *were* okay," he said in that horrible, detached tone he'd adopted.

"Of course we were, Roger, and we can be again. If only—"

Before I could finish my speech, he was gone.

I discussed the situation with Brenda over lunch at Pizzicotto, a cute little trattoria in Brentwood, not far from her condo.

"I've begged him to let me show him I've changed," I reported between forkfuls of pumpkin tortellini. "He won't listen."

It was my sister who wasn't listening. She was craning her neck to eavesdrop on the conversation going on at a nearby table.

"Brenda. I'm talking to you."

"Oh. Sorry." She leaned in and whispered, "I thought the blonde over there was Gwyneth Paltrow, but I was wrong."

"That must have been devastating for you."

"I *said* I was sorry."

"Right."

"Look, Elizabeth. If you promised him you've changed, then you've got to *prove* to him you've changed."

"Exactly. That's my game plan. The problem is, he acts as if I'm invisible. You can't prove anything to someone who refuses to acknowledge your presence."

"Then *make* him acknowledge it. This is no time for subtlety."

"Make him? How?"

"Well, he has a certain image of you—the same image we all have of you—that you're so compulsively neat and organized that you'd give your husband a potion to turn him into someone just as neat and organized.

Show him he's wrong, that you're not like that. And do it in a style that'll get his attention."

I was about to ask her for specific examples, but she was distracted again. The blonde at the nearby table *was* Gwyneth Paltrow, and Brenda was lost to me for the rest of the meal. Nevertheless, I took to heart what she'd suggested and came up with a few examples of my own.

The next morning, while Roger was sitting at the kitchen counter eating his English muffin and reading his newspaper, I toasted an English muffin for myself, pulled up a chair next to his, and chowed down. I made a conscious effort to get melted butter all over my hands and face and to leave those dreadful little seeds everywhere.

"So, Rogahw," I said unintelligibly, due to my mouthful of food. "Howdusleeplasnight?"

He glanced over at me, at the mess I'd made, but didn't seem particularly moved by it. "Fine," he said, and went back to his newspaper.

"See all the seeds?" I smiled widely, hoping for lots of muffin between my teeth. "Well, guess what? I'm not Dustbusting them up. I'm leaving them right there, for the entire day. Or maybe forever. Yes, I'm leaving them until they just disintegrate or get swallowed up by ants or grow into bigger seeds. Who cares? I don't. Not anymore. What do you think of that, huh?"

He thought I was pathetic, or so his expression indicated. Back to the drawing board.

When he got home that night, I had not only left the beds unmade, but I had tracked dirt from the garden all over the wall-to-wall carpet in the living room.

"Take a look at *this*," I said, pointing to the carpet stains. "But don't worry about it, because I'm not worried about it. In fact, I'm not even going to try to clean it up. I've decided that I sort of like the pattern it creates on the rug. It works for me in a comfy, lived-in kind of way."

"Elizabeth, really."

"What? I'm proving to you that I've changed, Roger. This is the new me, the me that has respect for the little messes of life."

"Congratulations," he said sourly and went straight to his bedroom.

I tried again. When he came home the next night, I handed him a Polaroid of an eight-week-old Irish setter.

"Isn't he the most adorable puppy you've ever seen?" I said with wild enthusiasm.

"What's this all about, Elizabeth?" said Roger.

"I went to the breeder," I said. "You've always wanted a dog—an Irish setter, especially. I thought I'd check and see whether she had any pups available, and she does."

"*You've* never wanted a dog."

"I know, but I've changed, as I've been telling you. I used to think dogs were messy, but now I understand that life is messy, that it's supposed to be messy. So what do you say? Should we bring this puppy home?"

Roger handed me back the photo. It was several seconds before he spoke. "These episodes of yours, Elizabeth, these attempts, these scenes . . ." He shook his head. "I realize that they're all about getting me to believe that you've changed—I'm not that dense. But what's keeping us apart has nothing to do with unmade beds or stains on the carpet or dog hairs on the furniture. It has to do with your inability to accept me as a fallible human being, to love me unconditionally despite my faults, to accept the fact that marriage isn't some fairy tale where everybody is beautiful and neat and tidy. You can talk all you want about your superficial changes, but how can I believe that you've changed in *here*?" He pointed to his heart. "How can I believe you've really given up your pursuit of perfection?"

He didn't wait for me to answer, not that I had an answer. The truth is, he wasn't far off the mark. Maybe I hadn't changed enough or in the right way. Maybe I still had work to do.

As luck would have it, I was forced to put my campaign for Roger on hold, temporarily, after receiving a phone call from Preston.

"Hello, Elizabeth dear," he said. "I've got another assignment for you."

"That's great," I said, happy to be back in his good graces. "Where am I off to?"

"New Orleans," he said. "You're going to inspect the new Worthington there. According to their promotional literature, this hotel is the jewel in their crown, the most luxurious in the chain. I wouldn't be surprised if you awarded it Five Keys, Elizabeth."

"It sounds heavenly," I said. "I can't wait to see it."

"Speaking of Five Keys," he said, "I've read several recent reviews of the Seaborne in Palm Beach, and they all came down rather hard on the hotel. Curious, isn't it? The fact that you recommended that it receive our highest designation and yet so many others have been less than complimentary about it?"

Swell. So it was only a matter of time before Preston found out that I took a bribe in exchange for the rating—an automatic and permanent heave-ho for an inspector. "It *is* curious," I said. "But evaluating hotels can be such a subjective process. Perhaps these other people brought their own prejudices with them to Palm Beach."

"Perhaps," said Preston. "If we begin to hear negative comments from our subscribers, however, we may have to give the Seaborne another look."

And give me my pink slip, I thought, crossing my fingers that he wouldn't probe any further into the Seaborne situation.

I left for New Orleans a week later. Roger bid me an unconvincing "Have a good trip" after I had asked him to use our few days apart to remember us the way we used to be, remember how much we loved each other. That was all I could do at that point—apologize over and over, plead with him to forgive me, remind him of better times. I took off for the Big Easy feeling that repairing our marriage would be anything but easy.

⟡

The Worthington New Orleans, like the Worthington Seattle, was a grand affair—a magnificent replica of an antebellum mansion combined with state-of-the-art amenities. Sitting majestically on legendary Canal Street, presiding over the Mississippi River and downtown shopping areas, it was a gorgeous property with enormous curb appeal. As I stepped out of the taxi, I had high hopes for its rating.

"Good afternoon, Ms. Stickler, and welcome to the Worthington Hotel New Orleans," said the registration clerk, who was professional, courteous, and neatly attired in her navy-blue uniform. She thanked me for coming, told me my room was still being cleaned, and, after apologizing for the inconvenience, announced that I was being upgraded from the deluxe room I'd reserved to a premier room in the Worthington Club, an entire floor of accommodations accessed by a special elevator key. "And please accept the champagne with our compliments."

"Champagne?" I said.

"Yes. Because of the inconvenience. I've just arranged for a bottle of Veuve-Clicquot to be delivered to your room. It should be chilling in your ice bucket by the time you get there."

"Thank you. That's very nice of you."

"Delighted to be of service."

Well, I thought, glancing at my watch. That was quite a check-in—mercifully brief and extremely gracious.

The bellman escorted me up to my premier room in the Worthington Club, and along the way he gave me a highly informative rundown of the hotel's amenities, as well as the options available to me should I be interested in exploring the city.

"If you're a museum person, there's the National D-Day Museum and the Memorial Hall," he said. "If you enjoy visiting historical sites, there's the French Quarter and the Natchez Riverboat. And if you're a music lover, well, New Orleans is the birthplace of jazz. There are jazz clubs galore here."

"I appreciate the information," I said.

"Delighted to be of service."

When we got to my room, I nearly died when I saw the size of it. It was twice as big as most hotel guest rooms and it overlooked the river.

"Is everything satisfactory, Ms. Stickler?" asked the bellman after guiding me through the room's various features.

"Very much so. Thank you," I said.

"Delighted to be of service," he said.

After he left, I began my inspection, noting in my manual that, among many other things, the AM/FM clock radio had a CD player built right in; the closet was supplied with extra pillows, both goosedown and foam; the sheets were one-hundred-percent cotton and bore the elegant "W," the Worthington's logo; and the bathroom, which was wall-to-wall marble, offered a complete line of Bulgari toiletries, generously sized terry bath towels, a lighted makeup mirror, a hair dryer, a razor, and a scale. I should add that the housekeeping was impeccable—not a stray hair in the place. As for the complimentary champagne, it was resting in its ice bucket, next to a small plate of truffles that were accompanied by a tasteful little note reading "Delighted to be of service."

Excellent on all counts, I wrote in my manual.

That evening, I dined at Frederick's Restaurant, named for the hotel's chef. The waiters were knowledgable, the food was served promptly and at the proper temperature and was artfully presented and prepared, and the wine recommended by the sommelier was as woody and flavorful as promised. I couldn't remember having a more flawless meal.

My room service breakfast the following morning was also without a misstep, as were the rest of my experiences at the Worthington New

Orleans. No matter where I explored or what I requested, I could find not a single demerit. Not a chandelier that hadn't been dusted. Not a sofa cushion that hadn't been plumped. Not a member of the hotel staff who didn't bow and scrape. The final test, I decided, would be Torture the Concierge.

"Good afternoon, Ms. Stickler. My name is Kevin, and I'm the concierge assigned to the Worthington Club rooms. How may I help you today?"

"Hello, Kevin." I went into my spiel about Roger's birthday. "My husband's a real geek, if you know what I mean. He just loves computers, wireless phones, anything electronic. I was thinking of sending him a wristwatch/laptop—one of those gadgets that can do everything but wash windows."

Kevin chuckled. AMLP doesn't specify that a concierge must laugh at a guest's jokes, but it helps. "That won't be any problem whatsoever," he said.

"Are you sure?" I said. "It's pretty late in the day and I need you to choose the merchandise, purchase it, and have it shipped in time to arrive in Santa Monica by tomorrow."

"The Worthington New Orleans has an expert in that."

"An expert in what?"

"Computers. He's our computer concierge, or, as some people call him, our technology butler."

"This hotel has a technology butler?"

"Absolutely. What I'd like to do is contact him right away and have him pay you a visit in your room, Ms. Stickler, so you can discuss your husband's electronics issues with him directly."

Electronics issues? Technology butler?

"Would that be satisfactory, Ms. Stickler?" asked Kevin.

"Oh, yes. Beyond satisfactory. Thank you."

"Delighted to be of service."

The technology butler came knocking on my door within five minutes, and he sent Roger a wristwatch/computer of some sort, and the Worthington New Orleans more than deserved Five Keys, I determined by the end of my stay. It deserved Six Keys. Seven. Maybe even ten. It was so perfect it deserved its own ratings system.

And I hated it.

I hated that the mini-bar was always stocked. I hated that the carpets were always being vaccumed. I hated that every single person who worked there trilled "Delighted to be of service," as if they were robots who'd been programmed. I hated that everything was so perfect as to be soulless, icy cold, completely lacking in the idiosyncracies that give a place charm and make you want to come back for more.

My God, I thought, as I put down my Standards Manual and focused on what I was feeling. *Perfection leaves you cold. Perfection is not charming. Perfection doesn't make you want to come back for more.*

I got up from the writing desk and walked across the room to the mirror over the dresser. When I peered at my reflection, I shuddered.

How had I let this career of mine—of seeking out perfection for a bunch of strangers—spill over into my personal life? I thought. How had I let it taint my marriage, spoil it, possibly forever? Why hadn't I seen that, while I'd been suited for my job, the job hadn't been suited for me, hadn't been healthy for me? Why hadn't I figured out that it had intensified my need for order and control, not balanced it, moderated it? And what was I going to *do* about it?

Find another way to earn a living, that's what.

The realization hit me hard, the way realizations should. Roger had been exactly right when he'd said that the changes in me were only superficial, that I hadn't changed in *here*. I knew exactly what he meant now. I prayed I could make him believe that.

As I was turning away from the mirror to start packing my suitcase, the phone in the room rang. I rushed to answer it.

"Roger?" I said hopefully.

"This is Preston, Elizabeth."

"Oh." He rarely called me while I was on an assignment, but I was glad he did. I had something I wanted to tell him.

"I'm afraid there's a problem," he said.

"What is it?"

"We've been getting quite a few complaints about the Seaborne in Palm Beach. No one but you seems to think it's a Five Key property, Elizabeth. As a result, I've been asked by the higher-ups to look into the matter."

"Look into the matter. That sounds ominous, Preston. Are you accusing me of something?"

"I'd rather not be, but you know as well as I do that an irregularity of this nature usually points to an inspector who got greedy."

"An inspector who took a payoff, you mean."

"Yes. Now, I'm certain *you* would never succumb to that sort of temptation, but I was enlisted to ask. I'm just following orders."

I smiled to myself. He was such a snake with his good cop/bad cop routine. Well, he was in for a jolt. "I'm guilty, Preston."

"Pardon?"

"I did take a payoff." I didn't tell him that the payoff involved a packet of herbs, not a wad of cash; that I had sold out not to make money but to save my husband. Let him think whatever he chose.

"I'm stunned. Stunned and disappointed. I was aware that you were having personal troubles, but to commit an act of such dishonesty after all your years with the company? It's inexcusable."

"I'll tell you what's really inexcusable—your standards for these hotels. You force them to conform to a ridiculous and arbitrary set of rules, and by doing so, you encourage them to lose all of their individuality. I agree that they should provide guests with excellent quality and service, but you can't measure excellence by checking off boxes on some stupid chart—or by expecting perfection. One person's idea of 'perfect' is another's idea of 'depressing.' What I'm saying, Preston, is that you don't have to fire me, because I quit."

"You quit?"

"Yes."

He started to lecture me, but I hung up on him before he could gather any steam.

Oh, Roger, I thought, wishing he could have heard my exchange with Preston. I've changed and this proves it. But I didn't change for you or for our marriage. I changed because it was time, because I was due, because I'm not following the old script anymore.

The airport limo dropped me off at the house at six-thirty or so. I didn't expect Roger to be home by then—he'd gone back to putting in long hours at the office—but I threw together a meal just in case he was hungry when he walked in the door.

And then I waited for him. Too excited to eat, I busied myself—flipped through a couple of magazines, watched TV, watered the plants, and fantasized about sharing my moment of self-discovery with him. I was dying to tell him I'd quit my job and why. Even if the news didn't impress him, even if he no longer cared what I did with my life, even if we never managed to reconcile, I had experienced a breakthrough and I wanted him to know about it. He was my best friend in all the world—or had been—and best friends are the ones you turn to when you've had a big-time revelation about yourself.

So where was he? Nine o'clock came and went. Ten o'clock passed. At eleven, I called his private line at the office, prepared to remind him that he needed some food and some sleep and that our house was the place for both. There was no answer.

Where could he be? I wondered. Since I'd given him the antidote, he'd stopped hanging out at dance clubs, stopped all his nocturnal adventures, in fact. So if he wasn't in his office, where the hell was he?

Naturally, my mind went straight to the women—to Nikki, Kim, Lucy, Gerta, and Carrie. Was he with one of them? Supposedly he wasn't interested in them, now that he'd been un-enhanced. At least, that's what he'd said. But what about them? Was it possible that *she* (the most persistent among them) had been so persuasive in her pleadings that he surrendered and agreed to see her?

He hadn't left me a message on the answering machine. Even during our worst of times, he'd always left me a message saying where he'd be if I needed him. But not that night. The only message on the machine was from Art Yarnell, who had, apparently, stepped up his harassment of me from letter writing to phone calling. The loser.

I also looked around the house for a note. Roger had never been a big one for notes, and as it turned out, that evening was no exception.

I checked the closet in the guestroom and was comforted to see his clothes still hanging there. Wherever he is, he's not planning a sleepover, I thought with enormous relief.

I fell asleep on the living room sofa, curled up in a ball with the TV still on. When the sound of a particularly loud car radio woke me up, I looked at my watch. Three A.M.

Maybe he *was* planning a sleepover, I decided, letting my jealousy get the better of me. Maybe he didn't remember which day I was flying home from my trip. It certainly wouldn't have been the first time.

Roger didn't show up at all that night, nor did he show up the following afternoon. I called the law firm and asked his secretary if he was there. He wasn't and hadn't been for two days.

"The last time I saw him he told me he wouldn't be coming in for a while," she said. "I assumed you knew, Mrs. Baskin."

You assumed wrong. "Did he mention any meetings out of the office?

Any closings he had scheduled? Any number where he could be reached?"

"No, he didn't. And that's not like Mr. Baskin at all."

I felt the fear, the panic, rising in my chest. Where was my husband? Where had he gone and with whom? Why would he have just taken off, leaving all his clothes behind?

Forget the clothes, I told myself. Roger couldn't care less about them in his un-enhanced state. He'd buy new ones if he had to, if he was in a big hurry to leave town.

But *had* he left town? Was I the reason he'd left? Had he come to the conclusion that he could never forgive me for giving him the potion and, in retaliation, allowed himself to be lured away by one of his femmes fatales?

Or was there a more sinister explanation? Had his strained relationships with either David or Brad put him in harm's way? Did Frankie's father, a deadbeat who was blaming Roger for his own weaknesses, finally act on his aggressive tendencies? Or was Roger the victim of a more random type of foul play?

Of course there was yet another possibility, a less likely possibility, to be sure, but one I couldn't discount. Did Roger's disappearance have something to do with the stud stimulant? Was there a chance, no matter how remote, that there really *was* a magical component to the potion Farkus had concocted? Magic often has its downside, doesn't it? What if there were ingredients in either the original packet of herbs or the antidote that actually had the property to make a person vanish into thin air? What then?

What then, indeed.

PART THREE

CHAPTER TWENTY-FIVE

He's gone," I announced to Clover, trying desperately to remain calm. Of course, I had help in the "remaining calm" department. An hour before placing the call to her, I popped a couple of Valium. "I said goodbye to him two days ago, went to New Orleans on business, and haven't seen him since. I'm as worried as I've ever been, Clover. Part of me thinks he's run off with a new love, and another part of me thinks it's the stud stimulant that could have—"

"Bud's gone too," she cut me off.

"*What?*"

"He hasn't been home in days."

"Are you saying he's still on his enhancement binge, carrying on until the wee hours, bouncing from nightspot to nightspot? Or are you saying he's gone, as in *gone*?"

"I'm saying he's vanished. Nobody has seen or heard from him, not even at the car dealerships. Oh, I'm so glad you're back, Elizabeth. I've been bursting to tell you about this."

"Wait. Just wait." Despite the Valium, I was starting to hyperventilate and had to bring my breathing back to normal. "So Bud has vanished too? They've both vanished?"

"It sure looks that way."

"Well, then maybe it *is* Farkus's potion that's responsible. Maybe, it sent our husbands up in a puff of smoke. One minute, they're around. The next, they're invisible. Presto-chango! Like magic!"

"Lord have mercy." I could practically hear Clover crossing herself. "We should call the police."

"And tell them what? That we gave our husbands some herbs from a doctor who's not a doctor and now they've disappeared? That we'd like to file a missing persons report on them? That we want their faces plastered all over milk cartons?"

"Why not?"

"Because until we find out otherwise, our husbands aren't really missing."

"Then what are they?"

"What are they? Well, if Farkus used magic on them and morphed them into some other life form, they could be rabbits, for all I know. Or birds. Yes. Maybe they've turned into birds now—big, white birds with wings that soar over the ocean and—"

"Elizabeth!"

"What?"

"Are you on some kind of drug?"

"Yes."

She sighed. "Usually, you're the one who stays strong and I'm the one who folds."

"I'm sorry. It's just that we did mess with Mother Nature by giving Roger and Bud the powder. Who knows what the consequences might be?"

"I certainly don't."

"Exactly. Look, Clover. Why don't we sleep on this, just for a day? I need a little time to recover from the news of Roger's disappearance, figure things out, consider possible scenarios. If he and Bud *have* been magically altered, the police aren't going to be any help to us."

She agreed to sleep on it. But neither of us ended up getting any sleep because Bud finally came home at two-thirty in the morning and she woke me up at three to tell me about it.

"You must be so relieved," I said, even though she was crying hysterically and didn't sound relieved in the slightest. "With Bud showing up, my theory about our husbands turning into birds flies right out the window."

"I wish he *had* turned into a bird," she wailed.

"Clover, you don't mean that."

"Yes, I do. Guess what he did turn into?"

"What?"

"A gay person."

"Bud's gay?"

There was a lot of sobbing and nose blowing on the other end of the phone. It was several seconds before she composed herself. "Apparently, he's been struggling with his problem—excuse me, his *sexual orientation*—for a long time, even before we got together."

"Oh, Clover. And you had no idea?"

"None. When we were first married, he was very attentive to me, very much the perfect husband. Then over the last couple of years he started to pull away. I just assumed he was in that 'settling-in phase,' as your sister calls it; that he was taking me for granted, acting the way men do when they've been married a while. But then I gave him the herbs and he became enhanced, and that's when he had his self-discovery. He started going to the opera and the wine tastings and the ballroom dance classes, and he realized that he wasn't being honest with himself or me.

What I'm leading up to, Elizabeth, is that the reason he didn't want to make love to me was that he wanted to make love to Quentin, his ballroom dancing instructor."

"You poor thing. You must be in shock."

"I am. But I'm grateful that Mama's not alive to see this. She was pretty narrow-minded, bless her heart."

Clover went on to explain that Bud would be moving out within the week and that, before long, she would be a lonely divorcée.

"You must feel as if all the money you spent on Farkus was a huge waste," I said.

"Not completely," she said. "If I hadn't given Bud the herbs, it would have taken him forever to come out of the closet. I may have lost him, Elizabeth, but the truth is, I never really had him. Not *that way*."

I was very proud of my friend. She was in terrible pain and yet she wasn't blaming Bud. She was accepting him for who he was, even though he'd hurt her. I only wished I had accepted Roger for who he was. If I had, he would be home with me, instead of out there in the world doing God knows what.

Now that Bud had reappeared, I ruled out the notion that Roger could have been mutated into some magic-induced life force. I had to face the reality that he had either left me of his own free will or met with foul play. Given the wretched state of our marriage before he disappeared, I was leaning toward the former rather than the latter, which is why I didn't call the police just yet. Why bring them in if we were only talking about a domestic matter? Husbands left their wives all the time. They even left their law practices, if they were really feeling like chucking it all. It was crappy, but it wasn't criminal.

The question I resolved to answer in short order was, Which woman had he left me for? I was going to have to piece together the events of Roger's life while he'd been under the influence of the powder and figure out very quickly which brazen hussy—Nikki, Lucy, Kim, Gerta, or Carrie—had seduced my man.

I began with Carrie, since she was the last woman I'd seen Roger with. They had been lovey-dovey in her office the day I'd stopped by to have lunch with him. And she'd always looked up to him, been grateful to him, for making her a partner in the firm. Had that gratitude turned to lust once he was enhanced? Did she now view him as a possible husband and father to her two kids? Had she, in fact, appropriated Roger for herself? It isn't uncommon for men and women who work in the same office together to develop a romantic relationship. Was that the case here? Was Roger holed up at Carrie's house while they decided how to break the news to me, to the other partners?

There was one way to find out. At nine o'clock that evening, when I was fairly sure that she would be home from work, I drove to Carrie's one-story brick ranch in the Cheviot Hills section of L.A. When I pulled up in front of the house, I didn't see Roger's car on the street, which was a relief. Of course, Carrie had a two-car garage. Maybe it was parked in there, out of sight of suspicious wives.

I rang the bell. One of her two daughters opened the door.

"Hello, Cassie," I said, bending down to pat her head.

"I'm Callie," she said, ducking away.

"Oh, sorry," I said, remembering that Cassie was the eight-year-old and Callie was the nine-year-old and Carrie was their supposedly intelligent mother, even though she'd given them cutesy and confusing names. "Is your mommy home?"

"Yeah, but she has company. A man."

I stiffened, felt my saliva dry up. "Where are they?"

"In Mommy's room."

Great. Now what? Did I really want to catch Roger in bed with Carrie *Boob*in? I know women are always saying, "I'd love to catch my son-of-a-bitch husband red-handed so I can see the expression on his face." But, personally, I had no interest in getting a look at my husband's red hand or the expression on his face. "Maybe I'll come back another time," I told Callie or Cassie or whoever she was.

I patted her on the head again and started for the door.

"Callie? Is someone there?" It was Carrie calling out to her daughter.

"It's a lady," Callie told her. "A lady from your work."

Before I knew it, Carrie was emerging from her bedroom, her fullsome figure wrapped in a powder-blue bathrobe. Her face was flushed, her hair mussed—the markings of afterglow, I thought, feeling a need for oxygen.

"Elizabeth! Gosh, what are you doing here?" she said, pulling her robe tighter around her in a phony display of modesty.

"Sorry if I'm interrupting," I said, staring her down. I despised her, suddenly. "Your daughter told me you have company."

"Well, yeah. I do have a guest tonight." She seemed uncomfortable. Wonder why. "Is there something you wanted to talk to me about? There must be, otherwise you would have waited until tomorrow, right? It's about Roger, isn't it."

"Bingo. You win the Samsonite luggage," I said with as much sarcasm as I could muster.

"Would you like to sit down?"

"Not particularly. What I'd like is for you to tell him to put his clothes on and come out here."

Now she was deeply offended, or so she pretended. "What business is it of yours whether he's dressed or undressed?"

"What business is it of *mine*?" I was seething.

"Yeah. I'm the one who sets the rules of conduct here. This is *my* house."

"Right, but that's *my* husband in your bedroom. I want him out of there. Now. With his clothes on and his fly zipped."

I'm ashamed to say that both of Carrie's daughters, Callie and Cassie, were huddled in the corner listening to all this. I was sorry that I had to put them through such a sordid ordeal, but given their mother's promiscuousness, it probably wasn't the first time.

"You think Roger's in my bedroom?" said Carrie, all innocence and purity.

"I'm betting on it. Now, if you won't make him come out of there, I'm going in."

Before she could stop me, I barreled past her and stormed down the hall toward what I assumed was the master bedroom. I was on automatic pilot now, on a mission to confront my husband. If our marriage was over, let him tell me to my face.

When I got to Carrie's room, I flung open the door, prepared to find Roger in his birthday suit, lying spread-eagled on the bed, his Freddy shriveled and spent.

"Oh my God!" I yelled and shut the door as fast as I'd opened it. The scene was too gruesome, too nauseating. I had never been in such an awkward situation in my entire life.

"Are you satisfied?" said Carrie, who was standing behind me, breathing down my neck.

"I . . . never expected . . ."

"Then you shouldn't go barging into people's houses uninvited," she said.

I nodded. I felt sad. Sad and sick. I wish I'd never seen him like that. I *really* wish I'd never seen him like that.

As I walked outside to my car, I tried to understand why marriages are such a slippery slope. Why can't two people just fall in love and live happily ever after? Why do they have to cheat on each other? Why do they have to hurt each other? Roger had accused me of having unrealistic, fairy-tale expectations about marriage, but I didn't know *how* unrealistic until I'd marched into Carrie's bedroom that night. What I did know was that the image of Brad—naked and flabby and without his toupée—would stay with me for a long, long time. Yes, it was Brad in there, not Roger. I wondered if Gerta suspected. And I wondered if she was striking back at her husband by coming on to mine.

Gerta, as I've mentioned, was a foreigner with an open disdain for American customs, one of which was taking a shower fairly regularly. When she arrived at my house for lunch the following afternoon, she had actual B.O., the kind that is easily remedied by a little water and a bar of soap.

"I vas so surprised vhen you called," she said upon entering the house. "I assumed you vould be too vorried about Roger to make social engagements. From vhat I hear, he's missing."

"I vanted—I mean, wanted—to talk to you about that, Gerta. But why don't we sit down first?"

I had prepared lunch and set it outside on the deck—a salad Nicoise for me, a bottle of Beaujolais for her. Well, not really. I made a salad for her too, but she always drank more than she ate. I was hoping she would get looped as usual and hold nothing back.

"So," I said, after she'd downed a couple of glasses of wine. "I hear that you and Roger had gotten pretty friendly before he took off for parts unknown."

"Yes. I probably shouldn't admit zis to you, Elizabett, but I didn't find him especially attractive vhen I first met him. He vas alvays sveet, of course, but quiet. I didn't pay much attention to him, frankly."

"What changed?"

"He changed. He became exciting to be around. A little too exciting."

I poured her another glass. "What do you mean by 'too exciting,' Gerta?"

"Hard to resist." She smiled. "If he veren't your husband, Elizabett, I vould have gone after him."

"But you already have a husband." A husband who's porking his law partner.

"Of course, and I love Brad very much." She pressed her lips together and made little kissing sounds. "But you don't really believe zat a voman must restrict herself to one lover, do you?"

"Actually, yes, Gerta. I do."

She waved her hand at me. "You Americans are so provincial. In Europe, vee believe zat it's not so terrible for a vife to sleep wiz a man ozer zan her husband. In many cases, the vife and za mistress are close confidentes."

"Okay. Pretend we're in Europe. Confide in me."

She laughed. "About vat?"

"You and Roger."

She laughed again. "All right. So I'll tell you the truth. I didn't sleep vith Roger. I vanted to, but he vasn't interested. I slept vith David instead."

"David?" I knocked over the bottle of wine. Fortunately, the placemats were washable.

"See how you reacted? I told you Americans are provincial."

"David?" I repeated, still reeling from this latest bombshell. "You're saying you slept with your husband's partner?" While your husband was sleeping with his other partner? How they got any work done at that law firm was beyond me.

"Yes, but only vonce. I had too much to drink that night."

What else was new? "Wow, Gerta. I never would have pictured you two together. Does Brad have any idea?"

She shook her head. "I vouldn't tell him. Men are so much more fragile zan vomen, no?"

"No." I fed her and sent her home. Call me provincial, but the way Roger and I were before his enhancement—monogamous, entrenched in our routines, secure in the knowledge that we could always count on each other—was starting to look better and better.

Over the next few days, I made contact with Nikki, Lucy, and Kim. I invited myself to their houses. I asked them impertinent questions about their sex lives. I demanded to know when they had last seen Roger. In the end, I was both heartened and discouraged. Heartened, because my husband hadn't left me for any of these women. Discouraged, because he still hadn't come home.

CHAPTER TWENTY-SIX

Where are you? I thought as I sat by the phone, praying Roger would call. Why can't you be here in this house with me—here in your stupid lounger, zonked out in front of the TV—here in the kitchen, slurping milk right out of the carton—here in our bed, snuggling up to me and telling me you love me? Why?

I moped and I mused, and when I couldn't sit still any longer, I got up and searched the house for the umpteenth time, hunting for clues, hoping to find a hint of where Roger could have gone, and coming up empty.

Should I call the police? I asked myself over and over. My interactions with them in the past hadn't been pleasant, and I really didn't expect them to get too excited about a case involving a missing husband who was mad at his wife for sneaking some herbs into his orange juice. "This is a private matter between you and Mr. Baskin," I was sure they'd say, squelching a laugh, rolling their eyes, thinking Roger and I were just another nutty L.A. couple with too much time and money on our hands.

Besides, I believed that Roger would come back to me. Oh, and Brenda believed he would come back to me. She believed it because that was how it played out in her favorite movies.

"Look at Billy Crystal in *When Harry Met Sally*," she said one night when she'd stopped by to hold my hand. "He came back. Look at Tom Cruise in *Jerry McGuire*. He came back. Look at Hugh Grant in *Notting Hill*. He came back."

"Look at Robert Redford in *The Way We Were*," I said. "He left and married someone else."

"Forget *The Way We Were*," said Brenda. "It was so manipulative."

"Why? Because it didn't have a happy ending?"

"Yeah. You had to sit through two hours with no payoff. Not my idea of a love story. My idea of a love story is *An Affair to Remember*. Cary Grant came back, even though Deborah Kerr lied to him about being hit by that car. All you did was lie to Roger about giving him some herbs. I'm telling you, he'll come back, Elizabeth."

I didn't bother to remind her that my life wasn't a movie. I was comforted by her visits, no matter how questionable her logic. But while I believed that Roger would come back, as I've said, I had a competing belief that he might be in trouble and would have to extricate himself before he came back. I know, I know. I had crossed his female admirers off the list of possible troublemakers. And I'd figured that although David and Brad had been angry with Roger, I might as well cross them off the list too, since they had found consolation in the beds of Gerta and Carrie, respectively. But there could be someone else he'd pissed off during the height of his enhancement, couldn't there?

Like Frankie's father, Dennis Wheeler. He was deeply disturbed, unpredictable, a loose cannon. He'd been verbally abusive to Roger since he'd crawled out from whatever rock he'd been living under. He was definitely worth checking out, I decided.

I drove to Venice, to Frankie's ramshackle house with its broken windowpanes and rotting asphalt roof and wood siding that was desperately in need of a paint job. While many of Venice's neighborhoods had been gentrified, providing plenty of shops and restaurants for the trendoids, there were pockets of town that had yet to be cleaned up, and the Wheelers lived in one of them. How could they afford otherwise? Dennis Wheeler never contributed a dime.

I arrived about eight in the evening. Frankie was the only one home.

"Where's your mom?" I asked after we'd shared a hug. He had lost weight. I wondered if anyone was bothering to feed him or buy groceries for him or, God forbid, pay attention to him.

"Working," he said. "She's a waitress at a diner now. She comes home around nine."

So Frankie was on his own for meals. No wonder he looked so malnourished. "And your dad? How about him?"

"He's . . . somewhere." Frankie turned away from me.

"Honey? What is it? You can tell me anything."

He kept his back to me. "No, I can't. Not this. I'd get in trouble, because it was just stuff I overheard between him and my mom."

"Frankie." I placed my hands on his bony shoulders and brought him around to face me. "What's your father done? Has he hurt you?"

He shook his head. "Not me."

"Your mother?"

"No. It's nothing like that." He lowered his eyes. "I can't tell you, Elizabeth. Sorry."

I didn't want to push him, but I did want to know what his no-good father was up to. "Has he gone away again, Frankie?"

"Yeah, but I can't tell you where."

"Okay. How about telling me why he's gone away?"

"I heard him say to my mom that he was going away to get us some money. He has a plan. He said that when he comes back, he's gonna have so much money we won't have to live here anymore."

"A plan, huh?" A plan, but not a job. I didn't like the sound of that.

"Yeah. He's gonna make us rich."

"Wow. Did he go away to borrow money from someone? Is that it?"

"Maybe, but I can't tell you where, like I said."

"Okay, Frankie. I won't ask again. The real reason I'm here is to tell you that Roger has gone away too." I wanted to soften the blow, to protect Frankie from any more surprises. He'd had enough turmoil in his young life.

"I already know that."

I blinked. "You do?" How was that possible? Could Roger have chosen Frankie to confide in? Had he shared his intentions with his Little Brother but not his wife?

As if realizing he'd just spilled the beans, Frankie clapped his hand over his mouth.

"Don't be afraid," I said. "You didn't do anything wrong. I only want you to confirm this for me: You already knew that Roger hasn't been home for a while?"

He nodded, his hand still covering his mouth. Gently, I pulled it away from his face and held it.

"I'm very worried about him, honey. He left without telling me where he was going. Do you know where he is?"

"Nope. Just that he went away, like my dad."

"So they're both gone?" I wondered if Frankie was just being fanciful, convincing himself that Roger and his father were pals who shared similar interests, buddies who hung out together. But he wasn't that sort of kid. He'd always been amazingly grounded for his age, didn't make up stories, didn't hide from reality.

"Yup. They're both gone. And when they come back, my dad will be rich."

Now I was really confounded. When *they* come back? That implied that Dennis and Roger were somehow a twosome, that both of them were involved in Dennis's so-called "plan." And yet the notion was preposterous. Roger would never go anywhere with Frankie's father. Not willingly and certainly not to tag along on some get-rich-quick scheme.

Suddenly, an idea dawned on me—an idea that filled me with dread. Was it possible that crazy Dennis Wheeler had kidnapped Roger, holding him hostage for money? Was it possible that he had forcibly taken Roger somewhere and threatened him into signing away his bank account? Was that the plan Frankie had overheard? Dennis had always resented Roger for what he believed to be Roger's "high and mighty attitude" toward the Wheelers, and he'd been acting even more peculiar than usual lately, according to Roger. But was he twisted enough to view his son's Big Brother as his meal ticket? Could he have dragged him off to some remote location and beaten him into handing over his money? Was that why no one had seen or heard anything about Roger—except Frankie?

Growing uneasier by the minute, I decided to wait for Mrs. Wheeler to come home before calling the police. I wanted to save my husband, but I didn't want to alienate Frankie if my suspicions were out of line. I would talk to her about her son's remarks and hear what she had to say.

It was close to nine-thirty by the time Eve Wheeler trudged in the door. A pitifully thin woman, whose lovely features were camouflaged by too much makeup and a grim, resigned expression, she seemed alarmed at the sight of me. Was it simply that Roger had been the more frequent visitor over the years? Or was it that she felt guilty around me, had something to hide? Our last encounter had been the previous November. Roger had invited her and Frankie to join us for Thanksgiving dinner, but she had declined, claiming she had to work. In what we'd thought was a generous gesture, Roger and I roasted an extra turkey with all the trimmings and delivered it to her that morning. Frankie was thrilled to have a real, home-cooked meal, but Eve seemed put out by our interference or was uncomfortable about taking "charity," and couldn't recognize that all we were doing was *being there* for her and her son.

"Oh," she said when she saw me. "I didn't know whose car that was outside."

"I hope you don't mind my dropping by," I said. "I had some news for Frankie."

"We may not have money, but we do have a telephone," she snapped.

"Yes, but I wanted to tell him in person. You see, Roger hasn't come home in a few days. I thought Frankie should know about it, since the two of them are so close, but, apparently, he already did."

Eve Wheeler raised an eyebrow at her son but didn't comment.

"I understand that Dennis hasn't been around either," I went on. "Frankie indicated that he was chasing down a financial opportunity."

"Frankie has no business going on about his father to strangers," she said.

"I'm hardly a stranger, Eve. I guess I'm wondering if Dennis's financial opportunity and Roger's disappearance are related. It's sort of a coincidence that they're both gone, isn't it?"

"Related? What are you hinting at?"

There was no point in beating around the bush. Not with Roger's life at stake. "Be honest with me. Is Dennis up to something? Is he holding Roger captive, hoping to extort money from him?"

She laughed. "You're way off the mark, lady. If your husband's not around, it's your problem, not mine."

"Yes, yes, I understand that you want to protect Dennis," I kept on. "I can certainly sympathize with that impulse, but it won't do Frankie or you any good if he spends the next ten years in prison. On the other hand, if you tell me the truth and we find Roger all in one piece, I'll make sure the police are lenient with him. Just tell me what's going on. Won't you do that? Won't you help me?"

Eve responded by throwing me out of her house, either because she was covering up for Dennis or because she was insulted by my accusation. All I knew was that despite Frankie's pleas to let me stay, she shooed me out the door, stone-faced.

Was she in on her husband's caper? I wondered as I got into the car. Was she covering up for him? Or had I misread the situation?

I couldn't take any chances. The fact that Frankie knew that Roger hadn't come home, coupled with his father's often erratic behavior, was enough to whip me into action.

Although it was late and I was dead tired, I drove straight to the Beverly Hills Police Department, hoping to have a talk with Detective Dembo or Detective Wasluski or both. Santa Monica has its own police force and it would have been the agency of choice, given that Roger was a Santa Monica resident and was last seen there, but I figured I might as well go where I knew people. If only for advice.

It was like Old Home Week when I walked into the B.H.P.D. and saw the familiar faces of the desk officer and the lieutenant who was in charge of public information and the sergeant who'd arrested Clover and me that fateful night at Farkus's office. They all remembered me and high-fived me and asked me if I'd been a good girl. It was sort of sweet.

"I came to see Detectives Dembo and Wasluski," I said. "It's not about the Farkus case, but I really need a few minutes with them. Are they around?"

"In their office," said the desk officer. "They've got someone in there with them, but I'll give them a buzz that you're here."

I thanked him and waited, trying not to picture Roger in a dark basement somewhere, his hands and feet bound, his mouth taped shut, his captor standing over him making terrifying demands. Before long, the desk officer pointed me in the direction of the detectives' office and sent me on my way.

"Hey, look who's here," said Dembo, greeting me at the door to his cubicle. "If it isn't the happy housewife."

"It's great to see you too," I said wryly.

"Come on in," he said, ushering me inside the tiny space. "There's someone who's dying to share old times with you."

"I'll bet," I said, assuming he was referring to Wasluski. I turned to my left and nearly fell over. "What on earth—" I was shocked to see another man standing there, next to Wasluski, a man I never imagined I'd see in that office.

"Surprised?" he said with that smarmy smirk of his.

"Of course, I'm surprised," I said, wondering whose nightmare I'd stepped into now. "What could you possibly be doing here? You told me you lived in Kansas City, among other lies."

Yup. It was Chris Eckersly, the letch who kept turning up in the least likely places. I never expected to run into him again, certainly not at the B.H.P.D.

"You're looking as luscious as ever," he said leeringly. "Maybe when your little conference with the detectives is over, you and I can pick up where we left off in Seattle."

"And maybe you can explain why you're hanging around this police station," I countered. "What did you do? Try to buy the services of an undercover cop, since you clearly can't get women to have sex with you for free?"

"Now, now. Mrs. Stickler. There's no need to get nasty."

"The name's Baskin," I corrected him. "Mrs. Roger Baskin."

"So I've heard from the detectives."

I looked at Dembo. "Will someone please tell me why this man is in your office tonight?"

"Mr. Eckersly is a private investigator," said Dembo. "He's the one I mentioned to you when we stopped by your house. He's been tracking our so-called Dr. Farkus for a client who wasn't particularly satisfied with her treatment or her preparation or whatever it was he gave her."

"He's a private investigator?" Another shocker. "He pretended he was an investment banker—an investment banker from Kansas City with a wife and four kids and a roving eye. But then being a creep must be part of his job description."

Eckersly smiled. "That's why they call us private *dicks*."

"Funny. So if you were hired to find Farkus, what were you doing in Seattle?"

"That was Farkus's place of business before he migrated down here to Beverly Hills."

"Really. What about the swanky restaurants? I didn't know private investigators ate at Spago."

"Farkus hung out with the swells wherever he set up shop. I went where he went. Besides, my client pays me well."

"How nice for you."

"Sure is, but let's talk about you. You're looking delicious as always, Elizabeth, or did I already say that?"

"Look, I've got enough problems right now without you slobbering all over me." I turned to the detectives. "Could I have a little time with you two? *Alone*?"

"Why not," said Wasluski, who told Chris Eckersly to scram. When it was just the three of us, I told the detectives that Roger was missing.

"I'd be missing too if I found out my wife had been arrested for a felony," said Dembo with a laugh.

"Please. This isn't a joke," I said. "It's true that he was angry at me for what I did and that our marriage was on shaky ground when he left, but it's been a few days now and I'm getting worried." I told them about

Dennis Wheeler, about his whole family. "Isn't it possible that this man is holding my husband against his will? And if so, is there anything you can do about it?"

Wasluski said that he'd take down the information and forward it to the Santa Monica Police Department for them to set an investigation in motion. "I'll also run a check on your guy, Wheeler, and see if he's got any priors."

"Now?"

"Now what?"

"Will you run the check on Dennis Wheeler now? While I wait?"

Wasluski rolled his eyes. "Be right back."

I paced outside the office while Dembo placed a few calls, conducted some business. After what seemed like an eternity, Wasluski returned with an answer. "Arrest records are confidential, but I can tell you that the guy's got one. It's not a mile long, but it's not pretty."

"I knew it. What happens from here? Can you go after him?"

"I can't, but I'll call a buddy of mine at the S.M.P.D. and let him handle it," said Dembo. "We'll find out what this Wheeler's up to, okay?"

"Okay, but hurry. Please hurry."

The next morning, the phone rang at eight-thirty, jolting me out of the half-sleep I'd finally fallen into after a night of tossing and turning.

"Roger?" I said, as I often did in my fantasy that he would call.

"It's Detective Wasluski," he said. "We found your Mr. Wheeler."

"Oh, that's wonderful!" I sat up in bed. "Is Roger all right?"

"They weren't together. The investigating officers followed a lead that the wife gave them. It turns out Wheeler *was* involved in a theft, but it didn't have anything to do with your husband. He robbed an electronics store in Hollywood, and they caught him and his buddies with the goods."

"So that was his plan to get rich," I said, thinking of poor Frankie and how he'd been disappointed yet again.

"Guess so. His wife seemed almost glad to tip off the officers."

"Maybe she was fed up with him and his schemes. Maybe she finally saw what a bad influence he was on their son." I hoped so.

"In any case, that puts us at square one with your husband."

"I realize that. I'm so worried about him, Detective. I don't know where he could be."

"Then here's some advice," he said straightforwardly, without all the macho crap. "I'm gonna speak to you as a guy, not as a cop. And what I want to tell you is this: Your husband has probably gone off to lick his wounds, to think things through. We men aren't big on talking about our problems the way women are. My hunch is that he just needed time to himself and he took it."

"But he didn't leave a message or a note or anything. He didn't even tell his office where he was going. That's not like Roger."

"He's mad at you. Mad at the world, right?"

"Yes."

"Madder than he's ever been?"

"Yes."

"Then forget about his good manners and start remembering his favorite haunts."

"I don't understand."

"Use your head, Elizabeth. Where does your husband go when he's upset? He's out there someplace. Figure out where."

I thanked the detective for his help, got out of bed, and made myself some coffee. When I was sufficiently caffeinated, I sat down with a pen and a pad of paper, poised to compile a list of possible "favorite haunts"—places where Roger might be licking his wounds. But I couldn't think of any. He wasn't the type to drown his sorrows at a bar. Nor was he the type to camp out at a friend's—

I dropped the pen. In an instant, I knew exactly where Roger was.

I hurried up to the attic and burrowed through the cartons and the clothes and the lampshades until I found just what I was looking for—nothing.

Yessss!

I pumped my fist in the air, because Roger's tent, along with the rest of his camping gear, was nowhere in sight.

It made perfect sense, I realized, as I ran back downstairs to get dressed. Whenever Roger needed to think, to relax, to escape the pressures of life, he went camping. Camping was his passion. "I can be myself when I'm camping," he always said. "I can feel free."

If there was ever a time when Roger needed to escape the pressures of life and feel free, this was it.

There was only one question that remained: *Where* had he gone camping? Southern California had lots of sites that appealed to him, so which of them had he chosen?

Did he drive all the way down to Anza-Borrego Desert State Park, near San Diego? Did he take a boat to one of the Channel Islands? Anacapa, maybe, or Santa Cruz? Or did he stay closer to home?

I tried to think of all the spots Roger had told me about over the years, but it wasn't until I recalled his most recent camping trip that I solved the puzzle. He'd walked in the door at the end of that weekend, unshaven but invigorated, and proclaimed that his "favorite haunt," as Detective Wasluski had put it, was the Manker Flats campground at Mt. Baldy, not only because it's so accessible from L.A. but because the mountain itself (Mount San Antonio, as it's more formally known) is the tallest peak in the San Gabriels, rising to its 10,064-foot elevation. Roger said that hiking up to the summit was a "high" for him, literally; that it afforded him a knockout view of Southern California—an expanse of mountain, desert, and coastal lowland; and that he never failed to be awed by it.

He took Frankie there just before I'd given him the herbs, I recalled.

He even took me there on my one-and-only camping trip with him. Yes, that's where he was now. There wasn't a doubt in my mind.

I threw on some sneakers, dug a sweater out of my dresser drawer, grabbed my *Thomas Guide* containing all the maps I'd ever need, and hopped in my car.

"Within an hour, I'll be with you, Roger," I said aloud as I pulled out of the driveway, en route to the San Bernadino Freeway. "Only fifty miles are separating us now."

No, I didn't care for camping or hiking, as I've indicated—communing with poison ivy wasn't my idea of rapture—but tough times called for tough measures.

CHAPTER TWENTY-SEVEN

I didn't suspect that I was being followed, not during the entire ride on the 10 freeway. It wasn't until I took the Euclid Avenue off-ramp and went north toward the mountains that I made a mental note of the white Nissan Sentra and the man sitting behind the wheel. I didn't recognize him or his car, and so I told myself not to be paranoid, that it was just a coincidence we were on the same trail, so to speak. Maybe he's going to Mt. Baldy too, I thought. Maybe lots of people leave Santa Monica on a Tuesday morning at the precise time I did and head for the hills. What else was I supposed to think?

Focusing my attention on getting to Roger, I continued up Euclid and eventually found myself on Mt. Baldy Road and in the center of the small village, where hikers and campers congregate. Across the street from the Mt. Baldy Lodge is the U.S. Forest Service's Visitor Center, my initial destination. In order to park my car and enter the campground, I had to purchase a five-dollar Adventure Pass—a small price to pay for the chance to patch things up with my husband, I thought.

"Can I help you?" asked the forest ranger manning the Visitor Center.

"I'd like to buy an Adventure Pass," I said.

"That'll be five dollars per vehicle," she said.

I gave her the money.

"You planning a day hike?" she said, handing me the pass and instructing me to place it on my dashboard.

I smiled. What I was planning was an extravagantly romantic reunion with Roger. I was going to find him, make up with him, and bring him home. "Yes. A day hike."

"Good," she said, "because if you were planning to camp overnight, I was gonna tell you that there's no toilets and no water, not since last week. We usually wait until November to shut everything off, but this has been a chilly October."

No toilets and no water? Well, I wouldn't be staying overnight, so what did it matter?

As I turned to leave, I nearly ran smack into the man who was standing next in line.

"Sorry," I said.

"You will be," he said.

I did a double take. "What?"

"I said, 'Happy hiking,' " he replied innocently, then asked the forest ranger for his Adventure Pass.

I kept moving, but I knew I had heard him right the first time and it shook me up. So did the fact that he appeared to be the guy in the Sentra, the guy I'd seen in my rearview mirror during the trip to Mt. Baldy. Same red hair. Same upturned nose. Same stocky build. *Was* he following me? Or was I just being silly?

I got back in my car and drove a couple of miles until I reached the

Manker Flats campground. I parked along the side of the road, grabbed my sweater, and went skipping off in search of Roger's car. The campground has twenty-two pull-in sites for vehicles, but since it was a weekday in late October—not exactly tourist season—I didn't expect the search to take long. And it didn't. Sandwiched between a couple of R.V.s was Roger's Volvo wagon, the car he'd wanted to trade for a Porsche when he was under the influence of the stud stimulant.

I was so thrilled to have found Roger that I raced toward the Volvo, thinking he'd be sitting in it and that, as soon as I tapped on the window and he realized how much I loved him, all would be well.

Dope. That's what I was. Roger hadn't driven to Mt. Baldy to hang out in his car. He was hiking, of course, and very likely wouldn't be back for hours.

Since the Volvo was locked, I couldn't open the door and wait for him there. And since his nearby tent lacked the comforts of even a decent chair, I had no interest in waiting for him there. Besides, I was pretty keyed up and wanted to talk to him as soon as humanly possible. There was only one thing to do, I decided. Get out on the trail and surprise him on his way back to camp.

Roger, unlike yours truly, was an experienced hiker, who relished the challenges brought on by the rough, steep trails. Such a Boy Scout, my husband. He was probably up at some ridiculously high elevation right that minute, maybe at the summit, fully equipped with his Swiss army knife and his water bottles and his emergency whistle. But regardless of his itinerary up the mountain that Tuesday morning, I knew from past chronicles that he would be returning to the campsite via Devil's Backbone and Baldy Notch and then down the Baldy fire road, a dirt road that meandered between the Manker Flats and the ski lift. It wasn't the quickest route back, but it was the one he preferred because it was less strenuous than the alternatives and, therefore, easier on his legs and feet after an arduous day of hiking. What's more, the final lap, the dirt road, was a stretch even I could navigate, which is why meeting him there seemed like a good idea at the time.

Before I took off, I reached into my shoulder bag for a pen and something to write on, my intention being to stick a note on the windshield of Roger's car to tell him I had arrived and had gone up the Baldy fire road looking for him. All I could find was my shopping list, so I scribbled my message on the back of it—complete with Xs and Os—and tucked it under the left windshield wiper.

Here goes nothing, I thought, tying the arms of my sweater around my waist and then lifting the strap of my handbag over my head so I could wear it knapsack style.

As I set out on my journey, I immediately wished I owned a pair of hiking boots. The ground was fairly flat—i.e., no boulders to climb—but my Nikes were the kind that are fine in aerobics class but don't really cut it on dirt roads. Nevertheless, I trudged on, passing a few hikers here and there. As I said, it was a weekday and not the busy season, so there weren't a lot of bodies around. As I walked, I took in the flora and fauna—Roger had taught me about the enormous incense cedars that are home to a variety of mountain birds—and I had to admit that it was refreshing to be surrounded by so much natural beauty and solitude. Perhaps for the first time, I got an inkling of what it was about camping and hiking that Roger found so restorative. It was the peacefulness, the sense of being one with the earth and sky, and the dramatic contrast between the serene setting and the hustle-bustle of L.A. that combined to make the experience unique. I was grateful that he had found such an outlet, a place to come to when he needed a respite from the world. I understood it now, even if, given my druthers, I would rather have been combing the sale racks at Saks.

I was about a half hour into my hike when I heard footsteps behind me. Assuming it was a fellow traveler, I stepped to the side, intending to let him or her pass. Roger had also taught me that it's proper "trail etiquette" to walk single file so a trail isn't widened by excessive use.

I waited for the person to continue on ahead of me. Instead, the footsteps came to a dead halt only inches from my back. I turned around, about to say hello or give a nod (another rule of trail etiquette), and instead stopped breathing.

"Alone at last," said the man—the man in the Nissan Sentra, the man in the Visitor Center, the man who, it was now abundantly clear from the gun he was pointing at me, had followed me after all.

"Oh, God!" I said, my mind scrambling to catch up with the current reality. For years I'd been suspicious of people, assumed everyone was a psycho unless proven otherwise, and it had only been Roger's trusting nature that had mellowed me. But there I was, nose to nose with an actual nut, and I had to stay calm somehow, had to keep myself from flipping out. "Do I know you?" I asked, wondering if he was one of those lunatics who commits random acts of violence or if he had sought me out because of some personal association.

"Let's just say you've never met me," he replied cryptically. His hair was red all right. Reddish orange. And he had more freckles than anyone I'd ever seen. The Freckled Fanatic, the newspapers would probably dub him after he killed me.

I glanced to my left and right, hoping another hiker would approach and scare this guy away, but we really were alone. And so I screamed.

He didn't care for that. He rushed toward me and thrust the barrel of the gun into my chest, squishing my left breast. It was worse than having a mammogram. And then he said, sounding like a movie gangster, "You try that again and I'll pull the trigger."

With that, he ripped my handbag off of me, then yanked my right arm behind my back, did the same with my left, and switched the position of the gun to the middle of my spine. This was not fun, this being contorted like a pretzel, even though I tried to pretend it was just another yoga position.

"Okay. Let's go," he said, shoving me forward.

"Where?" I managed, my teeth chattering with fear and cold. I wished I'd put on my sweater instead of left it dangling around my waist, but it was too late for a wardrobe adjustment.

"We're gonna take a little detour," he said. "I don't want anybody spoiling our fun, Elizabeth."

I jerked my head around after he said my name.

"Don't look at me," he commanded. "Just keep going."

So he *did* know me, I thought, discarding the idea of the random act. But *how* did he know me?

As we tramped along, veering well off the road and into the woods where nobody was likely to run into us, I wracked my brain, attempted to place my abductor. Perhaps he was someone with a score to settle against Roger, I thought. Someone who'd taken umbrage with him while he was parading around town, showing off his enhancement. I'd ruled out the lovesick women and the law partners and Frankie Wheeler's father as possible threats, but maybe this guy was the real threat and he simply hadn't popped up on my radar screen.

But if Roger was the object of his wrath, what was he doing with me? Why wouldn't he have followed Roger to Mt. Baldy and held *him* at gunpoint?

"Where are you taking me?" I said, as we trekked farther and farther from civilization.

He didn't answer me, except to penetrate the gun deeper into the skin on my back. I interpreted that as a "Shut up."

When we'd been hiking for about fifteen minutes—and I mean *hiking* as opposed to the sissy stuff I'd been doing when I'd first set out—and we were so far off the beaten path that I had to acknowledge that this guy was genuinely out to murder me, he spun me around to face him, then pushed me onto the ground.

"Okay," he said after I'd gone down rather ungracefully, clinging to a couple of tree branches, then landing on my ass. "It's time you and I had a talk."

"Sure," I said, "but would you mind if I put my sweater on? I talk better when my lips aren't frozen."

He shook his head. "As a matter of fact, I'm gonna need your sweater."

"It's not your size."

"I said, *give* it to me."

I didn't like his tone, but this was not the time to get huffy. "If you're cold too, why don't we just wander on back to the campground? We can shake hands, part as friends, pretend this never happened. How about it?"

"The sweater, Elizabeth." He was still holding the gun on me, so I handed over my Ralph Lauren cashmere crewneck. "And now your belt."

"My belt? What would you want with—"

He stuck the gun under my chin, which suggested that he meant business, so I reached down, unbuckled my leather belt (I forget whose it was, designer-wise), pulled it out of the loops of my jeans, and gave it to him.

"Good. And now I'd like you to remove your socks and sneakers."

Boy, I was really stumped. Stumped and shivering. "What is this? Strip poker without the poker?"

"Your socks and shoes, Elizabeth."

Old freckles wasn't fooling around. I gave him my socks and my Nikes and prayed we had come to the end of the disrobing.

Unfortunately, we hadn't. Freckles unbuckled his own belt and whipped it out of his jeans.

Dear Lord, I prayed again, harder this time. Don't let this guy be a murderer *and* a pervert. Take me to heaven if You feel You must, but leave my virtue, such as it is, intact. Amen.

"Would you mind telling me who you are and why you've gone to the trouble of following me here from Santa Monica?" I said.

"As soon as I finish up some chores," he said. Before I could put up much of a struggle, he began to tie my ankles together with his belt.

"Oh, please don't," I moaned, both because I wasn't thrilled with the implications of this and because he tied the belt so tight it was stopping my circulation.

"You asked for it," he said, then used my belt to bind my wrists together.

"I asked for it? How?" I was curled up on the ground with my hands and feet bound, and I was about as afraid and confused and uncomfortable as a person could be.

Freckles looked skeptical. "You're kidding, right? You really don't know?"

"Know what? Tell me who you are!"

"All right, all right. I'm Art Yarnell. Does the name ring a bell? Ding-a-ling?"

"You're—" Wait a second. This guy was the general manager of the Phoenician Paradise? The one who'd been sending me bullying letters and leaving equally bullying messages on my answering machine? The one who was enraged because I hadn't given his hotel Five stupid Keys?

"Ah. I thought you'd remember." He smiled. Even his lips had freckles. "I certainly remember you. I've been watching you for days, did you sense it? I was going to make my move the other night, when you were home all by yourself, but you've got neighbors right on top of you, and I didn't want any interruptions. So I decided to wait until you took a drive. Imagine my delight this morning when you got into your car and drove all the way here, to such a remote location. It was too perfect. Too wonderful. I couldn't be more pleased."

And I couldn't have been more stunned. I was still processing the fact that I was in the presence of a man who'd promised over and over again to make me pay, a man whose warnings I had ignored because I'd been so caught up in saving my marriage.

"In case you're wondering why I have so much leisure time, it's because I lost my job," he went on. "Yeah, the hotel sent me packing. They said I didn't have the leadership skills to run the hotel in the appropriate manner.' "

"But that's not my fault," I protested. "In my evaluation for AMLP, I was very specific in my criticism of the hotel. All the problems I enumerated could have been fixed. *You* could have fixed them. There had to be other reasons why you were let go." Like their discovery that they had a wacko for a general manager.

"No! It was you who checked into the hotel with your little notebook and inspected every nook and cranny; you who cost us millions of dollars in bookings; you who destroyed the owners' faith in me. Oh, it was pretty awful, believe me. Before they actually fired me, they let me become the butt of jokes, let me lose the respect of my employees, let me die a slow death. It was humiliating and horrible, and now it's your turn."

"My turn for what?"

"To die a slow death."

"Listen, Art. Please listen." I didn't like his drift. Not at all. "There's no need for you to blame me, because I don't work for AMLP anymore. I'll never be inspecting hotels again."

"You got that right." He laughed. "You'll never be doing much of anything again."

"Oh, please," I pleaded. "Why not rethink this plan of yours, Art. Why not untie me and then the two of us can hike back to the campsite, get a nice cup of coffee, chat about our career goals. Come on. Stranding me here isn't going to get you your job back."

"Maybe not, but it'll make me feel a helluva lot better." He laughed again. I realized then that there was no point in trying to reason with this looney tune.

"So you're going to leave me? Just leave me to die?"

"That's the general idea, yeah. I seriously doubt that anyone will find you in the middle of nowhere. Well, maybe they will—after the bears are finished with you."

God, no. Oh, God, no. I screamed again, and my pathetic shouts echoed out over the mountains, reverberating back at me like some cruel joke.

"That's enough of that," he said, then took both my socks, bunched them together in a tight little ball, and stuffed them into my mouth, effectively cutting off any further cries for help.

I tried to muscle my tongue against the socks, to force them out. I tried to manufacture saliva to spit them out. I tried to clamp my teeth down on them to reduce them enough so they would fall out. No luck.

"Don't exhaust yourself, Elizabeth," said Freckles, who tied the arms of my sweater around my head, across my mouth, rendering it impossible for me to eject the socks by any of the above techniques. "There. All done." He put the gun in his jacket pocket, since he wouldn't have any use for it now. He really wasn't planning to shoot me, it was clear. He was planning to let me rot in the wilderness, to die a slow death.

I made noises, attempted to form words, grunted out a "Please don't leave me here!" but nothing intelligible came out.

"Goodbye, Elizabeth. I sincerely hope you've learned your lesson." He turned to go, then changed his mind. "I should add"—he chuckled malevolently—"that there's no room service at this hotel. No valet service either. There isn't even a concierge."

With that parting shot, Art Yarnell gave me a little salute and, within a few minutes, disappeared from my line of vision.

CHAPTER TWENTY-EIGHT

People assume that when you live in southern California, you never have a bad hair day. The weather's so sunny and dry that there's virtually no frizz factor, right? Well, try getting stuck on Mt. Baldy and then tell me about it. The sky was clear when Art Yarnell faded into the distance, but by four o'clock the clouds had formed, and by five I was drenched by a passing shower, the dampness and humidity leaving my hair looking like the Bride of Frankenstein's. Not exactly the way I wanted to present myself to Roger when he found me and we reconciled and we vowed to resume our marriage in a spirit of honesty and sharing and unconditional love.

I know, I know. You're thinking, What's with this woman? She's bound and gagged and stranded in the wilderness, and she's obsessing about her *hair*? Where are her priorities?

I guess you'd have to understand my state of mind. I was on the verge of losing it, on the edge of actual creepiness.

On the physical side, I'd developed a nasty case of leather burn on my wrists and ankles, having spent hours trying to wriggle out of my restraints and failing. In addition, I'd been bitten all over my body by species of insects I didn't know existed. I'd become extremely dehydrated, both because I hadn't had a sip of water all day and because the socks in my mouth had sucked up all the moisture inside me. I'd suffered a bad chill that had caused me to feel dizzy and nauseous and very, very tired. And—okay, this one's embarrassing—I'd taken a whizz in my pants.

On the emotional side, I was terrified. Beyond terrified. I was in that scary, scary place in your brain where you're so beyond terrified that you don't really care what happens to you, or you care but you realize you can't do anything about it, or you care but you've gone so soft in the head that you don't even remember what "care" means. In other words, I wondered if I'd be rescued, then decided I would not be, then prayed I would be, then was absolutely sure I wouldn't be. And so on.

My thoughts, like my emotions, were all over the map. I thought about my childhood, about my mother's inability to provide a stable home for her daughters; about all the houses and schools and fathers that had passed through my life; about the survival mechanisms I'd adopted as a result of constantly being forced into the role of The New Kid; about the euphoria I'd felt when I left for college and was suddenly liberated from the constraints of the past, free to live in a way that made *me* happy. I thought about Roger, about our first meeting and our subsequent courtship and our eventual marriage; about how he was the first person who gave me a sense of safety and permanence and genuine friendship; about our good years, only our good years. I couldn't bear to drift into Farkus territory, into the period after Roger's enhancement. It was too painful, and I was in enough pain.

As the sun was beginning to set and darkness was poised to descend upon me, I focused in earnest on Roger as my beacon of light, my ray of hope, my one and only chance to make it out of the woods alive. He would rescue me, I buoyed myself. He would rescue me at Mt. Baldy just as he'd rescued me on the 405. There was a nice symmetry to this idea, and I clung to it for dear life.

Please come for me, I thought, tears rolling down my cheeks. No matter how you feel about me now, please come.

Unfortunately, what came wasn't Roger.

I was sitting there convincing myself he would save me when I heard someone or something stepping through the brush, snapping an occasional tree branch, working through the woods to get to me.

I perked up considerably at first, believing it was Roger rushing to my aid. But when I heard no cry of "Elizabeth? Are you in there?" I began to have my doubts.

Oh, God, I said silently. It isn't Roger. It's Art Yarnell, checking to see if I'm dead yet.

Wanting him to think I was so he wouldn't finish the job, I played possum. I closed my eyes, rolled my head backwards, and made my body go limp. I didn't have a mirror, of course, but in my mind I looked dead. Dead enough, anyway.

I remained in that fake, corpselike pose for several minutes, listening intently and with growing dread to the approaching footsteps. I was surprised that Yarnell hadn't muttered something, cursed me out, talked to himself about his daring abduction of me, but I continued to play possum. Just kept my eyes closed and my body still, and waited.

As it turned out, I'd gotten my mammals mixed up. While I was playing possum, it was a bear that was about to play with me. Yup. A big black bear—Smokey without the cute little outfit.

This fella (or gal) made his presence known to me by licking my nose with his eight-thousand-foot tongue.

I opened my eyes with a start, naturally, and came as close to having a stress-induced heart attack as a person can get.

But I did not scream. No. Even in my state of utter panic, I remembered what Roger had taught me about bears—don't provoke them. He also taught me that they're more interested in food than they are in people. The problem with that axiom was that I feared I might be food as well as people.

I sat there motionless, not moving a muscle, breathing shallowly if at all, while Smokey continued to inspect me. He sniffed my bare feet, then licked them too. I'm rather ticklish, so it took all my willpower not to jerk my legs away, *provoke* him, and send him on an eating binge.

His next move was to paw my shoulder. Since he needed a manicure—a nail-clipping at the very least—he succeeded in ripping right through my Donna Karan T-shirt and cutting my skin. A prelude to his first bite, I figured, bracing myself for him to devour me.

But he didn't devour me. He sniffed me some more, pawed me some more, licked me some more. It was almost sweet how he seemed to like me. Or was his liking me a negative? Was he merely examining me, the way one examines a piece of fruit at the market before deciding whether to buy it and *eat* it? Was he getting ready to open his mouth and swallow me whole?

Oh, God, Roger. Where are you? I thought, wishing he would come before I was reduced to a pile of bones. Or did bears eat those too?

I was contemplating this gruesome notion when my furry friend suddenly pricked up his ears, hesitated, and lumbered away. Just like that. Had he sensed there was something more appetizing nearby? A coyote, maybe? A family of squirrels? Or, perhaps, another wife who'd come looking for her husband and been thwarted by a crazed former hotel manager?

The important thing was that he was gone. Crisis averted.

But not for long. In the stillness of the dusk, I heard a sound. Several sounds, actually. The sort of sounds you hear on those National Geographic specials on PBS. The sounds of one animal eating another.

The first sound reminded me of the rattle you get when you shake a couple of maracas—the key word being "rattle." Even in my addled state, I recognized that I was not in the vicinity of a Brazilian dance band but of a poisonous snake. According to Roger, the Western rattlesnake, which was known to slither around the Mt. Baldy area, was a dangerous character, in terms of bites and venom and fatalities. You can imagine how thrilled I was to recall that bit of trivia.

The second sound was a high-pitched screech or yelp, followed by an eerie silence, which suggested strongly that the snake had attacked its prey, killed it, and was preparing to make a meal of it.

Was I next?

It was a logical assumption, given my circumstances and the fact that Roger had shared another little factoid with me: Rattlers will eat anything as long as it's alive and warm.

Okay, that's it, I decided, a jolt of adrenaline surging through my aching, weary body. That's it, that's enough, that's the end. I am not a contestant on *Survivor.* I am not interested in spending another second in these woods. I am not going to let myself become some creature's dinner!

Pumped with purpose and determination, I surveyed my surroundings in the diminishing light, searching for a sharp outcropping of rock—a piece angular enough to saw off the leather belt around my wrists.

There, I thought when I spotted such a rock, its jagged edge more than fitting the bill. There's my way out.

Using every ounce of strength I could summon up, I laid down on the ground face-up—an unwieldy proposition when your wrists are tied behind your back and your feet are bound at the ankles. And then I pushed upward with my legs against the hard earth, attempting to slide myself toward the rock.

Come on, Elizabeth. You can do this. You can.

I willed myself to keep going, despite the pain and the fatigue and the difficulty of the task.

Just push. Push. Push.

As I pushed, I said a little thank-you to the trainer at the gym for prodding me into doing those torturous plié squats, walking lunges, and standing hamstring curls. Whatever lower body strength was propelling me onward was a result of my exercise regimen, I was sure. The question was, Would that strength be my protection from the jaws of the rattlesnake? Would it prevent me from becoming a rattle*snack*?

On and on I slid, over and over I pushed, stopping only to catch my breath—a neat trick when your mouth is stuffed with your socks. When I'd finally managed to drag myself all the way to the rock, I actually wept with joy. Even if I wasn't able to cut the belt from my wrists, I would die knowing I'd tried.

Here we go, I said to myself, as I backed up to the edge of the rock and maneuvered my body into position.

Again and again I sawed the leather against the sharp angle of the rock, moving my arms up and down, urging myself on. It was pitch dark by this time, but I refused to let that deter me or sap my energy or depress me. The rattlesnake was great motivation.

At one point, though, I almost gave up. My muscles were so sore that I wondered if I'd torn them all. But after a brief rest, I went back to business, grinding away at the leather, bearing down on it, abrading it.

And then I felt sort of a pop, a snap, a break, and my arms flew open behind me.

Without even taking the time to massage my wrists or flex my fingers or pat myself on the back, I untied the sweater from around my head, pulled the socks out of my mouth, and freed my ankles. And then I stood, wobbly but alive, and yelled my lungs out.

"Roger! Help meeeeee!"

When nothing happened—i.e., the only voice I heard in response to my plea was my own, echoing back at me—I considered walking my way out of the woods, toward the dirt road that led to the campground. But

I quickly nixed that idea. For one thing, it was dark, and I was afraid I'd wander inadvertently into even more remote territory, if that were possible. For a second, I had no desire to barge in on the rattlesnake during his dinner hour. And for a third, I was shot, totally spent. And so I stayed put and shouted again, as loud as I could.

"It's Elizabeth! I'm not dead, Roger!"

What I heard next was not my own voice again but the roar of an engine and the *thump thump thump* of propeller blades.

It's a helicopter, I realized as the noises drew closer. It's a helicopter, all right, and it's up there looking for me.

I waved my arms in the air, trying frantically to signal the plane, but it took several more minutes until there was contact.

Before I knew what hit me, something hit me—a beam of light from the night sky. It shone down on me with such intensity that I had to shield my eyes from it.

Thank God, I thought, knowing instinctively that it was Roger in that helicopter, Roger who was coming for me, Roger who was and always would be my beacon of light.

"Elizabeth! I'm with the search and rescue team! Just stay where you are!"

He was calling to me through a bullhorn, hoping to be heard above the din.

"Elizabeth! We've spotted you down there! Everything's going to be okay!"

Such a nice guy, my husband. I couldn't wait to tell him about quitting AMLP and making discoveries about myself and understanding that it's the magic of love that transforms more effectively and enduringly than any potion.

"Camping is for wimps!" I yelled up to him, and promptly passed out.

CHAPTER TWENTY-NINE

When I woke up, I was in a bed. I had an IV needle stuck in a vein and an oxygen tube hooked into my nostrils and assorted bandages wrapped across my body. I also had Roger seated next to me in a chair. He was staring down at the floor, his expression one of concern as well as exhaustion.

"Hi," I said, startling him.

He looked up at me and smiled, flashing me his dimple, his sinkhole. "Welcome back, sleepyhead."

"It's nice to *be* back." I touched his arm. "Where am I?"

"You're at the San Antonio Community Hospital, about twelve miles from Mt. Baldy. We brought you here last night."

I didn't remember being brought anywhere. "Am I okay?"

"You're fine. You came down with a little hypothermia and dehydration, that's all, plus a few cuts and bruises. They're feeding you fluids and antibiotics and other tasty treats, so you should be up and around in no time."

"Maybe, but right now I feel like I've been hit by a tractor-trailer."

"It'll get better. I promise. You've been through a lot, don't forget."

"That's just it. I do forget. It's weird how my memory of last night is so in-and-out. The last thing I remember clearly is you, how you called to me from the helicopter. But I also have vague images of talking to people and telling them about Art Yarnell and—" I stopped when it occurred to me that he might still be on the loose.

"He's in custody," Roger said. "He won't hurt you ever again."

"How did they catch him?"

"They had your help. You were very brave, Elizabeth. You could hardly move, let alone stay awake, but you pulled yourself together enough to give the police a complete description of Yarnell, of his car, of the approximate time he'd left you in the woods, all of it. Your information enabled them to find him and lock him up."

"That's great news." I sighed with relief. "How did you find *me*, by the way?"

"You want the long version or the short version?"

"The short version. I might nod out again without warning."

"Okay. Here it is. I returned to the campsite, saw your note on my windshield, and raced back up the dirt road toward the ski lifts. Then I—"

"Wait. You *raced* back up the dirt road?"

"Sure. Because we should have run into each other long before then. I was worried."

"You were worried?" I was fishing. I was dying to know whether he still loved me, whether our estrangement was a thing of the past, whether we were "us" again. "Tell me about the 'worried' part, Roger."

"I thought you said you wanted the short version."

"I changed my mind."

"All right. I was worried sick, if you want the truth. I was well aware that you weren't exactly an advanced hiker."

"I am now."

He laughed. "Yes, but you weren't yesterday. So I rushed up the dirt road—"

"You *rushed?*"

"I raced, I rushed, I got my ass in gear, whatever. And then I found your handbag."

"My handbag! I forgot all about that too. Yarnell pulled it off of me and then was stupid enough to leave it on the road. I'm amazed nobody made off with it. I had all my credit cards in it."

"Your credit cards are safe, Elizabeth. You can thank the fact that Tuesday in late October is a slow day on the trails."

"Don't I know it. So you saw my handbag and then what?"

"I figured something had happened to you. I contacted the rescue people from the Mt. Baldy Volunteer Fire Department, and we began a search. When we didn't make any progress, they called in the San Bernandino County Sheriff's Department. After a frustrating few hours, we finally located you by helicopter, and once we did, the EMS technicians took over. They did a terrific job. So did you, Elizabeth."

"Me?"

"Absolutely. Look at you—you're all in one piece."

I didn't want to look at me. I knew without looking that my hair was a filthy mess and my face was wearing yesterday's makeup and my lips were not only cracked and dry but swollen, thanks to the bee that had stung me. I must have been a vision. Not the way I wanted Roger to see me for the first time in days.

"You're beautiful," he said, sensing my insecurity and taking my hand (the one without the IV needle in it). "Never more so than right now."

"Oh, Roger. You don't have to say things you don't mean. Now that we're done with the Robinson Crusoe story, we need to talk about us, about where we go from here."

"We go home, that's where we go. They're only keeping you here another night, for observation."

"So you're saying that *we* go home?" I asked hopefully. "You and I? Together?"

Before he could answer, Brenda burst into the room, her arms filled with flowers.

"My poor sister," she said, depositing the vase on a nearby table so she could hang over the side of my bed unencumbered. "How *are* you?"

"I'm tired," I said. "Sort of washed out."

"I'll bet you are. What an adventure."

"Yes, but it's over now."

"That's what you think." She laughed.

"Sorry, but I missed the joke, Brenda. Why isn't my adventure over?"

"Because you're a celebrity, Elizabeth. A genuine *star*!"

I glanced at Roger. "What's she talking about? Or is this just Brenda-speak for 'Get Well Soon?' "

"I called her last night," he said, "to tell her what had happened and to give her the name of the hospital, but she already knew everything."

"Of course, I knew!" she exclaimed. "I was watching the news on KNBC last night, and who was being carried out of some wilderness on a stretcher but my big sister! I nearly died!"

I was the one who'd nearly died, but that was beside the point. "I was on television?"

"And how. They devoted an entire segment to your rescue. You were on *before* the story about the man who taught his dog to play the piano and *after* the story about the woman who lives in a house wall-papered entirely in eight-by-tens of Elvis. You're going to be inundated with requests for interviews, Elizabeth, which is why I brought along the names of some really good publicists. I recommend that you hire one as soon as possible. And then after the interviews, you'll need an agent to handle the book and movie rights."

"I hate to disappoint you, Brenda, but I'm not interested in any of that. I just want a normal life. It's been quite a year, you know?"

"Sure, but think of the movie! Throw some hair extensions on Meg Ryan and she could play you in a heartbeat!"

After allowing Brenda to cast the other characters in the movie and volunteer her choices for director and screenwriter, Roger put his arm around her and gently escorted her out the door. "Elizabeth is supposed to rest," he said. "How about grabbing a bite to eat and coming back in a little while?"

"Okay, but doesn't she—"

"I love you, Brenda," I said, blowing her a kiss as she disappeared into the hall. "Thanks for the flowers."

A few minutes later, Roger returned, solo.

"I appreciate your help there," I said. "She's a wonderful sister, but she can be a bit *enthusiastic*."

"Well, now that she's gone, temporarily, you really should rest."

"Not a chance, Baskin. I'm not letting you off the hook that easily. Before Brenda blew in, I suggested that we needed to talk about us, about where we go from here, and you said we were going home, together."

"And we are. Unless you've decided you've had it with me. I have a lot of apologizing to do, I admit."

He had a lot of apologizing to do? Maybe the medicine they were pumping into me was affecting my hearing.

"This isn't the appropriate moment to burden you with my mea culpas," he went on. "You must be very weak."

"It *is* the appropriate moment." Hearing his mea culpas first would give me extra time to polish up mine.

"If you're sure." He sat back down and edged his chair closer to the bed. "For starters, I apologize for taking off to Mt. Baldy without telling you, without telling anyone."

"But you did tell someone, Frankie. You did, didn't you, Roger?"

He nodded. "I was with him the afternoon before I left. I blurted out that I was headed to Mt. Baldy but asked him to keep it a secret, just between us. It felt safe to tell him, Elizabeth. He was the only one I wasn't mad at."

"Go on."

"I was at a very low point, emotionally. I was angry and I didn't want to confront my feelings, so I tried to escape from them by running away from the world and hiding out in my tent. Like some pathetic kid, huh?"

"Like a kid who was hurting."

"I would say that's accurate. You see, I wasn't just angry at you, although I was still steaming about your pilgrimage to the magic doctor. I was angry at myself too, angry at the way I'd loved you but didn't show it enough; loved you but didn't work at it enough; loved you but took you for granted, let my job come first, let the 'routine' come first. I was lazy, Elizabeth. A lazy husband. I didn't keep the excitement alive. It never even occurred to me to try. I just kept grinding along, getting up in the morning and going to work and hating my job."

"You hate your job? You never said a word, Roger."

"That's what I'm talking about. I never said a word because I refused to let the notion sink in. I just kept going and going and going, never stopping to question what I was doing or ask myself why I was doing it. Real estate bores the piss out of me, and yet I worked harder on those deals than anyone in the office."

I was stunned by his confession. I had no idea that he'd been miserable in his career. "So you escaped from your partners the way you escaped from me."

"Yes, and it was wrong. I should have given all of you an explanation, or at least some sort of indication of when I'd be back. It was an irresponsible act, but I wasn't myself. That's the only excuse I can come up with."

I squeezed his hand. "Sounds like you had a lot to deal with."

"I did. But I'm at the end of the trail now, to use a camping metaphor. I can see my way clear. I love you, Elizabeth, and I want us to be happy. You have my word that I'll do whatever's necessary to make that happen."

He leaned over and kissed my cruddy lips—oxygen tube, IV needle, hospital breath and all. I was so moved by his honesty and his pain and his declaration of love for me that I couldn't speak for several minutes. I just lay there in that bed, holding on to his hand, thanking God we'd been given another chance. When the lump in my throat finally receded, I told Roger it was my turn to take the floor.

"Remember when you said I hadn't changed?" I began. "Remember how, despite the Farkus fiasco, I was still caught up in my unrealistic expectations? How I was the same Elizabeth, trying to control my environment, trying to make our lives perfect, trying to make *you* perfect? Do you remember that, Roger?"

"Of course, I do. All too well. You were so intent on proving to me that you'd changed that you didn't get the problem, which is that there isn't any such thing as a perfect person, just as there isn't any such thing as a perfect marriage."

"Well, I get it now. I quit my job, Roger."

"You're kidding."

"Nope. I was about to be fired, but that's another story."

"Why did you quit?"

"Let's just say that the last hotel I went to inspect taught me what you were trying to teach me. It was a property in New Orleans, and it was so perfect, so flawless, so Five Key in all categories that it left me cold. It was perfect but remote, Roger. It was perfect but without charm. It was perfect and I hated it, and I realized that finding fault with hotels for a living isn't good for the soul. Or for a marriage. Not mine, anyway."

"I'm very surprised. I thought you and that job were a match made in heaven."

"Not made in *heaven,* as it turns out."

"I see that. Will you look for something else within the company?"

"No. I'll be pounding the pavement with you, I guess, figuring out what I really want to do and then doing it."

"So you have changed, Elizabeth. No doubt about it."

"Glad you noticed. Oh, and there's something else."

"Yes?"

"I love you, Roger. I'll always love you."

"In spite of my imperfections?"

"Because of your imperfections. Although there is one thing I'd still like to fix about you."

"Oh? And what might that be?"

I ran my fingers over his sweater, across his chest. "Your heart. I'm afraid I broke it when I told you the truth about the potion. Did I break it, Roger? And can I ever truly mend it?"

He smiled at me with adoring, forgiving eyes, which told me everything I needed to know.

EPILOGUE

I think we should pickle the floors," said Clover as the two of us completed a walk-through of the house we'd purchased six months ago. It was a Tudor-style residence in a commercially zoned neighborhood in L.A.'s Los Feliz section. Now that we'd received our building permit, we were planning to convert it into a bed-and-breakfast inn and create a business investment for ourselves. I had the expertise in the hospitality industry, and Clover had the pile of money, both from her divorce settlement from Bud and her inheritance from Mama, so it seemed like a natural that we'd become partners in a B&B. We couldn't wait to redo the place, then hire a resident manager to run it for us, to embue it with the atmosphere we envisioned. It would be a charming, homey inn, we'd decided. The sort of friendly, quirky establishment that AMLP doesn't deign to inspect.

"I think we should leave the floors the way they are," I said. "They have character."

"Why don't we wait and see what Bud says?" Clover suggested. It was a year and a half since they'd ended their marriage, but they had remained good friends. They went to the opera together and had dinner together, and when Bud started dating his ballroom dancing instructor in earnest, the three of them had dinner together.

"And we'll get Roger's opinion," I said. It was Roger who'd handled the legal work on the house. He was still practicing real estate law then, and our property was one of his last closings. Shortly thereafter, he left the firm to start his own, specializing in environmental law, a subject about which he was passionate. The move had given him the proverbial new lease on life, and I'd never seen him happier. He was the only partner in the new outfit, but he'd recruited three associates and two paralegals. Oh, and there was a very recent addition to his payroll—Eve Wheeler. When Roger had learned that Dennis Wheeler was in prison, leaving Frankie and his mother in even more dire straits than before, he persuaded Eve that it was time to let go of her hostility toward him and allow him to help her. He sent her to secretarial school and she discovered she was a quick study, and as a result, she was now an employee in his office—and Frankie had a parent who was home at a decent hour.

"Here's what I really think," said Clover. "It's time for lunch."

I smiled. "Name the place."

She chose Fred 62, a retro joint open twenty-four hours a day that serves such tweaked diner offerings as scrambled tofu and homemade Pop-Tarts. According to Brenda, it was a hangout for the movie stars who lived in Los Feliz, and of course, she was "the authority." About a month after my stint in the hospital, she'd been wooed away from *In the Know* magazine and was currently an editor in the L.A. bureau of *People*. I didn't think it was possible for her to become more enmeshed in the celebrity culture, but she was.

Ironically, though, it wasn't Brenda who gave us the scoop about Lanie Duquette, the Australian screen siren Clover and I had visited at her

Malibu estate, posing as exterminators. Lanie had been despondent that day, confiding to us that without her monthly dose of Farkus's potion she had no desire to make films, no desire to get out of bed in the morning. A week or so after we'd spoken to her, she revealed to Barbara Walters that she was retiring from the movie business at the tender age of thirty-four. She retreated from public view, didn't show up at award ceremonies, didn't appear in magazines, didn't frequent the "in" spots. She also divorced her billionaire dot-com husband, or rather, he divorced her. I felt sorry for her, but I had troubles of my own at that point.

Anyhow, Clover and I sat there at Fred 62, munching on our smoked-salmon sandwiches and chatting about our new venture. After lunch, we drove back to her place to discuss fabrics and furniture and other decorating issues pertaining to our B&B. We were debating paint colors when we were distracted by the sound of the television set in the next room.

"It's the cleaning lady," said Clover. "She's addicted to that E! Network. She leaves it on even when she's in another part of the house. I'll go turn it off."

"No. Don't. I swear I just heard them say something about Lanie Duquette."

"Really? I thought she vanished from the face of the earth."

"Me too." After I had stumbled on Andrea in Palm Beach and discovered she had access to all of Farkus's herbal concoctions, I'd made several attempts to reach Lanie. I knew she was desperate for her preparations, and so I was eager to tell her where Andrea was, hoping it might bring her some relief. But she really had vanished. She'd sold her house in Malibu and left no forwarding address or phone number, and no one—not even Brenda—had a contact for her. Eventually, I'd given up. "I hope she's okay. We'd better get in there and see."

We hurried into Clover's den, where her cleaning lady had, indeed, left the set tuned to the entertainment channel.

"There she is," I marveled, when Lanie's image filled the small screen.

She looked beautiful, glamorous, every inch the star—the polar opposite of the woman who'd shared her angst with us. "It's a live press conference, I think."

"Let's listen."

We each pulled up a chair and sat with rapt attention.

"I'd like to announce," Lanie began, amid a throng of photographers and journalists, "that I am resuming my movie career."

"Wow. I wonder what made her change her mind," I said, before Clover shushed me.

"I have recharged my batteries," Lanie continued. "I have recovered my zest for acting. I have regained my sense of purpose."

"Did your move to Sante Fe last year have anything to do with your decision to come back?" asked a reporter. The question gave Clover and me pause because we'd had no idea that it was New Mexico where Lanie had been living.

"Yes." She smiled her high-wattage smile, the smile that made men swoon, the smile that was nowhere in evidence the day Clover and I met her. "Yes, my move to Sante Fe has meant a great deal to me."

"In what respect?" asked another reporter.

"Well, I don't want to delve too deeply into personal matters," she replied, "but in general terms, I can tell you that I was able to tap into a certain energy in Santa Fe. What I'm saying is that I've been enhanced since coming here. Yes, that's exactly how I would describe myself—*enhanced*."

Clover and I looked at each other, our mouths open, our eyes wide, our pulses off the charts. There were other questions from reporters and Lanie answered them, but we didn't care about the rest of the press conference. We were stuck on that word, the code word that had flipped our whole worlds upside down.

"You realize what this means," I said finally.

"That he's still out there practicing," she said. "In New Mexico."

"Amazing, isn't it? The cops couldn't find him. The private investigator couldn't find him. But Lanie found him."

"Or he found her."

"I guess we can forget about ever having to testify at his trial," I said.

"Right. Because they'll never catch him. He'll keep setting up shop and peddling his herbs and fiddling with people's lives."

"Do you think he's a magician, Clover? Do you think it's possible that he's got some sort of power we don't understand?"

"He's either a magician or a really clever con man, bless his heart."

I nodded, deciding that he just might be a little of both.